"We all make  **deliberately p** **e to help herself.**

Drakon Xanthis's and she wondered what would happen when it shattered completely. "Best thing you can do now is forgive yourself for making such a dreadful mistake, and move forward."

Fire flashed in his eyes and he leaned in, closing the gap between them so that his broad chest just grazed the swell of her breasts and she could feel the tantalizing heat of his hips so close to hers.

"Such an interesting way to view things," he said, his head dropping, his voice deepening. "With you as my mistake."

His lips were so close now; her lower back tingled and her belly tightened, and desire coursed through her veins, making her ache everywhere.

Morgan could feel his need, feel the desire, and her mouth dried, her heart hammering harder. He was going to kiss her. And she wanted the kiss, craved his kiss, even as a little voice of reason inside her head sounded the alarm….

Stop. Wait. Think.

She had to remember…remember the past… remember what had happened last time…. This wasn't just a kiss, but an inferno. If she gave in to this kiss, it would be all over.

Dear Reader,

We know how much you love Harlequin® Presents®, so this month we wanted to treat you to something extra special—a second classic story by the same author for free!

Once you have finished reading *The Fallen Greek Bride*, just turn the page for another stunning Greek hero from Jane Porter.

This month, indulge yourself with double the reading pleasure!

With love,

The Presents Editors

Jane Porter

THE FALLEN GREEK BRIDE

The Disgraced
COPELANDS

HARLEQUIN PRESENTS®

ISBN-13: 978-0-373-13129-7

THE FALLEN GREEK BRIDE

Copyright © 2013 by Harlequin Books S.A.

The publisher acknowledges the copyright holder of the individual works as follows:

THE FALLEN GREEK BRIDE
Copyright © 2013 by Jane Porter

AT THE GREEK BOSS'S BIDDING
Copyright © 2007 by Jane Porter

PLEASE RECYCLE · THIS PRODUCT IS RECYCLABLE

Recycling programs for this product may not exist in your area.

This edition published by arrangement with Harlequin Books S.A.

For questions and comments about the quality of this book, please contact us at CustomerService@Harlequin.com.

® and TM are trademarks of Harlequin Enterprises Limited or its corporate affiliates. Trademarks indicated with ® are registered in the United States Patent and Trademark Office, the Canadian Trade Marks Office and in other countries.

HARLEQUIN®
www.Harlequin.com

Printed in U.S.A.

CONTENTS

Ever wondered what life is like in the
unrelenting glare of the spotlight?

Don't miss this scorching new trilogy from Jane Porter

The Disgraced Copelands

A family in the headlines—for all the wrong reasons!

For the Copeland family, each day brings another tabloid
scandal. Their world was one of unrivaled luxury and
glittering social events. Now this privileged life is nothing
but a distant memory.

Staring the taunting paparazzi straight in the eye,
the Copeland heirs seek to start new lives—with no one to
rely on but themselves. At least, that's what they think….

*It seems fame and riches can't buy happiness—but they make
it more fun trying!*

Look out for more scandalous stories about

**The Disgraced Copelands
by Jane Porter**

Coming soon!

THE FALLEN GREEK BRIDE

For Randall Toye—
thank you for the friendship and support.

CHAPTER ONE

"Welcome home, my wife."

Morgan froze inside Villa Angelica's expansive marble and limestone living room with its spectacular floor-to-ceiling view of blue sky and sea, but saw none of the view, and only Drakon's face.

It had been five years since she'd last seen him. Five and a half years since their extravagant two-million-dollar wedding, for a marriage that had lasted just six months.

She'd dreaded this moment. Feared it. And yet Drakon sounded so relaxed and warm, so *normal,* as if he were welcoming her back from a little holiday instead of her walking out on him.

"Not your wife, Drakon," she said softly, huskily, because they both knew she hadn't been his anything for years. There had been nothing, no word, no contact, not after the flurry of legal missives that followed her filing for divorce.

He'd refused to grant her the divorce and she'd spent a fortune fighting him. But no attorney, no lawsuit, no amount of money could persuade him to let her go. Marriage vows, he'd said, were sacred and binding. She was his. And apparently the courts in Greece agreed with him. Or were bought by him. Probably the latter.

"You are most definitely still my wife, but that's not a conversation I want to have across a room this size. Do come in,

Morgan. Don't be a stranger. What would you like to drink? Champagne? A Bellini? Something a little stronger?"

But her feet didn't move. Her legs wouldn't carry her. Not when her heart was beating so fast. She was shocked by Drakon's appearance and wondered for a moment if it really was Drakon. Unnerved, she looked away, past his broad shoulders to the wall of window behind him, with that breathtaking blue sky and jagged cliffs and azure sea.

So blue and beautiful today. A perfect spring day on the Amalfi Coast.

"I don't want anything," she said, her gaze jerking back to him, although truthfully, a glass of cool water would taste like heaven right now. Her mouth was so dry, her pulse too quick. Her head was spinning, making her dizzy from nerves and anxiety. Who *was* this man before her?

The Drakon Xanthis she'd married had been honed, sleek and polished, a man of taut, gleaming lines and angles.

This tall intimidating man in front of the picture window was broader in the shoulders and chest than Drakon had ever been, and his thick, inky brown and black hair hung in loose curls to almost his shoulders, while his hard fierce features were hidden by a dark beard. The wild hair and beard should have obscured his sensual beauty, rendered him reckless, powerless. Instead the tangle of hair highlighted his bronzed brow, the long straight nose, the firm mouth, the piercing amber gold eyes.

His hair was still damp and his skin gleamed as if he'd just risen from the sea, the Greek god Poseidon come to life from ancient myth.

She didn't like it. Didn't like any of this. She'd prepared herself for one thing, but not this....

"You look pale," he said, his voice so deep it was almost a caress.

She steeled herself against it. Against him. "It was a long trip."

"Even more reason for you to come sit."

Her hands clenched into fists at her sides. She hated being here. Hated him for only seeing her here at Villa Angelica, the place where they'd honeymooned for a month following their spectacular wedding. It'd been the happiest month of her life. When the honeymoon was over, they had left the villa and flown to Greece, and nothing was ever the same between them again. "I'm fine here," she said.

"I won't hurt you," he replied softly.

Her nails pierced her skin. Her eyes stung. If her legs would function, she'd run. Protect herself. Save herself. If only she had someone else to go to, someone else who would help her, but there was no one. Just Drakon. Just the man who had destroyed her, making her question her own sanity. "You already did that."

"You say that, my love, and yet you've never told me how—"

"As you said, that isn't something to discuss across a room of this size. And we both know, I didn't come here to discuss us. Didn't come to rehash the past, bring up old ghosts, old pain. I came for your help. You know what I need. You know what's at stake. Will you do it? Will you help me?"

"Six million dollars is a lot of money."

"Not to you."

"Things have changed. Your father lost over four hundred million dollars of what I gave him."

"It wasn't his fault." She met his gaze and held it, knowing that if she didn't stand up to him now, he'd crush her. Just as he'd crushed her all those years ago.

Drakon, like her father, played by no rules but his own.

A Greek shipping tycoon, Drakon Sebastian Xanthis was a man obsessed with control and power. A man obsessed with amassing wealth and growing his empire. A man obsessed with a woman who wasn't his wife. Bronwyn. The stunning Australian who ran his Southeast Asia business.

Her eyes burned and her jaw ached.

But no. She wouldn't think of Bronwyn now. Wouldn't wonder if the willowy blonde still worked for him. It wasn't important. Morgan wasn't part of Drakon's life anymore. She didn't care whom Drakon employed or how he interacted with his female vice presidents or where they stayed on their business trips or what they discussed over their long dinners together.

"Is that what you really believe?" he asked now, voice almost silky. "That your father is blameless?"

"Absolutely. He was completely misled—"

"As you have been. Your father is one of the biggest players in one of the biggest Ponzi schemes ever. Twenty-five billion dollars is missing, and your father funneled five billion of that to Michael Amery, earning himself ten percent interest."

"He never saw that kind of money—"

"For God's sake, Morgan, you're talking to me, Drakon, your husband. I know your father. I know exactly who and what he is. Do not play me for a fool!"

Morgan ground her teeth together harder, holding back the words, the tears, the anger, the shame. Her father wasn't a monster. He didn't steal from his clients. He was just as deceived as they were and yet no one would give him an opportunity to explain, or defend himself. The media had tried and convicted him and everyone believed the press. Everyone believed the wild accusations. "He's innocent, Drakon. He had no idea Michael Amery was running a pyramid scheme. Had no idea all those numbers and profits were a lie."

"Then if he's so innocent, why did he flee the country? Why didn't he stay, like Amery's sons and cousins, and fight instead of setting sail to avoid prosecution?"

"He panicked. He was frightened—"

"Absolute rubbish. If that's the case, your father is a coward and deserves his fate."

She shook her head in silent protest, her gaze pinned to Drakon's features. He might not look like Drakon, but it was definitely him. She knew his deep, smooth voice. And those eyes. His eyes. She'd fallen in love with his eyes first. She'd met him at the annual Life ball in Vienna, and they hadn't danced—Drakon didn't dance—but he'd watched her all evening and at first she'd been discomfited by the intensity of his gaze, and then she'd come to like it. Want it. Crave it.

In those early weeks and months when he'd pursued her, Drakon had seduced her with his eyes, examining her, holding her, possessing her long before he'd laid a single finger on her. And, of course, by the time he did, she was his, completely.

The last five years had been brutal. Beyond brutal. And just when Morgan had found herself again, and felt hopeful and excited about her future, her world came crashing down with the revelation that her beloved, brilliant financier father, Daniel Copeland, was part of Michael Amery's horrific Ponzi scheme. And instead of her father handling the crisis with his usual aplomb, he'd cracked and run, creating an even bigger international scandal.

She drew a slow, unsteady breath. "I can't leave him in Somalia to die, Drakon. The pirates will kill him if they don't get the ransom money—"

"It would serve him right."

"He's my father!"

"You'll put yourself in debt for the rest of your life, just to buy his freedom, even though you know that his freedom will be short-lived?"

"Yes."

"You do understand that he'll be arrested the moment he tries to enter any North American or European country?"

"Yes."

"He's never going to be free again. He's going to spend the rest of his life in prison, just like Michael Amery will, once he's caught, too."

"I understand. But far better for my father to be in an American prison than held by Somali pirates. At least in the United States he could get medical care if he's sick, or medicine for his blood pressure. At least he could have visitors and letters and contact with the outside world. God knows what his conditions are like in Somalia—"

"I'm sure they're not luxurious. But why should the American taxpayer have to support your father? Let him stay where he is. It's what he deserves."

"Do you say this to hurt me, or is it because he lost so much of your money?"

"I'm a businessman. I don't like to lose money. But I was only in four hundred million of the five billion he gave to Amery. What about those others? The majority were regular people. People who trusted your father with their retirement money…their life savings. And what did he do? He wiped them out. Left them with nothing. No retirement, no security, no way to pay the bills now that they're older and frailer and unemployable."

Morgan blinked hard to clear her vision. "Michael Amery was my father's best friend. He was like family. Dad trusted him implicitly." Her voice cracked and she struggled to regain her composure. "I grew up calling him Uncle Michael. I thought of him as my family."

"Yes, that's what you told me. Just before I gave your father four hundred million dollars to invest for me. I nearly gave him more. Your father wanted more. Twice as much, as a matter of fact."

"I am so sorry."

"I trusted your father." His gaze met hers and held. "Trusted you. I know better now."

She exhaled slowly. "Does that mean you won't help me?"

"It means…" His voice faded, and his gaze narrowed as he looked at her, closely, carefully, studying her intently. "Probably not."

"Probably?" she repeated hoarsely, aware that if Drakon wouldn't help her, no one would. The world hated her father, and wanted him gone. They all hoped he was dead. And they all hoped he'd suffered before he died, too.

"Surely you must realize I'm no fan of your father's, *glykia mou.*"

"You don't have to be a fan of my father's to loan me the money. We'll draft a contract, a legal document that is between you and me, and I will pay you back in regular installments. It will take time, but it'll happen. My business is growing, building. I've got hundreds of thousands of dollars of orders coming in. I promise—"

"Just like you promised to love me? Honor me? Be true to me for better or worse, in sickness and in health?"

She winced. He made it sound as if she hadn't ever cared for him, when nothing could be further from the truth. The truth was, she'd cared too much. She'd loved him without reservation. And by loving him so much, she'd lost herself entirely. "So why haven't you divorced me then? If you despise me so much, why not let me go? Set me free?"

"Because I'm not like you. I don't make commitments and run from them. I don't make promises and then break them. I promised five and a half years ago to be loyal to you, and I have been."

His deep gravelly voice was making her insides wobble while his focused gaze rested on her, examining her, as if she were a prized pet that had been lost and found.

"Those are just words, Drakon. They mean nothing to me. Not when your actions speak so much louder."

"My actions?"

"Yes, your actions. Or your lack of action. You only do something if it benefits you. You married me because it benefited you…or you thought it would. And then when times were difficult…when I became difficult…you disappeared. You wouldn't grant me a divorce but you certainly didn't come after me, fight for me. And then when the world turned against us, where were you again? Nowhere. God knows you wouldn't want your name sullied by connection with the Copeland family!"

He studied her for an endless moment. "Interesting how you put things together. But not entirely surprising. You've inherited your mother's flair for the dramatic—"

"I hate you! I do." Her voice shook and her eyes burned, but she wouldn't cry, wouldn't give him the satisfaction. He'd taken everything from her, but not anymore. "I knew you'd mock me, humiliate me. I knew when I flew here, you'd make it difficult, but I came anyway, determined to do whatever I had to do to help my father. You'll let me plead with you, you'll let me beg—"

"That was a very passionate speech, so please forgive my interruption, but I'd like to clarify something. I don't believe you've begged. You've asked for money. You've demanded money. You've explained why you needed money. But there's been very little pleading, and absolutely no begging, at all."

A pulse beat wildly in her throat. She could feel the same wild flutter in her wrists and behind her ears. Everything in her was racing, raging. "Is that what you want? You'd like for me to beg you to help me?"

His head cocked, and he studied her, his gaze penetrating. "It'd certainly be a little more conciliatory, and far less antagonistic."

"Conciliatory." She repeated the word, rolling it over in her mouth, finding it sharp and bitter.

He said nothing, just watched her, and she felt almost

breathless at the scrutiny, remembering how it had been between them during their four weeks here on their honeymoon. It was in this villa she'd learned about love and lust, sex and pleasure, as well as pain and control, and the loss of control.

Drakon never lost control. But he'd made sure she did at least once a day, sometimes two or three times.

Their sex life had been hot. Explosive. Erotic. She'd been a virgin when she'd married him and their first time together had been uncomfortable. He was large and it had hurt when he entered her fully. He'd tried to make it pleasurable for her but she'd been so overwhelmed and emotional, as well as let down. She couldn't respond properly, couldn't climax, and she knew she was supposed to. Knew he wanted her to.

He'd showered with her afterward, and kissed her, and beneath the pulsing spray of the shower, he lavished attention on her breasts and nipples, the curve of her buttocks and the cleft between her thighs, lightly playing with her clit until he finally accomplished what he hadn't in bed—she came. One of his arms held her up since her legs were too weak to do the job, and then he'd kissed her deeply, possessively, and when she could catch her breath, he'd assured her that the next time he entered her, it wouldn't hurt. That sex would never hurt again.

It hadn't.

But that didn't mean sex was always easy or comfortable. Drakon liked it hot. Intense. Sensual. Raw. Unpredictable.

He loved to stand across the room from her—just as he was doing now—and he'd tell her what to do. Tell her what he wanted. Sometimes he wanted her to strip and then walk naked to him. Sometimes he wanted her to strip to just her panties and crawl to him. Sometimes he wanted her to wear nothing but her elegant heels and bend over...or put a foot on a chair and he'd tell her where to touch herself.

Each time Morgan would protest, but he'd look at her from

beneath his black lashes, his amber gaze lazy, his full mouth curved, and he'd tell her how beautiful she was and how much he enjoyed looking at her, that it gave him so much pleasure to see her, and to have her trust him....

Obey him...

She hated those words, hated the element of dominance, but it was part of the foreplay. They had good sex in bed, but then they had this other kind of sex—the sex where they played erotic games that pushed her out of her comfort zone. It had been confusing, but inevitably she did what he asked, and then somewhere along the way, he'd join her, and his mouth would be on her, between her legs, and his hands would hold her, fingers tight on her butt, or in her hair, or gripping her thighs, holding them apart, and he'd make love to her with his mouth and his fingers and his body and he'd arouse her so slowly that she feared she wouldn't ever come, and then just when the desire turned sharp and hurt, he'd relent. He'd flick the tip of his tongue across that small sensitive nub, or suck on her, or stroke her, or enter her and she'd break. Shatter. And the orgasms were so intense they seemed to go on forever. Maybe because he made sure they went on forever. And by the time he was finished, she was finished. There was nothing left. She was drained, spent, but also quiet. Compliant.

He loved her flushed and warm, quiet and compliant. Loved her physically that is, as long as she made no emotional demands. No conversation. No time, energy or patience. Required no attention.

Morgan's chest ached. Her heart hurt. She'd been so young then, so trusting and naive. She'd been determined to please him, her beautiful, sensual Greek husband.

Their honeymoon here, those thirty days of erotic lovemaking, had changed her forever. She couldn't even think of this villa without remembering how he'd made love to her in every single room, in every way imaginable. Taking her on chairs and beds, window seats and stairs. Pressing her naked back or breasts to priceless carpets, the marble floor, the cool emerald-green Italian tiles in the hall…

She wanted to throw up. He hadn't just taken her. He'd broken her.

"Help me out if you would, Drakon," she said, her voice pitched low, hoarse. "I'm not sure I understand you, and I don't know if it's cultural, personal or a language issue. But do you *want* me to beg? Is that what you're asking me to do?" Her chin lifted and tears sparkled in her eyes even as her heart burned as if it had been torched with fire. "Am I to go onto my knees in front of you, and plead my case? Is that what it would take to win your assistance?"

He didn't move a muscle and yet the vast living room suddenly felt very small. "I do like you on your knees," he said cordially, because they both knew that on her knees she could take him in her mouth, or he could touch her or take her from behind.

She drew a ragged breath, locked her knees, praying for strength. "I haven't forgotten," she said, aware that she was in trouble here, aware that she ought to go. Now. While she could. While she still had some self-respect left. "Although God knows, I've tried."

"Why would you want to forget it? We had an incredible sex life. It was amazing between us."

She could only look at him, intrigued by his memory of them, as well as appalled. Their sex life had been hot, but their marriage had been empty and shallow.

Obviously that didn't trouble him. It probably didn't even cross his mind that his bride had feelings. Emotions. Needs. Why should it? Drakon's desires were so much simpler. He just needed her available and willing, as if she were an American porn star in a rented Italian villa.

"So on my knees it is," she said mockingly, lifting the hem of her pale blue skirt to kneel on his limestone floor.

"Get up," he growled sharply.

"But this *is* what you want?"

"No. It's not what I want, not like this, not because you need something, want something. It's one thing if we're making love and there's pleasure involved, but there's no pleasure in seeing you beg, especially to me. The very suggestion disgusts me."

"And yet you seemed so charmed by the memory of me on my knees."

"Because that was different. That was sex. This is…" He shook his head, features tight, full mouth thinned. For a moment he just breathed, and the silence stretched.

Morgan welcomed the silence. She needed it. Her mind was whirling, her insides churning. She felt sick, dizzy and off balance by the contradictions and the intensity and her own desperation.

He had to help her.

He had to.

If he didn't, her father was forever lost to her.

"I've no desire to ever see my wife degrade herself," Drakon added quietly, "not even on behalf of her father. It actually sickens me to think you'd do that for him—"

"He's my father!"

"And he failed you! And it makes me physically ill that you'd beg for a man who refused to protect you and your sisters and your mother. A man is to provide for his family, not rob them blind."

"How nice it must be, Drakon Xanthis, to live, untouched and superior, in your ivory tower." Her voice deepened and her jaw ached and everything in her chest felt so raw and hot. "But I don't have the luxury of having an ivory tower. I don't have any luxuries anymore. Everything's gone in my family,

Drakon. The money, the security, the houses, the cars, the name…our reputation. And I can lose the lifestyle, it's just a lifestyle. But I've lost far more than that. My family's shattered. Broken. We live in chaos—"

She broke off, dragged in a breath, feeling wild and unhinged. But losing control with Drakon wouldn't help her. It would hurt her. He didn't like strong emotions. He pulled away when voices got louder, stronger, preferring calm, rational, unemotional conversation.

And, of course, that's what she'd think about now. What Drakon wanted. How he liked things. How ironic that even after five years, she was still worrying about him, still turning herself inside out to please him, to be what *he* needed, to handle things the way *he* handled them.

What about her?

What about what she needed? What she wanted? What about her emotions or her comfort?

The back of her eyes burned and she jerked her chin higher. "Well, I'm sorry you don't like seeing me like this, but this is who I am. Desperate. And I'm willing to take desperate measures to help my family. You don't understand what it's like for us. My family is in pain. Everyone is hurting, heartsick with guilt and shame and confusion—how could my father do what he did? How could he not know Amery wasn't investing legitimately? How could he not protect his clients… his friends…his family? My sisters and brother—we can't even see each other anymore, Drakon. We don't speak to each other. We can't handle the shame of it all. We're outcasts now. Bottom feeders. Scum. So fine, stand there and mock me with your principles. I'm just trying to save what I can. Starting with my father's life."

"Your father isn't worth it. But you are. Stop worrying about him, Morgan, and save yourself."

"And how do I do that, Drakon? Have you any advice for me there?"

"Yes. Come home."

"Home?"

"Yes, home to me—"

"You're not home, Drakon. You were never home."

She saw him flinch and she didn't like it, but it was time he knew the truth. Time he heard the truth. "You asked me a little bit ago why I'd want to forget our sex life, and I'll tell you. I don't like remembering. It hurts remembering."

"Why? It was good. No, it was great. We were unbelievable together—"

"Yes, yes, the sex was hot. And erotic. You were an incredibly skillful lover. You could make me come over and over, several times a day. But that's all you gave me. Your name, a million-dollar diamond wedding ring and orgasms. Lots and lots of orgasms. But there was no relationship, no communication, no connection. I didn't marry you to just have sex. I married you to have a life, a home. Happiness. But after six months of being married to you, all I felt was empty, isolated and deeply unhappy."

She held his gaze, glad she'd at last said what she'd wanted to say all those years ago, and yet fully aware that these revelations changed nothing. They were just the final nail in a coffin that had been needing to be sealed shut. "I was so unhappy I could barely function, and yet there you were, touching me, kissing me, making me come. I'd cry after I came. I'd cry because it hurt me so much that you could love my body and not love me."

"I loved you."

"You didn't."

"You can accuse me of being a bad husband, of being cold, of being insensitive, but don't tell me how I felt, because I know how I felt. And I did love you. Maybe I didn't say it often —"

"Or ever."

"But I thought you knew."

"Clearly, I didn't."

He stared at her from across the room, his features so hard they looked chiseled from stone. "Why didn't you tell me?" he said finally.

"Because you hated me talking to you." Her throat ached and she swallowed around the lump with difficulty. "Every time I opened my mouth to say anything you'd roll your eyes or sigh or turn away—"

"Not true, either."

"It is true. For me, it's true. And maybe you were raised in a culture where women are happy to be seen and not heard, but I'm an American. I come from a big family. I have three sisters and a brother and am used to conversation and laughter and activity and the only activity I got from you was sex, and even then it wasn't mutual. You were the boss, you were in control, dictating to me how it'd be. Strip, crawl, come—" She broke off, gasping for air, and shoved a trembling hand across her eyes, wiping them dry before any tears could fall. "So don't act so shocked that I'd beg you to help me save my father. Don't say it's degrading and beneath me. I know what degrading is. I know what degrading does. And I've been there, in our marriage, with you."

And then she was done, gone.

Morgan raced to the door, her heels clicking on the polished marble, her purse on the antique console in the grand hall close to the front door, her travel bag in the trunk of her hired car.

She'd flown to Naples this morning from London, and yesterday to London from Los Angeles, almost twenty hours of traveling just to get here, never mind the tortuous winding drive to the villa perched high on the cliffs of the coast between Positano and Ravello. She was exhausted and flattened. Finished. But she wasn't broken. Wasn't shattered, not the way she'd been leaving him the first time.

Count it as a victory, she told herself, wrenching open the front door and stepping outside into the blinding sunshine. *You came, you saw him and you're leaving in one piece. You did it. You faced your dragon and you survived him.*

CHAPTER TWO

DRAKON WATCHED MORGAN spin and race from the living room, her cheeks pale, her long dark hair swinging. He could hear her high-heeled sandals clicking against the gleaming floor as she ran, and then heard the front door open and slam shut behind her.

He slowly exhaled and focused on the silence, letting the stillness and quiet wash over him, calm him.

In a moment he'd go after her, but first he needed to gather his thoughts, check his emotions. It wouldn't do to follow her in a fury—and he was furious. Beyond furious.

So he'd wait. He'd wait until his famous control was firmly in check. He prided himself on his control. Prided himself for not taking out his frustrations on others.

He could afford to give Morgan a few minutes, too. It's not as if she would be able to go anywhere. Her hired car and driver were gone, paid off, dispensed with, and the villa was set off the main road, private and remote. There would be no taxis nearby. She wasn't the sort to stomp away on foot.

And so Drakon used the quiet and the silence to reflect on everything she'd said. She'd said quite a bit. Much of it uncomfortable, and some of it downright shocking, as well as infuriating.

She'd felt degraded in their marriage?

Absolute rubbish. And the fact that she'd dare say such a

thing to his face after all these years made him want to throttle her, which seriously worried him.

He wasn't a violent man. He didn't lose his temper. Didn't even recognize the marriage she described. He had loved her, and he'd spoiled her. Pampered her. Worshipped her body. How was that degrading?

And how dare she accuse him of being a bad husband? He'd given her everything, had done everything for her, determined to make her happy. Her feelings had been important to him. He'd been a respectful husband, a kind husband, having far too many memories of an unhappy childhood, a childhood filled with tense, angry people—namely his mother—to want his wife to be anything but satisfied and content.

His mother, Maria, wasn't a bad woman, she was a good woman, a godly woman, and she tried to be fair, just, but that hadn't made her affectionate. Or gentle.

Widowed at thirty-five when Drakon's father died of a heart attack at sea, Maria had found raising five children on her own overwhelming. The Xanthis family was wealthy and she didn't have to worry about money, but that didn't seem to give her much relief, not when she was so angry that Drakon's father, Sebastian, had died leaving her with all these children, children she wasn't sure she'd ever wanted. One child might have been fine, but five was four too many.

Drakon, being the second eldest, and the oldest son, tried to be philosophical about her anger and resentment. She came from a wealthy family herself and had grown up comfortable. He told himself that her lack of affection and attention wasn't personal, but rather a result of grief, and too many pregnancies too close together. And so he learned by watching her, that she was most comfortable around her children if they asked for nothing, revealed no emotion or expressed no need. Drakon internalized the lesson well, and by thirteen and fourteen, he became the perfect son, by having no needs, or emotions.

But that didn't mean he didn't enjoy pleasing others. Throughout his twenties he had taken tremendous pride in spoiling his girlfriends, beautiful glamorous women who enjoyed being pampered and showered with pretty gifts and extravagant nights out. The women in his life quickly came to understand that he didn't show emotion and they didn't expect him to. It wasn't that he didn't feel, but it wasn't easy to feel. There were emotions in him somewhere, just not accessible. His girlfriends enjoyed his lifestyle, and his ability to please them, and they accepted him for who he was, and that he expressed himself best through action—doing or buying something for someone.

So he bought gifts and whisked his love interests to romantic getaways. And he became a skilled lover, a patient and gifted lover who understood the importance of foreplay.

Women needed to be turned on mentally before they were turned on physically. The brain was their largest erogenous zone, with their skin coming in second. And so Drakon loved to seduce his partner slowly, teasing her, playing with her, whetting the appetite and creating anticipation, because sex was how he bonded. It's how he felt close to his woman. It was how he felt safe expressing himself.

And yet she hadn't felt safe with him. She hadn't even enjoyed being with him. Their lovemaking had disgusted her. He had disgusted her. He'd turned off Morgan.

Drakon's stomach heaved. He swallowed the bitter taste in his mouth.

How stupid he'd been. Moronic.

No wonder she'd left him. No wonder she'd waited until he had flown to London for the day. He had only been away for the day, having flown out early on his jet, returning for a late dinner. But when he had entered their villa in Ekali, a northern suburb of Athens, the villa had been dark. No staff. No dinner. No welcome. No Morgan.

He remembered being blindsided that night. Remembered thinking, he could go without dinner, could live without food, but he couldn't live without Morgan.

He'd called her that night, but she didn't answer. He'd left a message. Left another. Had flown to see her. She wasn't to be found.

He'd called again, left another message, asking her to come home. She didn't. She wouldn't even speak to him, forcing him instead to interact with her trio of attorneys as they informed him that their client was filing for divorce and moving on with her life, without him.

His surprise gave way to frustration and fury, but he never lost his temper with her. He tried to remain cool, focused, pragmatic. Things had a way of working out. He needed to be patient, and he refused to divorce her, insisting he wouldn't agree to a divorce until she met with him. Sat down and talked with him. In person.

She wouldn't. And so for two years her attorneys had battled on her behalf, while Drakon had battled back. His wife would not leave him without giving him a proper explanation. His wife could not just walk away on a whim.

While the Copeland attorneys filed their lawsuits and counter lawsuits, Drakon had made repeated attempts to see Morgan. But every attempt to reach her was stymied. Her cell phone was disconnected. He had no idea where she was living. Her family would only say she'd gone away indefinitely. Drakon had hired private investigators to find her, but they couldn't. Morgan had vanished.

For two and a half years she'd vanished into thin air.

And then in October she had reappeared, emerging again on the New York social scene.

The private investigators sent Drakon her address, a high-rent loft in SoHo, paid for by her father. She'd started her own business as a jewelry designer and had opened a small shop down the street from her loft, locating her little store close to big hitters.

Drakon immediately flew to New York to see her, going straight from the airport to her boutique, hoping that's where he'd find her at 11:00 a.m. on a Wednesday morning. Before he even stepped from his limousine, she walked out the shop's front door with her youngest sister, Jemma. At first glance they looked like any glamorous girls about town, slim and chic, with long gleaming hair and their skin lightly golden from expensive spray-on tans, but after that first impression of beauty and glamour, he saw how extremely thin Morgan was, dangerously thin. She looked like a skeleton in her silk tunic and low-waisted trousers. Wide gold bangles covered her forearms, and Drakon wondered if it was an attempt to hide her extreme slenderness, or perhaps accent her physique?

He didn't know, wasn't sure he wanted to know. The only thing he knew for certain was that she didn't look well and he was baffled by the change in her.

He let her go, leaving her with Jemma, and had his driver take him to her father's building on 53rd and Third Avenue. Daniel Copeland could barely hide his shock at seeing Drakon Xanthis in his office, but welcomed him cordially—he was, after all, taking care of Drakon's investment—and asked him to have a seat.

"I saw Morgan today," Drakon had said bluntly, choosing not to sit. "What's wrong with her? She doesn't look well."

"She hasn't been well," Daniel answered just as bluntly.

"So what's wrong with her?" he repeated.

"That's her business."

"She's my wife."

"Only because you won't let her go."

"I don't believe in divorce."

"She's not happy with you, Drakon. You need to let her go."

"Then she needs to come tell me that herself." He'd left Daniel's office after that, and for several weeks he'd expected a call from Morgan, expected an email, something to say she was ready to meet with him.

But she didn't contact him. And he didn't reach out to her. And the impasse had continued until three days ago when Morgan had called him, and requested a meeting. She'd told him up front why she wanted to see him. She made it clear that this had nothing to do with them, or their marriage, but her need for a loan, adding that she was only coming to him because no one else would help her.

You are my last resort, she'd said. *If you don't help me, no one will.*

He'd agreed to see her, telling her to meet him here, at Villa Angelica. He'd thought perhaps by meeting here, where they'd embarked on their married life, they could come to an understanding and heal the breach. Perhaps face-to-face here, where they had been happy, he could persuade Morgan to return to Athens. It was time. He wanted children, a family. He wanted his wife back where she was supposed to be—in his home, at his side.

Now he realized there was no hope, there never had been, and he felt stupid and angry.

Worse, he felt betrayed. Betrayed by the woman he'd vowed to love and protect, a woman he'd continued to love these past five years, because it was his duty to love her. To be faithful to her. To provide for her.

But he was done with his duty. Done with his loyalty. Done with her.

He wanted her gone.

It was time to give her what she wanted. Time to give them both what they needed—freedom.

Drakon ran a hand over his jaw, feeling the dense beard, a beard he'd started growing that day he'd learned she intended to end their marriage without uttering a single word, or explanation, or apology to him.

He'd vowed he'd grow his beard until his wife returned home, or until he'd understood what had happened between them.

It had been an emotional, impulsive vow, but he'd kept it. Just as he'd kept hope that one day Morgan, his wife, would return to him.

And she had returned, but only to tell him how much she hated him. How much she despised him. How degrading she'd found their marriage.

Drakon exhaled slowly, trying to control the hot rush of emotion that made his chest ache and burn. He wasn't used to feeling such strong emotions. But he was feeling them now.

He headed into the small sitting room, which opened off the living room to his laptop and his briefcase. He took a checkbook to his personal account out of his briefcase and quickly scrawled her name on a check and filled in the amount, before dating it and signing it. He studied the check for a moment, the anger bubbling up, threatening to consume him, and it took all of his control to push it back down, suppressing it with ruthless intent.

He wasn't a failure. She was the failure. She was the one who had walked out on him, not the other way around. He was the one who had fought to save their marriage, who had honored their vows, who had honored her by thinking of no other woman but his wife, wanting no other woman than Morgan.

But now he was done with Morgan. He'd give her the money she wanted and let her go and once she left, he wouldn't waste another moment of his life thinking or worrying about her. She wanted her freedom? Well, she was about to get it.

Morgan was standing on the villa's front steps gazing out at the sweeping drive, with the stunning view of the dark green mountains that dropped steeply and dramatically into the sapphire sea, anxiously rubbing her nails back and forth against her linen skirt, when she heard the front door open behind her.

Her skin prickled and the fine hair at her nape lifted. She knew without even turning around it was Drakon. She could feel his warmth, that magnetic energy of his that drew everything toward him, including her.

But she wouldn't allow herself to be drawn back into his life. Wouldn't give him power over her ever again.

She quickly moved down the front steps, putting distance between them. She refused to look at him, was unable to look at him when she was filled with so much anger and loathing.

"You had no right to send away my car," she said coolly, her gaze resolutely fixed on the dazzling blue and green colors of the coast, but unable to appreciate them, or the lushness of the dark pink bougainvillea blooming profusely along the stone wall bordering the private drive. Panic flooded her limbs. He was so close to her she could barely breathe, much less think.

"I didn't think you'd need it," he said.

She looked sharply at him then, surprised by his audacity, his arrogance. "Did you imagine I was going to stay?"

"I'd hoped," he answered simply.

She sucked in a breath, hating him anew. He could be so charming when he wanted to be. So endearing and real. And then he could take it all away again, just like that. "You really thought I'd take one look at you and forget my unhappiness? Forget why I wanted the divorce?"

"I thought you'd at least sit down and talk to me. Have a real conversation with me."

"You don't like conversation, Drakon. You only want information in bullet form. Brief, concise and to the point."

He was silent a moment, and then he nodded once, a short, decisive nod. "Then I'll be brief in return. The helicopter is on the way for you. Should be here soon. And I have this for you." He handed her a folded piece of paper.

Morgan took it from him, opened it. It was a check for seven million dollars. She looked up at Drakon in surprise. "What's this?"

"The money you begged for."

She flinched. "The pirates are only asking for six."

"There will be other expenses. Travel and rescue logistics. You'll want to hire an expert to help you. Someone with the right negotiation skills. There are several excellent firms out there, like Dunamas Maritime Intelligence—"

"I'm familiar with them."

"They won't be cheap."

"I'm familiar with their fees."

"Don't try to do it on your own, thinking you can. Better to pay for their expertise and their relationships. They know what they're doing, and they'll help you avoid a trap. The Somali pirates sound like they're a ragtag organization, but in truth, they're being funded by some of the wealthiest, most powerful people in the world."

She nodded, because she couldn't speak, not with her throat swelling closed. For the first time in a long, long time, she was grateful for Drakon Xanthis, grateful he had not just the means to help her, but knowledge and power. There weren't many people like Drakon in the world, and she was suddenly so very glad he had been part of her life.

"Use whatever is left after you pay your management fee to pay your father's travel expenses home. There should be enough. If there isn't, let me know immediately," he added.

"Thank you," she whispered huskily.

His jaw tightened. "Go to London before you return to New York, cash the check at the London branch of my bank. There won't be any problems. They'll give you the six million in cash you need for the ransom. You must have it in cash, and not new bills, remember that. But I'm sure your contact told you that?"

"Yes."

His lashes dropped, concealing his expression. "They're very particular, *agapi mou*. Follow the instructions exactly. If you don't, things could turn unpleasant."

"As if storming my father's yacht off the Horn of Africa, and killing his captain, wasn't unpleasant enough—" She broke off, hearing the distinctive hum of the helicopter. It was still a distance from them, but it would be here soon.

For a moment neither said anything, both listening to the whir of the helicopter blades.

"Why have you kept the news of your father's kidnapping private?" he asked her. "I would have thought this was something you'd share with the world…using the kidnapping to garner sympathy."

"Because it wouldn't garner sympathy. The American public hates him. Loathes him. And if they discovered he was kidnapped by Somali pirates, they'd be glad. They'd be dancing in the streets, celebrating, posting all kinds of horrible comments all over the internet, hoping he'll starve, or be killed, saying it's karma—"

"Isn't it?"

She acted as though Drakon hadn't spoken. "But he's my father, not theirs, and I'm not using their money. Not spending government funds, public funds or trust funds. We haven't gone to the police or the FBI, haven't asked for help from anyone. We're keeping this in the family, handling it on our own, and since my brother and sisters don't have the means, I'm using my money—"

"You mean my money."

She flushed, and bit hard into her lower lip, embarrassed. His money. Right. They weren't married, not really, and she had no right to spend his money, just because she had nothing left of her own.

"I stand corrected," she whispered. "Your money. I'm using your money. But I will pay you back. Every penny. Even if it takes me the rest of my life."

A small muscle popped in his jaw. "There is no need for that—" He paused, glancing up at the dark speck overhead. The helicopter.

One of the reasons Drakon had chosen this villa for their honeymoon five and a half years ago was that the outdoor pool had a special cover that converted it into a heli landing pad, making the remote villa far more appealing for a man who needed to come and go for meetings in Naples, Athens and London.

"No need to pay me back," Drakon said, picking up his broken train of thought, "because I'm calling my attorney this afternoon and asking him to process the paperwork for the divorce. He will make sure the dissolution is expedited. By the end of the month, it will be over."

It will be over. For a moment Morgan couldn't take this last bit in. What was he saying? He'd finally agreed to the divorce?

He was giving her the money *and* granting her the divorce?

She just looked up at him, eyes burning, too overwhelmed to speak.

He dipped his head and raised his voice in order to be heard over the hum of the helicopter, which had begun to descend. "You will receive your full settlement once the dissolution occurs. With the current state of affairs, I'd suggest you allow me to open a personal account for you in London or Geneva and I can deposit the funds directly into the account without fear of your government freezing it. I know they've frozen all your family accounts in the United States—"

"I don't want your money."

"Yes, you do. You came here for my money. So take what you came for—"

"I came to see you for my father, and that was the only reason I came here today."

"A point you made abundantly clear." He smiled at her but his amber gaze looked icy, the golden depths tinged with frost. "So I am giving you what you wanted, freedom and financial security, which fulfills my obligation to you."

She shivered at the hardness in his voice. She had never heard him speak to her with so much coldness and disdain and it crushed her to think they were ending it like this— with contempt and anger.

"I'm sorry," she whispered, her heart beating too fast and aching far too much.

He didn't answer her, his gaze fixed on the helicopter slowly descending. Morgan watched him and not the helicopter, aware that this just might be the last time she would see Drakon and was drinking him in, trying to memorize every detail, trying to remember him. This.

"Thank you," she added, wanting him to just look at her, acknowledge her, without this new terrible coldness.

But he didn't. He wouldn't. "I'll walk you to the landing pad," he said, putting his hand out to gesture the way without touching her or looking at her.

Perhaps it was better this way, she told herself, forcing herself to move. It was hard enough being near him without wanting to be closer to him. Perhaps if he'd been kind or gentle, she'd just want more of him, because she'd always wanted more of him, never less. The doctors had said she was addicted to him, and her addiction wasn't healthy. He wasn't the sun, they lectured her, and Drakon, despite his intense charisma and chemistry, couldn't warm her, nor could he actually give her strength. She was the only one who could give herself strength, and the only way she could do that was by leaving him, putting him behind her.

And so here she was again, leaving him. Putting him behind her.

So be strong, she told herself. *Prove that you're strong on your own.*

Morgan blinked to clear her vision, fighting panic as they rounded the villa and walked across the lawn for the open pool terrace where the helicopter waited, balancing like a peculiar moth on the high-tech titanium cover concealing the pool. The roar from the helicopter's spinning blades made conversation impossible, not that Drakon wanted to talk to her.

One of the household staff met them at the helicopter with Morgan's travel bag and Drakon set it inside the helicopter, then spoke briefly to the pilot before putting out his hand to assist Morgan inside.

She glanced down at his outstretched hand, and then up into his face, into those unique amber eyes that had captivated her from the start. "Thank you again, Drakon, and I hope you'll be happy."

His lips curved, but his eyes glittered with silent fury. "Is that a joke? Am I supposed to be amused?"

She drew back, stunned by his flash of temper. For a moment she could only stare at him, surprised, bewildered, by this fierce man. This was a different Drakon than the man she'd married. This was a Drakon of intense emotions and yet after they'd married she'd become convinced that Drakon felt no emotion. "I'm serious. I want you to be happy. You deserve to be happy—"

"As you said I'm not one for meaningless conversation, so I'm going to walk away now to save us from an embarrassing and uncomfortable goodbye," he said brusquely, cutting her short, to propel her into the helicopter. Once he had her inside, he leaned in, his features harsh, and shouted to her, "Don't try to cut corners, Morgan, and save money by handling the pirates yourself. Get help. Call Dunamas, or Blue Sea, or one of the other maritime intelligence companies. Understand me?"

His fierce gaze held hers, and she nodded jerkily, even as her stomach rose up, and her heart fell. If he only knew…

If he only knew what she had done….

And for a split second she nearly blurted the truth, how she had been negotiating with the pirates on her own, and how she'd thought she was in control, until it had all gone terribly wrong, which was why she was here…which was why she needed Drakon so much. But before she could say any of it, Drakon had turned around and was walking away from the helicopter.

Walking away from her.

Her eyes burned and her throat sealed closed as the pilot handed Morgan a set of headphones, but she couldn't focus on the pilot's instructions, not when she was watching Drakon stride toward the villa.

He was walking quickly, passing the rose-covered balustrade on the lower terrace then climbing the staircase to the upper terrace, and the entire time she prayed he'd turn around, pray he'd acknowledge her, pray he'd wave or smile, or just *look* at her.

He didn't.

He crossed the terrace to the old ballroom and disappeared into the great stone house without a backward glance.

So that was it. Done. Over. She was finally free to move on, find happiness, find love elsewhere.

She should be happy. She should feel at peace. But as the helicopter lifted off the pad, straight into the air, Morgan didn't feel any relief, just panic. Because she didn't get the help she needed, and she'd lost him completely.

It wasn't supposed to have gone like this. The meeting today…as well as their marriage. Because she had loved him. She'd loved him with everything she was, everything she had, and it hadn't been enough. It should have been enough. Why wasn't it enough? In the beginning she'd thought he was perfect. In the beginning she'd thought she'd found her soul mate. But she was wrong.

Seconds passed, becoming one minute and then another as the helicopter rose higher and higher, straight up so that the villa fell away and the world was all blue and green, with the sea on one side and the sharp, steep mountains on the other and the villa with its famous garden clinging to that bit of space on the rock.

Fighting tears, her gaze fell on the check she still clutched in her hand. Seven million dollars. Just like that.

And she'd known that he'd help her if she went to him. She'd known he'd come through for her, too, because he'd never refused her anything. Drakon might not have given her much of his time or patience, but he'd never withheld anything material from her.

Guilt pummeled her, guilt and fear and anxiety, because she hadn't accomplished everything she'd come to Villa Angelica to accomplish. She needed more from Drakon than just a check. She needed not just financial assistance, but his help, too. There were few men in the world who had his knowledge of piracy and its impact on the shipping industry. Indeed, Drakon was considered one of the world's leading experts in counter piracy, and he'd know the safest, quickest method for securing her father's release, as well as the right people to help her.

Morgan exhaled in a rush, heart beating too hard.

She had to go back. Had to face Drakon again. Had to convince him to help her. Not that he'd want to help her now, not after everything that was said.

But this wasn't about pride or her ego. This was life and death, her father's life, specifically, and she couldn't turn her back on him.

Swallowing her fear and misgivings, Morgan grabbed at her seat belt as if throwing on brakes. "Stop, wait," she said to the pilot through the small microphone attached to her headphones. "We have to go back. I've forgotten something."

The pilot was too well-trained, and too well-paid, to question her. For a moment nothing seemed to happen and then he shifted and the helicopter began to slowly descend.

Drakon didn't wait for the helicopter to leave. There was no point. She was gone, and he was glad. While climbing the stairs to his bedroom suite, he heard the helicopter lift, the throbbing of the rotary blades vibrating all the way through the old stone walls.

In his bathroom, Drakon stripped his clothes off and showered, and then dried off, wrapping the towel around his hips and prepared to shave. It would take a while. There was a lot of beard.

He gathered his small scissors and his razor and shaving cream, and as he laid everything out, he tried not to think, particularly not of Morgan, but that was impossible. He was so upset. So angry.

What a piece of work she was. To think he'd wanted her back. To think he'd loved her. But how could he have loved her? She was shallow and superficial and so incredibly self-centered. It was always about her…what she wanted, what she needed, with no regard for anyone else's needs.

As he changed the blade on his razor, he felt a heaviness inside, a dull ache in his chest, as if he'd cut his heart. And then Drakon took the razor to his beard.

He had loved her, and he had wanted her back. Wanted her home with him. But that was before he understood how disgusted she was with him, how disgusted she'd been by their marriage.

Disgust.

He knew that word, and knew disgust produced shame. His mother used to be disgusted by emotion, and as a young child, Drakon had felt constant shame in her presence, shame that he had such strong emotions, emotions she found appalling. He still remembered how wild he'd felt on the inside as a little boy, how desperate and confused he'd felt by her rejection, and how determined he'd been to win her affection, even if it meant destroying part of himself. And so that became the goal, his sole objective as a child. To master his hideous emotions. To master want and need, to stifle them, suppress them, thereby winning his mother's approval and love.

He succeeded.

Drakon rinsed the shaving cream from his face and studied his smooth, clean jaw in the mirror. He'd forgotten what his face looked like without a beard, had forgotten how lean his cheeks were above his jutting chin. He had a hard chin, a stubborn chin, which was fitting since he knew he'd become a very hard, stubborn man.

A knock sounded on the outer door of his suite. Drakon mopped his damp face, grabbed a robe and crossed his room to open the door, expecting one of the villa staff.

It wasn't one of the staff. It was Morgan.

Something surged in his chest, hot and fierce, and then it was gone, replaced by coldness. Why was she back? What game was she playing now? He leaned against the door frame, and looked her up and down, coolly, unkindly. "Need more money already?"

Color stained her cheeks, making her blue eyes even deeper, brighter. "You…shaved."

"I did."

"We need to talk."

He arched an eyebrow. "Thank you, but no. I've heard more than enough from you already. Now if you'd be so good as to see yourself out, and get back into the helicopter—"

"The helicopter is gone. I sent him away."

"That was foolish of you. How are you getting back home?"

"We'll figure that out later."

"You mean, you can figure that out later. There is no more we. I'm done with you, and done helping you. You've got your check, and in a month's time you'll receive your settlement, but that's it. That's all there is. I've nothing more for you. Now if you'll excuse me, I have things to do."

Her eyebrows lifted and she walked past him, into his room, glancing around the impressive bedroom where they'd spent the first month of their marriage. "Looks just as I remembered," she said, turning to face him. "But you don't. You've changed."

"Yes, I grew a beard, I know."

"It's not just the beard and hair. It's you. You're different."

"Perhaps you weren't aware. My wife left me. It wasn't an easy thing."

She gave him a long, level look. "You could have come after me."

"I did."

"You did not."

"I *did*."

"I'm not talking about phone calls, or emails or texts. Those don't count."

"No, they don't, and they don't work, either, not once you turned your phone off. Which is why I flew repeatedly to New York, drove up to Greenwich—"

"You didn't!"

His hands clenched at his sides. "Good God, if you contradict me one more time, I will throttle you, Morgan, I will. Because I did go after you, I wanted you back, I wanted you home and I did everything I could to save our marriage. I visited your father at work. I appeared on your parents' doorstep. I spoke—repeatedly—to each of your siblings—"

"I can't believe it," she whispered.

"Believe it," he said grimly, moving toward her, stepping so close he could smell the hint of fragrance from her shampoo, and the sweet clean scent of her perfume on her skin. He loved her smell. Loved her softness. Loved everything about his woman.

But that was then, and this was now, and he was so done with the craziness and the chaos that had followed their marriage.

His gaze caught hers, held, and he stared down into her eyes, drinking in that intense blue that always made him think of the sea around his home in Greece. Tiny purple and gold flecks shimmered against the deep blue irises…like the glimmer of sun on the surface of water. He used to think her eyes perfectly expressed who she was…a woman of magic and mystery and natural beauty.

Now he knew he'd been tricked. Tricked and deceived by a beautiful face, by stunning blue eyes.

Bitterness rolled through him and his gut clenched, his jaw hardening, anger roiling. He really didn't like remembering, and he really didn't like feeling the fury and rejection again, but it was what it was. They were what they were. Such was life.

"And if you don't believe me, make some enquiries. Ask your brother, or your sister Tori, or Logan, or Jemma. Ask them all. Ask why no one would tell me anything. Demand answers, if not for you, then for me. Find out why the entire Copeland family turned their backs on me. I still don't know why. Just as I don't know why you disappeared, or where you went, but you were gone. I even hired private investigators, but you were nowhere to be found."

Morgan bundled her arms across her chest and drew a slow, unsteady breath. A small pulse beat wildly at the base of her throat. "You really came after me?"

"Of course I came after you! You were my wife. You think I just let you go? You think I'd just let you leave?"

She swallowed hard, her blue eyes shining. "Yes."

He swore softly, and walked away from her, putting distance between them. "I don't know what kind of man you think you married, but I am not he. In fact, you, my wife, know nothing about me!"

She followed him, her footsteps echoing on the tiled floor. "Maybe that's because you never gave me a chance to get to know you, Drakon."

He turned abruptly to face her, and she nearly bumped into him. "Or maybe it's because you didn't stay long enough to get to know me, *Morgan*."

Morgan took a swift step backward, stunned by his blistering wrath. She squeezed her hands into fists, crumpling the check in her right hand.

The check.

She'd forgotten all about it. Her heart ached as she glanced down at the paper, creased and crumpled in her hand. "If that is truly the case," she said, voice husky, "I'm sorry."

"If," he echoed bitterly, his upper lip lifting. "I find it so ironic that you don't believe a word I say, and yet when you need something, you'll come running to me—"

"I didn't want to come to you."

"Oh, I'm quite sure of that." He made a rough sound and turned away, running a hand over his newly shaven jaw. "My God, what a joke. I can't believe I waited five years for this."

"What does that mean?"

"Forget it. I don't want to do this." He turned and looked at her, cheekbones jutting against his bronzed skin, his amber gaze hard. "I have finally come to the same realization you did five years ago. That we don't work. That we never worked. That there is no future. And since there is no future, I've nothing to say to you. You have the money, you have what you came for—"

"I didn't just come for money. I need your help."

"That's too bad, then, because the check is all you're getting from me."

She inhaled sharply. He sounded so angry, so bitter, so unlike her husband. "Drakon, please. You know how the pirates operate. You've dealt with them before—"

"No. Sorry. I'm not trying to be ugly, just honest. I'm done. Done with you. Done with your family. Done with your father—my God, there's a piece of work —but he's not my problem anymore, because I'm not his son-in-law anymore, either. And I never thought I'd say this, but I'm actually glad to be done…glad to have a complete break. You've exhausted every one of my resources, and I've nothing more to give. To you, or the rest of the Copeland family."

She winced and looked away, hoping he didn't see the tears that filled her eyes. "No one told me you came after me," she said faintly, her gaze fixed on the view of the sea beyond the window. "But then, in that first year after I left you, no one told me anything."

"I don't see how that is relevant now."

"It probably won't mean anything to you now, but it's relevant to me. It's a revelation, and a comfort—"

"A *comfort?*" he repeated sarcastically.

She lifted her chin a fraction, squared her shoulders. "Yes, a comfort, knowing you didn't give up on me quickly, or easily."

"Unlike you, who gave up so quickly and easily."

"I'm sorry."

"I'm sure you are, now that the privileged Copelands are broke."

She laughed to keep from crying. He was so very, very changed. "We're broke," she agreed, "every last one of us, and struggling, but my brother and sisters, they're smart. They'll be fine. They'll come out of this okay. Me...I'm in trouble. I'm stupid—"

"If this is a play for my sympathy, it's not working."

"No. I'm just telling you the truth. I'm stupid. Very, very stupid. You see, I didn't come to you first. I tried to handle the pirates on my own. And I've already given them money—"

"What?"

She licked her lower lip. "We didn't want it known about my father, and so we kept the details to ourselves, and I tried to manage freeing my father on my own, and I gave them money. But they didn't free my father."

Drakon just looked at her, his jaw clenched, his lips a hard flat line. She could see the pulse beating at the base of his throat. His amber gaze burned. He was furious.

Furious.

Morgan exhaled slowly, trying to calm herself, trying to steady her nerves, but it wasn't easy when her heart raced and the blood roared in her ears. "I didn't want to have to bother you, Drakon. I thought I could manage things better than I did."

He just kept staring at her, his spine stiff, his muscles tensed. He was clearly at war within himself and Morgan felt his anger and frustration. He wanted to kick her out of the villa but he didn't run from responsibilities, or from providing for his family.

He was Greek. Family was everything to him. Even if he didn't enjoy his family.

His tone was icy cold as he spoke. "You should have never tried to handle the pirates on your own. You should have gone to Dunamas or Blue Sea immediately—"

"I didn't have the money to pay for outside help or expertise," she said softly, cutting him short, unable to endure another lecture. "I didn't even have enough to pay the three million ransom. You see, that's what they asked for in the beginning. Three million. But I couldn't come up with exactly three million, and I'd run out of time, so I made the sea drop with what I had, thinking that almost three million was better than nothing, but I was wrong. The pirates were really angry, and accused me of playing games, and they were now doubling the ransom to six million and I had just two weeks or they'd execute Dad."

"How much were you short?"

"A hundred thousand."

"But you dropped two-point-nine million?"

She nodded. "I was so close to three million, and to get it I emptied my savings, sold my loft, liquidated everything I had, but I couldn't get more. I tried taking out personal loans from family and friends but no one was able to come up with a hundred thousand cash in the amount of time we had."

"You didn't come to me for the hundred thousand."

"I didn't want to involve you."

"You have now."

"Because there was no one else who would help me. No other way to come up with six million without my father's situation becoming public knowledge."

"One hundred thousand would have been a hell of a lot cheaper than six million."

"I know." Her stomach heaved. She felt so terribly queasy. "But then, I told you I was stupid. I was afraid to come to you, afraid to face you—"

"I wouldn't have hurt you."

"No, but I have my pride. And then there were all those feelings—" she broke off, and gulped air, thinking she might just throw up "—because I did have feelings for you, and they confused me, but in the end, I had to come. Had to ask you for help…help and money, because the pirates are playing games. They're toying with me and I'm scared. Scared of botching this, scared of never seeing my father again, scared that they have all the power and I have none."

She opened her fist, smoothed the creased check, studied the number and sum it represented. "I know you're angry with me, and I know you owe me nothing. I know it's I that owe you, but I need your help, Drakon. At the very least, I need your advice. What do I do now? How do I make sure that they will release my father this time?" Her gaze lifted, met his. "Who is to say that they will ever release him? Who is to say that he's even…he's even…" Her voice drifted off, and she gazed at him, unable to finish the thought.

But she didn't have to finish the thought. "You're afraid he might not be alive," Drakon said, brutally blunt.

She nodded, eyes stinging. "What if he isn't?"

"That's a good question."

"So you see why I need you. I've already given them three million. I can't give them another six without proof, but they refuse to let me speak to him, and I don't know what to do. I'm frightened, Drakon. And overwhelmed. I've been trying to keep it together, but I don't know how to do this—"

"You and your father sing the same tune, don't you?"

She just stared at him, confused. "What does that mean?"

"The only time I hear from you, or your father, is when one of the Copelands needs money. But I'm not a bank, or an ATM machine, and I'm tired of being used."

Morgan struggled to speak. "I never meant to use you, Drakon. And I certainly didn't marry you for money, and I'm ashamed my father asked you to invest in his company, ashamed that he'd put you in that position. I didn't agree with it then, and I'm shattered now that he lost so much of your personal wealth, but he is my father, and I can't leave him in Somalia. It might be acceptable…even fiscally responsible, but it's not morally responsible, not to me. And so I'm here, begging for your help because you are the only one who can help me."

She paused, swallowed, her gaze searching his face, trying to see a hint of softening on his part. "You might not want to hear this right now, Drakon, but you'd do the same if it were your family. I know you…I know who you are, and I know you'd sacrifice everything if you had to."

Drakon looked at her hard, his features harsh, expression shuttered, and then turned away, and walked to the window where he put his hand on the glass, his gaze fixed on the blue horizon. Silence stretched. Morgan waited for him to speak, not wanting to say more, or rush him to a decision, because she knew in her heart, he couldn't tell her no…it'd go against his values, go against his ethics as a man, and a protective Greek male.

But it was hard to wait, and her jaw ached from biting down so hard, and her stomach churned and her head throbbed, but she had to wait. The ball was in Drakon's court now.

It was a long time before he spoke, and when he did, his voice was pitched so low she had to strain to hear. "I have sacrificed everything for my family," he said roughly. "And it taught me that no good deed goes unpunished."

Her eyes burned, gritty, and her chest squeezed tight with hot emotion. "Please tell me I wasn't the one who taught you that!"

His hand turned into a fist on the window.

Morgan closed her eyes, held her breath, her heart livid with pain. She had loved him…so much…too much….

"I need to think, and want some time," Drakon said, still staring out the window, after another long, tense silence. "Go downstairs. Wait for me there."

CHAPTER THREE

DRAKON WAITED FOR the bedroom door to close behind Morgan before turning around.

His gut churned with acid and every breath he drew hurt.

He wasn't going to do it. There was no way in hell he'd actually help her free her father. For one—he *hated* her father. For another—Drakon had washed his hands of her. The beard was gone. The vigil was over. Time to move forward.

There was no reason he needed to be involved. No reason to do more than he had. As it was, he'd gone above and beyond the call of duty. He'd given her the money, he'd told her what to do, he'd made it clear that there were those who knew exactly what to do, he'd named the people to call...he'd done everything for her, short of actually dialing Dunamas on his cell phone, and good God, he would not do that.

Drakon stalked back to the bathroom, stared at his reflection, seeing the grim features, the cold, dead eyes, and then suddenly his face dissolved in the mirror and he saw Morgan's instead.

He saw that perfect pale oval with its fine, elegant features, but her loveliness was overshadowed by the worry in her blue eyes, and the dark purple smudges beneath her eyes, and her unnatural pallor. Worse, even here, in the expansive marble bathroom, he could still feel her exhaustion and fatigue.

She'd practically trembled while talking to him, her thin arms and legs still too frail for his liking and he flashed back to that day in New York where he'd spotted her walking out of her shop with Jemma. Morgan might not be sick now, but she didn't look well.

Someone, somewhere should be helping her. Not him… she wasn't his to protect anymore…but there should be someone who could assist her. In an ideal world, there would be someone.

He shook his head, not comfortable with the direction his thoughts were taking him. She's not your problem, he told himself. She's not your responsibility. Not your woman.

Drakon groaned, turned away from the mirror, walked out of the bathroom, to retrieve his phone. He'd make a few calls, check on a few facts, see if he couldn't find someone to work with her, because she'd need someone at her side. Not him, of course, but someone who could offer advice and assistance, or just be a source of support.

Standing outside on his balcony he made a few calls, and then he made a few more, and a few more, and each call was worse than the last.

Morgan Copeland was in trouble.

She'd lost her home, her company, her friends, her reputation. She was a social outcast, *and* she was broke. She was overdrawn in her checking account and she'd maxed out every credit card she owned.

Drakon hung up from his last call and tossed the phone onto the bed.

Dammit.

Dammit.

He was so angry with her….

And so angry with her rarified world for turning on her.

She had lost everything. She hadn't been exaggerating.

Morgan was standing in the living room by the enormous wall of windows when Drakon appeared, almost an hour after she'd left him in his bedroom. He'd dressed once again in the off white cashmere V-neck sweater he'd worn earlier, his legs long in the pressed khaki trousers, the sweater smooth over his muscular chest. He'd always had an amazing body, and his perfect build allowed him to wear anything and now with the beard gone she could see his face again and she couldn't look away.

She couldn't call him beautiful, his features were so strong, and his coloring so dark, but he had a sensuality and vitality about him that fascinated her, captivated her. "How long had you been growing that beard?" she asked.

"A long time."

"Years?"

"I'm not here to discuss my beard," he said curtly, crossing the room, walking toward her. "While upstairs I did some research, made a few phone calls, and you did sell your loft. Along with your boutique in SoHo."

Energy crackled around him and Morgan felt her insides jump, tumble. He was so physical, always had been, and the closer he got, the more the tension shifted, growing, building, changing, binding them together the way it always had. The way it always did. "I had to," she said breathlessly, "it was the only way to come up with the money."

"You should have told me immediately that you'd given the Somali pirates ransom money and that they'd failed to release your father."

"I thought you might not have helped me, if you knew…." Her voice faded as Drakon closed the distance between them. He was so alive, so electric, she could almost see little sparks shooting off him. Her heart pounded. Her tummy did another nervous, panicked flip.

She shouldn't have sent away the helicopter. She should have gone while she could. Now it was too late to run. Too late to save herself, and so she stared at him, waited for him, feeling the energy, his energy, that dizzying combination of warmth and heat, light and sparks. This was inevitable. He was inevitable. She could run and run and run, but part of her knew she'd never escape him. She'd run before and yet here she was. Right back where they'd honeymooned, Villa Angelica.

She'd known that coming here, to him, would change everything. Would change her.

It always did.

It already had.

Her legs trembled beneath her. Her heart pounded. Even now, after all these years, she felt almost sick with awareness, need. This chemistry and energy between them was so overwhelming. So consuming. She didn't understand it, and she'd wanted to understand it, if only to help her exorcise him from her heart and her mind.

But all the counselors and doctors and therapists in the world hadn't erased this…him.

Why was Drakon so alive? Why was he more real to her than any other man she'd ever met? After Drakon, after loving Drakon, there could be no one else…he made it impossible for her to even look at anyone else.

He'd reached her, was standing before her, his gaze fierce, intense, as it traveled across her face, making her feel so bare, and naked. Heat bloomed in her skin, blood surging from his close inspection.

"What did you do, Morgan?"

"I don't understand."

"You've sold everything," he added harshly. "You have nothing and even if you get your father back to the United States, you'll still have nothing."

"Not true," she said, locking her knees, afraid she'd collapse, overwhelmed by emotion and memories, overwhelmed by him. She'd been up for two days straight. Hadn't eaten more than a mouthful in that time. She couldn't, knowing she would soon be here, with him again. "I'd have peace of mind."

"Peace of mind?" he demanded. "How can you have peace of mind when you have no home?"

He could mock her, because he didn't know what it was like to lose one's mind. He didn't know that after leaving him, she'd ended up in the hospital and had remained there for far too long. It had been the lowest point in her life, and by far, the darkest part. But she didn't want to think about McLean Hospital now, that was the past, and she had to live in the present, had to stay focused on what was important, like her father. "I did what I had to do."

"You sacrificed your future for your father's, and he doesn't have a future. Your father—*if* alive, *if* released—will be going to prison for the rest of his life. But what will you do while he's in his comfortable, minimum security prison cell, getting three square meals a day? Where will you sleep? What will you eat? How will you get by?"

"I'll figure it out."

"You are so brave and yet foolhardy. Do you ever look before you leap?"

She flashed to Vienna and their wedding and the four weeks of honeymoon, remembering the intense love and need, the hot brilliant desire that had consumed her night and day. She hated to be away from him, hated to wake up without him, hated to breathe without him.

She'd lost herself completely in him. And no, she hadn't looked, hadn't analyzed, hadn't imagined anything beyond that moment when she'd married him and became his.

"No," she answered huskily, lips curving and heart aching. "I just leap, Drakon. Leap and hope I can fly."

If she'd hoped to provoke him, she'd failed. His expression was impassive and he studied her for a long moment from beneath his thick black lashes. "How long has it been since you've spoken to your father?"

"I actually haven't ever spoken to him. My mother did, and just that first day, when they called her to say they had him. Mother summoned us, and told us what had happened, and what the pirates wanted for a ransom "

"How long did she speak to your father?"

"Not long. Just a few words, not much more than that."

"What did he say to her?"

"That his yacht had been seized, his captain killed and he had been abducted, and then the pirates got back on the phone, told her their demands and hung up."

"Has anyone spoken with your father since?"

She shook her head. "No."

"Why not?"

"They won't let us. They say we haven't earned the right."

"But you've given them three million."

Her lips curved bitterly and her gaze lifted to meet his. "I can't sleep at night, knowing I was so stupid and so wasteful. Three million dollars gone! Three million lost forever. It would have been fine if we'd saved my father, but we didn't. I didn't. Instead it's all gone and now I must start over and worse, the ransom has doubled. I'm sick about it, sick that I made such a critical error. I didn't mind liquidating everything to save my father, but it turns out I liquidated everything for nothing—"

"Stop."

"You are right to despise me. I am stupid, stupid, stupid—"

He caught her by the shoulders and gave her a hard shake. "Enough. You didn't know. You didn't understand how the pirates operated, how mercurial they are, how difficult, how unpredictable. You had no way of knowing. There is no handbook on dealing with pirates, so stop torturing yourself."

With every sentence he gave her a little shake until she was thoroughly undone and tears filled her eyes, ridiculous tears that stung and she swiped at them, annoyed, knowing they were from fatigue, not sadness, aware that she was exhausted beyond reason, knowing that what she wanted was Drakon to kiss her, not shake her, but just because you wanted something didn't mean it was good for you. And Drakon wasn't good for her. She had to remember that.

He saw her tears. His features darkened. "We'll get your father back," he said, his deep voice rumbling through her, his voice as carnal as the rest of him, drawing her into his arms and holding her against his chest, comforting her.

For a moment.

Morgan pulled back, slipping from Drakon's arms, and took several quick steps away to keep from being tempted to return. He'd been so warm. He'd smelled so good. His hard chest, covered in cashmere, had made her want to burrow closer. She'd felt safe there, secure, and yet it was an illusion.

Drakon wasn't safe. He was anything but safe for her.

He watched her make her escape. His jaw jutted, his brow lowered, expression brooding. "We'll get your father back," he said, repeating his promise from a few moments ago. "And we'll do it without giving them another dollar."

She looked up at him, surprised. "How?"

"I know people."

She blinked at him. Of course he knew people—Drakon knew everyone—but could he really free her father without giving the pirates more money? "Is that possible?"

"There are companies…services…that exist just for this purpose."

"I've looked into those companies. They cost millions, and they won't help me. They loathe my father. He represents everything they detest—"

"But they'll work with me."

"Not when they hear who they are to rescue—"

"I own one of the largest shipping companies in the world. No maritime agency would refuse me."

Hope rose up within her, but she didn't trust it, didn't trust anyone or anything anymore. "But you said…you said you wouldn't help me. You said since you'd given me the check—"

"I was wrong. I was being petty. But I can't be petty. You're my wife—" he saw her start to protest and overrode her "—and as long as you are my wife, it's my duty to care for you and your family. It is the vow I made, and a vow I will keep."

"Even though I left you?"

"You left me, I didn't leave you."

Pain flickered through her. "You owe me nothing. I know that. You must know that, too."

"Marriage isn't about keeping score. Life is uneven and frequently unjust and I did not marry you, anticipating only fun and games. I expected there would be challenges, and there have been, far more than I anticipated, but until we are divorced, you are my wife, and the law is the law, and it is my duty to provide for you, to protect you, and I can see I have failed to do both."

She closed her eyes, shattered by his honesty, as well as his sense of responsibility. Drakon was a good man, a fair man, and he deserved a good wife, a wife less highly strung and sensitive…a wife who craved him less, a wife who could live and breathe without him at her side….

Morgan wasn't that woman. Even now she wanted to be back in his arms, to have his mouth on hers, to have him parting her lips, tasting her, filling her, possessing her so completely that the world fell away, leaving just the two of them.

That was her idea of life.

And it was mad and beautiful and impossible and bewitching.

"It's not your fault," she whispered, wrapping her arms around her, wishing she'd needed less talk and tenderness and reassurance. "It's mine. Maybe even my father's. He spoiled me, you know, and it infuriated my mother."

"Your mother did say at our wedding that you were your daddy's little girl."

Morgan's breath caught in her throat and she bit into her bottom lip. "Mother had Tori and Branson and Logan, and yes, I was Daddy's girl, but they were Mother's darlings, and you'd think since she had them living with her, choosing her, she wouldn't mind that I chose to live with Father, but she did."

"What do you mean, they lived with her, and you lived with Daniel? Didn't you all live together?"

Morgan shook her head. "Mother and Father lived apart most of the time. They'd put on a show for everyone else— united front for the public, always throwing big parties for the holidays or special occasions…Christmas party, New Year's party, birthdays and anniversaries. But behind closed doors, they could barely tolerate each other and were almost never in the same place at the same time, unless there was a photo shoot, or reporter about. Mother loved being in the society columns, loved having our lavish, privileged lifestyle featured in glossy magazines. She liked being envied, enjoyed her place in the sun. Father was different. He hadn't grown up with money like Mother, and wasn't comfortable in the spotlight. He lived far more quietly…he and I, and Jemma, when she joined us. We'd go to these small neighborhood restaurants and they weren't trendy in the least. We loved our Mexican food and Greek food and Indian food and maybe once every week or two, we'd send out for Chinese food. After dinner, once my homework was done, we'd watch television in the evening…we had our favorite show. We had our routines. It was lovely. He was lovely. And ordinary." She looked up at Drakon, sorrow in her eyes. "But the world now won't ever know that man, or allow him to be that man. In their eyes, he's a greedy selfish hateful man, but he wasn't. He really wasn't—" She broke off, drew a deep breath and then another.

"Mother used to say I was a demanding little girl, and she hated that Father humored me. She said he spoiled me by taking me everywhere with him, and turning me into his shadow. Apparently that's why I became so clingy with you. I shifted my attachment from my father onto you. But what a horrible thing for you…to be saddled with a wife who can't be happy on her own—"

"You're talking nonsense, Morgan—"

"No, it's true."

"Well, I don't buy it. I was never saddled with you, nor did I ever feel encumbered by you. I'm a man. I do as I please and I married you because I chose you, and I stayed married to you because I chose to, and that's all there is to it."

She looked away, giving him her profile. It was such a beautiful profile. Delicate. Elegant. The long, black eyelashes, the sweep of cheekbone, the small straight nose, the strong chin, above an impossibly long neck. The Copeland girls were all stunning young women, but there was something ethereal about Morgan…something mysterious.

"You're exhausted," he added. "I can see you're not eating or sleeping and that must change. I will not have you become skin and bones again. While you're here, you will sit and eat real meals, and rest, and allow me to worry about things. I may not have been the patient and affectionate husband you wanted, but I'm good at managing chaos, and I'm damn good at dealing with pirates."

He didn't know what he expected, but he didn't expect her to suddenly smile at him, the first smile he'd seen from her since she arrived, and it was radiant, angelic, starting in her stunning blue eyes and curving her lips and making her lovely face come alive.

For a moment he could only look at her, and appreciate

her. She was like the sun and she glowed, vital, beautiful, and he remembered that first night in Vienna when she'd turned and looked at him, her blue eyes dancing, mischief playing at her mouth, and then she'd spotted him, her eyes meeting his, and her smile had faded, and she'd become shy. She'd blushed and turned away but then she'd peek over her shoulder at him again and again and by the end of the ball he knew he would have her. She was his. She would always be his. Thank God she'd felt the same way. It would have created an international scandal if he'd had to kidnap her and drag her off to Greece, an unwilling bride.

"I am happy to allow you to take the lead when it comes to the pirates," she said, her smile slowly dying, "and you may manage them, but Drakon, you mustn't try to manage me. I won't be managed. I've had enough of that these past five years."

Drakon frowned, sensing that there was a great deal she wasn't saying, a great deal he wouldn't like hearing, and he wanted to ask her questions, hard questions, but now wasn't the time, not when she was so fragile and fatigued. There would be time for all his questions later, time to learn just what had dismantled his marriage, and who and what had been managing her, but he could do that when she wasn't trembling with exhaustion and with dark purple circles shadowing her eyes.

"I'm concerned about you," he said flatly.

"There's been a lot of stress lately."

He didn't doubt that, and it crossed his mind that if he'd been a real husband, and a more selfless man, he would have gone to Morgan, and offered her support or assistance before it'd come to this. Instead, he, like the rest of the world, had followed the Copeland family crisis from afar, reading about the latest humiliation or legal move in the media, and doing nothing.

"I can see that, but you'll be of no use to your father, if you fall apart yourself," he said. "I'll make some calls and the staff can prepare us a late lunch—"

"Do we really need lunch?"

"Yes, we do. And while I understand time is of the essence, not eating will only make things worse. We need clear heads and fierce resolve, and that won't happen if we're fainting on our feet."

Morgan suddenly laughed and she shook her head, once again giving him a glimpse of the Morgan he'd married… young and vivacious and full of laughter and passion. "You keep using 'we,' when we both know you mean me." She paused and her gaze lifted, her eyes meeting his. "But I do rather like the image of you fainting on your feet."

His gaze met hers and held and it was all he could do to keep from reaching for her. He wanted her. Still wanted her more than he'd wanted anyone or anything. "Of course you would," he said roughly. "You're a wicked woman and you deserve to be—"

Drakon broke off abruptly, balling his hands into fists and he realized how close he'd come to teasing her the way he'd once teased her, promising her punishment, which was merely foreplay to make her hot, to make her wet, to make her shudder with pleasure.

It used to give him such pleasure that he brought her pleasure. He wasn't good at saying all the right words, so he used his body to say how much he adored her, how much he desired her, how much he cherished her and would always cherish her.

But only now did he know she'd hated the way he'd pleasured her.

That she'd been disgusted—

"Don't," she whispered, reaching out to him, her hand settling on his arm. "Don't do that, don't. I know what you're thinking, and I'm sorry. I shouldn't have said what I did, shouldn't have said it how I did. It was wrong. I was wrong. I was upset."

His body hardened instantly at her touch, and he glanced down at her hand where it clung to his forearm. He could feel her warmth through the softness of the cashmere, and the press of her fingers, and it was nothing at all, and yet it was everything, too. Nothing and everything at the same time.

He looked away from her hand, up into her eyes, angry with her all over again, but also angry with himself. How could he have not known how she felt? How could he have not realized that she didn't enjoy…him…them?

"Rest assured that I will not take advantage of you while you are here," he said, trying to ease some of the tension rippling through him. "You are safe in the villa," he continued, hating that he suddenly felt like a monster. He wasn't a monster. Not even close. It's true he could be ruthless in business, and he had a reputation for being a fierce negotiator, a brilliant strategist, an analytical executive, as well as a demanding boss, but that didn't make him an ogre and he'd never knowingly hurt a woman, much less his wife. "You are safe from me."

"Drakon."

"I'll have your bag taken up to the Angelica Suite," he said. "It's the second master suite, on the third floor, the suite one with the frescoed ceiling."

"I remember it."

"It's in the opposite wing of where I'm staying but it should give you privacy and I think you'll find it quite comfortable. I can show you the way now."

"There's no need to take me there," she said hoarsely. "I remember the suite."

"Fine. Then I'll let you find your way, and as I have quite a few things to do, I'll eat as I work, and I'll have a light lunch sent to you in your room, but we'll need to meet later so I can fill you in on the arrangements I've been able to make for your father."

* * *

Morgan was glad to escape to her room, desperate to get away from Drakon and that intense physical awareness of him....

She'd hurt him. What she'd said earlier, about their sex life, about their marriage, it'd hurt him terribly and she felt guilty and sorry. So very sorry since she knew Drakon would never do anything to hurt her. He'd always been so protective of her but he was also so very physical, so carnal and sexual and she was a little afraid of it. And him. Not when she was with him, making love to him, but later, when he was gone, separated from her. It was then that she analyzed their relationship, and what they did and how they did it and how little control she had with him.

It frightened her that she lost control with him.

Frightened her that he had so much power and she had so little.

It had niggled at her during their honeymoon, but their picnics and dinners out and the afternoon trips on his yacht were so fun and romantic that she could almost forget how fierce and shattering the sex was when he was charming and attentive and affectionate. But in Athens when he disappeared into his work life, his real life, the raw nature of their sex life struck her as ugly, and she became ugly and it all began to unravel, very, very quickly.

Upstairs in her suite, Morgan barely had time to open the two sets of French doors before a knock sounded on the outer bedroom door, letting her know her overnight bag had arrived. She thanked the housemaid and then returned to the first of the two generous balconies with the stunning view.

She had never tired of this view. She couldn't imagine how anyone could tire of it.

The Amalfi Coast's intense blues and greens contrasted by rugged rock had inspired her very first jewelry collection. She'd worked with polished labradorite, blue chalcedony, pāua shell, lapis lazuli and Chinese turquoise, stones she'd acquired on two extensive shopping trips through Southeast Asia, from Hong Kong to Singapore to Bali.

It'd been a three-month shopping expedition that big sister Tori had accompanied her on for the first month, and then Logan came for the second month, and Jemma for the third.

By the time Morgan returned to New York, she'd filled two enormous trunks of stones and had a briefcase and laptop full of sketches and the first orders from Neiman Marcus and Bergdorf Goodman. The designs were pure fantasy—a stunning collection of statement-making collars, cuffs and drop earrings—and had cost her a fortune in stone. It had tested her ability to execute her ideas, but had ended up being worth every stress and struggle as the Amalfi Collection turned out to be a huge success, generating significant media attention, as well as the attention of every fashion designer and fashion publicist of note, never mind the starlets, celebrities and socialites who all wanted a Morgan Copeland statement piece.

Morgan's second collection, Jasper Ice, had been inspired by her love of the Canadian Rockies and ski trips to Banff and Lake Louise. The collection was something that an ice princess in a frozen tundra would wear—frosty and shimmering pieces in white, silver, blush, beige and pale gold. The second collection did almost as well as the first, and garnered even more media with mentions in virtually every fashion magazine in North America, Europe and Australia, and then photographed on celebrities and young royals, like the Saudi princess who had worn a gorgeous pink diamond cuff for her wedding.

Morgan was glad Jasper Ice did well, but the cool, frozen beauty of the collection was too much like her numb emotional state, when she'd been so fiercely, frantically alive and in love with Drakon Xanthis.

Drakon, though, was the last person she wanted to think

of, especially when she was enjoying the heady rush of success, and for a while she had been very good at blocking him out of her mind, but then one October day, she had been walking with Jemma to lunch and she had spotted a man in a limousine. He'd had a beard and his hair was long but his eyes reminded her so much of Drakon that for a moment she thought it was him.

She had kept walking, thinking she'd escaped, but then a block away from her shop, she'd had to stop, lean against a building and fight for air.

She'd felt like she was having a heart attack. Her chest hurt, the muscles seizing, and she couldn't breathe, couldn't get air, couldn't even speak. She opened her mouth, stared at Jemma, wanting, needing help, but she couldn't make a sound. Then everything went black.

When she woke up, she'd been in an ambulance, and then when she woke again, she was in a bed in the emergency room. She'd spent the next ten days in the hospital, six in ICU, being seen by cardiac specialists. The specialists explained that her extreme weight loss had damaged her heart, and they warned her that if she didn't make immediate and drastic changes, she could die of heart failure.

But Morgan hadn't been dieting. She didn't want to lose weight. She had just found it impossible to eat when her heart was broken. But she wasn't a fool, she understood the gravity of her situation, and recognized she was in trouble.

During the day they'd fed her special shakes and meals and at night she'd dreamed of Drakon, and the dreams had been so vivid and intense that she'd woke desperate each morning to actually see him. She made the mistake of telling Logan that she was dreaming about Drakon every night, and Logan had told their mother, who then told the doctors, and before Morgan knew it, the psychiatrists were back with their pills and questions and notepads.

Did she understand the difference between reality and fantasy?

Did she understand the meaning of wish fulfillment?

Did she want to die?

It would have been puzzling if she hadn't been through all this before at McLean Hospital in Massachusetts, and then at the Wallace Home for a year after that. But she had been through it before so she found the doctors with their clipboards and questions and colorful assortment of pills annoying and even somewhat amusing.

She'd refused the pills. She'd answered some questions. She'd refused to answer others.

She wasn't sick or crazy this time. She was just pushing herself too hard, working too many hours, not eating and sleeping enough.

Morgan had promised her medical team and her family she'd slow down, and eat better, and sleep more and enjoy life more, and for the next two plus years she did. She began to take vacations, joining her sisters for long holidays at the family's Caribbean island, or skiing in Sun Valley or Chamonix, and sometimes she just went off on her own, visiting exotic locations for inspiration for her jewelry designs.

She'd also learned her lesson. She couldn't, wouldn't, mention Drakon again.

Those ten days in the hospital, and her vivid, shattering dreams at night, had inspired her third collection, the Black Prince, a glamorous, dramatic collection built of ruby hues—garnets, red spinels, pink sapphires, diamonds, pave garnets, watermelon tourmaline, pink tourmaline. The collection was a tribute to her brief marriage and the years that followed, mad love, accompanied by mad grief. In her imagination, the Black Prince was Drakon, and the bloodred jewels represented her heart, which she'd cut and handed to him, while the pink sapphires and delicate tourmalines were the tears she'd cried leaving him.

But, of course, she had to keep that inspiration to herself, and so she came up with a more acceptable story for the public, claiming that her newest collection was inspired by the Black Prince's ruby, a 170-carat red spinel once worn in Henry V's battle helmet.

The collection was romantic and over-the-top and wildly passionate, and early feedback had seemed promising with orders pouring in for the large rings, and jeweled cuffs, and stunning pendulum necklaces made of eye-popping pale pink tourmaline—but then a week before the official launch of her collection, news of the Michael Amery scandal broke and she knew she was in trouble. It was too late to pull any of her ads, or change the focus of the marketing for her latest Morgan Copeland collection.

It was absolutely the wrong collection to be launched in the middle of a scandal implicating Daniel Copeland, and thereby tarnishing the Copeland name. The Black Prince Collection had been over-the-top even at conception, and the finished pieces were sensual and emotional, extravagant and dramatic, and at any other time, the press and fashion darlings would have embraced her boldness, but in the wake of the scandal where hundreds of thousands of people had been robbed by Michael Amery and Daniel Copeland, the media turned on her, criticizing her for being insensitive and hopelessly out of touch with mainstream America. One critic went so far as to compare her to Marie Antoinette, saying that the Black Prince Collection was as "frivolous and useless" as Morgan Copeland herself.

Morgan had tried to prepare herself for the worst, but the viciousness of the criticism, and the weeks of vitriolic attacks, had been unending. Her brother, Branson, a media magnate residing in London, had sent her an email early on, advising her to avoid the press, and to not read the things being written about her. But she did read them. She couldn't seem to help herself.

In the fallout following the Amery Ponzi scandal, the orders that had been placed for her lush Black Prince Collection were canceled, and stores that had trumpeted her earlier collections quietly returned her remaining pieces and closed their accounts with her. No one wanted to carry anything with the Copeland name. No one wanted to have an association with her.

It was crushing, financially and psychologically. She'd invested hundreds of thousands of dollars into the stones, as well as thousands and thousands into the labor, and thousands more into the marketing and sales. The entire collection was a bust, as was her business.

Fortunately, there was no time to wallow in self-pity. The phone call from Northern Africa, alerting her that her father had been kidnapped, had forced her to prioritize issues. She could grieve the loss of her business later. Now, she had to focus on her father.

And yet…standing here, on the balcony, with the bright sun glittering on the sapphire water, Morgan knew she wouldn't have had any success as a designer, or any confidence in her creative ability, if it hadn't been for her honeymoon here in this villa.

And Drakon.

But that went without saying.

CHAPTER FOUR

Morgan had only packed her traveling clothes and the one blue linen top and skirt she'd changed into after arriving in Naples, and so before lunch arrived, she slipped into her comfortable tracksuit to eat her lunch on the balcony before taking a nap. She hadn't meant to sleep the afternoon away but she loved the breeze from the open doors and how it fluttered the long linen curtains and carried the scents of wisteria and roses and lemon blossoms.

She slept for hours in the large bed with the fluffy duvet and the down pillows all covered in the softest of linens. The Italians knew how to make decadent linens and it was here on her honeymoon that she'd come to appreciate cool, smooth sheets and lazy afternoon naps. She'd fall asleep in Drakon's arms after making love and wake in his arms and make love yet again and it was all so sensual, so indulgent. It had been pure fantasy.

She'd dreamed of Drakon while she slept, dreamed they were still together, still happy, and parents of a beautiful baby girl. Waking, Morgan reached for Drakon, her hand slipping sleepily across the duvet, only to discover that the other side of her big bed was empty, cool, the covers undisturbed. Rolling onto her side, she realized it was just a dream. Yet more fantasy.

Tears stung her eyes and her heart felt wrenched, and the

heartbreak of losing Drakon felt as real as it had five years ago, when her family had insisted she go to McLean Hospital instead of return to Drakon in Greece.

You're not well. This isn't healthy. You're not healthy. You're too desperate. This is insanity. You're losing your mind....

Her throat swelled closed and her chest ached and she bit into her lip to keep the memories at bay.

If she hadn't left Drakon they probably would have children now. Babies...toddlers...little boys and girls...

She'd wanted a family with him, but once in Greece Drakon had become a stranger and she had feared they were turning into her own parents: distant, silent, destined to live separate lives.

She couldn't do it. Couldn't be like her parents. Wouldn't raise children in such an unhealthy, unsuitable environment.

Stop thinking about it, she told herself, flipping the covers back and leaving the bed to bathe before dinner. In her grand bathroom with the soaring frescoed ceiling and the warm cream-and-terra-cotta marble, she took a long soak in the deep tub before returning to the bedroom to put her tired linen skirt and blouse back on. But in the bedroom the crumpled blue skirt and blouse were gone and in their place was a huge open Louis Vuitton trunk sitting on the bench at the foot of the bed.

She recognized the elegant taupe-and-cream trunk—it was part of the luggage set her father had given her before her wedding and it was filled with clothes. Her clothes, her shoes, her jewelry, all from the Athens villa. Drakon must have sent for them. It was a thoughtful gesture and she was grateful for clean clothes and something fresh to wear, but it was painful seeing her beautiful wardrobe...so very extravagant, so much couture. So much money invested in a couple dozen dresses and blouses and trousers. Thousands more in shoes and purses.

Morgan sorted through the sundresses and evening dresses and chic tunics and caftans. Her sisters were far more fashionable than she was, and constantly pushing her to be a bit more trendy, but Morgan liked to be comfortable and loved floaty dresses that skimmed her body rather than hug every curve, but she needed something more fitted tonight, something to keep her together because she was so close to falling apart.

She settled on a white eyelet dress with a boned corset and small puffy sleeves that made her feel like a Gypsy, and she added gold hoop earrings and a coral red shawl worn loosely around her shoulders. Morgan didn't wear a lot of makeup and applied just a hint of color to her cheeks and lips, a little concealer to soften the circles that remained beneath her eyes and then a bit of mascara because it gave her confidence.

The sun was just starting to set as she headed downstairs. She remembered her way to the dining room, but one of the villa staff was on hand at the foot of the stairs to escort her there. Before she'd even entered the dining room she spotted Drakon on the patio, through the dining room's open doors. He was outside, leaning against the iron railing, talking on the phone.

She hesitated before joining him, content for a moment to just look at him while he was preoccupied.

He'd changed from the cashmere sweater to a white linen shirt and a pair of jeans for dinner. His choice in wardrobe surprised her.

Jeans.

She'd never seen him wear jeans before, and these weren't fancy European denim jeans, but the faded American Levi's style and they looked amazing on him. The jeans were old and worn and they outlined Drakon's strong thighs and hugged his hard butt and made her look a little too long at the button fly that covered his impressive masculine parts.

How odd this new Drakon was, so different from the sophisticated, polished man she'd remembered all these years ago. His beard and long hair might be gone, but he still wasn't the Drakon of old. He was someone else, someone new, and that kept taking her by surprise.

The Drakon she'd married had been an incredibly successful man aware of his power, his wealth, his stature. He'd liked Morgan to dress up, to wear beautiful clothes, to be seen in the best of everything, and Drakon himself dressed accordingly. He wouldn't have ever worn a simple white linen shirt halfway unbuttoned to show off his bronze muscular chest. He'd been too controlled, too tightly wound, while this man… he oozed recklessness. And sex.

Drakon had always had an amazing body, but this new one was even stronger and more fit now and Morgan swallowed hard, hating to admit it, but she was fascinated by him. Fascinated and a little bit turned on, which wasn't at all appropriate given the situation, especially considering how Drakon had promised not to touch her.…

Drakon suddenly turned, and looked straight at her, his amber gaze meeting hers through the open door. Despite everything, heat flickered in his eyes and she swallowed hard again, even as she blushed hotly, aware that she'd been caught staring.

Nervous, she squared her shoulders and briskly crossed the dining room before stepping outside onto the patio. Drakon had just ended his call as she joined him outside and he slipped the phone into the front pocket of his jeans.

Those damn faded jeans that lovingly outlined his very male body.

There was no reason a Greek shipping magnate needed a body like that. It was decadent for a man who already had so much. His body was beautiful. Sexual. Sinful. He knew how to use it, too, especially those lean hard hips. Never mind his skillful fingers, lips and tongue.

"Hope I didn't keep you waiting long," he said.

Cheeks hot, insides flip-flopping, she reluctantly dragged her gaze from his button fly up to his face with its newly shaven jaw and square chin. "No," she murmured, almost missing the dark thick beard and long hair. When she'd first arrived, he'd looked so primitive and primal. So undeniably male that she wouldn't have been surprised if he'd pushed her up against the wall and taken her there.

Perhaps a little part of her wished he had.

Instead he'd vowed to stay away from her, and she knew Drakon took his vows seriously. Was it so wrong of her to wish he'd kissed her properly before he'd made that vow? Was it wrong to crave his skin even though he'd made the vow already?

Just thinking of his skin made her glance at his chest, at that broad expanse of hard muscle, and her body reacted, her inner thighs tightening, clenching, while her lower belly ached with emptiness. She hadn't been honest with him. She had loved to make love with him, loved the way he felt inside of her, his body buried deeply between her thighs and how he'd draw back before thrusting back in, over and over until she raked her nails across his shoulders and gripped his arms and arched under him, crying his name.

And just remembering, she could almost feel the weight of him now, his arms stretching her arms above her head, his hands circling her wrists, his chest pressed to her breasts. He'd thrust his tongue into her mouth even as his hard, hot body thrust into hers, burying himself so deeply she couldn't think, feel, want anything but Drakon.

Drakon.

And now she was here with him. Finally. After all these years.

Morgan, it's not going to happen, she told herself. He's letting you go. You're moving on. There will be no sex against the wall, or sex on the floor, or sex on the small dining table painted gold and rose with the lush sunset.

But wouldn't it feel good? another little voice whispered.

Of course it'd feel good. Everything with Drakon had felt good. Sex wasn't the problem. It was the distance after the sex that was.

"Something to drink?" he asked, gesturing to the bar set up in the corner and filled with dozens of bottles with colorful labels. "I can make you a mixed drink, or pour you a glass of wine."

"A glass of wine," she said, as a breeze blew in from the sea, and caught at her hair, teasing a dark tendril.

"Red or white?"

"Doesn't matter. You choose."

He poured her a glass of red wine. "Were you able to sleep?" he asked, handing her the goblet, and their fingers brushed.

A frisson of pleasure rushed through her at the brief touch. Her pulse quickened and she had to exhale slowly, needing to calm herself, settle herself. She couldn't lose focus, had to remember why she was here. Her father. Her father, who was in so much danger. "Yes," she said, her voice pitched low, husky with a desire she could barely master, never mind hide.

Drakon stiffened at the sudden spike of awareness. Morgan practically hummed with tension, her slim figure taut, energy snapping and crackling around her. It was hot and electric, she was hot and electric, and he knew if he reached for her, touched her, she'd let him. She wanted him. Morgan had been right about the physical side of their relationship. There was plenty of heat…intense chemistry…but she'd been the one that brought the fire to their relationship. She'd brought it out in him. He'd enjoyed sex with other women, but with her, it wasn't just sex. It was love. And he'd never loved a woman before her. He'd liked them, admired them, enjoyed them... but had never loved, not the way he loved her, and he was quite sure he would never love any woman this way again.

"For hours," she added, blushing, her voice still husky. "It was lovely. But then, I always sleep well here."

"It's the air, I think," he said. "You look beautiful, by the way," he said.

Her cheeks turned pink and her blue eyes glowed with pleasure. She looked surprised, touched. His beautiful woman. Part of him wanted to shake her, kiss her, make her his again, and another part of him wanted to send her away forever.

"Thank you for sending for my clothes," she said, fighting the same tendril of hair, the one the breeze loved to tease. "That was very kind of you."

"Not kind, just practical," he answered. "Since you're not returning to Ekali, there's no point keeping your things at the villa there anymore. Which reminds me, I have another trunk with your winter clothes and ski things ready to go home with you when you leave for New York. It's in one of the storage rooms downstairs. Didn't see any reason to drag it up three flights of stairs only to drag it down again in a few days.

A shadow passed across her face. "Is that how long you think I need to be here?"

"We'll know better once Rowan arrives. I expect him in late tonight or early tomorrow."

"Rowan?"

"Rowan Argyros, from Dunamas Maritime Intelligence. He's the one I work with when my ships have been seized. His headquarters are in London, but when I phoned him this afternoon I learned that he's in Los Angeles and he's promised to fly out this afternoon."

"But if you are a maritime piracy expert, why do you need outside help?"

"Because while I know shipping, and I've becoming quite knowledgeable about counter-piracy, it takes more than money to free a seized ship, or crew being held hostage. It takes a team of experts, as well as information, strategy and decisive action, and in your father's case, it will take extraordinary action. As you can imagine, it's crucial to do everything exactly right. There is no room for error in something like this. Even a small mistake could cost his life."

She paled. "Perhaps it's too dangerous."

"Rowan won't act unless he's sure of a positive outcome."

He watched her bite nervously into her lower lip and his gaze focused on that soft bottom lip. For a few seconds, he could think of nothing but her mouth. He loved the shape, the color, the softness of it. Always had. Her lips were full and a tender pink that made him think of lush, ripe summer fruit—sweet strawberries and cherries and juicy watermelon.

"We don't even know if my father is alive," she said after a moment, looking up into his eyes.

He knew from her expression that she was looking for reassurance, but he couldn't give it, not yet, not until Rowan had finished his intelligence work. And yet at the same time, there was no reason to alarm her. Information would be coming soon. Until then, they had to be positive. "We don't know very much about his condition at the moment, but I think it's important to focus on the best outcome, not the worst."

"When do you think this…Rowan…will have news for us?"

"I expect he'll have information when he arrives."

Morgan's eyes searched his again and her worry and fear were tangible and he fought the impulse to reach for her, comfort her, especially when she was so close he could feel her warmth and smell her light, delicate fragrance, a heady mix of perfume and her skin.

"It's difficult waiting," she said softly, the tip of her tongue touching her upper lip. "Difficult to be calm and patient in the face of so much unknown."

The glimpse of her pink tongue made him instantly hard. He wanted her so much, couldn't imagine not wanting her. It was torture being this close and yet not being able to kiss her, hold her, and he hardened all over again at the thought of kissing her, and tasting her and running his tongue across the seam of her lips.

He'd been with no one since Morgan left. For five years he'd gone without a woman, gone without closeness, intimacy, gone without even a kiss, and he suddenly felt starved. Ravenous. Like a man possessed. He needed her. She was his. His wife, his woman—

Drakon stopped himself. He couldn't go there, couldn't think of her like that. She might be his legally, but the relationship itself was over. "But that is life," he said grimly. "It is nothing but the unknown."

His staff appeared on the patio, lighting candles and sconces, including the heavy silver candelabra on the round white-linen covered table. "It appears dinner is ready," he added, glad for the diversion. "Shall we sit?"

Morgan realized with a start that the sun had dropped significantly and now hung just above the sea, streaking the horizon red, rose and gold. It would be a stunning sunset and they'd be here on the patio to see it. "Yes, please," she said, moving toward the table, but Drakon was already there, holding a chair for her.

She felt the electric shock as she sat down, her shoulder briefly touching his chest, and then his fingers brushing across the back of her bare arm. Her shawl had slipped into the crook of her elbow and the unexpected sensation of his skin on hers made her breath catch in her throat and she held the air bottled in her lungs as she pressed her knees tightly together, feeling the hot lick of desire and knowing she had to fight it.

"It will be a gorgeous sunset," she said, determined to think of other things than the useless dampness between her thighs and the coiling in her belly that made her feel so empty and achy.

His amber gaze met hers, and the warm tawny depths were piercing, penetrating, and it crossed her mind that he *knew*.

He knew how she felt, he knew she wanted him, and it was suddenly too much…being here, alone with him.

"Must grab my camera," she said, leaping to her feet. "Such an incredible sunset."

She rushed off, up to her room, where she dug through her things and located her phone, which was also her camera, but didn't return to the dining room immediately, needing the time to calm herself and pull her frayed nerves back together.

He's always done this to you, she lectured herself. *He seduced you with his eyes long before he ever touched you, but that doesn't mean anything. It's lust. He's good at sex. That doesn't mean he should be your husband.*

Morgan returned downstairs, head high. As she approached the patio through the dining room, the sunset bathed the patio in soft golden light. The small, round dining table seemed to float above the shimmering green tiles on the patio. The same green tiles extended all the way into the dining room and from the kitchen she caught a whiff of the most delicious aromas—tomato and onion, garlic, olive oil, herbs—even as the breeze rustled her skirts, tugging at her air, whispering over her skin.

So much light and color and sound.

So much sensation. So much emotion. It was wonderful

and terrible...bittersweet. Drakon and Villa Angelica had made her feel alive again.

Drakon rose as she stepped out onto the patio. "The sun is almost gone," he said, holding her chair for her.

She glanced out at the sea, and he was right. The bright red ball of sun had disappeared into the water. "I did miss it," she said, hoping she sounded properly regretful as she sat back down.

"Maybe next time," he said, with mock sympathy.

She looked up at him and then away, aware that he was playing her game with her. Pretending she'd wanted a photo when they both knew she just needed to escape him.

"I'll have to keep my phone close by," she said, reaching for her water glass and taking a quick sip.

His gaze collided with hers and then held, his expression one of lazy amusement. "Photos really help one remember things."

She felt herself grow warm. "I have a purely professional interest in the scenery."

"Is that so?"

She hated the way one of his black eyebrows lifted. Hated that curl of his lips. It was sardonic, but also quite sexy, and she was sure he knew it. "I use them for inspiration, not souvenirs," she said coolly, wanting to squash him, and his amusement. There was no reason for him to take pleasure in her discomfiture. No reason for him to act superior.

"Interesting," he drawled, and Morgan had to restrain herself from kicking him beneath the table because she knew he didn't mean it. And he didn't believe her. He probably was sitting there arrogantly thinking she was completely hung up on him...and imagining she was obsessing about having great sex with him...which was ludicrous because she wasn't thinking about having great sex with him anymore. At least not when she was talking about the scenery and inspiration.

"I use the inspiration for my work," she said defiantly, not even sure why she was getting so upset. "But you probably don't consider it work. You probably think it's silly. Superficial."

"I never said that."

"Perhaps you didn't say it, but you think it. You know you do."

"I find it interesting that you feel compelled to put words into my mouth."

His ability to be so calm and detached when she was feeling so emotional made her even more emotional. She leaned toward him. "Surely you've wondered what drove you to marry a flighty woman like me...a woman so preoccupied with frivolous things."

"Are you flighty?"

"You must think so."

He leaned forward, too, closing the distance between them. "I'm not asking you to tell me what I think. I'm asking you— are you flighty?"

Her chin jerked up. "No."

"Are you preoccupied with frivolous things?" he persisted.

Her cheeks burned hot and her eyes felt gritty. "No."

"So you're not flighty or frivolous?"

"No."

His eyes narrowed. "Then why would I think you are?"

She had to close her eyes, overwhelmed by pain and the wave of grief that swept over her.

"Morgan?"

She gave her head a small shake, refusing to open her eyes until she was sure they were perfectly dry. "I am sorry," she said huskily. "You deserved better than me."

"And I'd like to hear more about your jewelry and your ideas, unless you're determined to hold onto this bizarre fantasy of yours that I don't care for you or what's going on inside that beautiful, but complicated head."

She suddenly seethed with anger. Why was he so interested in her thoughts now, when he hadn't been interested in anything but her body when they'd lived together? "I loved what I did," she said shortly. "I was really proud of my work, and I am still proud of those three collections."

She glared at him, waiting for him to speak, but he simply sat back in his chair and looked at her, and let the silence grow, expand and threaten to take over.

The silence was beginning to feel uncomfortable and he was examining her a little too closely. She felt herself grow warm, too warm. "They were jewelry, yes," she said, rushing now to fill the silence, "but they were also miniature works of art, and each collection had a theme and each individual piece told a story."

"And what were those stories?"

"Life and death, love and loss, hope and despair…" Her voice faded, and she looked away, heart aching, because the collections had really been about him, them, their brief fierce love that became so very dangerous and destructive.

"I liked them all, but my favorite collection was your last one. The one you called a failure."

Her head jerked up and she had to blink hard to keep tears from welling up. "You're familiar with my three collections?"

"But of course."

"And you liked my designs?"

"You have such a unique vision. I admired your work very much."

She exhaled slowly, surprised, touched, grateful. "Thank you."

"I was proud of you, my wife. I still am."

The tears she'd been fighting filled her eyes and she didn't know what affected her more—his words or his touch. "My short-lived career," she said, struggling to speak, trying to sound light, mocking, but it had hurt, closing her business. She'd truly loved her work. Had found so much joy in her work and designs.

He caught one of her tears before it could fall. "I don't think it's over. I think you're in the middle of a transition period, and it may feel like death, but it's just change."

"Well, death certainly is a change," she answered, deadpan, flashing him a crooked smile, thinking she liked it when Drakon talked to her. She'd always liked his perspective on things. She found it—him—reassuring, and for her, this is how she connected to him. Through words. Language. Ideas.

If only they'd had more of this—time and conversation—perhaps she wouldn't have felt so lost in Greece. Perhaps they'd still be together now.

He suddenly reached out and stroked her cheek with his thumb, making her heart turn over once again.

"I liked it when you smiled a moment ago," he said gruffly, his amber gaze warm as he looked at her. "I have a feeling you don't smile much anymore."

For a moment she didn't speak, she couldn't, her heart in her mouth and her chest filled with hot emotion.

She was still so drawn to him, still so in love with him. But there was no relationship anymore. They were mostly definitely done—finished. No turning back.

He was helping her because she needed help, but that was all. She had to remember what was important—her father and securing his release—and not let herself get caught up in the physical again because the physical was maddening, disorienting and so incredibly addictive. She hadn't known she had such an addictive personality, not until she'd fell for Drakon.

"There hasn't been a great deal to smile about in the past few months," she said quietly. "Everything has been so grim and overwhelming, but just being here, having your support, gives me hope. If you hadn't agreed to help me, I don't know what I would have done. I'm so very grateful—"

"Your father's not home yet."

"But with your help, he soon will be."

"Careful, my love. You can't say that. You don't know that."

She averted her head and blinked hard, gazing out across the water that had darkened to purple beneath a lavender sky. The first stars were appearing and the moon was far away, just a little crescent of white.

"I'm not saying that it's hopeless," Drakon said. "Just that there is still a great deal we do not know yet."

"I understand. I do."

CHAPTER FIVE

MORGAN PASSED ON coffee and returned to her room, finding it far too painful to sit across from Drakon and look at him, and be so close to him, and yet not be part of his life anymore. Better to return to her suite and pace the floor in privacy, where he couldn't read her face or know how confused she felt.

How could she still want him so much even now? How could she want him when she knew how dangerous he was for her?

She needed to go home, back to New York, back to her family. There was no reason to remain here. Surely this man, Rowan whatever-his-name-was, from Dunamas Intelligence, didn't need her here for his work. He could email her, or call, when he had news....

Morgan nearly returned downstairs to tell Drakon she wanted to leave tonight, that she insisted on leaving tonight, but as she opened her door she realized how ridiculous she'd sound, demanding to go just when Rowan was set to arrive. No, she needed to calm down. She was being foolish. As well as irrational. Drakon wouldn't hurt her. He wasn't going to destroy her. She just needed to keep her head, and not let him anywhere close to her body.

Morgan went to bed, thinking she'd be too wound up to sleep, but she did finally sleep and then woke up early, her room filled with dazzling morning sunlight. After showering, she dressed simply in slim white slacks and one of her favorite colorful tunics and headed downstairs to see if she could get a coffee.

One of the maids gestured to the breakfast room, which was already set for two. Morgan shook her head. "Just coffee," she said, unable to stomach the idea of another meal with Drakon. "An Americano with milk. Latte," she added. "But nothing to eat."

The maid didn't understand and gestured again to the pretty table with its cheerful yellow and blue linens and smiled winningly.

"No, no. Just coffee. Take away." Morgan frowned, wondering why she couldn't seem to remember a single word of Italian. She used to know a little bit, but her brain wasn't working this morning. She was drawing a total blank.

The maid smiled. "Coffee. Americano, *si. Prego.*" And she gestured to the table once more.

Morgan gave up and sat down at the table, needing coffee more than argument. She ended up having breakfast alone and enjoyed her warm pastries and juice and strong hot coffee, which she laced with milk.

The sun poured in through the tall leaded windows, and light dappled the table, shining on the blue water glasses and casting prisms of delicate blue on the white plaster walls.

Morgan studied the patches of blue glazing the walls. She loved the color blue, particularly this cobalt-blue glass one found on the Amalfi coast, and could imagine beautiful jewelry made from the same blue glass, round beads and square knots mixed with gold and shells and bits of wood and other things that caught her fancy.

Her fingers suddenly itched to pick up a pencil and sketch some designs, not the extravagant gold cuffs and collars from her Amalfi collection, but something lighter, simpler. These pieces would be more affordable, perhaps a little bit of a splurge for younger girls, but within reach if they'd saved their pennies. Morgan could imagine the trendy jet-setters buying up strands of different colors and textures and pairing them with easy bracelets, perfect to wear to dinner, or out shopping on a weekend, or on a beach in Greece.

"What are you thinking about?" Drakon asked from the doorway.

Startled, she gazed blankly at him, having forgotten for a moment where she was. "Jewelry," she said, feeling as if she'd been caught doing something naughty. "Why?"

"You were smiling a little…as if you were daydreaming."

"I suppose I was. It helps me to imagine designing things. Makes the loss of my company less painful."

"You'll have another store again."

"It'd be fiscally irresponsible. My last collection nearly bankrupted me."

One of the kitchen staff appeared with an espresso for Drakon and handed it to him. He nodded toward the table. "May I join you?"

"Of course you may, but I was just about to leave," she said.

"Then don't let me keep you," he answered.

His voice didn't change—it remained deep, smooth, even—but she saw something in his face, a shadow in his eyes, and she suddenly felt vile. Here he was, helping her, supporting her, extending himself emotionally and financially, and she couldn't even be bothered to sit with him while he had breakfast?

"But if you don't mind my company," she added quickly, "I'll have another coffee and stay."

There was another flicker in his eyes, this one harder to read, and after sitting down across from her, he rang the bell and ordered another coffee for her, along with his breakfast.

They talked about trivial things over breakfast like the

weather and movies and books they'd read lately. Morgan was grateful their talk was light and impersonal. She was finding it hard to concentrate in the first place, never mind carry on a conversation. Drakon was so beautiful this morning with his dark hair still slightly damp from his shower and his jaw freshly shaven. The morning light gilded him, with the sun playing across his strong, handsome features, illuminating his broad brow, his straight Greek nose, his firm full mouth.

It was impossible to believe this gorgeous, gorgeous man had been her husband. She was mad to leave him. But then, living with him had made her insane.

Drakon's black brows tugged. "It's going to be all right. Rowan should be here in the next hour. We'll soon have information about your father."

"Thank you," she said quietly.

"Last night after you'd gone to bed I was thinking about everything you said yesterday—" He broke off, frowning. "Am I really such an ogre, Morgan? Why do you think I would judge you...and judge you so harshly?"

His gaze, so direct, so piercing, unnerved her. She smoothed the edge of the yellow square cloth where it met the blue underskirt. "Your corporation is worth billions of dollars and your work is vital to Greece and world's economy. I'm nothing. I do nothing. I add little value—"

"Life isn't just about drudgery. It is also about beauty, and you bring beauty into the world." The heat in his eyes reminded her of their courtship, where he'd watched her across ballrooms with that lazy, sensual gleam in his eyes, his expression one of pride and pleasure as well as possession. She'd felt powerful with his eyes on her. Beautiful and important.

"But I don't think important thoughts. I don't discuss relevant topics."

"Relevant to whom?"

"To you! I bore you—"

"Where do you get these ideas from?"

"From you." She swallowed hard and forced herself to hold his gaze even though it was so incredibly uncomfortable. "I annoyed you when we lived together. And I don't blame you. I know you find people like me irritating."

His black eyebrows pulled and his jaw jutted. "People like you? What does that mean?"

She shrugged uneasily, wishing she hadn't said anything. She hadn't meant anything by it.

No, not true. She had. She still remembered how he had shut down her attempts at conversation once their honeymoon had ended and they'd returned to Greece, remembered their silent lonely evenings in their sprawling modern white marble villa. Drakon would arrive home from work and they'd sit in the dining room, but it'd been a silent meal, with Drakon often reviewing papers or something on his tablet and then afterward he'd retreat to a chair in the living room and continue reading until bed. Once in the bedroom, things changed. Behind the closed door, he'd want hot, erotic sex, and for twenty minutes or sixty, or even longer depending on the night, he'd be alive, and sensual, utterly engrossed with her body and pleasure, and then when it was over, he'd fall asleep, and in the morning when she woke, he'd be gone, back to his office.

"People like me who don't read the business section of the newspaper. People like me who don't care passionately about politics. People like me who don't make money but spend it." She lifted her chin and smiled at him, a hard dazzling smile to hide how much those memories still hurt. "People who can only talk about fashion and shopping and which restaurants are considered trendy."

He tapped his finger on the table. "I do not understand the way you say, 'people like you.' I've never met anyone like you. For me, there is you, and only you."

She leaned forward, her gaze locking with his. "Why did you marry me, Drakon?"

"Because I wanted you. You were made for me. Meant for me."

"What did you like about me?"

"Everything."

"That's not true."

"It is true. I loved your beauty, your intelligence, your warmth, your passion, your smile, your laugh."

She noticed he said *loved,* past tense, and it hurt, a hot lance of pain straight through her heart. Perhaps it was merely a slip, or possibly, a grammatical error, but both were unlikely. Drakon didn't make mistakes.

"But you know that," he added brusquely.

"No," she said equally roughly, "I didn't know that. I had no idea why you cared about me, or if you even cared for me—"

"How can you say such a thing?"

"Because you never talked to me!" she cried. "After our honeymoon ended, you disappeared."

"I merely went back to work, Morgan."

"Yes, but you worked twelve- and fourteen-hour days, which would have been fine, but when you came home, you were utterly silent."

"I was tired. I work long days."

"And I was home alone all day with servants who didn't speak English."

"You promised me you were going to learn Greek."

"I did, I took lessons at the language school in Athens, but when you came home at night, you were irritated by my attempts to speak Greek, insisting we converse in English—" She compressed her lips, feeling the resentment and frustration bubble up. "And then when I tried to make friends, I kept bumping into your old girlfriends and lovers. Athens is full of them. How many women have you been with, Drakon?"

"You make it sound like you met dozens of exes, but you bumped into just three."

"You're right, just three, and in hindsight, they were actually much nicer than the Greek socialites I met who were furious that I'd stolen Greece's most eligible bachelor from under their noses." Morgan's eyes sparkled dangerously. "How could I, a trashy American, take one of Greece's national treasures?"

"It wasn't that bad."

"It was that bad! Everybody hated me before I even arrived!" She leaned across the table. "You should have warned me, Drakon. Prepared me for my new married life."

"I didn't know…hadn't realized…that some of the ladies would be so catty, but I always came home to you every night."

"No, I didn't have you. That was the problem."

"What do you mean?"

Morgan laughed coolly. "You came home to dinner, a bed and sex, but you didn't come home to me, because if you had, you would have talked to me, and tried to speak Greek to me, and you would have helped me meet people, instead of getting annoyed with me for caring what Greek women thought of me."

He swore violently and got up from the table, pacing the floor once before turning to look at her. "I can't believe this is why you left me. I can't believe you'd walk out on me, and our marriage, because I'm not one for conversation. I've never been a big talker, but coming home to you was my favorite part of the day. It's what I looked forward to all day long, from the moment I left for my office."

She swallowed around the lump filling her throat. "And

yet when Bronwyn called you at home, you'd talk to her for hours."

"Not for hours."

"For thirty minutes at a time. Over and over every night."

"We had business to discuss."

"And could nothing wait until the morning? Was everything really a crisis? Or could she just not make a decision without you?"

"Is that why you left me? Because of Bronwyn?"

Yes, she wanted to say. Yes, yes, yes. But in her heart she knew Bronwyn Harper was only part of the issue. Drakon's close relationship with his Australian vice president only emphasized how lonely and empty Morgan felt with him. "Bronwyn's constant presence in our lives didn't help matters. Every time I turned around, she was there, and you did talk to her, whereas you didn't talk to me."

The fight abruptly left her, and once her anger deserted her, she was exhausted and flattened, depressed by a specter of what they had been, and the illusion of what she'd hoped they'd be. "But it's a moot point now. It doesn't matter—" She broke off. "My God! You're doing it now. Rolling your eyes! Looking utterly bored and annoyed."

"I'm frustrated, Morgan, and yes, I do find this entire conversation annoying because you're putting words in my mouth, telling me how I felt, and I'm telling you I didn't feel that way when we were married."

"Don't you remember telling me repeatedly that you had people—*women*—talking at you at work, and that you didn't need me talking at you at home? Don't you remember telling me, you preferred silence—"

"I remember telling you that *once,* because I did come home one day needing quiet, and I wanted you to know it wasn't personal, and that I wasn't upset with you, that it had simply been a long day with a lot of people talking at me."

He walked toward her, his gaze hard, his expression forbidding. "And instead of you being understanding, you went into hysterics, crying and raging—"

"I wasn't hysterical."

"You had no right to be upset, though." He was standing before her now. "I'd just lost two members of my crew from a hijacked ship and I'd had to tell the families that their loved ones were gone and it was a bad, bad day. A truly awful day."

"Then tell me next time that something horrific has happened, and I'll understand, but don't just disappear into your office and give me the silent treatment."

"I shouldn't have to talk if I don't want to talk."

"I was your wife. If something important happens in your world, I'd like to know."

"It's not as if you could do anything."

"But I could care, Drakon, and I would at least know what's happening in your life and I could grieve for the families of your crew, too, because I would have grieved, and I would have wanted to comfort you—"

"I don't need comforting."

"Clearly." Hot, sharp emotions rushed through her, one after the other, and she gave her head a fierce, decisive shake. "Just as you clearly didn't need me, either, because you don't need anything, Drakon Xanthis. You're perfect and complete just the way you are!"

She brushed past him and walked out, not quickly, or tearfully, but resolutely, reassured all over again that she had done the right thing in leaving him. He really didn't want a wife, or a partner, someone that was equal and valuable. He only wanted a woman for physical release. In his mind, that was all a woman was good for, and thank God she'd left when she had or he would have destroyed her completely.

Drakon caught up with her in the narrow stairway at the back of the villa. It had once been the staircase for the servants and was quite simple with plain plaster walls and steep, small stairs, but it saved Morgan traversing the long hallway.

He clasped her elbow, stopping her midstep. "You are so very good at running away, Morgan."

She shook him off and turned to face him. He was standing two steps down but that still put them on eye level and she stared into his eyes, so very full of anger and pain. "And you are so good at shutting people out!"

"I don't need to report to you, Morgan. You are my wife, not my colleague."

"And funny enough, I would rather have been your colleague than your wife. At least you would have talked to me!"

"But then there would have been no lovemaking."

"Perhaps it will surprise you to know that I'm actually far more interested in what's in your brain than what's in your trousers." She saw his incredulous expression and drew a ragged breath, horrified all over again that their entire relationship had been based on sex and chemistry. Horrified that she'd married a man who only wanted her for her body. "It's true. Lovemaking is empty without friendship, and we had no friendship, Drakon. We just had sex—"

"Not this again!"

"Yes, this again."

"You're being absurd."

"Thank God we'll both soon be free so we can find someone that suits us both better. You can go get another pretty girl and give her an orgasm once or twice a day and feel like a real man, and I'll find a man who has warmth and compassion, a man who cares about what I think and feel, a man who wants to know *me*, and not just my body!"

He came up one step, and then another until they were on the same narrow stair, crowding her so that her back was against the plaster of the stairwell, and his big body was almost touching hers.

A dangerous light shone in his eyes, making her blood hum in her veins and her nerves dance. "Is that all I'm interested in? Your body?" he growled, a small muscle popping in his jaw.

She stared at his jaw, fascinated by that telling display of temper. He was angry and this was all so new...his temper and emotion. She'd always thought of him as supremely controlled but his tension was palpable now. He practically seethed with frustration and it made her skin tingle, particularly her lips, which suddenly felt unbearably sensitive. "Apparently so."

He stepped even closer, his eyes glittering down at her. "I wish I'd known that before I married you. It would have saved me half a billion dollars, never mind years of trouble."

"We all make mistakes," she taunted, deliberately provoking him, but unable to help herself. Drakon Xanthis's famous icy control was cracking and she wondered what would happen when it shattered completely. "Best thing you can do now is forgive yourself for making such a dreadful mistake and move forward."

Fire flashed in his eyes and he leaned in, closing the gap between them so that his broad chest just grazed the swell of her breasts and she could feel the tantalizing heat of his hips so close to hers.

"Such an interesting way to view things," he said, his head dropping, his voice deepening. "With you as my mistake."

His lips were so close now and her lower back tingled and her belly tightened, and desire coursed through her veins, making her ache everywhere.

She could feel his need, feel the desire and her mouth dried, her heart hammering harder. He was going to kiss her. And she wanted the kiss, craved his kiss, even as a little voice of reason inside her head sounded the alarm....

Stop. Wait. Think.

She had to remember...remember the past...remember

what had happened last time…this wasn't just a kiss, but an inferno. If she gave in to this kiss, it'd be all over. Drakon was so dangerous for her. He did something to her. He, like his name, Drakon, Greek for dragon, was powerful and potent and destructive.

But he was also beautiful and physical and sensual and he made her *feel*. My God, he made her feel and she wanted that intensity now. Wanted him now.

"My beautiful, expensive mistake," he murmured, his lips brushing across the shell of her ear, making her breath catch in her throat and sending hot darts of delicious sensation throughout her body, making her aware of every sensitive spot.

"Next time, don't marry the girl," she said, trying to sound brazen and cavalier, but failing miserably as just then he pushed his thigh between her legs. The heat of his hard body scalded her, and the unexpected pressure and pleasure was so intense she gasped, making her head spin.

"Would you have been happier just being my mistress?" he asked, his tongue tracing the curve of her ear even as his muscular thigh pressed up, his knee against her core, teasing her senses, making her shiver with need.

She was wet and hot, too hot, and her skin felt too tight. She wanted relief, needed relief, and it didn't help that she couldn't catch her breath. She was breathing shallowly, her chest rising and falling while her mouth dried.

"Would you have been able to let go more? Enjoyed the sex without guilt?" he added, biting her tender earlobe, his teeth sharp, even as he wedged his thigh deeper between her knees, parting her thighs wider so that she felt like a butterfly pinned against the wall.

"There was no guilt," she choked, eyes closing as he worked his thigh against her in a slow maddening circle. He was so warm and she was so wet and she knew it was wrong, but she wanted more, not less.

His teeth scraped across that hollow beneath her ear and she shuddered against him, thinking he remembered how sensitive she was, how her body responded to every little touch and bite and caress.

"Liar." He leaned in closer, his knee grinding and his hips pressing down against her hips, making her pelvis feel hot and yet hollow, and the muscles inside her womb clench. "You liked it hot. You liked it when I made you fall apart."

And it was true, she thought, her body so tight and hot and aching that she arched against him, absolutely wanton. There was no satisfaction like this, though, and she wanted satisfaction. Wanted him. Wanted him here and now. Wanted him to lift her tunic and expose her breasts and knead and roll the tight, aching nipples between his fingers. He'd made her come that way before, just by playing with her nipples, and he'd watched her face as she came, watched every flicker of emotion that crossed her face as he broke her control....

If only he'd peel her clothes off now, if only she could feel his skin on her skin, feel him in her, needing the heat and fullness of him inside her, craving the pleasure of being taken, owned, possessed—

Morgan's eyes flew open.

Owned?

Owned? My God. She was insane.

Visions of her months at McLean Hospital filled her head and it dragged her abruptly back to reality. She had to be smart. Couldn't destroy herself again. Never wanted to go back to McLean Hospital again.

The very memory of McLean was enough for her to put her hands on his chest and push him back, and she pushed hard, but he didn't budge and all she felt was the warm dense plane of muscle that banded his ribs, and the softness of his cashmere sweater over the dense carved muscle.

"Get off," she panted, pushing harder, putting all of her weight into the shove but Drakon was solid, immoveable. "I'm not a toy, Drakon, not here for your amusement."

His hand snaked into her hair, twisting the dark length around his fist, holding her face up to his. "Good, because I'm not amused."

"No, you're just aroused," she answered coldly, furious with herself for responding to him with such abandon. So typical. So pathetic. No wonder her family had locked her up.

He caught one of her hands and dragged it down his body and between their hips to cup his erection. "Yes," he drawled, amber gaze burning, "so I am."

She inhaled sharply, her fingers curving around him, clasping his thick shaft as if measuring the hard length, and it was a terrible seductive pleasure, touching him like this. She remembered how he felt inside her—hot, heavy—and how the satin heat of his body would stretch her, stroke her, hitting nerve endings she hadn't even known she had.

Curiosity and desire warred with her sense of self-preservation, before overriding her common sense.

Morgan palmed the length of him, slowly, firmly running her hand down his shaft and then, as if unable to stop herself, back up again to cup the thick, rounded head. She'd never thought a man's body was beautiful before she'd met Drakon, but she loved every muscle and shadow of his body, loved the lines and the planes and the way his cock hung heavy between his muscular legs. He was such a powerfully built man, and yet the skin on his shaft was so smooth and sensitive, like silk, and the contradiction between his great, hard body and that delicate skin fascinated her.

But then he fascinated her. No, it was more than that, more

than fascination. It was an obsession. She needed him so much she found it virtually impossible to live without him.

"You want me," he said. "You want me to peel your trousers and knickers off and take you here, on these steps, don't you?"

Fire surged through her veins, fire and hunger and shame. Because yes, she did want him and her orgasms were the most intense when he pushed it to the edge, making every touch into something dangerous and erotic. "You do like to dominate," she answered breathlessly.

He tugged on her hair, and it hurt a little, just as he'd intended, making her nipples harden into tight, aching buds even as she stiffened against him, her body rippling with need.

"And you do like to be dominated," he rasped in her ear.

CHAPTER SIX

SHE SHOVED AWAY from him and this time he let her go and Morgan ran the rest of the way up the stairs, racing back to her room, his voice echoing in her head. *And you like to be dominated...*.

Morgan barely made it to her bed before her legs gave out, the mocking words making her absolutely heartsick, because he wasn't completely wrong. Part of her did like it. It was sexy...hot...exciting.

But she shouldn't like it. It wasn't politically correct. She couldn't imagine her mother approving. Not that she wanted to think about her mother and sex at the same time...or even about sex in general since she wasn't going to be having sex anytime soon and God help her, she wanted to.

She wanted to be ravished. Stripped. Tied up. Taken. Tasted. Devoured—

Oh, God, she was mad, she was. What sane woman wanted to be ravished? What kind of woman ached to be tied up and taken? Tasted?

What was wrong with her?

Before Drakon she'd never had these thoughts. She'd never imagined that sex could make one feel absolutely wild. She'd never dreamed that desire could be an uncontrollable fire that made one lose all perspective...as well as one's reason....

But desire was an inferno, and she felt absolutely consumed by need now. Lying facedown on her bed, her body ached with need. Her skin burned, her senses swam. Every muscle in her body felt taut and every nerve ending far too tight. She wanted relief, craved release, and the fact that she couldn't have it made the aching emptiness worse.

Morgan buried her face in a pillow and knotted her fists and screamed. And screamed some more.

She wanted him. She wanted him, wanted him, wanted him and he could give her what she wanted, too. He'd do it. He'd do anything she wanted and yet it was wrong. They weren't together, they hadn't been together in years, and she couldn't use him to scratch an itch…no matter how powerful the itch.

And yet, oh, God, her body ached and throbbed and she felt wild…hot and tense and so very raw.

Dammit. Damn him. Damn that kiss in the stairwell. Damn this terrible incredible unforgettable chemistry.

It wasn't right to want him this much still. Wasn't fair to still feel so much, either, especially when she knew how bad he was for her, how very destructive. She couldn't blame him entirely. The doctors said the problem was hers…that she didn't have proper boundaries. She didn't have a clear or strong sense of self and the only way she'd achieve a strong, mature sense of self was by leaving Drakon….

As if it were that easy…

Just leave him. Forget him. Forget he ever existed…

And now he was downstairs, so intense and real, so physical, so sensual, so fiercely beautiful.

Morgan beat the bed with her fist, maddened by the futility of her desire. Blood drummed in her veins, need coiled tightly, hotly in her belly, and her entire body ached with emptiness. How could emptiness throb and pulse? How could emptiness burn? But it did. And she felt wild and furious and frustrated beyond reason.

If only she could go to him, and beg for him to help her, beg him to give her release. Beg for pleasure.

She'd happily crawl for him, crawl to him, if it meant that he could tame the beast inside her...that voracious hunger that made her feel too wild, too frantic, too much.

Drakon stood just inside the doorway of Morgan's suite and watched her beat her fist against the bed, her dark hair gleaming, her tunic riding high on her thighs, the soft fabric clinging to the firm, rounded curves of her hips and butt.

She had a gorgeous butt, and it made him want to spank her, restrain her, knowing it'd arouse her, make things hotter, make her wet and anxious and hungry for him.

And then he'd make love to her.

With his mouth, his tongue, his teeth, his hands, his cock. He loved the softness of her skin and the scent of her, the way she blushed, the way her tongue traveled across the bow of her upper lip and the way she'd squirm beneath him, her slim body arching, her hips grinding up to meet his, her legs opening for him.

"Undress," he said, his voice pitched so low it sounded like a growl.

Morgan swiftly sat up, eyes enormous in her face, cheeks flushed.

"Do it," he said, folding his arms across his chest.

Her lips parted in silent protest and yet he knew she was tempted, seriously tempted, because she wanted the same thing he did—excitement, pleasure, release.

"And what?" she whispered, her tongue darting to her lower lip, moistening it.

He was already hard. Now he wanted to explode. "And let me look at you. I want to see you, my beautiful wife."

"I'm not your wife."

"Oh, you are my wife. And have been my wife and will

be my wife until the day the divorce is granted. Then…you'll be someone else's woman, but until then, you are mine. And you know you are. That is why you came here to me, wanting my help. You knew I'd refuse you nothing."

He saw the flicker in her eyes, that recognition of truth. "Just as you know I've never refused you anything," she whispered, her voice unsteady.

No, she hadn't, he thought, his shaft growing even harder, making him hotter, remembering how she always responded to him.

He'd known plenty of women who liked hot sex, but he'd never been with anyone as passionate as Morgan. She wasn't comfortable with her passionate nature, though, and during their six months together she'd struggled with the concept of physical pleasure, and resisted giving in to her sensual side, viewing it as a weakness, or something shameful, instead of an intimacy that brought them closer together…binding, bonding, making them one. "But I've never forced you, Morgan—"

"Not forced, no, but you have pushed me, pushed me beyond what I was comfortable doing."

"Isn't that exciting, though? To try new things…explore new things…to know and then go outside your comfort zone?"

Another flicker of emotion passed over her lovely face. She had such fine, elegant features, as well as that famous Copeland reserve, a trait shared by her equally glamorous sisters. The reserve came from the way they'd been raised… from birth they'd been privileged, and had enjoyed a luxurious lifestyle of private schools, private jets, private islands. Their money attracted attention, and men, lots and lots of men, and by the time the four Copeland girls had become women, they knew they were special. Unique. They believed they deserved better.

Drakon had been drawn to Morgan's beauty, but also her

reserve. He'd viewed it as a challenge to break through her cool, haughty exterior to discover the warm woman underneath.

And once he'd touched her, she'd been more than warm. She'd burned as if consumed by a fever and during their honeymoon, those four weeks here at Villa Angelica, he'd enjoyed discovering the depths of her passion and exploring her desires, her fears and her limits.

"But everything with you was outside my comfort zone," she said, trying to hide the quiver of her lower lip. "Everything was overwhelming."

She'd said this once before to him, during the last week of their honeymoon after an erotic afternoon on a private island, and he'd been startled that her memory of lovemaking on the pristine ivory beach had been so different from what he'd felt. Returning to his yacht, which had been anchored off the island while they picnicked on the beach, he had never felt closer to her, or more committed, and he'd been shocked when she accused him of taking advantage of her. Shocked and sickened.

He was Greek—a man of surprisingly simple tastes. He valued his family, his friends and his culture, which included good food, good drink and great sex. He wouldn't apologize for enjoying sex, either, or enjoying his wife's beautiful body. What did she expect him to do? Pretend he didn't like sex? Act as though he didn't find pleasure in her warmth and softness?

Back in Athens after the honeymoon, Drakon had tried to be the husband she wanted. He stopped reaching for her quite as often, and then when he did reach for her, he changed the way he touched her, holding back to keep from overwhelming her. He knew she didn't like it when he expressed hunger, or focused too much on her pleasure, and so instead of just being with her, and enjoying her, he practiced control and distance, hoping that a less passionate husband would be more to her liking.

Instead she'd left.

And just remembering how he'd turned himself inside out trying to please her, trying to give her what she wanted, made him angry all over again now.

He'd hated second-guessing himself back then, hated not being able to please her, hated failing as a husband.

His gaze swept over her, slowly, critically, examining her as if he owned her, and he did…at least for a few more weeks.

"Undress," he said roughly, feeling raw and so very carnal, and liking it. Enjoying it. "I want to see my wife. It doesn't seem like too much to ask for, not after giving you seven million dollars."

One of her eyebrows lifted. "At least you didn't mention the four hundred million."

"That was to your father, not to you."

"I wonder what he had to do for four hundred million."

"You think I should have asked for some sexual favors, do you?"

"You like sex a lot."

"I liked it with you a lot." He suddenly reached down, palmed his erection through his trousers, and he saw her gaze settle on his shaft, measuring the length and size.

Dark pink color stormed her cheeks and she licked her lower lip, once and again, before finding her voice. "That's obscene," she whispered.

"You did it a moment ago."

"You made me."

"You liked it. But you'll tell me you didn't. You'll tell me sex is disgusting. You'll tell me I'm disgusting, but if I touched you now, my woman, you'd be dripping wet—"

"Disgusting."

"And I'd open you and lick you and taste you and make you

come." His head cocked and he shoved his hands in his trouser pockets. "When is the last time you came? How long has it been since you had an orgasm? A day? A week? A month?"

"It's none of your business."

"I did it in the shower yesterday, before you arrived. Stroked myself as I thought about you, picturing your breasts and your pale thighs and how much I enjoy being between them."

"Is there any point to this, Drakon? Or do you just wish to humiliate me?"

"Humiliate you, how? By telling you how much I want you, even now, even after you walked out on me?"

"But you don't want me, you just want to have sex with me."

"That's right. You don't believe you're attached to your body, or that your body is part of you. Instead it's a separate entity, which makes me think of a headless chicken—"

"Don't be rude."

"Then stop jumping to conclusions. Just because I like your body, doesn't mean I don't appreciate the rest of you."

"Humph!"

His eyebrows shot up, his expression mocking. "Is that the best you can do?"

She crossed her arms over her chest, her chin jerking up. "I get nowhere arguing with you."

"Very wise. Much better to just dispense with the clothing and let me have what I want." He paused, and his gaze moved slowly, suggestively over her. "And what I know you want, too. Not that you'll admit it."

Her chin lifted another notch. "And what do I want?"

"Satisfying sex without pushing the limits too far."

Dark pink color stormed her cheeks. "Without pushing the limits at all."

The corners of his mouth curled. So she did want sex. Just

nice-girl sex…sweet, safe missionary-position sex. His cock throbbed at the thought. He'd like some sweet, safe-missionary sex as well. "I'll see what I can do. But first, I'd like to see you. But I'm getting bored by all the discussion. Either we're going to do this, or we're not—"

"Your shirt first."

"Excuse me?"

"You want to do this? Then we'll do this. But you're not the boss and I'm not taking orders." Her tone was defiant and her eyes flashed and she'd never been angry before when they'd played these games. She'd been shy and nervous, but also eager to please. She wasn't eager to please now. "You don't get to have all the power anymore."

"No?"

"No. I'm not your servant or slave—"

"Which is good, since I don't make love with my servants, and I don't have slaves."

"The point is, you might be able to bark orders at Bronwyn, but not at me."

"I had no idea you were so hung up on Bronwyn," he drawled, liking this new feisty Morgan. She was a very different woman from the one he'd married and that intrigued him.

"I wasn't hung up on her. You were."

"Is that how it was?"

"Yes."

"So are we going to talk about Bronwyn, or are we going to have sweet, safe missionary-position sex?"

Her lips compressed primly. "You're horrible. You know that, don't you?"

"Horribly good, and horribly hard, and horribly impatient. Now, are we, or aren't we?" he asked, sauntering toward her, relaxed, easy, his arms loose at his sides. But it was a deceptive ease, and they both knew it as the temperature in the luxurious bedroom seemed to soar and the air sparked with heat and need, the tension between them thick and hot and electric.

Closing the gap between them, Drakon could feel Morgan tense, her hands squeezing in convulsive fists, even as her eyes widened and her lips parted with each quick shallow breath.

"You're trembling," he said, "but there's no need for that. I won't eat you. Not unless you want me to."

"Drakon." Her voice sounded strangled and her cheeks were crimson, making her blue eyes darken and shimmer like the sapphire sea beyond the window.

"I hope you'll want me to. I love how you taste, and how soft you are in my mouth…so sweet. But is that too risky for you? Pushing the limits too much?"

"You love to torment me."

"Yes, I do," he agreed, circling her slowly, enjoying just looking at her, and watching the color come and go in her exquisite porcelain complexion, and listening to her soft desperate gasps of air. "But this is nothing, Morgan. I haven't even gotten started." He stopped in front of her, gazed down at her, thinking she looked very young and very uncertain and very shy, much like his virgin bride. "Now tell me, what should I do to you first?"

Morgan's heart was pounding so fast she couldn't catch her breath, and she opened her mouth, lips parting, to gulp in shallow gasps of air. She felt as if she were balancing on the edge of a volcano while little voices inside her head demanded she throw herself in.

She needed to leave, to escape the villa, to summon the helicopter and fly far, far away. Remaining here with Drakon was stupid and destructive. She might as well fling herself into that volcano…the outcome would be the same.

And yet, wasn't she already there, in the fiery pit? Because molten lava seemed to be seeping through her veins, melting her bones and muscles into mindless puddles of want and need.

She actually felt sick with need right now. But could she do this…go through with this…knowing it would be just sex, not love? Knowing Drakon wanted her body but not her heart?

"Are you crying?" he asked, his voice dropping, deepening with concern, as his hands wrapped around her arms, holding her up.

She shook her head, unable to look him in the eye.

"What's wrong?" he asked.

She swallowed hard, tried to speak, but no sound would come out. Not when her throat ached and her heart was still thundering in her chest.

He reached up to smooth a dark tendril of hair back from her face. "Have I frightened you?" His deep voice was suddenly gentle, almost painfully tender.

Hot tears scalded the back of her eyes. She bit hard into her lower lip so that it wouldn't quiver.

"I would never hurt you, Morgan," he murmured, drawing her against him, holding her in his arms, holding her securely against his chest.

She closed her eyes as the heat of his body seeped into her hands, warming her. He felt good. Too good. It was so confusing. This was confusing.

She didn't push him away, and yet she couldn't relax, waiting for the moment he'd let her go. But she didn't want him to let her go. She wanted him closer. Wanted to press her face to his chest and breathe him in. She could smell a hint of his spicy fragrance and loved that fragrance—his own scent, formulated just for him—and what it did to his skin. He smelled like heaven. Delicious and warm and good and intoxicating. He smelled like everything she wanted. He smelled like home. He *was* home. He was everything to her, but wasn't that the problem? With him, she lost herself. With him, she lost her mind.

With a strangled cry, Morgan slid a hand up across his chest, to push him back, and just like before, once she touched him, she couldn't take her hand away. She stroked across the hard plane of muscle of his chest, learning again the shape of his body and how the dense smooth pectoral muscle curved and sloped beneath her palm. God, he was beautiful. And without his shirt, his skin would feel so good against hers. She loved the way his bare chest felt against her bare breasts, loved the friction and the heat and the delicious, addictive energy—

"Can't do this," she choked, shaking her head. "We can't, we can't."

"Ssshh," he murmured, cupping her face, his thumbs stroking lightly over her cheekbones, sweeping from the curve of the bone to her earlobes. "Nothing bad will happen—"

"Everything bad will happen," she protested, shivering with pleasure from the caress. She loved the way he touched her. He made her feel beautiful, inside and out, and she struggled to remember what bad things would happen if he touched her....

"You are so beautiful," he murmured, hands slipping from her face to tangle in her hair.

"And mad, Drakon, certifiably insane—"

"That's okay."

"Drakon, I'm serious!"

"I am, too." His head dipped lower and his lips brushed hers, lightly, slowly, and she shuddered, pressed closer, a stinging sensation behind her eyes. One kiss...could it be so bad? One kiss...surely she could be forgiven that?

His lips found hers again and the kiss was surprisingly gentle, the pressure of his mouth just enough to tease her, send shivers of desire racing up and down her spine. This was all so impossible. They couldn't do this, couldn't give in to this, it's all they had and while the chemistry was intense, chemistry wasn't enough. Sex wasn't enough. She needed more. She needed a relationship, love, intimacy, commitment, but right now, she also needed this.

She'd missed him so much. Missed his skin and his scent, his warmth and his strength, and her defenses caved as his hands framed her face, and he held her face to his, deepening the kiss, drinking her in.

She could feel him and smell him and taste him now and she was lost. Nothing felt better than this. Nothing felt better than him. He wasn't just her husband, he was home and happiness—

No. No, no, no. Couldn't think that way, couldn't lose sight of reality. He wasn't home or happiness. And he'd finally agreed to let her go. After five years of wanting out, and she *did* want out, she was free.

And yet when his tongue stroked the seam of her lips, she arched and gasped, opening her mouth to him. Drakon deepened the kiss, his tongue flicking the inside of her lip, making every little nerve dance. One of his hands slid from the back of her head, down over her shoulders to her waist before settling in the small of her spine, urging her closer, shaping her against his powerful body.

She shuddered with pleasure as his tongue filled her mouth and the fingers of his hand splayed wider on her back, making her lower belly throb, ache, just like her thighs ached.

Every thrust of his tongue shot another bright arc of sensation through her, sensation that surged to the tips of her breasts, tightening them into hard, sensitive peaks, and then deep into her belly and even deeper to her innermost place, and yet it wasn't enough, not even close. Morgan dug her nails into his shoulders, pressing her breasts to his chest, practically grinding herself against his hips to feel the ridge of his erection rub against her sensitive spot at the junction of her thighs and the heat of his palm against her lower back.

It was still so electric between them, still fierce and wild, and she felt overwhelmed by desire, overwhelmed by the memory of such dizzying, maddening pleasure and the knowledge that he was here, and there could be more. And right now, she wanted more. She literally ached for him and could feel her body soften and warm for him, her body also clearly remembering that nothing in the world felt better than him in her. Him with her.

And then his hand was slipping slowly across the curve of her hip, to cup the roundness of her butt, and she nearly popped out of her skin. "Drakon," she groaned against his mouth, feeling as if he were spreading fire through her, fire and such fierce, consuming need.

She trembled as he stroked the length of her, from her hip to her breast and down again. His hands were everywhere now, pinching a nipple, stroking the cleft of her buttocks, shaping her thighs. She wanted his hand between her thighs, wanted him to touch her, fill her, wanted him more than she'd wanted anything—

Wait.

Wait.

She struggled to focus, clear her head, which was impossible with Drakon's amazing hands on her body and his mouth taking hers, promising her endless pleasure.

She had to move back, away, had to, now.

But then his hands were up, under her tunic, his skin so warm against hers, and when he unhooked her bra to cup her breasts, his thumbs grazing her tight, swollen nipples, she gave up resisting, gave up thinking and gave in to him.

He stripped off her clothes while kissing her, his hands never leaving her body as the clothes fell away, giving her no time to panic or reconsider.

Once naked, he carried her to the bed, and set her on her back in the middle of the enormous bed. The room's windows and doors were open and the sunlight spilled across the floor, splashing on the walls while the heady sweet scent of wisteria filled the room.

Morgan watched Drakon's face as he moved over her, his hard, powerful body warm, his skin a burnished gold, his strong features taut with passion. But it was his eyes that once again captivated her, and the burning intensity of his gaze. When he looked at her he made her feel extraordinary…desirable…rare…impossibly valuable. She knew he didn't feel that way about her, not anymore, but with him stretched out over her, his skin covering her, warming her, it didn't seem to matter.

She lifted her face to his, and his mouth met hers in a blistering kiss that melted everything within her. There was nothing she wouldn't give him. And as he settled his weight between her thighs, his hips pressing down against hers, she shivered with pleasure.

He was resting his weight on his forearms, but she wanted more pressure, not less, and Morgan arched up, pressing her breasts to his bare chest, loving the friction of his nipples on hers even as she opened her thighs wider, letting him settle deeper into her.

"I want you," she whispered against his mouth, her arms circling his shoulders, her hands sliding into his thick hair, fingers curling into the crisp strands at his nape. He felt good and smelled good and in this moment, everything was right in the world…at least, everything was right in her world. "I want you in me. I need you in me."

"It's been a long time."

"Too long," she said, lifting her hips, grinding up against him, not wanting any more foreplay, not wanting anything but him, and his body meshed deeply with hers.

"Patience," he answered, kissing the corner of her mouth and the line of her jaw, smoothing her hair back from her face. "There's no need to rush— "

But there was. She didn't want to wait, had enough teasing and words and thinking, had enough of everything but him. And right now she just wanted him. She reached between them, caught his hard shaft and gripped it firmly, the way she knew he liked it, and rubbed his head up and down her, the warm, rigid shaft sliding across her damp opening, making him slick, and then bringing the silken head up to her sensitive nub, drawing moisture up over her clit.

She heard him groan deep in his throat, a hoarse, guttural sound of pleasure, and it gave her a perverse thrill, knowing she could make Drakon feel something so strong that he'd groan aloud.

His hands stroked the outsides of her thighs and then down the inside and she shifted her hips, positioning him at her wet, slick core. "Do you want me?" she whispered, her lips at his ear.

"Yes," he groaned, his voice so low that it rumbled through her. "Yes, always."

And then he took control, lowering his weight, forearms pressed to the bed, and kissed her, deeply, his tongue plunging into her mouth even as he entered her body, thrusting all the way until they were one, and for a nearly a minute he remained still, kissing her, filling her, until she felt him swell inside her, stretching her, throbbing inside her, making her throb, too. Her pulse raced and her body tingled and burned, her inner muscles clenching and rippling with exquisite sensation. He was big and hard and warm and she could come like this, with her body gripping him, holding him, and Drakon knew it, knew how just being inside her could shatter her.

"Not yet," she gasped, hands stroking over his broad shoulders and down the smooth, hard, warm planes of his back, savoring the curve and hollow of every thick, sinewy muscle. Men were so beautiful compared to women, and no man was more beautiful than Drakon. "Don't let me come, not yet. I want more. I want everything."

And maybe this was just the plain old missionary position, but it felt amazing, felt hot and fierce and intense and emotional and physical and everything that was good. Sex like this was mind-blowingly good, especially with Drakon taking his time, thrusting into her in long smooth strokes that hit all the right places, that made her feel all the right things. Morgan wished it could last forever, but she was already responding, the muscles inside her womb were coiling tighter and tighter, bringing her ever closer to that point of no return. Morgan's head spun with the exquisite sensation, the tension so consuming that it was difficult to know in that moment if it was pleasure or pain, and then with one more deep thrust, Drakon sent her over the edge and her senses exploded, her body rippling and shuddering beneath his.

Drakon came while she was still climaxing and he ground out her name as he buried himself deeply within her. She could feel him come, feel the heat and liquid of him surging within her, and it hit her—they hadn't used a condom. On their honeymoon they had never used protection. Drakon wanted children and she wanted to please him and so they had never used birth control, but this was different. They were divorcing. She'd soon be single. There was absolutely no way she could cope with getting pregnant now.

"What have we done?" she cried, struggling to push him off of her. "What did we do?"

Drakon shifted his weight and allowed her to roll away from him, even as a small muscle jumped in his jaw. "I think you know what we just did."

"We shouldn't have. It was wrong."

"Doesn't feel wrong to me," he said tersely, watching her

slide to the edge of the bed and search for her tunic, or something to cover up with.

She grabbed Drakon's shirt, and slipped it over her arms into the sleeves and buttoned up the front. "Well, it was. We didn't use birth control, Drakon, and we shouldn't have even thought about sex without using a condom."

"But we never used a condom."

"Because we were newlyweds. We were hoping to have children, we both wanted a big family, but it's different now. We're separated. Divorcing. A baby would be disastrous, absolutely the worst thing possible—"

"Actually, I can think of a few things worse than a baby," he interrupted, getting off the bed and reaching for his trousers. He stepped into one leg and then the other before zipping them closed. "Like famine. Disease. Pestilence. Or someone swindling billions of dollars—"

"Obviously I didn't mean that a baby was a tragedy," she retorted, crossing her arms over her chest to hide the fact that she was trembling. Just moments ago she'd been so relaxed, so happy, and now she felt absolutely shell-shocked. How was it possible to swing from bliss to hell in thirty seconds flat? But then, wasn't that how it had always been with them?

"No, I think you did," he countered. "It's always about you, and what's good for you—"

"That's not true."

"Absolutely true. You're so caught up in what you want and need that there is no room in this relationship for two people. There certainly was never room for me."

Her eyes widened. "You can't be serious, Drakon. You're the most controlling person I've ever met. You controlled everything in our marriage, including me—"

"Do I look like I'm in control?" he demanded tautly, dark color washing the strong, hard planes of his face.

He was breathing unsteadily, and her gaze swept over him,

from his piercing gaze to the high color in his cheekbones to his firm full mouth, and she thought he looked incredible. Beautiful. Powerful. Her very own mythic Greek god. But that was the problem. He was too beautiful, too powerful. She had no perspective around him. Would throw herself in the path of danger just to be close to him.

Good God. How self-destructive was that?

Before she could speak, she heard the distinctive hum of a helicopter.

"Rowan," Drakon said, crossing to the balcony and stepping outside to watch the helicopter move across the sky. "He'll have news about your father."

"Then I'd better shower and dress."

CHAPTER SEVEN

MORGAN REFUSED TO think about what had just happened in her bed, unable to go there at all, and instead focused on taking a very fast shower before drying off and changing into a simple A-line dress in white linen with blue piping that Drakon had shipped over from the Athens house with the rest of the wardrobe.

In the steamy marble bathroom, she ran a brush through her long hair before drawing it back into a sleek ponytail and headed for her door, careful to keep her gaze averted from the bed's tousled sheets and duvet.

The maid would remake the bed while she was gone, and probably change the sheets, and Morgan was glad. She didn't want to remember or reflect on what had just changed there. It shouldn't have happened. It was a terrible mistake.

She took the stairs quickly, overwhelmed by emotion—worry and hope for her father, longing for Drakon, as well as regret. Now that they'd made love once, would he expect her to tumble back into bed later tonight?

And what if he didn't want to make love again? What if that was the last time? How would she feel?

In some ways that was the worst thought of all.

It wasn't the right way to end things. Couldn't be their last time. Their last time needed to be different. Needed more, not less. Needed more emotion, more time, more skin, more love…

Love.

She still loved Drakon, didn't she? Morgan's eyes stung, knowing she always would love him, too. Saying goodbye to him would rip her heart out. She only hoped it'd be less destructive than it had been the first time. Could only hope she'd remember the pain was just grief…that the pain would eventually, one day, subside.

But she wouldn't go there, either. Not yet. She was still here with him, still feeling so alive with him. Better to stay focused on the moment, and deal with the future when it came.

Reaching the bottom stair she discovered one of Drakon's staff was waiting for her. "Mrs. Xanthis, Mr. Xanthis is waiting for you in the terrace sunroom," the maid said.

Morgan thanked her and headed down the final flight of stairs to the lower level, the terrace level.

The sunroom ran the length of the villa and had formerly been a ballroom in the nineteenth century. The ballroom's original gilt ceiling, the six sets of double glass doors and the grand Venetian glass chandeliers remained, but the grand space was filled now with gorgeous rugs and comfortable furniture places and potted palms and miniature citrus trees. It was one of the lightest, brightest rooms in the villa and almost always smelled of citrus blossoms.

Entering the former ballroom, Morgan spotted Drakon and another man standing in the middle of the enormous room, talking in front of a grouping of couches and chairs.

They both turned and looked at her as she entered the room, but Morgan only had eyes for Drakon. Just looking at him made her insides flip, and her pulse leap.

She needed him, wanted him, loved him, far too much.

Her heart raced and her stomach hurt as she crossed the

ballroom, her gaze drinking in Drakon, her footsteps muffled
by the plush Persian rugs scattered across the marble floor.

He looked amazing…like Drakon, but not like Drakon
in that soft gray knit shirt that hugged his broad shoulders
and lovingly molded to his muscular chest, outlining every
hard, sinewy muscle with a pair of jeans. In America they
called shirts like the one he was wearing Henleys. They'd
been work shirts, worn by farmers and firemen and lumber-
jacks, not tycoons and millionaires and it boggled her mind
that Drakon would wear such a casual shirt, although from
the look of the fabric and the cut, it wasn't an inexpensive
one—but it suited him.

He looked relaxed…and warm. So warm. So absolutely
not cold, or controlled. And part of her suddenly wondered,
if he had ever been cold, or if she'd just come to think of
him that way as they grew apart in those last few months of
their marriage?

Which led to another question—had he ever been that
much in control, too? Or had she turned him into something
he wasn't? Her imagination making him into an intimidating and controlling man because she felt so out of control?

God, she hoped not. But there was no time to mull over the
past. She'd reached Drakon's side and felt another electric jolt
as his gaze met hers and held. She couldn't look away from
the warmth in his amber eyes. Part of him still burned and it
made her want to burn with him. Madness, she told herself,
don't go there, don't lose yourself, and yet the air hummed
with heat and desire.

How could she not respond to him?

How could she not want to be close to him when he was
so fiercely alive?

"It's going to be all right," he murmured, his deep voice
pitched so low only she could hear.

Her lovely, lovely man that made her feel like the most

beautiful woman in the entire world. Her lovely, lovely man that had pushed her to the brink, and beyond, and he still didn't know…still had no idea where she'd been that first year after leaving him, or what had happened to her trying to separate herself from him.

Part of her wanted to tell him, and yet another part didn't want to give him that knowledge, or power. Because he could break her. Absolutely destroy her. And she wasn't strong enough yet to rebuild herself again…not yet. Not on top of everything else that had happened to her father and her family with the Amery scandal.

"I promise you," he added.

She heard his fierce resolve and her heart turned over. This is how she'd fallen in love with him—his strength, his focus, his determination. That and the way he smiled at her… as if she were sunshine and oxygen all rolled into one. "Yes," she murmured, aware that once upon a time he'd been everything to her…her hope, her happiness, her future. She missed those days. Missed feeling as if she belonged somewhere with someone.

There was a flicker in his eyes, and then he made the introductions. "Morgan, this is Rowan Argyros, of Dunamas. Rowan, my wife, Morgan Copeland Xanthis."

Morgan forced her attention from Drakon to the stranger and her jaw nearly dropped. *This* was Rowan Argyros? *This* was one of the founders of Dunamas Maritime Intelligence?

Her brows tugged. She couldn't mask her surprise. Argyros wasn't at all what she'd expected.

She'd imagined Drakon's intelligence expert to look like one, and she'd pictured a man in his forties, maybe early fifties, who was stocky, balding, with a square jaw and pugilistic nose.

Instead Rowan Argyros looked like a model straight off

some Parisian runway. He was gorgeous. Not her type at all, but her sister Logan would bed him in a heartbeat.

Tall and broad-shouldered, Argyros was muscular without any bulk. He was very tan, and his eyes were light, a pale gray or green, hard to know exactly in the diffused light of the ballroom. His dark brown hair was sun-streaked and he wore it straight and far too long for someone in his line of work. His jaw was strong, but not the thick bulldog jaw she'd come to associate with testosterone-driven males, but more angular... elegant, the kind of face that would photograph beautifully, although today that jaw was shadowed with a day-old beard.

"Mrs. Xanthis," Rowan said, extending a hand to her.

It bothered her that he hadn't even bothered to shave for their meeting, and she wondered how this could be the man who would free her father?

Rowan Argosy looked as if he'd spent his free time hanging out on obscenely big yachts off the coast of France, not planning daring, dangerous life-saving missions.

She shook his hand firmly and let it go quickly. "Mr. Argyros," she said crisply. "I would love to know what you know about my father. Drakon said you have information."

"I do," Rowan said, looking her straight in the eye, his voice hard, his expression as cool and unfriendly as hers.

Morgan's eyebrows lifted. Nice. She liked his frosty tone, and found his coldness and aloofness reassuring. She wouldn't have trusted him at all if he'd been warm and charming. Military types...intelligence types...they weren't the touchy-feely sort. "Is he alive?"

"He is. I have some film of him taken just this morning."

"How did you get it?"

"Does it matter?"

"No." And her legs felt like Jell-O and she took a step back, sitting down heavily in one of the chairs grouped behind them. Her heart was thudding so hard and fast she thought she might be sick and she drew great gulps of air, fighting waves of nausea and intense relief. Dad was alive. That was huge. "Thank God."

For a moment there was just silence as Morgan sat with the news, overwhelmed that her father was indeed alive. After a moment, when she could trust herself to speak, she looked up at Rowan. "And he's well? He's healthy?"

He hesitated. "We don't know that. We only have his location, and evidence that he is alive."

So Dad could be sick. He probably didn't have his heart medicine with him. It'd probably been left behind on his boat. "What happens now?" she asked.

"We get your father out, take him to wherever you want him to go."

"How does that happen, though?"

"We're going to have you call your contact, the one in Somalia you've been dealing with, and you're going to ask to speak to your father. You'll tell them you need proof that he's alive and well if they are to get the six million dollars."

"They won't let me speak to him. I tried that before."

"They will," Drakon interjected, arms folded across his chest, the shirt molded to his sculpted torso, "if they think you're ready to make a drop of six million."

She looked at him. "What if they call our bluff? Wouldn't we have to be prepared to make the drop?"

"Yes. And we will. We'll give them a date, a time, co-ordinates for the drop. We'll tell them who is making the drop, too."

"But we're not dropping any money, are we?" she asked, glancing from him to Rowan and back again.

"No," said Rowan. "We're preparing a team right now to move in and rescue your father. But speaking to your father gives us important information, as well as buys us a little more time to put our plan in place."

She nodded, processing this. "How long until you rescue him?"

"Soon. Seventy-two hours, or less."

She looked at Rowan, startled. "That is soon."

"Once we have our plan in place, it's better to strike fast." Rowan's phone made a low vibrating noise and he reached into his pocket and checked the number. "I need to take this call," he said, walking away.

Morgan exhaled as Rowan exited through the sunroom, into the stairwell that would take him back up to the main level of the villa.

"You okay?" Drakon asked, looking down on her, after Rowan disappeared.

"Things can go wrong," she said.

"Yes. And sometimes they do. But Dunamas has an impressive track record. Far more successes than failures. I wouldn't have enlisted their help if I didn't think they'd succeed."

She hesitated. "If Rowan's team didn't succeed…people could die."

"People *will* die even if they do succeed. They're planning a raid. The pirates are heavily armed. Dunamas's team will be heavily armed. It's not going to be a peaceful handover. It'll be explosive and violent, and yet the team they're sending are professionals. They're prepared to do whatever they have to do to get him out alive."

So some of them—or all of them—could end up dying for her father?

Nauseated all over again, Morgan moved from her chair, not wanting to think of the brave, battle-tested men, men the world viewed as heroic, risking their lives for her father, who wasn't a hero.

Stomach churning, she pushed open one of the sunroom's tall arched glass doors and stepped onto the terrace, into the sunshine. She drank in a breath of fresh air, and then another. Was she being selfish, trying to save her father? Should she not do this?

Panic and guilt buffeted her as she leaned against the terrace's creamy marble balustrade and squeezed her eyes closed.

Drakon had followed her outside. "What's wrong?"

She didn't answer immediately, trying to find the right words, but what were those words? How did one make a decision like this? "Am I doing the wrong thing?" she asked. "Am I wrong, trying to save him?"

"I can't answer that for you. He's your father. Your family."

"You know I tried everything before I came to you. I asked everyone for help. No one would help me."

"Who did you approach?"

"Who didn't I?" She laughed grimly and glanced out across the terraced gardens with the roses and hedges and the pool and the view of the sea beyond. "I went to London to see Branson, and then to Los Angeles to see Logan, and then to Tori in New York, and back to London, but none of them would contribute money toward Dad's ransom. They're all in tight financial straits, and they all have reasons they couldn't give, but I think they wouldn't contribute to the ransom because they're ashamed of Dad. I think they believe I'm wasting money trying to rescue him. Mom even said he's better off where he is…that people will find it easier to forgive us—his kids—if Dad doesn't come back."

"You mean, if the pirates kill him?" Drakon asked.

She nodded.

"Your mother is probably right," he said.

She shot him a swift glance before pushing away from the railing to pace the length of the terrace. For a long minute she just walked, trying to master her emotions. "Maybe," she said, "maybe Mom is right, but I don't care. I don't care what people think of me. I don't care if they like me. I care about what's right. And while what Dad did, just blindly giving Michael the money, wasn't right, it's also not right to leave him in Somalia. And maybe the others can write him off, but I can't."

She shivered, chilled, even though the sun was shining warmly overhead. "I can't forget how he taught me to swim and ride a bike and he went to every one of my volleyball games in high school. Dad was there for everything, big and small, and maybe he was a terrible investment advisor, but he was a wonderful father. I couldn't have asked for better—" Morgan broke off, covering her mouth to stifle a sob. She couldn't help it, but she missed him, and worried about him, and there was just no way she could turn her back on him now. No way at all.

"I think you have your answer," Drakon said quietly. "You have to do this. Have to help him. Right or wrong."

They both turned at the sound of a squeaky gate. Rowan was heading up toward them from the lower garden.

"And if anybody can get your father home, it's Argyros," Drakon said.

Morgan wrinkled her nose. "He looks like a drug smuggler."

The corner of Drakon's mouth lifted. "He isn't what one expects. That's what makes him so successful."

"As long as you trust him."

"I do."

On reaching their side, Rowan announced that his office was now ready for Morgan to try to phone her pirate contact in Somalia. "We have a special line set up that will allow us to record the conversation," he said. "And my team is standing by now, to listen in on the call."

"But I can only use my phone," she answered. "And my number. They know my number—"

"We know. And we can make it appear to look like your number. Today's technology lets us do just about anything."

In the villa's dark-paneled library they attempted the call but no one answered on the other end. Morgan left a message, letting her contact know that she had six million in cash, in used bills, and was ready to make the drop but she wanted to speak to her father first. "I need to know he's alive," she said, "and then you'll have the money."

She hung up, glanced at Rowan and Drakon. "And now what?"

"We wait for a call back," Rowan said.

They had a light lunch in the library while waiting, but there was no return call. Morgan wanted to phone again but Rowan said it wasn't a good idea. "We're playing a game," he explained. "It's their game, but we're going to outplay them. They just don't know it yet."

The afternoon dragged. Morgan hated waiting as it made her restless and anxious. She wanted to hear her father's voice, and she wanted to hear it sooner than later. After a couple hours, she couldn't sit still any longer and began to walk in circles. She saw Morgan and Drakon exchange glances.

"What?" she demanded. "Am I not allowed to move out of my chair?"

Drakon smiled faintly. "Come, let's go get some exercise and fresh air."

Stretching her legs did sound nice, but Morgan didn't want to miss the call. "What if the pirate calls back and I'm not here?"

"He'll leave a message," Drakon said.

"Won't he be angry?" she asked.

Rowan shrugged. "They want your money. They'll call back."

It was close to four when Morgan and Drakon left the

house to walk down to the water, and the afternoon was still bright, and warm, but already the sun was sitting lower in the sky. Morgan took a deep breath, glad to have escaped the dark cool library and be back outside.

"Thank you for getting me out of there," she said to Drakon as they crossed the lawn, heading for the stone and cement staircase that hugged the cliff and took them down to the little dock, where they used to anchor the speedboat they used to explore the coast.

"You were looking a little pale in there," Drakon said, walking next to her. "But your father's going to be all right."

"If I was pale, it's because I was thinking about what we did earlier." Her fingers knotted into fists. "Or what we shouldn't have done." She glanced up at him as he opened the second wrought-iron gate, this one at the top of the stairs.

"Which was?" he asked innocently.

She shot him a disbelieving look and his golden brown eyes sparked, the corner of his sexy mouth tugging in a slow, wicked smile and just like that the air was suddenly charged, and Morgan shivered at the sudden snap and crackle of tension and the spike of awareness. God, it was electric between them. And dangerous.

"It can't happen again," she whispered, her gaze meeting his.

"No?" he murmured, reaching out to lift a soft tendril of hair back from her cheek, but then he couldn't let it go and he let the strand slide between his fingers, before curling it loosely around his finger and thumb.

Her breath caught in her throat and she stared up at him, heart pounding, mouth drying. She loved the way he touched her and he was making her weak in the knees now. "It confuses me."

"Confuses you, how?"

The heat between them was intense. Dizzying. So much

awareness, so much desire, so impossible to satisfy. She swayed on her feet and he immediately stepped between her and the edge of the stairs, pressing her up against the wall. "I can't think around you," she whispered, feeling his dazzling energy before her, and the sun warmed rock at her back.

"Thinking is overrated," he murmured, moving in closer to her, brushing his lips across her forehead.

She closed her eyes, breathing in his light clean fragrance and savoring the teasing caress. "Is it?"

"Mmm-hmm."

"Does that mean you're not going to think, either?"

She felt the corners of his mouth curve against her brow. He was smiling. And God, didn't that turn her on?

She locked her knees, her inner thighs clenching, wanting him, needing. Damn him.

"One of us should probably keep our heads," he answered, his hands cupping her face, thumbs stroking her cheekbones. "Less frantic that way."

"And I suppose you think that should be you?" she breathed, trying to resist the pleasure of his hands pushing deep into her hair, his fingers wrapping around the strands, his knuckles grazing her scalp. He was so good at turning her on, making her feel, and he was making her feel now with a little tug, a touch, and just like that, desire rushed through her...hot, consuming, intense.

"Of course," he said, leaning in to her, his mouth lightly kissing down from her brow, over her cheekbone, to the soft swell of her lips.

"Why?"

"Because no one has ever loved you the way I loved you."

Her eyes flew open and she stared into his eyes. "Don't say that."

"It's true. You know how I feel about you. You know I can not refuse you anything."

"Not true. For five years you refused to grant me the divorce."

"Because I didn't want to lose you."

"Five years is a long time to wait for someone."

"I would have waited forever for you, Morgan."

Her heart was pounding again, even harder. "That doesn't make sense, Drakon. Nothing about this…us…makes sense."

"Who said love was supposed to make sense?"

She exhaled hard, in a quick, desperate rush, and she had to blink hard to clear her vision. "Did you *really* love me?"

"How can you doubt it?"

She frowned, thinking, trying to remember. Why had she doubted it? Why had she not felt loved? How did she get from besotted bride to runaway wife?

He reached out, tipped her chin up, so he could look deeper into her eyes. "Morgan, tell me. How could you doubt me?"

"Because after our honeymoon…after we left here…I didn't feel loved…." Her voice drifted off as she struggled to piece it together. How lost she'd felt in Athens, how confused waiting for him all day, needing him so much that when he walked through the door, she didn't know if she should run to him, or hide, ashamed for feeling so empty. "But then, after a while, I didn't feel anything anymore—" She broke off, bit down into her lip, piercing the skin. "No, that's not true. I did feel something. I felt crazy, Drakon. I felt crazy living with you."

"Don't say that."

"It's true."

He stepped away from her, turned and faced the sea, then rubbed his palm across the bristles on his jaw.

Morgan watched him just long enough to see the pain in his eyes. She'd hurt him. Again.

Hating herself, hating what they did to each other, she

slipped past him and continued down the stairs to the water's edge.

She had to get out of here. And she had to get out of here soon.

CHAPTER EIGHT

HE SWORE SOFTLY, and shook his head.

God, that woman was frustrating. And to think he hadn't just fallen in love with her, but he'd married her.

Married her.

Long before his wedding day, Drakon had been warned by other men that getting married changed things. He'd been warned that wives—and marriage—were a lot of work. But Drakon hadn't been daunted. He didn't mind work. He'd succeeded because he'd always worked hard, put in long hours, never expecting life to be easy.

But marriage to Morgan hadn't started out difficult. It'd been amazing initially. She'd been amazing, and everything had been easy, since Morgan had been easiness herself…joyful, uncomplicated, undemanding. And then they moved into the new villa in Ekali, the affluent Athens neighborhood, and she'd changed…expressing worries, and then doubts, and then needs which came to sound like demands.

Be home from work early.

Don't work too late.

Why aren't you ever here?

And if he were honest, he had worked long hours, really long hours, and the more Morgan pressured him to come home, the more he wanted to be at the office, and he'd told himself he was working late to provide for her, working late to ensure she had everything she needed, when deep inside he knew he was just avoiding going home to her. It wasn't that he didn't love her…but he was suddenly so aware of how she now depended on him for everything. It overwhelmed him. How could he meet all those needs? How could he manage her, and his work, and his responsibilities?

While he grew more distant, she grew more emotional, her sunny smiles fading until they were gone, replaced by a woman who looked fragile and haunted, her eyes sad, her lovely face taut, her expression stricken.

It made him angry, this change in her. Made him angry that she couldn't be like his other women…happy to shop and visit salons and spas and just enjoy being spoiled, enjoy the prestige of being Drakon Xanthis's pampered wife. It was good enough for his other women. Why not for her?

Why did Morgan want more? More to the point, what did she want from *him?*

He'd never told her—or anyone—but in his mind, she'd become like his mother. Drakon loved his mother, he was a dutiful son, but he didn't want to be around her, and that's what happened with Morgan. Morgan made him feel inadequate and he dealt with it by avoiding her.

And then one day Morgan disappeared, abruptly returning to America, and he had exploded.

How could she have just walk away from him like that? How could she give up? How *dare* she give up? He hadn't been happy all those years ago, but he hadn't walked away from her. He hadn't felt the magic, either, but he wasn't a quitter—

And then it struck him. He had quit on her. Maybe he hadn't physically left, but he'd checked out emotionally.

And only now he could see that her needs hadn't been so overwhelming. She hadn't asked for that much. But the fact that she'd asked for anything—time, tenderness, reassurance—had triggered the worst in him, and he'd reacted like the boy he'd once been, retreating, hiding, rejecting.

He'd given her money but not affection.

He'd given her toys but not his heart.

He'd given her stuff…as long as she didn't engage him, want him, need him. Don't bother him because he couldn't, wouldn't, deal with anyone else's problems—he had plenty of his own.

Ah.

And there it was. The ugly, ugly truth.

Drakon Xanthis was a selfish, shallow, stunted man. A man that looked strong on the outside but was just an angry child on the inside. And that's when he knew, that he'd wronged Morgan…badly. Cruelly. He'd taken a twenty-two-year-old woman from her home and her country and dropped her into his white marble house and told her to be silent and to not feel and to not need. To not express emotion, to not reach out, to not cry, to not talk, to not be human.

My God.

He'd done to her what his mother had done to him. Be there, Drakon, but do not need. Be present, Drakon, but do not feel.…

Five years ago Drakon went in search of Morgan, seeking to right the wrongs, but she was gone. She'd vanished…completely disappeared…and his anger with himself grew. He'd loved Morgan and he'd treated her so badly. He'd taken the person who loved him, wanted him, the real him—the man, not the name, the bank account, the status—and crushed her.

He'd broken her.

He knew it. And all he'd wanted was to find her, apologize, fix everything. And he couldn't. Morgan was gone again. And Drakon was shattered. Until she came back, until he could make things right, he was a man in hell.

Now, from the top of the stairs, he watched Morgan step

onto the platform down below, her brown hair gleaming in the sunlight, spilling down her back. His chest hurt, heavy and aching with suppressed emotion.

Morgan. His woman. His.

She stood on the platform, a hand shadowing her eyes as she looked out across the water. A wooden rowboat, the color of a robin's egg, was tethered to the platform and bobbed next to her. The blue rowboat, and dark sapphire sea, perfectly framed Morgan in her fitted white dress, which accented her slim curves.

She looked fresh and young standing on the platform, and when she slipped off her shoes and sat down on the pier's edge, pulling her crisp skirts high on her thigh so that she could put her bare feet in the water, he felt a fierce surge of emotion.

It had been his job to love her, cherish her and protect her. And he'd failed in all three counts.

Watching her, Drakon's chest grew tight. He'd vowed five years ago to make things right, and he hadn't made them right yet. Giving her a check and a divorce wasn't right. It was easy. Easier to let her go than to change, or struggle to save them. But he didn't want easy. He wanted Morgan. And she was worth fighting for, and she was worth changing for, and she was worth everything to him.

She was everything to him.

He'd known it the moment he'd lost her.

And now that she was here, he realized that he could not give up on her. Could not give up on them. Not because he needed to win her back, not because he needed to prove anything—for God's sake, he was Drakon Xanthis, and the world was his oyster—but because he loved *her,* Morgan Copeland.

And for the past five years, Morgan Copeland had tied him up in knots. But he was a smart man. He could figure out how to untie the knots. He could figure out how to reach her, how to make this—them—work.

It was a challenge, but he liked challenges. He'd never been afraid of tackling difficult situations. What was it that his father used to say? Problems were just opportunities in disguise?

Morgan being here was an opportunity. And Drakon would make the most of the opportunity.

"It was a mistake making love without protection," Drakon said quietly. "And I accept full responsibility should you get pregnant."

Morgan stiffened. She hadn't heard Drakon approach, but now she felt him there behind her, and her nape prickled, the hair on her arms lifted, and a shiver raced through her as she remembered how it felt being with him in her room, his skin on her skin, his mouth taking hers, his body giving her so much pleasure.

It had been so good. So intense and physical that she lost perspective. Forgot what was important. But then, hadn't that always been his effect on her?

"What does that mean?" she asked quietly, reaching up to pluck a fine strand of hair away from her eyelashes as she kept her gaze fixed on the watery horizon, where the sunlight shimmered in every direction. "That you will accept full responsibility if I get pregnant?"

"I'll assume full financial responsibility, for you and the child, and once the baby is born, I will assume full physical custody of the child—"

"What?" she choked, cutting him short as she turned to look at him where he was standing on the narrow stair landing behind her, leaning against the rock wall. "You'll take my baby?"

"Our baby," he calmly corrected, broad shoulders shifting,

"and I am quite able to raise a child on my own, Morgan. I will get help, of course, but I'll be a good father—"

"You'd take the baby away from me?"

"If that would make you feel better—"

"It wouldn't."

"You said earlier that you didn't want to be a single mother."

"I don't. It wouldn't be right for the baby. But that doesn't mean you can have him or her."

He walked toward her. "But I'm ready to be a father, and you're not wanting to be a mother right now—"

"You can't say that. You don't know that. My God, Drakon! Where are you getting this from?"

"First of all, right now, as far as we know, there's no baby. And secondly, *should* you conceive, then of course I'd want to support my child—financially, emotionally, physically. I won't be an absentee father."

Her skin prickled as he stood above her. The man was pure electricity. The air practically pulsed with energy. "No, I don't want to be pregnant right now, it's not high on my to-do list at the moment, with my father being held hostage and my family in chaos, but if I was pregnant, I'd manage."

"That's not good enough. My child deserves better than that. If you are pregnant, we'll have to do the right thing for our child, which means raising him or her in a calm, stable home, without chaos."

"Then you'd be stuck with me, Drakon, because I'm not handing over my child."

"Our child."

"Which might not even exist."

"Which probably doesn't exist, because when we were newlyweds and having unprotected sex every day, twice a day, for months, you didn't get pregnant."

She bit into her lip, hating the panic rushing through here.

This was just a conversation of hypotheticals. "Does that mean if I do conceive, you'd want the baby and me to live with you?"

"Yes."

It's not real, she reminded herself, don't freak out. "And we'd be divorced?"

"No."

"No?"

He shook his head. "Absolutely not. If you're pregnant, we'll stay together. If you're not, I'll have my attorney file the divorce papers. But as we won't know that for a couple more weeks, I won't have my attorney file until we know for certain."

"Awfully convenient," she muttered under her breath.

"Happily so," he answered, not rising to the bait. "This way there would be no stigma attached to the child. We're still legally married. The baby would be a result of our reconciliation."

"And if I'm not pregnant?"

"You'll be free—single—within a couple months."

Morgan didn't immediately speak. Instead she looked out across the water and listened to the waves break and felt the breeze catch and lift her hair. She might appear calm, but her thoughts were tangled and her emotions intense. "And should the unthinkable happen, should I conceive...we would all live together, as a family?"

"Yes."

She turned to look at him. "Where would we raise the baby?"

"Greece," he said firmly.

She made a rough sound, tucking a strand of hair behind her ear. "I'd prefer not to raise a child in Greece."

"Why not?"

"I don't like Greece."

"How can you not like Greece? It's beautiful and warm and so full of life."

"I found it excruciatingly isolating, and horribly boring—"

"There was no reason for you to be bored. You had money, a driver, you could have gone shopping. The salesclerks would have loved you. They would have waited on you hand and foot."

Battling her temper, Morgan drew her feet out of the water, wrapped her arms around bent knees. "Not all women live to shop."

"Most women do."

"You can't generalize like that. It's not true." He started to protest and she overrode him. "Obviously one or more of your past girlfriends managed to convince you that retail therapy was the answer for everything, but I'm not one of them." She rose to her feet. "Shopping when I'm lonely just makes me feel worse…wandering alone from store to store looking for something to buy…how pathetic is that?"

"It would have been better than you sitting sulking at home."

Heat rushed through her, and her cheeks suddenly burned. "Sulking? Shopping? Why in God's name did you even marry shallow, materialistic me?"

"You were young. I thought you'd change."

"I can't believe you just said that! I can't believe you think you're so perfect…that you had no blame in our failed marriage."

"So what did I do wrong?" he asked.

"You didn't talk to me."

He laughed. "*That's* my mistake?"

Her eyes blazed. "Fine, laugh, but it's true. Our marriage ended because we didn't talk to each other. It ended because we both kept everything bottled inside and I think it's time we started talking, and saying those things that aren't comfortable, but true—"

"It's not going to change anything."

"No, but at least it'll clear the air. Perhaps give us better understanding of what happened…maybe help me understand you."

"Me?" he said incredulously. "What is there to understand about me?"

"Everything! I married one person and yet I ended up with another."

He drew back, shocked. "I didn't change. Morgan, it was you. When we married, you were strong and confident, and then before I knew what happened, you turned into an angry, silent woman who only responded when I touched her. So I touched you, as often as I could, as much as I could, trying to get you back."

"Words would have worked. Words and conversation."

"I don't trust words. Don't put much stock in conversation."

"Obviously, but would it have killed you to ask me about my day, or tell me about your day—" She broke off, averting her head, unable to look at him when her heart felt so bruised and tender. What a mistake it had been…falling in love… thinking it would work. "Let's just hope I'm not pregnant," she added hoarsely. "Because I don't want to go through life like this, trying to explain myself, trying to be accepted, only to be mocked by you."

Drakon shook his head, muttering something under his breath, something with quite a few syllables and from his inflection, sounded far from flattering.

"What did you just say?" she demanded.

"Doesn't matter."

"No, it does. I want to hear this. I want to hear everything you wouldn't tell me before."

"You gave up on us so quickly, Morgan. You didn't give

yourself time to adjust to married life, nor did you try to make friends."

"Maybe I did give up too soon, but you could have tried to help me adjust to Athens. Instead you dropped me off at the house and expected me to keep myself busy until you returned every night."

"I had a job to do."

"You could have made more of an effort to help me adjust. You could have taken the time to show me around, or cut your day short now and then so we could take a walk, or visit a nearby beach, or even have people over."

Drakon looked bewildered. "Have people over? For what?"

"Have dinner, visit, socialize." She could see by his expression that he still didn't get it. "Surely, you're used to entertaining…having some friends over for a barbecue or a party."

"To my house?"

"Yes."

"Never have."

"Why not?"

"My family didn't. I never did. I don't have time, nor is it something I'd want to do. I work long days, and when I go home, I want to relax, rest, focus on what I need to do the next day."

"But while you were working twelve- and fourteen-hour days, Drakon, what was I supposed to do?"

"Read a book…take language courses…learn to cook?" He shrugged, sighed, running a hand through his cropped dark hair. "Eventually we would have had children. And then, of course, you had the house."

"The *house?*" Morgan suppressed a sudden urge to throw rocks at his head. "Did you actually just say I had the *house?*"

"Yes, the house. The one I had built for you."

"You did not build that marble mausoleum for me. You bought it for me—"

"No, I bought the lot, scrapped the old house that was there and built our home for you."

"I *hated* the villa."

"What?"

Her eyebrows lifted, her lips twisting. "Yes. I hated it. It's awful. It was too white and sterile, never mind cold, modern and boxy—"

"It's a ten-million-dollar architectural masterpiece, Morgan."

"Or merely an outrageously expensive ice cube tray!"

His eyes sparked. "You disappoint me."

"Yes, so I've gathered. You work twelve-hour days while I'm home learning Greek, and how to cook, and hopefully getting pregnant." She shuddered. "What a horrendous life that would have been. Thank God I escaped when I did!"

He reached out, his fingers wrapping around her biceps to haul her against him. "Do you know how many women would be thrilled to live in that house?"

"I have no idea, although I'm sure Bronwyn would love to be one." She flung her head back to look him in the eye. "How is she, by the way? Doing well?"

"She's fine."

"I bet she is."

"What does that mean?"

"What do you think it means, Drakon?"

"I think it means you're petty and irrational when it comes to Bron. She's never been anything but polite to you—"

"Give me a break!"

"—ordering you flowers, arranging for your birthday cake," he continued, as if she'd never interrupted.

Morgan shook his hand off her arm. "How nice of her to get me flowers from you and order birthday cake for me. It makes me feel so good to know that your vice president of

Southeast Asia was able to do those little things to make my birthday special since you were too busy to do it yourself."

He tensed and his jaw popped. "That's not why I didn't do it."

"No? Then why didn't you do it?" She dragged in a breath of air, holding it a moment, fighting for control, not wanting to cry now. She would not cry while discussing Bronwyn. Would not lose it now when she needed to be strong. "Because I didn't want flowers picked out by the woman who is spending all day at the office with you. I didn't want a cake ordered by her, either. She's not my friend. She's not my family. She doesn't like me and is only trying to get closer to you."

"She was doing me a favor."

"Ah. I knew it. It was about you."

"What does that mean?"

"It means, that her favor to you, was not just unnecessary, but it actually hurt me."

"That's ridiculous."

And this was why she and Drakon weren't together. This was why she'd left him, and this was why they'd never be together.

Even though part of her would always love him, they couldn't be together, because outside the bedroom, they simply didn't work. There was no real understanding, no meeting of the minds. The only time they connected, the only time they made sense, was when they were having sex. But sex was just a part of a relationship, it couldn't be the relationship.

She looked up at him, her expression fierce. "Perhaps you will permit me to give you a little advice. Maybe I can do something for the future Mrs. Xanthis. Don't let Bronwyn, or any other woman, intrude so much in your personal life. The women you work with shouldn't be allowed to overshadow the woman you live with. And should you want to send your wife flowers, or a gift, do it yourself or don't do it at all."

His eyes glittered and he looked almost pale beneath his tan. "Anything else, Morgan?"

"Yes, actually. Next time you marry, ask your bride what kind of home she wants to live in. Or better yet, include her on the design process, or take her with you when you go house hunting. That way your poor wife might actually like her cage."

"Cage?" he choked out, expression furious.

She shrugged, shoulders twisting. "It's what it felt like," she said, slipping past him to climb the stone and cement stairs that led back up to the house. And then halfway up the staircase, she paused. "But I'm not your pet, Drakon, and I won't be kept!"

And then with her skirts in her hands, she raced on up, half hoping he'd follow and end this terrible fight the only way they knew how to end things—through sex.

Because right now she wanted him and needed him, not to make her come, but to make her feel safe. Sane. Only she didn't know how to ask him for comfort, and he didn't know how to give comfort. Just raw, carnal pleasure.

But even raw, carnal pleasure would be better than nothing right now, and as she continued up toward the house, she tried not to think how good it'd feel to have him push her back against the rock wall and capture her hands in his and hold her immobile all the while kissing her senseless, kissing her until she was wet and ready for him and he could take her here, in the sun, near the sea, with the tang of salt in her nose and the sweet heady fragrance of jasmine perfuming the air, and the taste of Drakon—her husband, and her heart—on her tongue.

CHAPTER NINE

THERE WAS NO call back from the pirates and Morgan spent the rest of the afternoon in her bedroom. She didn't have to stay in her room, but she thought it safer than wandering around the villa or the extensive grounds, where she might bump into Drakon.

In her room, Morgan tried napping and she actually fell asleep, but didn't sleep long, as her mother called, waking her. It was a brief, meaningless conversation about social events and it infuriated Morgan that her mother would even ask, much less expect, Morgan to drop everything to attend a charity fund-raiser with her.

"I'm in Italy working to bring Dad home," Morgan told her mother.

"No one is going to give you the money, Morgan." Her mother paused. "And if they do, they are fools."

After hanging up, Morgan tried to fall back asleep, but she couldn't, too unsettled from the call. So she took a long bath, trying to forget the things her mother said, remaining in the tub until the water turned cold and the skin on her fingers shriveled up.

Morgan was chilled by the time she got out of the bath, and she blew her hair dry and dressed carefully for dinner, trying to fill her time, trying to stay busy so she wouldn't go find Drakon.

She wanted Drakon. She missed him. Didn't want to be at the villa with him and yet not with him. The last time she was here, on that delicious, luxurious honeymoon, they spent almost every moment together and it didn't seem right being at the villa and not seeing him.

But then, life didn't seem right without him in it.

But finally, thankfully, she'd managed to get through the afternoon and now it was almost dinner, and time for the nightly *aperitivo*.

Morgan was the first to the living room for the Italian *aperitivo*. The pre-dinner drink was a tradition at Villa Angelica, one she and Drakon had come to enjoy during their honeymoon.

In the living room, Morgan went to the antique table that had been set up as the bar with a selection of alcohol and juices, sodas, sparkling water and tonic water and other cocktail mixes. Morgan bypassed the mixes for the pitcher of Campari. Tonight it was Campari with pomegranate. Tomorrow night it might be Campari orange. The cocktail changed every night and Morgan enjoyed sampling the different variations.

She wandered now with her cocktail to the window to watch the sunset. It would be another stunning sunset and the sky was a fiery red orange at the moment and she sipped the cocktail, basking in the warm rays of the sun reaching through the glass.

This was like a dream, she thought, one of those dreams she had when she was at McLean Hospital, when she'd dream of Drakon every night, and in her dreams they were together still, and happy…so very, very happy.…

Suddenly footsteps sounded in the stairwell and Morgan turned to watch Drakon descend the final flight of stairs and step into the grand entry. Her heart turned over in her chest as she watched him. He moved with such ease, and so much grace, that he made other men look clumsy. But then, he'd always had confidence, and a physicality that other men didn't have. She'd wondered if growing up on boats, working on cargo ships as if he were a deckhand instead of the owner's son, had given him that awareness and balance.

As he crossed the hall and joined her in the living room, the enormous Venetian chandelier bathed him in light and she sucked in a breath, struck all over again by his intensity and that strong, hard face with those intensely observant eyes.

He was looking at her now. She grew warm under his inspection, remembering how much she'd wanted to go to him earlier, how much she'd craved him all afternoon.

"Hello," she said, hoping he couldn't see her blush.

"Hello," he answered, the corner of his mouth quirking as if amused.

His smile did something to her and she felt a frisson of pleasure race through her. Flustered, Morgan lifted her drink to her lips, sipped her cocktail and studied Drakon covertly over the rim of her glass. He was wearing a crisp white dress shirt open at the collar and fine trousers and he looked like the Drakon she'd married—polished, elegant, handsome— but she'd learned something new about him during the last twenty-four hours. He wasn't as controlled as she'd imagined. If anything he was a man of passion.

And that was both good and bad. Good, because he met her intensity and answered her fierce need for touch and sensation. Bad, because soon he'd be out of her life again and she couldn't imagine ever feeling this way about any other man. Couldn't imagine ever wanting any other man.

"Were you able to get a nap?" he asked, turning away to pour himself a drink.

He, too, chose the Campari cocktail and for some reason that made her happy. "I did lie down," Morgan answered, her back now to the window so she could face Drakon, "but the moment I finally fell asleep, my phone rang. It was my mother."

"Calling to get news about your father?"

"No. She just wanted to know if I'd be home to attend a fund-raiser in Greenwich with her this weekend." Morgan shook her head incredulously. "A black-tie fund-raiser! Can you imagine?"

"You used to attend events like that all the time."

"Yes, when we were socially desirable, but we're not anymore. We're hated, loathed, but Mom doesn't get it. She's trying to carry on as if everything is the same, but nothing's the same. Only Mom refuses to face facts, refuses to accept that no one wants us at their balls or parties or fund-raisers anymore." Morgan tried to laugh but couldn't quite pull it off. "Dad's being held hostage in Somalia and Mom's trying to find a date for this Saturday's symphony gala. What a horrible family you married into, Drakon!"

His amber gaze suddenly locked with hers. "I didn't marry them. I married you."

"And I'm the craziest of them all!"

He said nothing for a long moment and then he smiled, a slow, wicked smile that put an equally wicked gleam in his eye. "Is that why sex was always so much fun?"

She blushed but was saved from answering by the sudden appearance of Rowan. "Your contact from Somalia just phoned," he said, entering the living room. "He left a message. They're not going to let you speak with your father. But since you have the money ready, they want to arrange the drop, and give you instructions on where you'll find your hostage."

Morgan's smile died on her lips and she glanced at Drakon, and then back at Rowan. "Did they really say it like that?"

Rowan nodded and Morgan paled and swallowed hard. "They make my father sound like a carcass," she whispered, sickened.

"We're not dealing with sensitive people," Rowan answered.

"But don't panic," Drakon added. "I'm sure he's still alive."

She drew a quick breath and lifted her chin. "I want him out of there."

"He will be," Drakon said.

Rowan nodded. "Soon.

It took them a while to move from the living room to the dining room for dinner, but once they got there, the dining room glowed with candlelight. The dining room's antique chandelier was filled with tapers, and the iron and glass sconces on the white walls reflected onto the ceiling making every surface gleam and dance with light. But the meal was definitely subdued. Morgan was both angry and heartsick and felt impossibly distracted. Rowan barely spoke and Drakon didn't say much more than Rowan. But every now and then Morgan looked up to find Drakon watching her, his expression shuttered and impossible to read.

Perhaps if she and Drakon had been alone, she would have asked him what he was thinking, but with Rowan present, Morgan left Drakon to his own thoughts, and she tried not to dwell on her father, or his conditions in Somalia.

As Drakon said, her father would be home soon. Rowan had agreed with him.

She had to focus on that, cling to that, not allow herself to slide into panic or doubt.

Finally the dinner dishes were being cleared away and coffee was served. But sitting in silence with coffee proved even more uncomfortable than eating in silence.

"I hate them," she choked out, unable to remain silent another moment. "I hate how they've taken him and are treating him like he's nothing…nobody…just an object to be bartered."

"It is horrendous," Drakon agreed quietly.

"But it's on the rise, isn't it?" She looked up at him as she added another half teaspoon of sugar to her coffee and gave it a brisk stir. "From what I read, attacks have doubled in the last few years."

Drakon's dark head inclined. "Last year there were more hostages taken than ever before."

"Nearly twelve hundred," Morgan murmured, having done a fair amount of research on her own, trying to understand what had happened to her father. "With many being held for nine months or more. Unthinkable. But it's real. It's happening."

"At least your father will be freed," Rowan said brusquely. "There are hundreds of hostages who haven't been ransomed...that will never be ransomed."

Morgan's insides twisted. She couldn't imagine being one of the unfortunate crew who were never freed. How terrible to sit day after day, week after week, month after month waiting for a ransom that might never come. "Because someone isn't willing to pay the ransom?" she asked.

"Or able to pay it. Not all shipping companies have insurance that will pay it, and most ordinary people can't come up with millions of dollars, not even to save a loved one," Drakon answered.

Morgan put her spoon down, her eyes burning, guilt eating at her because she was able to help her father. She was able to do something and yet she felt for those who couldn't. "Fortunately, I understand the counter-piracy measures put in place this past year seem to be helping. From what I read, piracy was down during the first quarter of the year—not enough of course to give cause for celebration, but enough to know that the experts might be on to something."

"That's true," Drakon agreed. "Right now there's a concerted international effort to check piracy, and it's helping, but it certainly hasn't stopped the pirates. It's just slowed them a little."

"How do you stop them?"

"Put a stable, strong, and effective government in place. Change their economic structure. Take out the group who is arming the pirates, and profiting from the hostage ransoms." Rowan's lips curved, his expression hard. "But if that were easy, it would have been done already. And so we do the next best thing—increase maritime intelligence and continue international cooperation on monitoring the water off the Horn of Africa."

"Until I began researching piracy I didn't realize that until recently, few countries worked together...that for the most part, most countries just focused on their own pirated vessels," Morgan answered.

Rowan shrugged. "Typical nationalistic reaction."

"How so?"

"Every country has its own navy, military intelligence and sources, so it's not easy getting everyone on the same page. Governments are protective of their military and don't want to share resources," he answered her.

Morgan frowned. "But you're military?"

"Former, yes. Just as most of us in maritime intelligence have served in one arm of the navy or another."

"Were you in the Royal Navy?" she asked.

"I've actually served in both the U.S. Navy and the Royal Navy, but at different times and in different capacities."

Morgan glanced to Drakon and then back to Rowan. "How is that possible?"

"I have dual nationalities...I was born in Northern Ireland to an Irish mother, and an American Greek father, giving me both American and British citizenship."

"Irish, too," Drakon said.

"They let you have all those passports?" Morgan asked, rather amazed.

Rowan shrugged. "If you're good at what you do."

"And you are good, I take it?"

His lips curved but the smile didn't reach his eyes. "Have to be. There's a lot at stake—" He broke off as the sound of high heels clicking briskly on hard tiles echoed in the hallway.

They were all listening to the footsteps and Morgan stiffened, her shoulders drawing back as unease rolled through her in a huge dark wave.

Bronwyn.

Morgan went hot and then cold. But no, it couldn't be. What would Bronwyn be doing here?

And yet no one else walked that way. No one else sounded so fiercely confident in high stiletto heels.

Then there she was, appearing in the dining room doorway as if she owned Villa Angelica, as tall and blonde and statuesque as ever, dressed tonight in a formfitting red jersey knit that clung to her curves, making the most of her voluptuous body. Bronwyn, a stunning blonde with brilliant blue eyes and a dark golden tan, knew how to make an entrance.

"Hope I haven't kept you waiting," she said, smiling, as her gaze swept the dining room, before lingering on Drakon.

Morgan's stomach hurt as she saw the way Bronwyn looked at Drakon. Drakon had always said that Bronwyn was just part of his management team, a valuable employee and nothing more, but from the possessive expression on Bronwyn's face, Morgan knew that Bronwyn was fiercely attached to Drakon.

"You haven't kept us waiting," Drakon answered, rising and gesturing to a chair at the table. "Join us. Have you eaten? Would you like coffee? Something sweet?"

Bronwyn flashed Drakon a grateful smile as she moved

around the dining room table to take an empty chair. "A glass of wine would be perfect. You know what I like."

Morgan ground her teeth together as she glanced from Bronwyn to Drakon and then back to Bronwyn again. How could he have invited her here, now, when they were in the middle of a crisis? How could he possibly think it was appropriate?

Bronwyn sat down and crossed one leg over the other, then gave her head a small toss, sending her long, artfully layered blond hair spilling over her shoulders down to the tops of her high full breasts. "Drakon, next time, send the helicopter for me, not a driver. I was nauseous from Sorrento on. Such a grueling drive. So many hairpin curves."

Drakon didn't respond; too busy speaking to one of the kitchen staff, requesting Bronwyn's wine.

Bronwyn turned to Rowan. "Haven't seen you in a while. How are you?"

"Busy," he answered flatly, expression hard.

"But it must be nice to be in a business that is booming," she retorted.

"Not if there are people's lives at stake," Morgan said, unable to remain silent.

Bronwyn waved her hand in a careless gesture. "Most crews on hijacked ships aren't hurt. Most are eventually released when the ransom's paid."

"Most," Morgan said, hanging on to her temper by a thread. "But that's not all, and not a cause to celebrate."

Bronwyn smiled, her long lashes dropping over her eyes, but not before Morgan caught the glittering animosity in the blue depths. "Was I celebrating? I hope not. That would be most insensitive of me, considering your father is being held hostage as we speak."

For a moment Morgan couldn't breathe. The air caught in her throat and she balled her hands into fists. "We'll have him home soon, though," she answered, struggling to sound calm. "Drakon's brought in the best to secure his release."

Bronwyn flashed Rowan an amused glance. "The best, yes, as well as the most expensive. What will the job cost Drakon this time, Rowan? Seven million? Ten? More?"

"That's none of your business, Bronwyn," Drakon said gruffly.

The Australian turned wide blue eyes on him. "You assigned me the task of improving the corporation's bottom line, which includes cutting unnecessary spending—"

"And you know perfectly well that I will pay Dunamas Maritime Intelligence from my personal account, not the corporation, so enough." Drakon's tone was cool and firm, but not cold or firm enough for Morgan.

Why did he put up with Bronwyn? Why did he allow his vice president to speak to him the way he did? He wouldn't tolerate it from anyone else, Morgan was sure of that.

"Yes, boss," Bronwyn answered, rolling her eyes even as she glanced in Morgan's direction, the exasperation in Bronwyn's eyes replaced by bruising disdain.

Interesting, Morgan thought, air catching in her throat. *Bronwyn doesn't like me, either.*

Morgan had sensed it five years ago, and had mentioned her concern to Drakon, but Drakon had brushed Morgan off, telling her not to be petty, that Bronwyn was far too professional to have any ill will toward his new wife. Morgan had felt ashamed for being petty—if that's what how she was behaving—and properly chastised, tried not to object to Bronwyn's frequent intrusions into their personal life, but it was almost impossible. Bronwyn called constantly, appeared on their doorstep at strange moments, felt perfectly comfortable drawing Drakon out of the living room and off into his study for long, private business conversations.

Morgan hated it, and had come to resent Bronwyn, all

the while feeling guilty for resenting someone that Drakon viewed as so indispensible to his work.

But now Morgan knew she'd been right to object to Bronwyn's intrusiveness. Because Bronwyn meant to be intrusive. Bronwyn wanted Drakon. She'd wanted him five years ago, and she still wanted him now.

Of course, Morgan had no proof, just her female intuition and that nagging gut instinct that told her something was wrong…the same gut instinct that was telling her now that Bronwyn was still a problem.

Abruptly Morgan stood, unable to remain one more moment in the same room with Bronwyn.

"It's late and I'm still jet-lagged," Morgan said, her voice sharper than usual. "If you'll excuse me, I think I'll head to bed."

CHAPTER TEN

THE NEXT MORNING Morgan had coffee brought to her in her room and she sat on her balcony, sipping her coffee, trying to figure out how she could avoid going downstairs today. She'd slept like hell, dreaming of Bronwyn, as well as Bronwyn and Drakon frolicking in the pool, and the ballroom, and everywhere else, and the last person Morgan wanted to see was the real Bronwyn, who Morgan knew was up and about, as she could hear her voice wafting up from one of the terraces below.

Morgan glared down into her coffee as Bronwyn's laugh spiraled up again. Why was Bronwyn here? What was Drakon thinking?

"More coffee? A pastry?" a deep, distinctive male voice coming from the bedroom behind her, asked.

Morgan glanced over her shoulder, to where Drakon lounged in the doorway, looking horribly handsome and very rested. "You should knock," she said tartly, hating him for bringing Bronwyn here, to the villa, when Morgan was here feeling overwhelmed and out of control.

"I did. You didn't answer."

"Then maybe you shouldn't have come in."

"I needed to speak with you."

"But it's not polite to barge in on ladies in the morning."

"Not even if I have an invitation for an outing?"

That did give her pause, and Morgan eyed him suspiciously, excited at the idea of escaping the villa for a few hours, before realizing that she needed to be here, available, in case the pirates tried to contact her. "How can we just leave right now in the middle of everything? What if the pirates want to talk to me? Or change their demands?"

"They're not going to change their demands. They're anticipating six million dollars being delivered any day now."

He was probably right, and yet she found it hard to contemplate doing something pleasurable when her father was still in such trouble. "I wish I knew if he had his heart medicine. I wish I knew he was okay...healthy...strong. Then I'd feel better about things. But I don't know, and the not knowing is really scary."

"It's always the scariest part." His broad shoulders shifted. "But worrying doesn't change his situation, it just makes you sick, and makes it more difficult for you to cope with stress. Which is why I'm taking you out for a couple hours. Fresh air and a change of scenery will give you some perspective."

"And we could be reached if something happens?"

"Absolutely."

She hesitated. "So who would be going?"

"Just you and me, if that's all right."

Her gaze slowly swept over his face with the high cheekbones, straight nose, firm, sensual mouth, before dropping to his body. God, she loved his body...his narrow hips, his long lean, muscular torso and those sinfully broad shoulders. She glanced back up into his face, noting his arched eyebrow and his amused expression. She blushed. "Yes, that's all right."

His warm golden brown eyes, framed by those long, dense black lashes, glinted. "I'm glad."

She looked at him for a long moment, wondering what Drakon had up his sleeve, and why he'd decided to be charming today. He was reminding her of the Drakon of their courtship, the Drakon of their honeymoon—mellow, amusing, easygoing, attentive. She liked this Drakon, very much, but why was he here now? And what did he want? "When do we leave?"

"When can you be ready?"

They took the helicopter towards Naples, flying above the stunning Italian coastline, where the blue sea butted against the green swell of land, before rising up into the hills and the slopes of Mount Vesuvius, the volcano that had erupted and wiped out Pompeii.

"So beautiful," Morgan murmured, her fingers pressed against the slick helicopter window, her gaze fixed on the landscape below. "And so deceptively screne."

"Because Vesuvius is still active?"

"Isn't it considered one of the world's deadliest volcanoes?"

"Unfortunately, yes. Its Plinian eruptions aren't a good fit for the three million people living at the base, as well as up and down the slopes."

"I'd be afraid to live there."

"Scientists believe they can predict an eruption before it happens, and they do have an emergency evacuation plan.

She shivered. "I understand ancient Pompeii was beautiful."

"The villas that were on the outskirts of town would rival the finest villas today."

"I'd love to see it."

"Good. Because we're on our way there now."

Morgan clasped his arm in delight. "Really?"

"Really."

A bubble of warmth formed in her chest, rising. "I'm so glad!"

Drakon glanced down at her hand where it rested on his arm. He'd hardened the moment she touched him, it was how he always responded to her.

He drew a breath and exhaled, trying to ease some of the tightness in his gut. "I hope you'll enjoy today," he said, grateful he could sound controlled even when he didn't feel that way. "I'm hoping you will find something in Pompeii to inspire you and your next jewelry collection."

"I don't think there will be another—"

"Yes, there will be."

"I made terrible mistakes—"

"Everyone makes mistakes, but that doesn't mean you should give up. You have a gift. You're an artist. I believe in your vision."

She looked up into his eyes, fear and hope in the blue depths. "Do you really mean that?"

"Absolutely. You will have more collections, and you will succeed."

"How can you be so certain?"

"Because I've seen what you can do, and I know you. You're truly talented, Morgan. There's no one else like you."

Drakon's car was parked at a helipad outside Pompeii, waiting for them, and the driver whisked them to the ancient city to meet a private guide who was going to take them on a behind-the-scenes tour of the ruined city.

Morgan was glad she'd worn flat leather sandals since they walked from one end of the city to another, and she listened closely to everything the guide said, captivated by his stories of first century Pompeii, a thriving city of approximately ten thousand people. She was fascinated by the buried city and its restaurants and hotels and brothels, as well as the artwork revealed…frescoes and mosaics and sculptures.

"Pompeii is the most incredible place," she said as they made their way through the extraordinary villa, House of the Faun, and back into the sunlight. "But Pompeii also breaks my heart. It was such a beautiful city, and so full of life and people and passion—and then it was all wiped out. Gone in a matter of hours."

"Are you sorry I brought you today?"

She shook her head. "No. It's amazing. All of it. The houses, the streets, the restaurants, the statues and pots and artifacts. But it hurts, too. Life is so fragile, and unpredictable. There are no guarantees. Not for anyone."

"Your life changed overnight, didn't it?"

She looked at him, suddenly wary. "You mean, with the revelation of Michael's Ponzi scheme?"

Drakon nodded and Morgan bit down into her lip. "It did," she agreed softly. "I still find it hard to believe what's happened at home. Who would have thought a year ago…even three months ago…that my father would become one of the most hated men in America? That we'd lose everything… that so many others would lose everything, too, through his, and Michael's, actions?"

They'd come to a stop next to the cordoned-off fountain with its bronze statue of a dancing faun. This beautiful solitary faun was all that was left of this once glorious, elegant garden, and she held her breath a moment, pressing a fist to her chest, as if somehow she could control the pain, ease the tenderness.

"My father was horrified when he discovered that all his clients, all his investors, had lost their money. He found out on his way to a Valentine's Day soiree—another one of those black-tie balls my mother loves—when he got the text from Michael to say that it was over. That agents from the federal government had just left his house and there would be arrests made, and that Dad should flee, rather than be indicted." Her voice faded and she struggled to continue. "At first Dad didn't believe it. None of us could believe it. And then when the shock wore off, there was anger, and shame."

Morgan worked her lip between her teeth, tasting blood but

thinking nothing of it, because everything hurt now, all the time. Pain was constant. Pain and that endless, overwhelming shame. "Dad wanted to kill himself. My brother talked him out of it, telling Dad that if he was innocent, then he owed it to his family, his friends and his clients to prove his innocence, and try to recoup as much of the lost investments as he could. But then Dad vanished, and Mom said Dad would have been better off killing himself. That by disappearing, Dad had left us in a worse situation. Maybe Mom was right. Maybe Dad should have died—"

"You don't really feel that way," Drakon said brusquely. "Or you wouldn't be trying so hard to help him now."

"I guess part of me keeps hoping that if he returns, he can fix this…salvage something. Branson, you know, is determined to see all the investors paid back—"

"That's impossible."

"I know, but Branson can't escape his name. Women can marry and take a new surname. But Branson's a man. He'll be one of those hated Copelands forever."

"Someday people will forget. There will be other news that will become more urgent and compelling. There will be disasters and tragedies that will eventually cover this scandal, burying it."

Just as the volcano had buried Pompeii.

Morgan's gaze drifted slowly across the columns and walls and the sunken garden, feeling the emptiness, hearing the silence. Everything was so still here, and yet once this villa had bustled with life, with the comings and goings of the family and its household servants and pets. And all that activity and laughter and anger, all the fears and needs and dreams, ended that August day, and for hundreds of years this city lay buried beneath layers of ash and soil, grass and the development of new towns. New construction. New lives. New dreams.

"Come," Drakon said, putting his hand on her bare arm,

his touch light, but steadying. "Let's walk. This place is making you sad, and I didn't bring you here to be sad. I brought you here to inspire you."

"I am inspired, and moved. Gives one perspective…and certainly a great deal for me to be thankful for." She flashed Drakon an unsteady smile, allowing him to steer her from the garden and back to the street. "Like life. And air. And sunlight."

"Good girl. Count your blessings. Because you have many, you know. You have your health, and your creativity, and your brother and your sisters—"

"And you," she said, catching his hand, giving it a quick squeeze. "You've been here for me, and have hired Rowan to help rescue Dad. I am so grateful- –"

"Please don't thank me."

"Then let me at least apologize, because I am sorry, Drakon, I am so, so sorry for what my father did, and deeply ashamed, too."

"You didn't do it, love. You aren't responsible."

"But he's my father."

"And maybe he didn't know that Amery was just depositing all that money into his own account. Maybe he had no idea. Perhaps you're right. Perhaps we wait to judge and try him, until he is back, and he can answer the charges, answer everyone's questions?"

Her heart surged, a little rush of hope, and she turned quickly to face him. "Do you really think he could be innocent? Do you think—" And then she abruptly broke off when she saw Drakon's face.

He didn't think her father was innocent. He still despised her father. Drakon was merely trying to soften the blow for her. Make her disillusionment and pain more bearable.

Her eyes burned and she looked away. "You don't have to do that," she whispered. "There's no need to say things you don't mean just to make me feel better. I'd rather hear the truth from you."

"And I'd rather protect you, *agapi mou*."

Agapi mou. My love. Her chest squeezed, aching. "I remember when I really was your love."

"You will always be my love."

"But not the same way. It will never be the same."

"No, it won't be the same. It can't be."

He'd spoken gently, kindly, and for some reason that made it all even worse. "I hate what I did to us," she said. "Hate that I destroyed us."

"What did happen, Morgan? You were there one morning, and then gone that night. I just want to understand."

She hadn't planned on talking about what really happened, not here, not like this. "I wasn't prepared for life as a newlywed," she said, stumbling a little over the words. "I…I had unrealistic expectations of our life in Greece."

"What did you think it would be like?"

"Our honeymoon."

"But you know I had to return to work."

"Yes, but I didn't know work for you meant twelve-hour days, every day." Her hands twisted anxiously. "And I understand now, that's just how you work, and I'm not criticizing you. But I didn't understand then, how it would be, and it didn't leave much time for me. I married you because I wanted to be with you, not because I wanted your money or a villa in Greece."

"Looking back, I know now I wasn't very flexible with my hours. I regret how much I worked."

"You loved your work."

"But I loved you more, Morgan."

She'd looked into his eyes as he said it and for a moment she was lost, his amber gaze that intense, searing heat of old, and her heart felt wrenched and she fought to hold back the tears.

She couldn't cry…couldn't cry…wouldn't cry….

"So where do we go now?" she murmured, holding back the tears by smiling hard, smiling to hide her pain and how much she'd missed Drakon, and how much she'd always love Drakon. "What's next on our tour?"

"Lunch," he said lightly, smiling back at her. "I've a restaurant in mind, it's on our way home in Sorrento."

They didn't actually eat in Sorrento, but at a restaurant just outside the city, on the way to Positano. The simple one-story restaurant was tucked high into the mountain, off the beaten path, with a beamed ceiling and breathtaking views of the coast.

Normally the restaurant just served dinner, but today they'd opened for them for lunch, and Morgan and Drakon had the place to themselves.

With the expansive windows open, and course after course of the most delicious seafood and pasta arriving at their table, Morgan felt the tension easing from between her shoulders. After finishing her coffee, she leaned back in her chair. "This was really lovely, Drakon. I feel almost optimistic again. Thank you."

"I've done very little, Morgan."

"You've done everything. You've brought in Rowan and his team, and while they work to free Dad, you're keeping me occupied and encouraging me to think about life, down the road. You've shown me incredible things today, and given me ideas for future designs, and best of all, peace of mind. You're my hero…my knight in shining armor."

"So much better than a husband."

"Husbands are overrated," she teased.

"Apparently so," he answered drily.

And then reality hit her, and the memory of what had happened to them. Her smile slowly, painfully faded. "I've cost you a pretty penny, haven't I? Four hundred million here, seven million there—"

"I don't think about the money when I look at you."

"What do you think about?"

"You."

She dipped her head, and while this is what she wanted to hear, she did feel guilty. Love shouldn't be this expensive. Love shouldn't have cost Drakon so much. "I want to pay for Dunamas's services."

"They're expensive."

"But my father isn't your responsibility, and I can't allow you to keep picking up the tab, taking hits and losses, because you got tangled up with me."

"Tangled? Is that what they call wives and weddings these days?"

"Don't try to distract me. I'm serious about paying you back. It will take me some time. I'll pay in installments, but I'll pay interest, too. It's what the banks would do. And I may be one of those entitled Copelands, but I'm not entitled to your money, and I insist on making sure you are properly compensated—"

"You're ruining my lunch."

"You've finished eating, already."

"Then you're ruining my coffee."

"You've finished that, too." She held up a finger. "And before you think of anything else I'm ruining, please know I'm immensely grateful, which is why I'm trying to make things right, as well as make them fair."

"How is it fair for me to take what little money you earn over the next ten years? I'd be ashamed to take your money."

"And you don't think I'm ashamed that I had to come back to you, with my hand out, begging for assistance?"

Frowning, he pushed his empty cup. "We should go."

She reached across the table and caught his hand in hers. "Don't be angry, Drakon. Branson's not the only one who wants to put things right. If I could, I'd pay every one of my father's investors back—"

"You're not your father, Morgan. You're not responsible."

"I *feel* responsible."

"You'll make yourself sick, obsessing about this."

"And you don't obsess about what my father did to you?"

Drakon looked down at their hands, where their fingers were laced together. "Yes, I did lose a fortune," he said after a moment, his fingers tightening on hers. "But losing you five years ago was so much worse."

"No."

"Yes." He squeezed her fingers again. "There is always more money to be made, *gynaika mou*. But there is only one of you."

The driver stopped before the villa's great iron gates, waiting for them to open to give them access to the old estate's private drive and exquisite gardens. But Morgan wasn't ready to be back at the villa with Bronwyn and Rowan and the villa staff. After so many years of not being with Drakon, it was such a joy to have him to herself.

"We'll soon find out if Rowan's heard anything," Drakon said, glancing out the window as the four-story white marble villa came into view.

"Hopefully he has," she said, feeling guilty because for the past hour she hadn't thought of her father, not once. She'd been so happy just being with Drakon that she'd forgotten why she was here in Italy on the Amalfi Coast.

"And hopefully you had a good day," he added. "I'd thought perhaps you'd be inspired by Pompeii, but it can be overwhelming, too."

"I loved it. Every minute of it."

And it was true, she thought, as the car stopped in front of the villa's entrance and the driver stepped out to come around to open their door. But it wasn't just Pompeii she loved. She loved every minute of being with him today. This was what life was supposed to feel like. This is what she'd missed so much—his warmth, his strength, his friendship, his love.

His love.

She frowned, confused, suddenly caught between two worlds—the memories of a complicated past and the changing present. In this moment, the present, anything could happen. In this moment, everything was fluid and possible.

She and Drakon were possible. Life was possible. Love was possible.

She and Drakon could make different decisions, be different people, have a different future.

Could it be a future together?

"I enjoyed today, too," Drakon said.

"I hope we can do it again."

"Visit Pompeii?"

"Not necessarily Pompeii. But another outing…another adventure. It was fun."

Drakon suddenly leaned forward and swept the back of his hand over her cheek. "It was. And good to get away from here, and all this."

Her heart ached at the gentle touch. She'd forgotten how extraordinarily tender he could be. Over the years she'd focused on his control and his aloofness, in contrast to the wild heat of their lovemaking, and she'd turned him into someone he wasn't…someone cold and hard and unreachable. But that wasn't really Drakon. Yes, he could be aloof, and hard, and cold, but that wasn't often, and only when he was angry. And he wasn't always angry. In fact, he'd never been angry during their engagement or the first couple months of their marriage. It was only later, after they'd gone to Athens and gotten stuck in that terrible battle for control, a battle that had come to include Bronwyn, that they'd both become rigid and antagonistic.

She reached up, caught his hand, pressed it to her cheek. "Promise me we'll do this again soon. Please?"

"I promise," he said, holding her gaze as the driver opened the door to the back of the car.

Drakon stepped out and Morgan was just about to follow when heavy footsteps crunched the gravel drive and Rowan appeared at their side.

"Where have you been?" Rowan demanded. "I've been trying to reach you for the past hour."

"My mobile didn't ring," Drakon answered.

"I called," Rowan said. "Repeatedly." He turned to look at Morgan, his expression apologetic. "Your father was moved from his village today and we don't know where he is at the moment. But my office is gathering intelligence now that should help us understand what happened, why and where he's being held now."

CHAPTER ELEVEN

Morgan paced the living room, unable to stop moving, unable to be still.

How could her father have vanished? Where had he been taken? And why? Had he gotten sick? Had he died? What were his captors reason for moving him?

She reached the end of the living room, turned and started back again. She'd traveled this path for ten minutes now but there was no way she could sit, not when fear bubbled up in her, consuming her.

Drakon was at the opposite end of the living room, watching her, keeping her company. "Where did they take him, Drakon?" she said, stopping midstep. "Why did they move him?"

She'd asked him the same questions already, several times, as a matter of fact, but he answered just as patiently now. "As Rowan explained, high-profile hostages are often moved from one location to another to stymie rescue attempts."

"Do you think they knew we were planning something?"

"I doubt it. Rowan doesn't think so, either, but we don't know for sure. Fortunately, his office is diligently gathering intelligence now and we should know more soon. Believe me, your father is at the top of Dunamas's priority list."

"He's right," Bronwyn said, entering the living room with a brisk step, her deceptively simple knit dress, the color of ripe plums, making the most of her lush shape. "Dunamas is pulling all their sources and resources from other tasks to gather information on your father, leaving dozens of ships, countless sailors and hundreds of millions of dollars of cargo vulnerable to attack."

"That's not necessary, Bron," Drakon said, rebuking her.

"But it's true." She leaned on the back of a wing chair, her blond hair smooth and sleek and falling forward in an elegant golden shimmer. The expression in her blue eyes was mocking and she shot Drakon a challenging glance. "I know you don't like to discuss business in front of your wife, but shouldn't she know the truth? That Dunamas is dropping everything, and everyone, because Morgan Copeland's criminal father has changed village locations?"

Morgan flinched at Bronwyn's words. "Is that true? Has Dunamas pulled all its surveillance and protection from its other clients?"

"No," Drakon said flatly. "It's not true. While Dunamas has made your father a priority, it continues its surveillance and protective services for each ship, and every customer, it's been hired to protect."

"But at tremendous personal expense," Bronwyn retorted.

"That's none of your business," he answered, giving her a look that would have crushed Morgan, but Bronwyn wasn't crushed.

"Funny how different you are when she's around." Bronwyn's blue gaze met his and held.

Drakon's jaw thickened. "I'm exactly the same."

"No. You're not. Normally Drakon Xanthis rules his shipping empire with a cool head, a critical eye and shrewd sense…always fiscally conservative, and cautious when it comes to expenses and investments." Bronwyn's lips pursed. "But the moment Morgan Copeland enters the picture, smart, insightful, strategic Drakon Xanthis loses his head. Suddenly money is no object, and common sense is thrown out the window—"

"Bronwyn," he growled.

The Australian jerked her chin up, her expression a curious mixture of anger and pain. "You're just a fool for love, aren't you?"

Drakon looked away, his jaw tight, his amber gaze strangely bleak. Morgan glanced from Drakon to Bronwyn and back again, feeling the tension humming in the room, but this wasn't the sparky, sexy kind of tension that zinged between her and Drakon, but something altogether different. This tension was dark and heavy and overwhelming....

It felt like death...loss...

Why? What had happened between them? And what bound Drakon to Bronwyn, a woman Morgan disliked so very intensely.

But then on her own accord, Bronwyn walked out, pausing in the doorway to look at Drakon. "Don't be putty in her hands," she said. "You know what happens to putty."

The pressure in Morgan's chest should have eased after Bronwyn left. There should have been a subtle shift in mood, an easing of the tension, some kind of relief.

But Morgan felt no relief, and from Drakon's taut features, she knew there would be no relief.

Whatever it was that Bronwyn had just said to Drakon—and Morgan had heard her, but hadn't understood the significance, only felt the biting sarcasm—it'd hit the mark. Drakon had paled and was now ashen, his strong jaw clenched so tightly the skin along the bone had gone white.

"What just happened?" Morgan asked, her voice cracking.

Drakon didn't answer. He didn't even look at her.

She flushed as silence stretched and it became evident that he wasn't going to answer her, either.

"What was she saying, Drakon?" Morgan whispered, hat-

ing the way shame crept through her, shame and fear and that
terrible green-eyed monster called jealousy, because she was
jealous of Bronwyn, jealous that Bronwyn could have such a
powerful effect on Drakon.

But once again Morgan's question was met with stony silence. And the silence hurt. Not merely because he wasn't
talking to her, but because Bronwyn had done this to him—
to *them*—again.

Again.

Morgan's hands fisted at her sides. What was Bronwyn's
power? Because she certainly had something…some strange
and rather frightening influence over Drakon….

Something had to have happened between Drakon and
Bronwyn. Something big…

Something private and powerful…

Morgan's head pounded as she left the living room. She
needed space and quiet, and headed downstairs to the sunroom, and then outside to the broad terrace beyond. But the
terrace still felt too confining and Morgan kept walking,
down more stairs, to the lower garden, through manicured
boxwood and fanciful hedges to the old rose garden and the
herb garden and then to the miniature orchard with its peek-
aboo views of the sea.

She walked the narrow stone path through the orchard
before reaching the twisting path that followed the cliff, the
path dotted with marble benches. Morgan finally sat down in
one of these cool marble benches facing the sea, and drew a
slow breath, trying to process everything, from her father's
disappearance, to Drakon and Bronwyn's peculiar relationship, to her own relationship with Drakon. There was a lot
to sort through.

She sat on the bench, just breathing in the heady, fragrant
scent of wisteria and the blossoms from the citrus trees in the
small orchard, when she heard someone talking.

It was Rowan approaching on the path, talking on the phone, speaking English to someone, his tone clipped, no-nonsense, and his low brusque voice was such a contrast to his appearance. He looked like sex, but talked like a soldier. And suddenly the warrior king from the film *Spartacus* came to mind.

Rowan spotted her and ended his call.

"Any news about my father?" she asked him as he stopped before her bench.

"Not yet. But don't panic."

"I'm trying not to."

"Good girl."

The sun had dropped significantly and the colors in the sky were deepening, the light blue turning to rose gold.

"It's going to be another beautiful sunset," she said. "I love the sky here, the red and orange sunsets."

"You do know its pollution, ash and smoke just scattering away the shorter-wavelength part of the light spectrum."

Morgan made a face. "That's so not romantic."

He shrugged. "As Logan will tell you, I'm not a romantic guy."

Shocked, Morgan turned all the way to look at him. "You know my sister?"

"Drakon didn't tell you?"

"No."

"Thought he had."

"How do you know her?"

"I live in L.A. Malibu."

Which made sense as Logan lived in Los Angeles, too. "How well do you know her?"

He hesitated, just a fraction too long, and Morgan realized that he *knew* her, knew her, as in the Biblical knowing. "You guys...dated?"

"Not dated, plural. One date. Met at a celebrity fund-raiser."

"What fund-raiser?" she asked, finding it impossible to imagine Rowan Argyros at a charity event.

"It's inconsequential."

But from his tone, she knew it wasn't, and Morgan fought the sudden urge to smile. There was much more to the Rowan-Logan story than what he was telling her, and Morgan eyed him with new interest, as well as appreciation, because Logan might be her fraternal twin, but Logan and Morgan were polar opposites. Morgan was quieter and shyer, and Logan was extremely confident and extroverted, as well as assertive, especially when it came to men. Morgan had married Drakon, her first love, while Logan didn't believe in love.

"How did you two get along?" she asked now, lips still twitching, amused by the idea of Logan and Rowan together. They were both so strong—it would have been an interesting date…an explosive date.

"Fine."

"I doubt that."

Rowan looked at her from beneath a cocked brow, smiling, clearly amused. "Why do you say that?"

"Because I know Logan. She's my sister. And I've met you."

"Whatever happened—or didn't happen—is between your sister and me, but I will say she talked about you that night we were together. Told me…things…about you, and your past, not knowing I was connected to Drakon."

"Did you tell her you knew Drakon?"

"No."

"Well, there you go."

He stared down at her, expression troubled. He looked as if he wanted to say something but wasn't going to.

Morgan sighed. "What is it? What's on your mind?"

"Have you told Drakon about the year following your separation? Does he know what happened?"

Morgan eyed him warily. "About what?"

"About you being…ill."

She opened her mouth, and then closed it, shaking her head instead.

"Maybe you should. Maybe it's time."

Morgan turned back to the sea, where the horizon was now a dramatic parfait of pink and orange and red, with streaks of luscious violet. So beautiful it couldn't be real. "I don't think it'd change anything…if he knew."

"I think it would change a great deal. Maybe not for you, but for him."

She shot Rowan a cynical glance, feeling impossibly raw. "How so?"

"You weren't the only one who had a hard year after you left. Drakon's world fell apart, too."

Drakon was in his room, just stepping out of the shower when he heard a knock at his door. He dried off quickly, wrapped the towel around his hips and headed to the bedroom door. Opening it, he discovered Morgan in the hall.

"You okay?" she asked, looking up at him, a shadow of concern in her eyes.

He nodded. "I was just going to dress and come find you."

"Do you mind if I come in?"

He opened the door wider, and then once she was inside, he closed the door behind him.

"You look nice," she said, her voice low and husky.

"Almost naked?"

Color swept her cheeks. "I always liked you naked. You have an amazing body."

He folded his arms across his chest and stared at her. "I can't believe you came here to compliment my body."

"No…no. But it kind of…relates…to what I was going to say."

He rocked back on his hips, trying not to feel anything, even though he was already feeling too much of everything. But wasn't that always the way it was when it came to Morgan? He felt so much. He loved her so much.

"Can I kiss you?" she blurted breathlessly.

He frowned, caught off guard.

"Just a kiss, for courage," she said, clasping her hands, nervously. "Because I don't know how to tell you this, and I'm not sure what you'll say, but I probably should tell you. 'Cause I don't think anyone did tell you--"

He drew her to him, then, silenced her stream of words with a kiss. His kiss was fierce, and she kissed him back with desperation, with the heat and hunger that had always been there between them.

He let the kiss go on, too, drawing her close to his body, cupping the back of her head with one hand while the other slid to the small of her back and urged her even closer to his hips. Just like that he was hard and hot and eager to be inside her body, wanting to fill her, needing to lose himself in her, needing to silence the voices in his head…voices of guilt and anger, failure and shame….

But then Morgan ended the kiss and lifting her head she looked up into his eyes, her blue eyes wet, her black lashes matted. "I'm not right in the head." Her voice quavered. She tried to smile even as tears shimmered in her eyes. "I'm crazy."

"You're not crazy."

She nodded, and her lower lip quivered. "That's why you couldn't find me after I left you. I had a nervous breakdown. My family had me hospitalized."

Drakon flinched and stepped backward. "Why are you saying this?"

"It's what happened. I left you and I fell apart. I couldn't stop crying, and I couldn't eat, and I couldn't sleep, and everybody said it was this or that, but I just missed you. I wanted you."

"So why didn't you come back?"

"They wouldn't let me."

Drakon's gut churned, and his hands clenched involuntarily at his side. "*Who* wouldn't let you?"

"The doctors. The hospital. My family. They made me stay there at McLean. It's a…mental…hospital."

"I know what McLean is." Drakon looked at her in barely masked horror. "I don't understand, Morgan. You were there…why?"

"Because I was crazy."

"You *weren't* crazy!"

"They said I was." She walked away from him, moving around his room, which had been their room on their honeymoon. She touched an end table, and the foot of the bed, and then the chaise in the corner before she turned to look at him. "And I did feel crazy…but I kept thinking if I could just get to you, I'd feel better."

"So why didn't you come home to me?"

"I couldn't." She struggled to smile, but failed. "I couldn't get to you, couldn't call you or write to you. They wouldn't let me do anything until I calmed down and did all the therapy and the counseling sessions—"

"What do you mean, they wouldn't let you out? Didn't you check yourself in?"

She shook her head, and sat down on the chaise, smoothing her skirt over her knees. "No. My parents did. My mother did. My dad approved, but it was Mother who insisted. She said you would never want me back the way I was." Morgan looked up at him, eyes bright, above the pallor of her cheeks. "So I went through the treatment, but it didn't help. It didn't work. They wanted me to say I could live without you, and I couldn't."

"Why not?"

Her slim shoulders lifted and fell. "Because I couldn't."

"So why did you leave me in the first place?"

"I started falling apart in Ekali. I was fine when we first got there, but after the first month, something happened to me. I began to cry when you were at work and I tried to hide it from you when you came home, but you must have known, because you changed, too. You became colder and distant, and maybe it wasn't you…maybe it was all me…because I needed too much from you, and God knows, my needs weren't healthy—"

"And who told you that you needs weren't healthy?" he growled, trying desperately hard to hang on to his temper. "Your parents?"

"And the doctors. And the therapists."

"Christ," he muttered under his breath, dragging a hand through his hair. "That's not true, you know," he said, looking at her. "You were young and isolated and lonely and I wasn't there for you. I know that now. I know I wasn't fair to you. I worked ridiculous hours, and expected you to be able to entertain yourself, and I owe you an apology. Actually, I owe you many, many apologies."

She managed a small, tight smile. "It's hard to remember… hard to go back…because what we had was good, so good, and then it all became so bad…." She sighed and rubbed her head. "I wish we could go back, and do it all again, and make different decisions this time."

"There's no going back, though, only going forward."

Morgan nodded. "I know, and I'm trying. And seeing Pompeii with you today made me realize that we have to go forward. We have to have hope and courage and build new lives."

He came to her, crouched before her, his hands on either

side of her knees, his gaze searching hers. "I know I failed you—"

"No more than I failed you, Drakon."

"But you didn't fail me. You were perfect…you were warm and real and hopeful and sensitive."

"So why did you pull away? Why shut me out…because it felt like you did—"

"I did. I definitely shut you out, and you weren't imagining that I pulled away, because I did that, too."

"Why?"

He hesitated a moment and then drew a breath. "Because I loved you so much, and yet I was overwhelmed by feelings of inadequacy…I couldn't make you happy, I couldn't meet your needs, I couldn't be who or what you wanted, so I… pushed you away."

Her eyes searched his. "It wasn't my imagination?"

"No."

"I wasn't crazy when I left you then?"

"No."

She made a soft, hoarse sound. "So I just went crazy when I left you."

"You were never crazy, Morgan."

She smiled, sadly. "But I was. Leaving you tore me apart. I felt my heart break when I left you. Everyone kept telling me I was developing this disorder or that disorder but they didn't understand…I just needed you. I just wanted you. And they wouldn't let me have you." Tears filled her eyes. "No one believed that I could love you that deeply…but why was it wrong to love you so much? Why did it make me bad…and mad…to miss you that much?"

"They were wrong, Morgan. And I was wrong. And I know you weren't insane, because I felt the same way, too. And I couldn't get to you, either. I couldn't find you, and all I wanted was to find you and apologize, and fix things, and change things, so that we could be happy. I knew we could be happy. I just needed you home."

She reached up to knock away a tear before it could fall. "But I didn't come back."

"No. But I wouldn't give up on you, or us. I still can't give up on us." He reached out to wipe her cheek dry with his thumb. "Tell me, my love, that I haven't waited in vain. Tell me there's a place in your life for me. Give me hope, Morgan."

She just looked at him, deep into his eyes, for a long moment before leaning forward and kissing him. "Yes," she whispered against his mouth. "Yes, there's a place in my life for you. There will always be a place in my life for you. I need you, Drakon. Can't live without you, Drakon."

His mouth covered hers, and he kissed her deeply, but it wasn't enough for her. Morgan needed more, craved more, and she wrapped her arms around his neck, and opened her knees so he could move between them, his big body pressed against hers. Still kissing her, he pressed her back onto the chaise, his towel falling off as he stretched out over her, his hand sliding up her rib cage to cup her breast.

Morgan hissed a breath as his fingers rubbed her nipple, making the sensitive peak pucker and tighten. His other hand was moving down her torso, tugging up the hem of her dress, finding her bare inner thigh, his touch sending lightning forks of sensation zinging through her body, making her body heat and her core melt. She wanted him, wanted him so much, and she sucked on his tongue, desperate for him to strip her and feel his warm, bare skin on hers.

And then his phone rang on the bedside table, chiming with a unique ringtone that Morgan had never heard before.

He lifted his head, listened, frowning. "Damn."

"What?"

He shook his head and rolled away from her, leaving the chaise to pick up his phone from the table near the bed.

"Damn," he muttered, reading the message. "She needs to talk to me before she returns to Athens."

Morgan didn't even need to ask who "she" was, knowing perfectly well it was Bronwyn. "Now?"

"She's leaving soon. Tonight."

"Surely she can wait a half hour?"

He didn't answer immediately, simply rolled away, his towel falling off in the process. "I won't be long."

"You really have to go now?"

"I'll be back in less than fifteen minutes."

Morgan watched him walk, without a stitch of clothing, to the closet. Dressed, Drakon Xanthis was a handsome, sophisticated man. Naked, he was absolutely beautiful.

He was beautiful now, and her mouth dried, her heart hurting as he disappeared into the closet, his body tan, skin gleaming, his muscles taut. Honed. He had those big shoulders and broad chest and lean flat abs and long strong legs, and between those legs hung his thick shaft, impressive even now, when he wasn't erect.

As the closet light came on, Morgan felt a surge of jealousy, hating that Drakon and his beautiful, hard, honed body was leaving her to go meet Bronwyn.

When he emerged a few minutes later, buckling the belt on his trousers, buttoning his shirt and tucking it into the waistband, Morgan felt almost sick.

Suddenly she felt like the young bride she'd been five years ago…uncertain, insecure, overwhelmed by her new life as Drakon Xanthis's American bride.

Drakon must have seen her fear because his brow furrowed as he gazed down at her. "There's no need to be threatened by Bronwyn. She works for me, but you're my wife."

But she'd been his wife before, and it hadn't helped her feel secure, or close to him. And while she'd been home alone for twelve, fourteen, sometimes sixteen hours a day, he'd been at the office with Bronwyn. Even if there was nothing sexual between him and Bronwyn, by virtue of being his trusted right hand, Bronwyn still got to spend time with Drakon…time Morgan would love to have. Not because Morgan couldn't be alone and needed Drakon to prop her up, but because she loved Drakon and enjoyed his company more than anyone else.

"I just don't want to feel as if I have to fight Bronwyn for you anymore," she said quietly, calmly, grateful that her voice could sound so steady when her heart was racing so fast.

"But you don't have to fight Bron for me. You never have."

And while this conversation was brutal, it was also necessary and long overdue. They should have talked about Bronwyn years ago. Morgan should have told Drakon how uncomfortable she was around her when they first married, but she hadn't, too afraid of displeasing him. And so the wound had festered, and her fear grew, until their entire relationship had become stunted and toxic.

"You love me?" she whispered.

"How can you doubt it?"

She bit down into her lip, holding back her fears, and her need to be reassured, knowing that her fears were irrational. Drakon wouldn't be here, helping her, if he didn't want to be. Drakon wouldn't have brought in Rowan to rescue her father if he didn't care about her. It was time she stopped panicking and stopped allowing her insecurities to get the upper hand. Drakon loved her. Drakon had always loved her. But he wasn't a woman…he was a man, a Greek man that had been raised to conceal vulnerabilities and avoid emotion. "I don't doubt it," she whispered. "I know you love me. Without question."

"There is no competition between you and Bron," he said roughly, his handsome, chiseled features hard.

She nodded, wanting to believe it, needing to believe it, but as he'd told her once, actions spoke louder than words. If he stayed at his office night after night until ten, making decisions, talking with Bronwyn, how was Morgan supposed to feel?

She felt a twinge of panic at the idea of returning to that life, but she had to be strong and confident. She believed in Drakon, and she had to believe that Drakon would do what was right for her…for them.

"Promise me you're not threatened by her," he said, stalking closer to her, forcing her to tilt her head back to meet his eyes.

"Promise me you won't be upset if I have to work long days, and late into the night, with her," he added.

Morgan's mouth opened, closed. She wanted to tell him she'd be fine, and she would try to be fine with it, but she couldn't promise him she'd be perfectly comfortable. She didn't know any woman who'd be perfectly comfortable with her husband being alone with a gorgeous woman night after night…day after day. Working in such close proximity created an intimacy that could lead to other things…and Morgan was sure Bronwyn did have feelings for Drakon. In fact, Morgan was sure Bronwyn was the problem here, not Drakon, but how could she tell him that?

She couldn't. But she also couldn't lie. And so with her heart racing, she swallowed convulsively. "I'm here for the long haul, Drakon. I'm here to stay. I'm playing for keeps."

His amber gaze drilled into her. "Playing for keeps," he repeated softly.

She licked her dry lips. "Yes."

"Is that a threat or a promise?"

"It's whatever you want it to be."

He laughed once, the mocking sound such a contrast to the sudden fire in his eyes. And then he was gone, walking out, leaving the door wide open behind him.

CHAPTER TWELVE

HE WASN'T GONE just a few minutes. He was gone a long time, over an hour, and Morgan returned to her room, wondering if she should dress for dinner, or if dinner would even be served tonight as it was growing late, well past the time they normally gathered in the living room for *aperitivos*.

Morgan eventually did change and go downstairs. Rowan was in the living room, having a drink.

"Can I pour you something?" he offered as she entered the candle lit living room.

"The Campari," she said, even as she tried to listen to the house, trying to hear where Drakon and Bronwyn might be.

Rowan filled her glass, handed her the cocktail. "They're outside," he said. "Or they were."

She sipped the cocktail. Campari and orange. It was tart and sweet at the same time. "Why do you say, 'were'?"

"A car arrived a half hour ago, and it just pulled away a few minutes ago." Rowan turned, nodded at the hall. "And here he is. Drakon Xanthis in the flesh." Rowan raised his glass. "I've a few calls to make. I'll have more privacy elsewhere. Cheers." And then Rowan walked out, leaving Drakon and Morgan alone.

Drakon walked past Morgan without saying a word, going to the bar where he made himself a drink. Morgan watched him, wondering what had happened between him and Bronwyn.

Drakon carried his drink to the window, where he sipped it and stared out at the dark sky.

"She's gone," he said at last. "Back to Athens."

Morgan looked at his rigid back, and the set of his shoulders. "Did something happen?" she asked quietly.

"I let her go."

"What?"

"I let her go. Fired her. Terminated her employment. Whatever you want to call it."

"Why?"

"I watched her here, how she behaved around you, and I didn't like it. She has worked for me for a long time—eight years—and she was good at what she did, but I won't have any woman snubbing you, not anymore. I won't look the other way, especially if it's my employee, or a friend of mine. It's not acceptable, and you shouldn't have to endure slights and snubs…not from anyone."

Morgan heard what he was saying and appreciated everything he was saying, but there was something else happening here. Drakon was upset…angry…but Morgan didn't understand who he was upset with—Bronwyn, himself, or Morgan.

"You didn't have to fire her because of me," Morgan said, choosing her words carefully. "I meant it when I said, I was sticking around. I'm not going to let anyone scare me away. I'm not twenty-two anymore. I'm twenty-seven and I know a lot more about the world now, and a lot more about myself."

He sipped his cocktail. "I agree you've changed, but I've also changed, and Bronwyn has, too. There was a time I needed her— and she saved me, I owe her a lot, if not everything—but that was four years ago, and things are different and it's time for her to move on. It'll be better for her."

Morgan's inside flipped nervously. "How did she save you?"

He took another long drink from his crystal tumbler and

then looked over his shoulder at Morgan. "If it weren't for her, I wouldn't have a company. I wouldn't have this villa. I wouldn't have anything."

"I don't understand."

"I know you don't." He sighed, shrugged, took another quick drink before continuing. "I would prefer you didn't know, and I'd promised Bron years ago I wouldn't tell you, she didn't want me to tell you. She said you wouldn't like it… you wouldn't respect me…but that's a risk I'll have to take."

Morgan sat down in one of the chairs. "Please tell me."

He walked the length of the room, and it was a long room, before dropping into a chair not far from hers. "A number of years ago, I made a mistake. Normally it wouldn't be an issue, but with the situation being what it was, the mistake was serious. It nearly bankrupted me."

He closed his eyes, shook his head, then opened them again and looked at her. "I was close to losing everything. And I mean everything. The company. The ships. The contracts. Our offices. Our homes. The cars, planes, yachts… everything…" His voice faded and for a moment there was just silence, a heavy, suffocating silence that blanketed the room. "And the worst of it was, I didn't care."

Drakon was still looking at her, but he didn't seem to see her. He seemed to be seeing something else, his expression tortured. "I didn't care," he repeated lowly, strangely detached.

Morgan had never heard him talk this way, or sound this way, and her heart thumped uncomfortably and she wasn't sure if she wanted to hear more, but there was no way she would stop him from talking.

After a long, uneasy moment Drakon continued. "I wasn't able to make good decisions during this time, and I didn't do what I should have done to protect my company, my future, or my employees. I was willing to lose it all. But Bronwyn refused to just stand there, a witness, as my company and life imploded."

"So she took over," he continued. "She stepped into my empty shoes and vacant office and became me…became president and CEO and no one knew it was Bronwyn Harper forging my signature, shifting funds, slashing spending, liquidating assets." Drakon's gaze met Morgan's. "Not all of her decisions were the right ones. Some of her actions had negative consequences, but if she hadn't stepped in when she did, there would be nothing here today."

It was hard for Morgan to hear Drakon speak of Bronwyn so reverently, because Morgan wished she'd been the one who had been there for Drakon when he needed someone. "I'm glad she helped you," Morgan said huskily. "Glad she was able to help you, because I couldn't have, even if I'd wanted to."

He looked at her, amber gaze piercing. "So yes, she helped me, but she was never more than a valuable employee. She was never your rival. I never once wanted her. I have only wanted you."

"Then why fire her? If she was such a help, and you feel so grateful—"

"She wanted more than what we had." His mouth curved but the smile didn't reach his eyes. "She made it clear she wanted more, that she was in love with me, but I didn't feel that way about her. I loved you, and only you, and Bronwyn knew that."

"But she stuck around all these years…she stuck around because she had to hope she had a chance."

He shrugged. "Maybe. Probably. But she didn't. If I couldn't have you, there wouldn't have been anyone else for me. It was you or nobody."

Morgan exhaled slowly, her head spinning. "She must be heartbroken right now."

"She'll be fine. She's strong. She's smart. She'll have a

better life now, away from me." Drakon drew Morgan into his arms and pressed a kiss to her temple, and then another to her cheekbone. "It's you I'm worried about."

"You don't need to worry about me."

"Rowan hasn't found your father yet."

"But he hasn't given up."

"No. And Rowan won't, not until we find your father. There is no one better than Rowan and Dunamas. They will continue looking for your father, until he is found."

"What if it takes weeks…months…years?"

"Doesn't matter. I promise you, we will never forget him, and never give up."

CHAPTER THIRTEEN

THEY ATE DINNER, just the two of them, as Rowan was nowhere to be found, and then skipping coffee and dessert, they headed upstairs to Drakon's room, where they made love, soundlessly, wordlessly, so quiet in the dark silent night.

Their lovemaking wasn't fierce and hot, or carnal and raw, but slow, careful, tender, so tender that Morgan wept after she climaxed because she'd never felt this way with Drakon before, had never made love with him like this before, their bodies so close, so connected, they'd felt like one.

Afterward, they lay side by side, his body wrapped around hers, his muscular arm holding her close to him, and still they said nothing, because there were no words, at least not the right ones. So much had happened since they'd met. So much love and yet so much loss. So much anger and pain and heartbreak…

But words right now wouldn't help, words would just get in the way, so they didn't talk, but instead lay close, filled with emotion, intense emotion that surged and ached and trembled and twisted.

Lying there in the dark, wrapped in Drakon's warmth and listening to him breathe, Morgan knew these things—she still loved him, deeply, passionately.

She also knew she wouldn't leave him. Not ever again.

But for them to have a future, they would have to talk

more, and they'd need patience, forgiveness, courage and strength.

She knew she was willing to fight for Drakon and her marriage, but there were still things she didn't understand about Drakon, things she didn't understand about the past.

And when, a half hour later, he kissed her shoulder but eased away to climb from the bed, she was filled with unease.

Turning over, she watched as he stepped into his cotton pajama pants, settling the drawstring waist low on his hips, leaving that magnificent torso bare. She watched him walk to the French door and push open the curtains. Propping an arm against the glass, he stared out at the sea, which rippled silver with moonlight.

She sat up and wrapped an arm around her knees, pressing the covers closer to her legs. "I've been thinking about what you said earlier, and how you feel so grateful to Bronwyn for saving your company…and saving you…when you made a mistake and nearly lost everything. But I know you. You don't make mistakes. What mistake did you make, that could have possibly cost you your company?"

He said nothing right away and Morgan was afraid he wouldn't speak, but then he shrugged. "I was distracted. Wasn't focused on work. And suddenly there was no money. No money to pay anybody, no money for taxes, no money at all."

"How could there be no money? Where did it go?"

Again, another long, excruciating silence. "Bad investments."

Ice filled her veins and she flashed to her father, and Michael Amery. No…he wouldn't…not a second time. She held her breath, even as her heart began to race. "You said…bad investments….plural." Morgan swallowed around the lump of panic forming in her throat. "Did you mean, investments, plural, or was there just that one horrible, huge loss to my father?"

He was silent so long that bile rose up in her throat, and she knew, she knew, there was more. She knew something else had happened, something he'd never told her. "Drakon, *agapo mou,* please, please tell me."

Drakon shifted his weight, muscles ripping across his shoulders and down his back, and then he turned toward her, the moonlight glancing briefly over his features until he'd turned his back to the window, with the light behind him, shadowing his face again. "Your father came to me asking for help after you'd left me."

Pain shot through her. Tears filled her eyes. "You gave him more money."

Drakon's lips compressed. "He was your father. He needed help."

"How much did he ask for?"

"A billion."

"Oh, my God." She pressed her hand to her mouth. "Drakon, no. You didn't..."

"What was I to do, Morgan? He was in trouble. I was his son-in-law, and I loved you. Family is family—"

"But I'd left you!"

"But I hadn't left you."

She ground her teeth together, tears blinding her, her stomach churning in bitter protest. "I can't believe this."

He laughed hollowly. "When your father came to me, telling me he was in trouble...that he had investors who needed their money back, but he didn't have the liquidity to give them their money...I thought it was my chance to win you back. But I didn't have that kind of money sitting in an account, no one has money like that, so I took loans from banks, as well as other resources, to come up with the money for your father."

"And you didn't get me back, did you?" she whispered.

For a minute there was just silence, and an almost unbearable pain, and then Drakon shook his head. "No. I gave him the money but Daniel refused to tell me where you were. Said that you'd contact me when you were ready."

"And I couldn't contact you, not at McLean." She blinked to clear her eyes. "And then what happened?"

"The economy started crashing. My creditors and lenders began to call their loans. But there was no money to give them. There was nothing I could do but file for bankruptcy, and fold. And I was fine with that, because without you, I didn't care."

"You're breaking my heart," Morgan whispered.

"I was pathetic. Bron said you'd find me pathetic—"

"Pathetic? How could I find you, who sacrificed everything for me, pathetic?" She rose up on her knees. "You were a hero. You loved me. You fought for me. You were willing to sacrifice everything for me."

He turned and looked at her, his face still shadowed but she felt his intensity. "I don't want to live without you, Morgan. I don't like life without you. And maybe that's weak—"

"Not weak," she said, leaving the bed to go to him, wrap her arms around his waist. She held him tightly, chilled by what he had told her, as well as chilled by the reality of her parents taking her to McLean and leaving her there when they knew Drakon wanted her, when they knew Drakon loved her. She didn't understand their motivations, but then, their lives were about money and appearances and Morgan knew she'd embarrassed them by coming home from Greece, heartbroken and hysterical.

He slid a hand down her back, shaping her to him. "I don't think you understand how much I loved you," he said roughly. "How much I will always love you." His voice cracked, turned hoarse. "There is no one else for me, but you. You aren't just my wife. You are my world."

"And you are mine."

"Why did you leave then?"

"I was honestly falling apart."

"Why?"

"I loved you so much, it scared me. I'd never felt for anyone what I felt for you…but the feelings were so intense, it made me feel out of control. And then when we made love… that started to do something to my head. Played games with me, made me afraid."

"Afraid? Why? How?"

"I had so little experience when I met you, and you had so much, and in bed you're…hot. Erotic. Demanding. You make everything hot and erotic, too."

"I demanded too much of you?"

"There were times I felt overwhelmed."

"Thus, your disgust."

"You never disgusted me. I shouldn't have said that. It wasn't true. I was just angry and hurt, and trying desperately hard to keep you at arm's length since I find you impossible to resist."

He stepped away from her and went to flip the light switch, turning on the small wall sconces so the room glowed with soft yellow light. "Maybe I didn't disgust you, but I must have scared you at times for you to even say such a thing."

"I never minded it being…hot…when you were relaxed with me, and spent a lot of time with me, but once we returned to Athens, I didn't see you often and then we weren't talking and it didn't feel the same. It didn't feel as warm and safe. It felt more dangerous."

"But you always came."

"Because you've got great technique." She managed an unsteady smile. "But I'd rather not come, and just be close to you, feel close to you, than have erotic sex and have you feel like a stranger."

He sat down on the side of the bed. "Come here." He smiled crookedly. "Please."

Morgan walked to him, heart thumping, and feeling painfully shy. "Yes?"

He drew her down onto the bed next to him, and kissed her, once and again, before lifting his head to look down into her eyes. "I love how sensual you are. I love your passionate nature. But I never want you to be uncomfortable with me again…in bed, or out of bed. I love you too much to hurt you or scare you or to push you away. But you have to tell me when something is too much. You have to tell me when I'm being distant or when you feel nervous or lonely or afraid."

"You want me to talk to you," she said.

"Yes. I want you to talk to me."

"That means you have to talk to me, too."

He smiled even more crookedly. "I know."

"Okay."

"But I don't want you bored…especially in bed."

"My God, Morgan, I could never be bored in bed with you."

"No?"

"No! When we're together it's not about sex…its about me showing you how much you mean to me. How much I cherish you. How much I worship you. When I touch you, Morgan, I'm telling you that nothing is more important to me than you, and that I love you with all of my heart, and all of my soul."

"Really?"

"Really." His gaze searched hers. "All I have wanted for these past five years is to have you come home. I want you home. Morgan, please come home with me—"

"Yes." She reached up, cupped his cheek, drawing his face toward hers. She kissed him, deeply, and a shiver raced through her as his tongue met hers, teasing her. "Yes. I'm staying with you, going home with you, back to Athens."

"Even though you hate that white ice cube tray?" he asked, turning his mouth into her hand and kissing her palm.

Another delicious shiver ran through her and she smiled. "But would you mind if I added a few colorful rugs? A few paintings...some throw pillows?"

"Maybe what we really need is a new house for a fresh start—"

"No."

"Yes. I don't like the house, either."

"What?"

He laughed softly. "I hate it. It's awful. I never liked it. Not while they were building it, and not even when we moved in, but I thought you did like it, so I never told you."

"I think we have a slight communication problem," she said drily.

"You think?" he teased, pressing her backward onto the bed, and then stretching out over her, his long hard body covering hers.

"We need to work on it."

"Mmm," he agreed, kissing her throat and pushing the covers down to bare her breasts. "We're going to have to start talking more," he said, alternately kissing and licking the slope of her breast.

She sighed and arched as he latched onto one of her tight, pebbled nipples. "Okay," she gasped, desire coiling in her belly.

"Do you like this?" he asked, as he stroked down her flat belly.

"Um, yes."

"And this?" he asked, his fingers slipping between her legs.

She gasped as he caressed her most sensitive spot. "Yes. And I'm glad we're talking...but do we have to do it now?"

She felt his silent laughter as his teeth scraped her nipple.

"No," he answered. "I'd much rather just concentrate on you, and making you come."

"Good."

She gasped again as his fingers slipped down, where she was slick and wet, and then caressed up over the nub again. "Drakon?"

"Yes, *gynaika mou?*"

"Make love to me. And love me. Forever."

He shifted, bracing his weight on his arms and looked down into her eyes for an endless moment. "Always. Always, and forever, until I die."

EPILOGUE

"WILL YOU DO it, Logan? Cover for me for a few days so Drakon and I can have a brief getaway?" Morgan asked, speaking calmly into the phone, trying to sound relaxed, even though she was frustrated with Logan for dodging her calls for the past week. "You'd just be a point person for a few days, if there are any communication issues, but I doubt there will be."

"I can't drop everything and take over Dad's search just so you and Drakon can have a second honeymoon," Logan said, her voice sharp on the speakerphone. "Some of us have jobs, Morgan. Some of us must work as we don't have wealthy husbands to take care of us."

"Would you like a wealthy husband, Logan?" Drakon said, unable to remain silent in his seat across from Morgan's on his private jet. They were still on the ground, hadn't closed the doors, because Morgan had refused to take off until Logan promised she'd help. "You know it can be arranged."

"No, thank you, Drakon. I am quite capable of taking care of myself," Logan retorted crisply.

Drakon smiled. "You might actually enjoy a strong Greek husband…almost as much as he'd enjoy managing you."

"Not going to happen," Logan snapped. "But if it will help me get off this call, then yes, Morgan, I will be your contact person should something happen while you and Drakon are doing whatever you and Drakon do."

Drakon arched a brow at Morgan, and Morgan shook her head at him, blushing. "I seriously doubt anything will happen, though. We're only going to be gone a few days…just for a long weekend—"

"I got it. You're just gone a few days. Dunamas is doing all the intelligence work and orchestrating the rescue. They'll call me if they can't reach you should there be developments." Logan paused. "Did I forget anything?"

Morgan grimaced. "No. That's pretty much it."

"Good. Now go…scram. Enjoy your trip. And try to have fun. Dad's going to be okay." Logan's voice suddenly softened. "I'll make sure he is, I promise."

Morgan hung up and looked at Drakon, who had just signaled to his flight crew that they were ready to take off. "Why am I worrying so much?"

His amber gaze met hers. "Because you deliberately withheld information from her, knowing she'd never agree to help us if she thought she'd have to deal with Rowan."

Morgan chewed on her lip. "Let's just hope she doesn't have to deal with him. Otherwise there's going to be hell to pay."

"Rowan said the exact same thing."

* * * * *

AT THE GREEK BOSS'S BIDDING

For two of my favourite heroes, my brothers,
Dr. Thomas W. Porter and Robert George Porter.

PROLOGUE

THE HELICOPTER SLAMMED against the rocky incline of the mountain thick with drifts of snow.

Glass shattered, metal crunched and red flames shot from the engine, turning what Kristian Koumantaros knew was glacial white into a shimmering dance of fire and ice.

Unable to see, he struggled with his seatbelt. The helicopter tilted, sliding a few feet. Fire burned everywhere as the heat surged, surrounding him. Kristian tugged his seatbelt again. The clip was jammed.

The smoke seared his lungs, blistering each breath.

Life and death, he thought woozily. Life and death came down to this. And life-and-death decisions were often no different than any other decisions. You did what you had to do and the consequences be damned.

Kristian had done what he had to do and the consequences damned him.

As the roar of the fire grew louder, the helicopter shifted again, the snow giving way.

My God. Kristian threw his arms out, and yet there was nothing to grab, and they were sent tumbling down the mountain face. Another avalanche, he thought, deafened by the endless roar—

And then nothing.

CHAPTER ONE

"Oʜɪ. No." Tʜᴇ deep, rough voice could be none other than Kristian Koumantaros himself. "Not interested. Tell her to go away."

Standing in the hall outside the library, Elizabeth Hatchet drew a deep breath, strengthening her resolve. This was not going to be easy, but then nothing about Kristian Koumantaros's case had been easy. Not the accident, not the rehab, not the location of his estate.

It had taken her two days to get here from London—a flight from London to Athens, an endless drive from Athens to Sparta, and finally a bone-jarring cart and donkey trip halfway up the ridiculously inaccessible mountain.

Why anybody, much less a man who couldn't walk and couldn't see, would want to live in a former monastery built on a rocky crag on a slope of Taygetos, the highest mountain in the Peloponnese, was beyond her. But now that she was here, she wasn't going to go away.

"Kyrios." Another voice sounded from within the library and Elizabeth recognized the voice as the Greek servant who'd met her at the door. "She's traveled a long way—"

"I've had it with the bloody help from First Class Rehab. First Class, my ass."

Elizabeth closed her eyes and exhaled slowly, counting to ten as she did so.

She'd been told by her Athens staff that it was a long trip to the former monastery.

She'd been warned that reaching rugged Taygetos, with its severe landscape but breathtaking vistas, was nearly as exhausting as caring for Mr. Koumantaros.

Her staff had counseled that traveling up this spectacular mountain with its ancient Byzantine ruins would seem at turns mythical as well as impossible, but Elizabeth, climbing into the donkey cart, had thought she'd been prepared. She'd thought she knew what she was getting into.

Just like she'd thought she knew what she was getting into when she agreed to provide Mr. Koumantaros's home health care after he was released from the French hospital.

In both cases she had been wrong.

The painfully slow, bumpy ride had left her woozy, with a queasy stomach and a pounding headache.

Attempting to rehabilitate Mr. Koumantaros had made her suffer far worse. Quite bluntly, he'd nearly bankrupted her company.

Elizabeth tensed at the sound of glass breaking, followed by a string of select and exceptionally colorful Greek curses.

"*Kyrios,* it's just a glass. It can be replaced."

"I hate this, Pano. Hate everything about this—"

"I know, *kyrios.*" Pano's voice dropped low, and Elizabeth couldn't hear much of what was said, but apparently it had the effect of calming Mr. Koumantaros.

Elizabeth wasn't soothed.

Kristian Koumantaros might be fabulously wealthy and able to afford an eccentric and reclusive lifestyle in the Peloponnese, but that didn't excuse his behavior. And his behavior was nothing short of self-absorbed and self-destructive.

She was here because Kristian Koumantaros couldn't keep a nurse, and he couldn't keep a nurse because he couldn't keep his temper.

The voices in the library were growing louder again. Elizabeth, fluent in Greek, listened as they discussed her.

Mr. Koumantaros didn't want her here.

Pano, the elderly butler, was attempting to convince Mr. Koumantaros that it wouldn't be polite to send the nurse away without seeing her.

Mr. Koumantaros said he didn't care about being polite.

Elizabeth's mouth curved wryly as the butler urged Mr. Koumantaros to at least offer her some refreshment.

Her wry smile disappeared as she heard Mr. Koumantaros answer that as most nurses from First Class Rehab were large women Ms. Hatchet could probably benefit from passing on an afternoon snack.

"Kyrios," Pano persisted, "she's brought a suitcase. Luggage. Ms. Hatchet intends to stay."

"Stay?" Koumantaros roared.

"Yes, *kyrios.*" The elderly Greek's tone couldn't have been any more apologetic, but his words had the effect of sending Kristian into another litany of curses.

"For God's sake, Pano, leave the damn glass alone and dispense with her. Throw her a bone. Get her a donkey. I don't care. Just do it. *Now.*"

"But she's traveled from London—"

"I don't care if she flew from the moon. She had no business coming here. I left a message two weeks ago with the service. That woman knows perfectly well I've fired them. I didn't ask her to come. And it's not my problem she wasted her time."

Speaking of which, Elizabeth thought, rubbing at the back of her neck to ease the pinch of pain, she *was* wasting time standing here. It was time to introduce herself, get the meeting underway.

Shoulders squared, Elizabeth took a deep breath and

pushed the tall door open. As she entered the room, her low heels made a faint clicking sound on the hardwood floor.

"Good afternoon, Mr. Koumantaros," she said. Her narrowed gaze flashed across the shuttered windows, cluttered coffee table, newspapers stacked computer-high on a corner desk. Had to be a month's newspapers piled there, unread.

"You're trespassing, and eavesdropping." Kristian jerked upright in his wheelchair, his deep voice vibrating with fury.

She barely glanced his way, heading instead for the small table filled with prescription bottles. "You were shouting, Mr. Koumantaros. I didn't need to eavesdrop. And I'd be trespassing if your care weren't my responsibility, but it is, so you're going to have to deal with me."

At the table, Elizabeth picked up one of the medicine bottles to check the label, and then the others. It was an old habit, an automatic habit. The first thing a medical professional needed to know was what, if anything, the patient was taking.

Kristian's hunched figure in the wheelchair shuddered as he tried to follow the sound of her movements, his eyes shielded by a white gauze bandage wrapped around his head, the white gauze a brilliant contrast to his thick onyx hair. "Your services have already been terminated," he said tersely.

"You've been overruled," Elizabeth answered, returning the bottles to the table to study him. The bandages swathing his eyes exposed the hard, carved contours of his face. He had chiseled cheekbones, a firm chin and strong jaw shadowed with a rough black beard. From the look of it, he hadn't shaved since the last nurse had been sent packing.

"By whom?" he demanded, leaning crookedly in his chair.

"Your physicians."

"My physicians?"

"Yes, indeed. We're in daily contact with them, Mr. Koumantaros, and these past several months have made them question your mental soundness."

"You must be joking."

"Not at all. There is a discussion that perhaps you'd be better cared for in a facility—"

"Get out!" he demanded, pointing at the door. "Get out now."

Elizabeth didn't move. Instead she cocked her head, coolly examining him. He looked impossibly unkempt, nothing like the sophisticated, powerful tycoon he'd reportedly been, with castles and estates scattered all over the world and a gorgeous mistress tucked enticingly in each.

"They fear for you, Mr. Koumantaros," she added quietly, "and so do I. You need help."

"That's absurd. If my doctors were so concerned, they'd be here. And you…you don't know me. You can't drop in here and make assessments based on two minutes of observation."

"I can, because I've managed your case from day one, when you were released from the hospital. No one knows more about you and your day-to-day care than I do. And if you'd always been this despondent we'd see it as a personality issue, but your despair is new—"

"There's no despair. I'm just tired."

"Then let's address that, shall we?" Elizabeth flipped open her leather portfolio and scribbled some notes. One couldn't be too careful these days. She had to protect the agency, not to mention her staff. She'd learned early to document everything. "It's tragic you're still in your present condition—tragic to isolate yourself here on Taygetos when there are people waiting for you in Athens, people wanting you to come home."

"I live here permanently now."

She glanced up at him. "You've no intention of returning?"

"I spent years renovating this monastery, updating and converting it into a modern home to meet my needs."

"That was before you were injured. It's not practical for you to live here now. You can't fly—"

"Don't tell me what I can't do."

She swallowed, tried again. "It's not easy for your friends or family to see you. You're absolutely secluded here—"

"As I wish to be."

"But how can you fully recover when you're so alone in what is undoubtedly one of the most remote places in Greece?"

He averted his head, giving her a glimpse of a very strong, very proud profile. "This is my home," he repeated stubbornly, his tone colder, flintier.

"And what of your company? The businesses? Have you given those up along with your friends and family?"

"If this is your bedside manner—"

"Oh, it is," she assured him unapologetically. "Mr. Koumantaros, I'm not here to coddle you. Nor to say pretty things and try to make you laugh. I'm here to get you on your feet again."

"It's not going to happen."

"Because you like being helpless, or because you're afraid of pain?"

For a moment he said nothing, his face growing paler against the white gauze bandaging his head. Finally he found his voice. "How dare you?" he demanded. "How dare you waltz into my home—?"

"It wasn't exactly a waltz, Mr. Koumantaros. It took me two days to get here and that included planes, taxis, buses and asses." She smiled thinly. This was the last place she'd wanted to come, and the last person she wanted to nurse. "It's been nearly a year since your accident," she continued. "There's no medical reason for you to be as helpless as you are."

"Get out."

"I can't. Not only have I nowhere to go—as you must know, it's too dark to take a donkey back down the mountain."

"No, I don't know. I'm blind. I've no idea what time of day it is."

Heat surged to her cheeks. Heat and shame and disgust. Not for her, but him. If he expected her to feel sorry for him, he had another think coming, and if he hoped to intimidate her, he was wrong again. He could shout and break things, but she wasn't about to cower like a frightened puppy dog. Just because he was a famous Greek with a billion-dollar company didn't mean he deserved her respect. Respect was earned, not automatically given.

"It's almost four o'clock, Mr. Koumantaros. Half of the mountain is already steeped in shadows. I couldn't go home tonight even if I wanted to. Your doctors have authorized me to stay, so I must. It's either that or you go to a rehab facility in Athens. *Your* choice."

"Not much of a choice."

"No, it's not." Elizabeth picked up one of the prescription bottles and popped off the plastic cap to see the number of tablets inside. Three remained from a count of thirty. The prescription had only been refilled a week ago. "Still not sleeping, Mr. Koumantaros?"

"I *can't.*"

"Still in a lot of pain, then?" She pressed the notebook to her chest, stared at him over the portfolio's edge. Probably addicted to his painkillers now. Happened more often than not. One more battle ahead.

Kristian Koumantaros shifted in his wheelchair. The bandages that hid his eyes revealed the sharp twist of his lips. "As if you care."

She didn't even blink. His self-pity didn't trigger sympathy. Self-pity was a typical stage in the healing process—an early stage, one of the first. And the fact that Kristian Koumantaros hadn't moved beyond it meant he had a long, long way to go.

"I do care," she answered flatly. Elizabeth didn't bother

to add that she also cared about the future of her company, First Class Rehab, and that providing for Kristian Koumantaros's medical needs had nearly ruined her four-year-old company. "I do care, but I won't be like the others—going soft on you, accepting your excuses, allowing you to get away with murder."

"And what do you know of murder, Miss Holier-Than-Thou?" He wrenched his wheelchair forward, the hard rubber tires crunching glass shards.

"Careful, Mr. Koumantaros! You'll pop a tire."

"*Good.* Pop the goddamn tires. I hate this chair. I hate not seeing. I despise living like this." He swore violently, but at least he'd stopped rolling forward and was sitting still while the butler hurriedly finished sweeping up the glass with a small broom and dustpan.

As Kristian sat, his enormous shoulders turned inward, his dark head hung low.

Despair.

The word whispered to her, summing up what she saw, what she felt. His black mood wasn't merely anger. It was bigger than that, darker than that. His black mood was fed by despair.

He was, she thought, feeling the smallest prick of sympathy, a ruin of a great man.

As swiftly as the sympathy came, she pushed it aside, replacing tenderness with resolve. He'd get well. There was no reason he couldn't.

Elizabeth signaled to Pano that she wanted a word alone with his employer and, nodding, he left them, exiting the library with his dustpan of broken glass.

"Now, then, Mr. Koumantaros," she said as the library doors closed, "we need to get you back on your rehab program. But we can't do that if you insist on intimidating your nurses."

"They were all completely useless, incompetent—"

"All six?" she interrupted, taking a seat on the nearest armchair arm.

He'd gone through the roster of home healthcare specialists in record fashion. In fact, they'd run out of possible candidates. There was no one else to send. And yet Mr. Koumantaros couldn't be left alone. He required more than a butler. He still needed around-the-clock medical care.

"One nurse wasn't so bad. Well, in some ways," he said grudgingly, tapping the metal rim of his wheelchair with his finger tips. "The young one. Calista. And believe me, if she was the best it should show you how bad the others were. But that's another story—"

"Miss Aravantinos isn't coming back." Elizabeth felt her temper rise. Of course he'd request the one nurse he'd broken into bits. The poor girl, barely out of nursing school, had been putty in Kristian Koumantaros's hands. Literally. For a man with life-threatening injuries he'd been incredibly adept at seduction.

His dark head tipped sideways. "Was that her last name?"

"You behaved in a most unscrupulous manner. You're thirty—what?" She quickly flipped through his chart, found his age. "Nearly thirty-six. And she was barely twenty-three. She quit, you know. Left our Athens office. She felt terribly demoralized."

"I never asked Calista to fall in love with me."

"*Love?*" she choked.."Love didn't have anything to do with it. You seduced her. Out of boredom. And spite."

"You've got me all wrong, Nurse Cratchett—" He paused, a corner of his mouth smirking. "You *are* English, are you not?"

"I speak English, yes," she answered curtly.

"Well, Cratchett, you have me wrong. You see, I'm a lover, not a fighter."

Blood surged to Elizabeth's cheeks. "That's quite enough."

"I've never forced myself on a woman." His voice dropped, the pitch growing deeper, rougher. "If anything, our dear delightful Calista forced herself on me."

"Mr. Koumantaros." Acutely uncomfortable, she gripped her pen tightly, growing warm, warmer. She hated his mocking smile and resented his tone. She could see why Calista had thrown the towel in. How was a young girl to cope with him?

"She romanticized me," he continued, in the same infuriatingly smug vein. "She wanted to know what an invalid was capable of, I suppose. And she discovered that although I can't walk, I can still—"

"Mr. Koumantaros!" Elizabeth jumped to her feet, suddenly oppressed by the warm, dark room. It was late afternoon, and the day had been cloudless, blissfully sunny. She couldn't fathom why the windows and shutters were all closed, keeping the fresh mountain air out. "I do not wish to hear the details."

"But you need them." Kristian pushed his wheelchair toward her, blue cotton sleeves rolled back on his forearms, corded tendons tight beneath his skin. He'd once had a very deep tan, but the tan had long ago faded. His olive skin was pale, testament to his long months indoors. "You're misinformed if you think I took advantage of Calista. Calista got what Calista wanted."

She averted her head and ground her teeth together. "She was a wonderful, promising young nurse."

"I don't know about wonderful, but I'll give you naïve. And since she quit, I think you've deliberately assigned me nurses from hell."

"We do not employ nurses from hell. All of our nurses are professional, efficient, compassionate—"

"And stink to high heaven."

"Excuse me?" Elizabeth drew back, affronted. "That's a crude accusation."

"Crude, but true. And I didn't want them in my home, and I refused to have them touching me."

So that was it. He didn't want a real nurse. He wanted something from late-night T.V.—big hair, big breasts, and a short, tight skirt.

Elizabeth took a deep breath, fighting to hang on to her professional composure. She was beginning to see how he wore his nurses down, brow-beating and tormenting until they begged for a reprieve. *Anyone but Mr. Koumantaros. Any job but that!*

Well, she wasn't about to let Mr. Koumantaros break her. He couldn't get a rise out of her because she wouldn't let him. "Did Calista smell bad?"

"No, Calista smelled like heaven."

For a moment she could have sworn Kristian was smiling, and the fact that he could smile over ruining a young nurse's career infuriated her.

He rolled another foot closer. "But then after Calista fled you sent only old, fat, frumpy nurses to torture me, punishing me for what was really Calista's fault. And don't tell me they weren't old and fat and frumpy, because I might be blind but I'm not stupid."

Elizabeth's blood pressure shot up again. "I assigned mature nurses, but they were well-trained and certainly prepared for the rigors of the job."

"One smelled like a tobacco shop. One of fish. I'm quite certain another could have been a battleship—"

"You're being insulting."

"I'm being honest. You replaced Calista with prison guards."

Elizabeth's anger spiked, and then her lips twitched. Kristian Koumantaros was actually right.

After poor Calista's disgrace, Elizabeth had intentionally assigned Mr. Koumantaros only the older, less responsive nurses, realizing that he required special care. Very special care.

She smiled faintly, amused despite herself. He might not be walking, and he might not have his vision, but his brain worked just fine.

Still smiling, she studied him dispassionately, aware of his injuries, his months of painful rehabilitation, his prognosis. He was lucky to have escaped such a serious accident with his life. The trauma to his head had been so extensive he'd been expected to suffer severe brain damage. Happily, his mental faculties were intact. His motor skills could be repaired, but his eyesight was questionable. Sometimes the brain healed itself. Sometimes it didn't. Only time and continued therapy would tell.

"Well, that's all in the past now," she said, forcing a note of cheer into her voice. "The battleaxe nurses are gone. I am here—"

"And you are probably worse than all of them."

"Indeed, I am. They whisper behind my back that I'm every patient's worst nightmare."

"So I can call you Nurse Cratchett, then?"

"If you'd like. Or you can call me by my name, which is Nurse Hatchet. But they're so similar, I'll answer either way."

He sat in silence, his jaw set, his expression increasingly wary. Elizabeth felt the edges of her mouth lift, curl. He couldn't browbeat or intimidate her. She knew what Greek tycoons were. She'd once been married to one.

"It's time to move on," she added briskly. "And the first place we start is with your meals. I know it's late, Mr. Koumantaros, but have you eaten lunch yet?"

"I'm not hungry."

Elizabeth closed her portfolio and slipped the pen into the

leather case. "You need to eat. Your body needs the nutrition. I'll see about a light meal." She moved toward the door, unwilling to waste time arguing.

Kristian shoved his wheelchair forward, inadvertently slamming into the edge of the couch. His frustration was written in every line of his face. "I don't want food—"

"Of course not. Why eat when you're addicted to pain pills?" She flashed a tight, strained smile he couldn't see. "Now, if you'll excuse me, I'll see to your meal."

The vaulted stone kitchen was in the tower, or *pyrgos,* and there the butler, cook and senior housekeeper had gathered beneath one of the medieval arches. They were in such deep conversation that they didn't hear Elizabeth enter.

Once they realized she was there, all three fell silent and turned to face her with varying degrees of hostility.

Elizabeth wasn't surprised. For one, unlike the other nurses, she wasn't Greek. Two, despite being foreign, she spoke Greek fluently. And three, she wasn't showing proper deference to their employer, a very wealthy, powerful Greek man.

"Hello," Elizabeth said, attempting to ignore the icy welcome. "I thought I'd see if I could help with Mr. Koumantaros's lunch."

Everyone continued to gape at her until Pano, the butler, cleared his throat. "Mr. Koumantaros doesn't eat lunch."

"Does he take a late breakfast, then?" Elizabeth asked.

"No, just coffee."

"Then when does he eat his first meal?"

"Not until evening."

"I see." Elizabeth's brow furrowed as she studied the three staffers, wondering how long they'd been employed by Kristian Koumantaros and how they coped with his black moods and display of temper. "Does he eat well then?"

"Sometimes," the short, stocky cook answered, wiping

her hands across the starched white fabric of her apron. "And sometimes he just pecks. He used to have an excellent appetite—fish, *moussaka, dolmades,* cheese, meat, vegetables—but that was before the accident."

Elizabeth nodded, glad to see at least one of them had been with him a while. That was good. Loyalty was always a plus, but misplaced loyalty could also be a hindrance to Kristian recovering. "We'll have to improve his appetite," she said. "Starting with a light meal right now. Perhaps a *horiatiki salata,*" she said, suggesting what most Europeans and Americans thought of as a Greek salad—feta cheese and onion, tomato and cucumber, drizzled with olive oil and a few drops of homemade wine vinegar.

"There must be someplace outside—a sunny terrace—where he can enjoy his meal. Mr. Koumantaros needs the sun and fresh air—"

"Excuse me, ma'am," Pano interrupted, "but the sun bothers Mr. Koumantaros's eyes."

"It's because Mr. Koumantaros has spent too much time sitting in the dark. The light will do him good. Sunlight stimulates the pituitary gland, helps alleviate depression and promotes healing. But, seeing as he's been inside so much, we can transition today by having lunch in the shade. I assume part of the terrace is covered?"

"Yes, ma'am," the cook answered. "But Mr. Koumantaros won't go."

"Oh, he will." Elizabeth swallowed, summoning all her determination. She knew Kristian would eventually go. But it'd be a struggle.

Sitting in the library, Kristian heard the English nurse's footsteps disappear as she went in search of the kitchen, and after a number of long minutes heard her footsteps return.

So she was coming back. Wonderful.

He tipped his head, looking up at nothing, since everything was and had been dark since the crash, fourteen months and eleven days ago.

The door opened, and he knew from the way the handle turned and the lightness of the step that it was her. "You're wrong about something else," he said abruptly as she entered the library. "The accident wasn't a year ago. It was almost a year and a half ago. It happened late February."

She'd stopped walking and he felt her there, beyond his sight, beyond his reach, standing, staring, *waiting*. It galled him, this lack of knowing, seeing. He'd achieved what he'd achieved by utilizing his eyes, his mind, his gut. He trusted his eyes and his gut, and now, without those, he didn't know what was true, or real.

Like Calista, for example.

"That's even worse," his new nightmare nurse shot back. "You should be back at work by now. You've a corporation to run, people dependent on you. You're doing no one any good hiding away here in your villa."

"I can't run my company if I can't walk or see—"

"But you *can* walk, and there might be a chance you could see—"

"A less than five percent chance." He laughed bitterly. "You know, before the last round of surgeries I had a thirty-five percent chance of seeing, but they botched those—"

"They weren't botched. They were just highly experimental."

"Yes, and that experimental treatment reduced my chances of seeing again to nil."

"Not nil."

"Five percent. There's not much difference. Especially when they say that even if the operation were a success I'd still never be able to drive, or fly, or sail. That there's too much trauma for me to do what I used to do."

"And your answer is to sit here shrouded in bandages and darkness and feel sorry for yourself?" she said tartly, her voice growing closer.

Kristian shifted in his chair, and felt an active and growing dislike for Cratchett. She was standing off to his right, and her smug, superior attitude rubbed him the wrong way. "Your company's services have been terminated."

"They haven't—"

"I may be blind, but you're apparently deaf. First Class Rehab has received its last—*final*—check. There is no more coming from me. There will be no more payments for services rendered."

He heard her exhale—a soft, quick breath that was so uniquely feminine that he drew back, momentarily startled.

And in that half-second he felt betrayed.

She was the one not listening. She was the one forcing herself on him. And yet—and yet she was a woman. And he was—or had been—a gentleman, and gentlemen were supposed to have manners. Gentlemen were supposed to be above reproach.

Growling, he leaned back in his chair, gripped the rims on the wheels and glared at where he imagined her to be standing.

He shouldn't feel bad for speaking bluntly. His brow furrowed even more deeply. It was her fault. She'd come here, barging in with a righteous, high-handed, bossy attitude that turned his stomach.

The accident hadn't been yesterday. He'd lived like this long enough to know what he was dealing with. He didn't need her telling him this and that, as though he couldn't figure it out for himself.

No, she—Nurse Hatchet-Cratchett, his nurse number seven—had the same bloody mentality as the first six. In their eyes the wheelchair rendered him incompetent, unable to think for himself.

"I'm not paying you any longer," he repeated firmly, determined to get this over and done with. "You've had your last payment. You and your company are finished here."

And then she made that sound again—that little sound which had made him draw back. But this time he recognized the sound for what it was.

A laugh.

She was laughing at him.

Laughing and walking around the side of his chair so he had to crane his head to try to follow her.

He felt her hands settle on the back of his chair. She must have bent down, or perhaps she wasn't very tall, because her voice came surprisingly close to his ear.

"But *you* aren't paying me any longer. Our services have been retained and we are authorized to continue providing your care. Only now, instead of you paying for your care, the financial arrangements are being handled by a private source."

He went cold—cold and heavy. Even his legs, with their only limited sensation. *"What?"*

"It's true," she continued, beginning to push his chair and moving him forward. "I'm not the only one who thinks it's high time you recovered." She continued pushing him despite his attempt to resist. "You're going to get well," she added, her voice whispering sweetly in his ear. "Whether you want to or not."

CHAPTER TWO

KRISTIAN CLAMPED DOWN on the wheel-rims, holding them tight to stop their progress. "Who is paying for my care?"

Elizabeth hated playing games, and she didn't believe it was right to keep anyone in the dark, but she'd signed a confidentiality agreement and she had to honor it. "I'm sorry, Mr. Koumantaros. I'm not at liberty to say."

Her answer only antagonized him further. Kristian threw his head back and his powerful shoulders squared. His hands gripped the rims so tightly his knuckles shone white. "I won't have someone else assuming responsibility for my care, much less for what is surely questionable care."

Elizabeth cringed at the criticism. The criticism—slander?—was personal. It was her company. She personally interviewed, hired and trained each nurse that worked for First Class Rehab. Not that he knew. And not that she wanted him to know right now.

No, what mattered now was getting Mr. Koumantaros on a schedule, creating a predictable routine with regular periods of nourishment, exercise and rest. And to do that she really needed him to have his lunch.

"We can talk more over lunch," Elizabeth replied, beginning to roll him back out onto the terrace once more. But, just like before, Kristian clamped his hands down and gripped the wheel-rims hard, preventing him from going forward.

"I don't like being pushed."

Elizabeth stepped away and stared down at him, seeing for the first time the dark pink scar that snaked from beneath the sleeve of his sky-blue Egyptian cotton shirt, running from elbow to wrist. A multiple fracture, she thought, recalling just how many bones had broken. By all indications he should have died. But he hadn't. He'd survived. And after all that she wasn't about to let him give up now and wither away inside this shuttered villa.

"I didn't think you could get yourself around," she said, hanging on to her patience by a thread.

"I can push myself short distances."

"That's not quite the same thing as walking, is it?" she said exasperatedly. If he could do more…if he could walk… why didn't he? *Ornio,* she thought, using the Greek word for ornery. The previous nurses hadn't exaggerated a bit. Kristian was as obstinate as a mule.

He snorted. "Is that your idea of encouragement?"

Her lips compressed. Kristian also knew how to play both sides. One minute he was the aggressor, the next the victim. Worse, he was succeeding in baiting her, getting to her, and no one ever—*ever*—got under her skin. Not anymore. "It's a statement of fact, Mr. Koumantaros. You're still in the chair because your muscles have atrophied since the accident. But initially the doctors expected you to walk again." *They thought you'd want to.*

"It didn't work out."

"Because it hurt too much?"

"The therapy wasn't working."

"You gave up." She reached for the handles on the back of his chair and gave a hard push. "Now, how about that lunch?"

He wouldn't release the rims. "How about you tell me who is covering your services, and then we'll have lunch?"

Part of her admired his bargaining skill and tactics. He

was clearly a leader, and accustomed to being in control. But she was a leader, too, and she was just as comfortable giving direction. "I can't tell you." Her jaw firmed. "Not until you're walking."

He craned to see her, even though he couldn't see anything. "So you *can* tell me."

"Once you're walking."

"Why not until then?"

She shrugged. "It's the terms of the contract."

"But you know this person?"

"We spoke on the phone."

He grew still, his expression changing as well, as though he were thinking, turning inward. "How long until I walk?"

"It depends entirely on you. Your hamstrings and hip muscles have unfortunately tightened, shortening up, but it's not irreparable, Mr. Koumantaros. It just requires diligent physical therapy."

"But even with *diligent* therapy I'll always need a walker."

She heard his bitterness but didn't comment on it. It wouldn't serve anything at this point. "A walker or a cane. But isn't that better than a wheelchair? Wouldn't you enjoy being independent again?"

"But it'll never be the same, never as it was—"

"People are confronted by change every day, Mr. Koumantaros."

"Do not patronize me." His voice deepened, roughened, revealing blistering fury.

"I'm not trying to. I'm trying to understand. And if this is because others died and you—"

"Not one more word," he growled. "Not one."

"Mr. Koumantaros, you are no less of a man because others died and you didn't."

"Then you do not know me. You do not know who I am, or who I was before. Because the best part of me—the good in me—died that day on the mountain. The good in me perished while I was saving someone I didn't even like."

He laughed harshly, the laugh tinged with self-loathing. "I'm not a hero. I'm a monster." And, reaching up, with a savage yank he ripped the bandages from his head. Rearing back in his wheelchair, Kristian threw his head into sunlight. "Do you see the monster now?"

Elizabeth sucked in her breath as the warm Mediterranean light touched the hard planes of his face.

A jagged scar ran the length of the right side of his face, ending precariously close to his right eye. The skin was still a tender pink, although one day it would pale, lightening until it nearly matched his skin tone—as long as he stayed out of the sun.

But the scar wasn't why she stared. And the scar wasn't what caused her chest to seize up, squeezing with a terrible, breathless tenderness.

Kristian Koumantaros was beautiful. Beyond beautiful. Even with the scar snaking like a fork of lightning over his cheekbone, running from the corner of his mouth to the edge of his eye.

"God gave me a face to match my heart. Finally the outside and inside look the same," he gritted, hands convulsing in his lap.

"You're wrong." Elizabeth could hardly breathe. His words gave her so much pain, so much sorrow, she felt tears sting her eyes. "If God gave you a face to match your heart, your heart is beautiful, too. Because a scar doesn't ruin a face, and a scar doesn't ruin a heart. It just shows that you've lived—" she took a rough breath "—and loved."

He said nothing and she pressed on. "Besides, I think the scar suits you. You were too good-looking before."

For a split second he said nothing, and then he laughed, a

fierce guttural laugh that was more animal-like than human. "Finally. Someone to tell me the truth."

Elizabeth ignored the pain pricking her insides, the stab of more pain in her chest. Something about him, something about this—the scarred face, the shattered life, the fury, the fire, the intelligence and passion—touched her. Hurt her. It was not that anyone should suffer, but somehow on Kristian the suffering became bigger, larger than life, a thing in and of itself.

"You're an attractive man even with the scar," she said, still kneeling next to his chair.

"It's a hideous scar. It runs the length of my face. I can feel it."

"You're quite vain, then, Mr. Koumantaros?"

His head swung around and the expression on his face, matched by the cloudiness in his deep blue eyes, stole her breath. *He didn't suit the chair.*

Or the chair didn't suit him. He was too big, too strong, too much of everything. And it was wrong, his body, his life, his personality contained by it. Confined to it.

"No man wants to feel like Frankenstein," Kristian said with another rough laugh.

She knew then that it wasn't his face that made him feel so broken, but his heart and mind. Those memories of his that haunted him, the flashes of the past that made him relive the accident over and over. She knew because she'd once been the same. She, too, had relived an accident in endless detail, stopping the mental camera constantly, freezing the lens at the first burst of flame and the final ball of fire. But that was her story, not his, and she couldn't allow her own experiences and emotions to cloud her judgment now.

She had to regain some control, retreat as quickly as possible to professional detachment. She wasn't here for him; she was here for a job. She wasn't his love interest. He had one in Athens, waiting for him to recover. It was this lover of his who'd insisted he walk, he function, he see, and that was why she was here. To help him recover. To help him return to her.

"You're far from Frankenstein," she said crisply, covering her suddenly ambivalent emotions. She rose to her feet, smoothed her straight skirt and adjusted her blouse. "But, since you require flattery, let me give it to you. The scar suits you. Gives your face character. Makes you look less like a model or a movie star and more like a man."

"A man," he repeated with a bitter laugh.

"Yes, a man. And with some luck and hard work, soon we'll have you acting like a man, too."

Chaotic emotions rushed across his face. Surprise, then confusion, and as she watched the confusion shifted into anger. She'd caught him off guard and hurt him. She could see she'd hurt him.

Swallowing the twinge of guilt, she felt it on the tip of her tongue to apologize, as she hadn't meant to hurt his feelings so much as provoke him into taking action.

But even as she attempted to put a proper apology together, she sensed anything she said, particularly anything sympathetic, would only antagonize him more. He was living in his own hell.

More gently she added, "You've skied the most inaccessible mountain faces in the world, piloted helicopters in blizzards, rescued a half-dozen—"

"Enough."

"You can do anything," she persisted. His suffering was so obvious it was criminal. She'd become a nurse to help those wounded, not to inflict fresh wounds, but sometimes patients were so overwhelmed by physical pain and mental misery that they self-destructed.

Brilliant men—daring, risk-taking, gifted men—were particularly vulnerable, and she'd learned the hard way that these same men self-destructed if they had no outlet for their anger, no place for their pain.

Elizabeth vowed to find the outlet for Kristian, vowed she'd channel his fury somehow, turning pain into positives.

And so, before he could speak, before he could give voice to any of his anger, or contradict her again, she mentioned the pretty table setting before them, adding that the cook and butler had done a superb job preparing their late lunch.

"Your staff have outdone themselves, Mr. Koumantaros. They've set a beautiful table on your terrace. Can you feel that breeze? You can smell the scent of pine in the warm air."

"I don't smell it."

"Then come here, where I'm standing. It really is lovely. You can get a whiff of the herbs in your garden, too. Rosemary, and lemongrass."

But he didn't roll forward. He rolled backward, retreating back toward the shadows. "It's too bright. The light makes my head hurt."

"Even if I replace the bandages?"

"Even with the bandages." His voice grew harsh, pained. "And I don't want lunch. I already told you that but you don't listen. You won't listen. No one does."

"We could move lunch inside—"

"I don't want lunch." And with a hard push he disappeared into the cooler library, where he promptly bumped into a side-table and sent it crashing, which led to him cursing and another bang of furniture.

Tensing, Elizabeth fought the natural inclination to hurry and help him. She wanted to rush to his side, but knew that doing so would only prolong his helpless state. She couldn't become an enabler, couldn't allow him to continue as he'd done—retreating from life, retreating from living, retreating into the dark shadows of his mind.

Instead, with nerves of steel, she left him as he was, muttering and cursing and banging into the table he'd overturned, and headed slowly across the terrace to the pretty lunch table, with its cheerful blue and white linens and cluster of meadow flowers in the middle.

And while she briefly appreciated the pretty linens and fresh flowers, she forgot both just as quickly, her thoughts focused on one thing and only one—Kristian Koumantaros.

It had cost her to speak to him so bluntly. She'd never been this confrontational—she'd never needed to be until now—but, frankly, she didn't know what else to do with him at this point. Her agency had tried everything—they'd sent every capable nurse, attempted every course of therapy— all to no avail.

As Elizabeth gratefully took a seat at the table, she knew her exhaustion wasn't just caused by Kristian's obstinance, but by Kristian himself.

Kristian had gotten beneath her skin.

And it's not his savage beauty, she told herself sternly. It couldn't be. She wasn't so superficial as to be moved by the violence in his face and frame—although he had an undeniably handsome face. So what was it? Why did she feel horrifyingly close to tears?

Ignoring the nervous flutter in her middle, she unfolded her linen serviette and spread it across her lap.

Pano appeared, a bottle of bubbling mineral water in his hand. "Water, ma'am?"

"Please, Pano. Thank you."

"And is Mr. Koumantaros joining you?"

She glanced toward the library doors, which had just been shut. She felt a weight on her heart, and the weight seemed to swell and grow. "No, Pano, not today. Not after all."

He filled her glass. "Shall I take him a plate?"

Elizabeth shot another glance toward the closed and shuttered library doors. She hesitated but a moment. "No. We'll try again tonight at dinner."

"So nothing if he asks?" The butler sounded positively pained.

"I know it seems hard, but I must somehow reach him. I must make him respond. He can't hide here forever. He's too young, and there are too many people that love him and miss him."

Pano seemed to understand this. His bald head inclined and, with a polite, "Your luncheon will be served immediately," he disappeared, after leaving the mineral water bottle on the table within her reach.

One of the villa's younger staff served the lunch—*souvlaki*, with sliced cucumbers and warm, fresh pita. It wasn't the meal she'd requested, and Elizabeth suspected it was intentional, the cook's own rebellion, but at least a meal had been prepared.

Elizabeth didn't eat immediately, choosing to give Kristian time in case he changed his mind. Brushing a buzzing fly away, she waited five minutes, and then another five more, reflecting that she hadn't gotten off to the best start here. It had been bumpy in more ways than one. But she could only press on, persevere. Everything would work out. Kristian Koumantaros would walk again, and eventually return to Athens, where he'd resume responsibility for the huge corporation he owned and had once single-handedly run. She'd go home to England and be rid of Greece and Greek tycoons.

After fifteen minutes Elizabeth gave up the vigil. Kristian wasn't coming. Finally she ate, concentrating on savoring the excellent meal and doing her best to avoid thinking about the next confrontation with her mulish patient.

Lunch finished, Elizabeth wiped her mouth on her serviette and pushed away from the table. Time to check on Kristian.

In the darkened library, Kristian lifted his head as she entered the room. "Have a nice lunch?" he asked in terse Greek.

She winced at the bitterness in his voice. "Yes, thank you. You have an excellent cook."

"Did you enjoy the view?"

"It is spectacular," she agreed, although she'd actually spent most of the time thinking about him instead of the view. She hadn't felt this involved with any case in years. But then, she hadn't nursed anyone directly in years, either.

After her stint in nursing school, and then three years working at a regional hospital, she'd gone back to school and earned her Masters in Business Administration, with an emphasis on Hospital and Medical Administration. After graduating she had immediately found work. So much work she had realized she'd be better off working for herself than anyone else—which was how her small, exclusive First Class Rehab had been born.

But Kristian Koumantaros's case was special. Kristian Koumantaros hadn't improved in her company's care. He'd worsened.

And to Elizabeth it was completely unacceptable.

Locating her notebook on the side-table, where she'd left it earlier, she took a seat on the couch. "Mr. Koumantaros, I know you don't want a nurse, but you still need one. In fact, you need several."

"Why not prescribe a fleet?" he asked sarcastically.

"I think I shall." She flipped open her brown leather portfolio and, scanning her previous notes, began to scribble again. "A live-in nursing assistant to help with bathing, personal hygiene. Male, preferably. Someone strong to lift you in and out of your chair since you're not disposed to walk."

"I can't walk, Mrs.—"

"*Ms.* Hatchet," she supplied, before crisply continuing, "And you could walk if you had worked with your last four physical therapists. They all tried, Mr. Koumantaros, but you were more interested in terrifying them than in making progress."

Elizabeth wrote another couple of notes, then clicked her pen closed. "You also require an occupational therapist, as you desperately need someone to adapt your lifestyle. If you've no intention of getting better, your house and habits will need to change. Ramps, a second lift, a properly outfitted bathroom, rails and grabs in the pool—"

"No," he thundered, face darkening. "No bars, no rails, and no goddamn grabs in this house."

She clicked her pen open again. "Perhaps it's time we called in a psychiatrist—someone to evaluate your depression and recommend a course of therapy. Pills, perhaps, or sessions of counseling."

"I will never talk—"

"You are now," she said cheerfully, scribbling yet another note to herself, glancing at Kristian Koumantaros from beneath her lashes. His jaw was thick, and rage was stiffening his spine, improving his posture, curling his hands into fists.

Good, she thought, with a defiant tap of her pen. He hadn't given up on living, just given up on healing. There was something she—and her agency—could still do.

She watched him for a long, dispassionate moment. "Talking— counseling— will help alleviate your depression, and it's depression that's keeping you from recovering."

"I'm not depressed."

"Then someone to treat your rage. You *are* raging, Mr. Koumantaros. Are you aware of your tone?"

"*My* tone?" He threw himself back in his chair, hands flailing against the rims of the wheels, furious skin against steel. "*My* tone? You come into my house and lecture about my tone? Who the hell do you think you are?"

The raw savagery in his voice cut her more than his words,

and for a moment the library spun. Elizabeth held her breath, silent, stunned.

"You think you're so good." Kristian's voice sounded from behind her, mocking her. "So righteous, so sure of everything. But would you be so sure of yourself if the rug was pulled from beneath *your* feet? Would you be so callous then?"

Of course he didn't know the rug *had* been pulled from beneath her feet. No one got through life unscathed. But her personal tragedies had toughened her, and she thought of the old wounds as scar tissue…something that was just part of her.

Even so, Elizabeth felt a moment of gratitude that Kristian couldn't see her, or the conflicting emotions flickering over her face. Hers wasn't a recent loss, hers was seven years ago, and yet if she wasn't careful to keep up the defenses the loss still felt as though it had happened yesterday.

As the silence stretched Kristian laughed low, harshly. "I got you on that one." His laughter deepened, and then abruptly ended. "Hard to sit in judgment until you've walked a mile in someone else's shoes."

Through the open doors Elizabeth could hear the warble of a bird, and she wondered if it was the dark green bird, the one with the lemon-yellow breast, she'd seen while eating on the patio terrace.

"I'm not as callous as you think," she said, her voice cool enough to contradict her words. "But I'm here to help you, and I'll do whatever I must to see you move into the next step of recovery."

"And why should I want to recover?" His head angled, and his expression was ferocious. "And don't give me some sickly-sweet answer about finding my true love and having a family and all that nonsense."

Elizabeth's lips curved in a faint, hard smile. No, she'd never dangle love as a motivational tool, because even that could be taken away. "I wasn't. You should know by now that's not my style."

"So tell me. Give it to me straight. Why should I bother to get better?"

Why bother? Why bother, indeed? Elizabeth felt her heart race—part anger, part sympathy. "Because you're still alive, that's why."

"That's it?" Kristian laughed bitterly. "Sorry, that's not much incentive."

"Too bad," she answered, thinking she *was* sorry about his accident, but he wasn't dead.

Maybe he couldn't walk easily or see clearly, but he was still intact and he had his life, his heart, his body, his mind. Maybe he wasn't exactly as he had been before the injury, but that didn't make him less of a man…not unless he let it. And he was allowing it.

Pressing the tip of her finger against her mouth, she fought to hold back all the angry things she longed to say, knowing she wasn't here to judge. He was just a patient, and her job was to provide medical care, not morality lessons. But, even acknowledging that it wasn't her place to criticize, she felt her tension grow.

Despite her best efforts, she resented his poor-me attitude, was irritated that he was so busy looking at the small picture he was missing the big one. Life was so precious. Life was a gift, not a right, and he still possessed the gift.

He could love and be loved. Fall in love, make love, shower someone with affection—hugs, kisses, tender touches. There was no reason he couldn't make someone feel cherished, important, unforgettable. No reason other than that he didn't want to, that he'd rather feel sorry for himself than reach out to another.

"Because, for whatever reason, Mr. Koumantaros, you're still here with us, still alive. Don't look a gift horse in the mouth. Live. Live fully, wisely. And if you can't do it for yourself, then do it for those who didn't escape the avalanche that day with you." She took a deep breath. "Do it for Cosima. Do it for Andreas."

CHAPTER THREE

COSIMA AND ANDREAS. Kristian was surprised his English Nurse Cratchett knew their names, as it was Cosima and Andreas who haunted him. And for very different reasons.

Kristian shifted restlessly in bed. His legs ached at the moment. Sometimes the pain was worse than others, and it was intense tonight. Nothing made him comfortable.

The accident. A winter holiday with friends and family in the French Alps.

He'd been in a coma for weeks after the accident, and when he'd come out of it he'd been immobilized for another couple weeks to give his spine a chance to heal. He'd been told he was lucky there was no lasting paralysis, told he was lucky to have survived such a horrific accident.

But for Kristian the horror continued. And it wasn't even his eyes he missed, or his strength. It was Andreas, Andreas—not just his big brother, but his best friend.

And while he and Andreas had always been about the extreme—extreme skiing, extreme diving, extreme parasailing—Andreas, the eldest, had been the straight arrow, as good as the sun, while Kristian had played the bad boy and rebel.

Put them together—fair-haired Andreas and devilish Kristian—and they'd been unstoppable. They'd had too much damn fun. Not that they hadn't worked—they'd worked hard—but they had played even harder.

It had helped that they were both tall, strong, physical. They'd practically grown up on skis, and Kristian couldn't even remember a time when he and Andreas hadn't participated in some ridiculous, reckless thrill-seeking adventure. Their father, Stavros, had been an avid sportsman, and their stunning French mother hadn't been just beautiful, she'd once represented France in the Winter Olympics. Sport had been the family passion.

Of course there had been dangers, but their father had taught them to read mountains, study weather reports, discuss snow conditions with avalanche experts. They'd coupled their love of adventure with intelligent risk-taking. And, so armed, they had embraced life.

And why shouldn't they have? They'd been part of a famous, wealthy, powerful family. Money and opportunity had never been an issue.

But money and opportunity didn't protect one from tragedy. It didn't insure against heartbreak or loss.

Andreas was the reason Kristian needed the pills. Andreas was the reason he couldn't sleep.

Why hadn't he saved his brother first? Why had he waited?

Kristian stirred yet again, his legs alive and on fire. The doctors said it was nerves and tissue healing, but the pain was maddening. Felt like licks of lightning everywhere.

Kristian searched the top of his bedside table for medicine but found nothing. His nurse must have taken the pain meds he always kept there.

If only he could sleep.

If he could just relax maybe the pain would go away. But he wasn't relaxing, and he needed something—anything—to take his mind off the accident and what had happened that day on Le Meije.

There had been ten of them who had set off together for a final run. They'd been heli-skiing all week, and it had been their next to last day. Conditions had looked good, the ski guides had given the okay, and the helicopter had taken off. Less than two hours later, only three of their group survived.

Cosima had lived, but not Andreas.

Kristian had saved Cosima instead of his brother, and that was the decision that tormented him.

Kristian had never even liked Cosima—not even at their first meeting. From the very beginning she'd struck him as a shallow party girl who lived for the social scene, and nothing she'd said or done during the next two years had convinced him otherwise. Of course Andreas had never seen that side in her. He'd only seen her beauty, her style, and her fun— and maybe she was beautiful, stylish, but Andreas could have done better.

Driven to find relief, Kristian searched the table-top again, before painfully rolling over onto his stomach to reach into the small drawers, in case the bottles had been put there. Nothing.

Then he remembered the bottle tucked between the mattresses, and was just reaching for it when his bedroom door opened and he heard the click of a light switch on the wall.

"You're still awake." It was dear old Cratchett, on her night rounds.

"Missing the hospital routine?" he drawled, slowly rolling onto his back and dragging himself into a sitting position.

Elizabeth approached the bed. "I haven't worked in a hospital in years. My company specializes in private home healthcare."

He listened to her footsteps, trying to imagine her age. He'd played this game with all the nurses. Since he couldn't see, he created his own visual images. And, listening to Elizabeth Hatchet's voice and footsteps, he began to create a mental picture of her.

Age? Thirty-something. Maybe close to forty.

Brunette, redhead, black-haired or blonde?

She leaned over the bed and he felt her warmth even as he caught a whiff of a light fresh scent—the same crisp, slightly sweet fragrance he'd smelled earlier. Not exactly citrus, and not hay—possibly grass? Fresh green grass. With sunshine. But also rain.

"Can't sleep?" she asked, and her voice sounded tantalizingly near.

"I never sleep."

"In pain?"

"My legs are on fire."

"You need to use them, exercise them. It'd improve circulation and eventually alleviate most of the pain symptoms you're experiencing."

For a woman with such a brusque bedside manner she had a lovely voice. The tone and pitch reminded him of the string section of the orchestra. Not a cello or bass, but a violin. Warm, sweet, evocative.

"You sound so sure of yourself," he said, hearing her move again, sensing her closeness.

"This is my job. It's what I do," she said. "And tell me, Mr. Koumantaros, what do *you* do—besides throw yourself down impossibly vertical slopes?"

"You don't approve of extreme skiing?"

Elizabeth felt her chest grow tight. Extreme skiing. Jumping off mountains. Dodging avalanches. It was ridiculous—ridiculous to tempt fate like that.

Impatiently she tugged the sheets and coverlet straight at the foot of the bed, before smoothing the covers with a jerk on the sheet at its edge.

"I don't approve of risking life for sport," she answered. "No."

"But sport is exercise—and isn't that what you're telling me I must do?"

She looked down at him, knowing he was attempting to bait her once again. He wasn't wearing a shirt, and his chest was big, his shoulders immense. She realized that this was all just a game to him, like his love of sport.

He wanted to push her—had pushed her nurses, pushed all of them. Trying to distract them from doing their job was a form of entertainment for him, a diversion to keep him from facing the consequences of his horrific accident.

"Mr. Koumantaros, there are plenty of exercises that don't risk life or limb—or cost an exorbitant amount of money."

"Is it the sport or the money you object to, Nurse?"

"Both," she answered firmly.

"How refreshing. An Englishwoman with an opinion on everything."

Once again she didn't rise to the bait. She knew he must be disappointed, too. Maybe he'd been able to torment his other nurses, but he wouldn't succeed in torturing her.

She had a job to do, and she'd do it, and then she'd go home and life would continue—far more smoothly once she had Kristian Koumantaros out of it.

"Your pillows," she said, her voice as starchy as the white blouse tucked into cream slacks. Her only bit of ornamentation was the slender gold belt at her waist.

She'd thought she'd given him ample warning that she was about to lean over and adjust his pillows, but as she reached across him he suddenly reached up toward her and his hand became entangled in her hair.

She quickly stepped back, flustered. She'd heard all about Kristian's playboy antics, knew his reputation was that of a lady's man, but she was dumbfounded that he'd still try to pull that on her. "Without being able to see, you didn't realize I was there," she said coolly, wanting to avoid all allegations of improper conduct. "In the future I will ask you to move before I adjust your pillows or covers."

"It was just your hair," he said mildly. "It brushed my face. I was merely moving it out of the way."

"I'll make sure to wear it pulled back tomorrow."

"Your hair is very long."

She didn't want to get into the personal arena. She already felt exceedingly uncomfortable being back in Greece, and so isolated here on Taygetos, at a former monastery. Kristian Koumantaros couldn't have found a more remote place to live if he'd tried.

"I would have thought your hair was all short and frizzy," he continued, "or up tight in a bun. You sound like a woman who'd wear her hair scraped back and tightly pinned up."

He was still trying to goad her, still trying to get a reaction. "I do like buns, yes. They're professional."

"And you're so *very* professional," he mocked.

She stiffened, her face paling. An icy lump hit her stomach.

Her former husband, another Greek playboy, had put her through two years of hell before they were finally legally separated, and it had taken her nearly five years to recover. One Greek playboy had already broken her heart. She refused to let another break her spirit.

Elizabeth squared her shoulders, lifted her head. "Since there's nothing else, Mr. Koumantaros, I'll say goodnight." And before he could speak she'd exited the room and firmly shut the door behind her.

But Elizabeth's control snapped the moment she reached the hall. Swiftly, she put a hand out to brace herself against the wall.

She couldn't do this.

Couldn't stay here, live like this, be tormented like this.

She despised spoiled, pampered Greeks—particularly wealthy tycoons with far too much time on their hands.

After her divorce she'd vowed she'd never return to Greece, but here she was. Not just in Greece, but trapped on a moun-

tain peak in a medieval monastery with Kristian Koumantaros, a man so rich, so powerful, he made Arab sheikhs
look poor.

Elizabeth exhaled hard, breathing out in a desperate, painful rush.

She couldn't let tomorrow be a repeat of today, either. She
was losing control of Koumantaros and the situation already.

This couldn't continue. Her patient didn't respect her,
wasn't even listening to her, and he felt entirely too comfortable mocking her.

Elizabeth gave her head a slight dazed shake. How was
this happening? She was supposed to be in charge.

Tomorrow, she told herself fiercely, returning to the bedroom the housekeeper had given her. Tomorrow she'd prove
to him she was the one in charge, the one running the show.

She could do this. She had to.

The day had been warm, and although it was now night,
her bedroom retained the heat. Like the other tower rooms,
its plaster ceiling was high, at least ten or eleven feet, and
decorated with elaborate painted friezes.

She crossed to open her windows and allow the evening
breeze in. Her three arched windows overlooked the gardens, now bathed in moonlight, and then the mountain valley beyond.

It was beautiful here, uncommonly beautiful, with the ancient monastery tucked among rocks, cliffs and chestnut trees.
But also incredibly dangerous. Kristian Koumantaros was a
man used to dominating his world. She needed him to work
with her, cooperate with her, or he could destroy her business
and reputation completely.

At the antique marble bureau, Elizabeth twisted her long
hair and then reached for one of her hair combs to fasten the
knot on top of her head.

As she slid the comb in, she glanced up into the ornate

silver filigree mirror over the bureau. Glimpsing her reflection—fair, light eyes, an oval face with a surprisingly strong chin—she grimaced. Back when she'd done more with herself, back when she'd had a luxurious lifestyle, she'd been a paler blonde, more like champagne, softer, prettier. But she'd given up the expensive highlights along with the New York and London stylists. She didn't own a single couture item anymore, nor any high-end real estate. The lifestyle she'd once known—taken for granted, assumed to be as much a part of her birthright as her name—was gone.

Over.

Forgotten.

But, turning back suddenly to the mirror, she saw the flicker in her eyes and knew she hadn't forgotten.

Medicine—nursing—offered her an escape, provided structure, a regimented routine and a satisfying amount of control. While medicine in and of itself wasn't safe, medicine coupled with business administration became something far more predictable. Far more manageable. Which was exactly what she prayed Kristian would be tomorrow.

The next morning Elizabeth woke early, ready to get to work, but even at seven the monastery-turned-villa was still dark except for a few lights in the kitchen.

Heartened that the villa was coming to life, Elizabeth dressed in a pale blue shirt and matching blue tailored skirt— her idea of a nursing uniform—before heading to find breakfast, which seemed to surprise the cook, throwing her into a state of anxiety and confusion.

Elizabeth managed to convince her that all she really needed was a cup of coffee and a bite to eat. The cook obliged with both, and over Greek coffee—undrinkable—and a *tiropita,* or cheese pie, Elizabeth visited with Pano.

She learned that Kristian usually slept in and then had coffee in his bed, before making his way to the library where he spent each day.

"What does he do all day?" she asked, breaking the pie into smaller bites. Pano hesitated, and then finally shrugged.

"He does nothing?" Elizabeth guessed.

Pano shifted his shoulders. "It is difficult for him."

"I understand in the beginning he did the physical therapy. But then something happened?"

"It was the eye surgery— the attempt to repair the reti-nas." Pano sighed heavily, and the same girl who'd served Elizabeth lunch yesterday came forward with fresh hot cof-fee. "He'd had some sight until then—not much, but enough that he could see light and shadows, shapes—but something went wrong in the repeated surgeries and he is now as you see him. Blind."

Elizabeth knew that losing the rest of his sight would have been a terrible blow. "I read in his chart that there is still a slight chance he could regain some sight with another treat-ment. It'd be minimal, I realize."

Elderly Pano shrugged.

"Why doesn't he do it?" she persisted.

"I think…" His wrinkled face wrinkled further. "He's afraid. It's his last hope."

Elizabeth said nothing, and Pano lifted his hands to try to make her understand.

"As long as he postpones the surgery, he can hope that one day he might see again. But once he has the surgery, and it doesn't work—" the old man snapped his fingers "—then there is nothing else for him to hope for."

And that Elizabeth actually understood.

But as the hours passed, and the morning turned to noon, Elizabeth grew increasingly less sympathetic.

What kind of life was this? To just sleep all day?

She peeked into his room just before twelve and he was

still out, sprawled half-naked between white sheets, his dark hair tousled.

Elizabeth went in search of Pano once more, to inquire into Kristian's sleeping habits.

"Is it usual for Kirios Koumantaros to sleep this late?" she asked.

"It's not late. Not for him. He can sleep 'til one or two in the afternoon."

Unable to hide her incredulity, she demanded, "Did his other nurses allow this?"

Pano's bald head shone in the light as he bent over the big table and finished straightening the mail and papers piled there. "His other nurses couldn't control him. He is a man. He does as he wants to do."

"No. Not when his medical care costs thousands and thousands of pounds each week."

Mail sorted and newspapers straightened, Pano looked up at her. "You don't tell a grown man what to do."

She made a rough sound. "Yes, you do. If what he's doing is destructive."

Pano didn't answer, and after a glance at the tall library clock—it was now five minutes until one—she turned around and headed straight for Kristian's bedroom. What she found there, on his bedside table, explained his long, deep sleep.

He'd taken sleeping pills. She didn't know how many, and she didn't know when they'd been taken, but the bottle hadn't been there earlier in the evening when she'd checked on him.

She'd collected the bottles from the small table in the library and put them in her room, under lock and key, so for him to have had access to this bottle meant he had a secret stash of his own to medicate himself as he pleased.

But still, he couldn't get the prescriptions filled if Pano or another staff member weren't aiding him. Someone—and she suspected Pano again—was making it too easy for Kristian to be dependent.

Elizabeth spoke Kristian's name to wake him. No response. She said his name again. "Mr. Koumantaros, it's gone noon—time to wake up."

Nothing.

"Mr. Koumantaros." She stepped closer to the bed, stood over him and said, more loudly, "It's gone noon, Mr. Koumantaros. Time to get up. You can't sleep all day."

Kristian wasn't moving. He wasn't dead, either. She could see that much. He was breathing, and there was eye movement beneath his closed lids, but he certainly wasn't interested in waking up.

She cleared her throat and practically shouted, "Kristian Koumantaros—it's time to get up."

Kristian heard the woman. How could he not? She sounded as if she had a bullhorn. But he didn't want to wake.

He wanted to sleep.

He needed to keep sleeping, craved the deep dreamless sleep that would mercifully make all dark and quiet and peaceful.

But the voice didn't stop. It just grew louder. And louder.

Now there was a tug on the covers, and in the next moment they were stripped back, leaving him bare.

"Go away," he growled.

"It's gone noon, Mr. Koumantaros. Time to get up. Your first physical therapy session is in less than an hour."

And that was when he remembered. He wasn't dealing with just any old nurse, but nurse number seven. Elizabeth Hatchet. The latest nurse, an English nurse of all things, sent to make his life miserable.

He rolled over onto his stomach. "You're not allowed to wake me up."

"Yes, I am. It's gone noon and you can't sleep the day away."

"Why not? I was up most of the night."

"Your first physical therapy session begins soon."

"You're mad."

"Not mad, not even angry. Just ready to get you back into treatment, following a proper exercise program."

"No."

Elizabeth didn't bother to argue. There was no point. One way or another he would resume physical therapy. "Pano is on his way with breakfast. I told him you could eat in the dining room, like a civilized man, but he insisted he serve you in bed."

"Good man," Kristian said under his breath.

Elizabeth let this pass, too. "But this is your last morning being served in bed. You're neither an invalid nor a prince. You can eat at a table like the rest of us."

She rolled his wheelchair closer to the bed. "Your chair is here, in case you need it, and I'll be just a moment while I gather a few things." And with that she took the medicine bottle from the table and headed for the bathroom adjoining his bedroom. In the bathroom she quickly opened drawers and cupboard doors, before returning to his room with another two bottles in her hands.

"What are you doing?" Kristian asked, sitting up and listening to her open and close the drawers in his dresser.

"Looking for the rest of your secret stash."

"Secret stash of what?"

"You know perfectly well."

"If I knew, I wouldn't be asking."

She found another pill bottle at the back of his top drawer, right behind his belts. "Just how much stuff are you taking?"

"I take very little—"

"Then why do you have enough prescriptions and bottles to fill a pharmacy?"

It was his turn to fall silent, and she snorted as she finished checking his room. She found nothing else. Not in the armchair in the corner, or the drawer of the nightstand, nor between the mattresses of his bed. Good. Maybe she'd found the last of it. She certainly hoped so.

"Now what?" he asked, as Elizabeth scooped up the bottles and marched through the master bedroom's French doors outside to the pool.

"Just finishing the job," she said, leaving the French doors open and heading across the sunlit patio to the pool and fountain.

"Those are mine," he shouted furiously.

"Not anymore," she called back.

"I can't sleep without them—"

"You could if you got regular fresh air and exercise." Elizabeth was walking quickly, but not so fast that she couldn't hear Kristian make the awkward transfer from his bed into his wheelchair.

"*Parakalo,*" he demanded. "Please. Wait a blasted moment."

She did. Only because it was the first time she'd heard him use the word *please.* As she paused, she heard Kristian hit the open door with a loud bang, before backing up and banging his way forward again, this time managing to get through. Just as clumsily he pushed across the pale stone deck, his chair tires humming on the deck.

"I waited," she said, walking again, "but I'm not giving them back. They're poison. They're absolutely toxic for you."

Kristian was gaining on her and, reaching the fountain, she popped the caps off the bottles and turned toward him.

His black hair was wild, and the scar on his cheek like face paint from an ancient tribe. He might very well have been one of the warring Greeks.

"Everything you put in your body," she said, trying to slow the racing of her heart, as well as the sickening feeling that she was once again losing control, "and everything you do to your body is my responsibility."

And with that she emptied the bottles into the fountain, the splash of pills loud enough to catch Kristian's attention.

"You did it," he said.

"I did," she agreed.

A line formed between his eyebrows and his cheekbones grew more pronounced. "I declare war, then," he said, and the edge of his mouth lifted, tilted in a dark smile. "War. War against your company, and war against you." His voice dropped, deepened. "I'm fairly certain that very soon, Ms. Hatchet, you will deeply regret ever coming here."

CHAPTER FOUR

ELIZABETH'S HEART THUMPED hard. So hard she thought it would burst from her chest.

It was a threat. Not just a small threat, but one meant to send her to her knees.

For a moment she didn't know what to think, or do, and as her heart raced she felt overwhelmed by fear and dread. And then she found her backbone, and knew she couldn't let a man—much less a man like Kristian—intimidate her. She wasn't a timid little church mouse, nor a country bumpkin. She'd come from a family every bit as powerful as the Koumantaros family—not that she talked about her past, or wanted anyone to know about it.

"Am I supposed to be afraid, Mr. Koumantaros?" she asked, capping the bottles and dropping them in her skirt pocket. "You must realize you're not a very threatening adversary."

Drawing on her courage, she continued coolly, "You can hardly walk, and you can't see, and you depend on everyone else to take care of you. So, really, why should I be frightened? What's the worst you can do? Call me names?"

He leaned back in his wheelchair, his black hair a striking contrast to the pale stone wall behind him. "I don't know whether to admire your moxie or pity your naïveté."

The day hadn't started well, she thought with a deep sigh,

and it was just getting worse. Everything with him was a battle. If he only focused half his considerable intelligence and energy on healing instead of baiting nurses he'd be walking by now, instead of sitting like a wounded caveman in his wheelchair.

"Pity?" she scoffed. "Don't pity me. You're the one that hasn't worked in a year. You're the one that needs your personal and business affairs managed by others."

"You take so many liberties."

"They're not liberties; they're truths. If you were half the man your friends say you are, you wouldn't still be hiding away and licking your wounds."

"Licking my wounds?" he repeated slowly.

"I know eight people died that day in France, and I know one of them was your brother. I know you tried to rescue him, and I know you were hurt going back for him. But you will not bring him back by killing yourself—" She broke off as he reached out and grasped her wrist with his hand.

Elizabeth tried to pull back, but he didn't let her go. "No personal contact, Mr. Koumantaros," she rebuked sternly, tugging at her hand. "There are strict guidelines for patient-nurse relationships."

He laughed as though she'd just told a joke. But he also swiftly released her. "I don't think your highly trained Calista got that memo."

She glanced down at her wrist, which suddenly burned, checking for marks. There were none. And yet her skin felt hot, tender, and she rubbed it nervously. "It's not a memo. It's an ethics standard. Every nurse knows there are lines that cannot be crossed. There are no gray areas on this one. It's very black and white."

"You might want to explain that one to Calista, because she *begged* me to make love to her. But then she also asked me for money—confusing for a patient, I can assure you."

The sun shone directly overhead, and the heat coming off the stone terrace was intense, and yet Elizabeth froze. "What do you mean, she asked you for money?"

"Surely the UK has its fair share of blackmail?"

"You're trying to shift responsibility and the blame," she said, glancing around quickly, suppressing panic. Panic because if Calista *had* attempted to blackmail Mr. Koumantaros, one of Greece's most illustrious sons...oh...bad. Very, very bad. It was so bad she couldn't even finish the thought.

Expression veiled, Kristian shrugged and rested his hands on the rims of his wheelchair tires. "But as you say, Cratchett, she was twenty-three—very young. Maybe she didn't realize it wasn't ethical to seduce a patient and then demand hush money." He paused. "Maybe she didn't realize that blackmailing me while being employed by First Class Rehab meant that First Class Rehab would be held liable."

Elizabeth's legs wobbled. She'd dealt with a lot of problems in the past year, had sorted out everything from poor budgeting to soaring travel costs, but she hadn't seen this one coming.

"And you *are* First Class Rehab, aren't you, Ms. Hatchet? It is your company?"

She couldn't speak. Her mouth dried. Her heart pounded. She was suddenly too afraid to make a sound.

"I did some research, Ms. Hatchet."

She very much wished there was a chair close by, something she could sit down on, but all the furniture had been exiled to one end of the terrace, to give Mr. Koumantaros more room to maneuver his wheelchair.

"Calista left here months ago," she whispered, plucking back a bit of hair as the breeze kicked in. "Why didn't you come to me then? Why did you wait so long to tell me?"

His mouth slanted, his black lashes dropped, concealing

his intensely blue eyes. "I decided I'd wait and see if the level of care improved. It did not—"

"You refused to cooperate!" she exclaimed, her voice rising.

"I'm thirty-six, a world traveler, head of an international corporation and not used to being dependent on anyone—much less young women. Furthermore, I'd just lost my brother, four of my best friends, a cousin, his girlfriend, and her best friend." His voice vibrated with fury. "It was a lot to deal with."

"Which is why we were trying to help you—"

"By sending me a twenty-three-year-old former exotic dancer?"

"She wasn't."

"She was. She had also posed topless in numerous magazines—not that I ever saw them; she just bragged about them, and about how men loved her breasts. They were natural, you see."

Elizabeth was shaking. This was bad—very bad—and getting worse. "Mr. Koumantaros—" she pleaded.

But he didn't stop. "You say you personally hire and train every nurse? You say you do background reports and conduct all the interviews?"

"In the beginning, yes, I did it all. And I still interview all of the UK applicants."

"But *you* don't personally screen every candidate? You don't do the background checks yourself anymore, either. Do you?"

The tension whipped through her, tightening every muscle and nerve. "No."

He paused, as though considering her. "Your agency's literature says you do."

Sickened, Elizabeth bit her lip, feeling trapped, cornered. She'd never worked harder than she had in the past year. She'd never accomplished so much, or fought so many battles, either. "We've grown a great deal in the past year. Doubled in size. I've been stretched—"

"Now listen to who has all the excuses."

Blood surged to her cheeks, making her face unbearably warm. She supposed she deserved that. "I've offices in seven cities, including Athens, and I employ hundreds of women throughout Europe. I'd vouch for nearly every one of them."

"*Nearly?*" he mocked. "So much for First Class Rehab's guarantee of first-class care and service."

Elizabeth didn't know which way to turn. "I'd be happy to rewrite our company mission statement."

"I'm sure you will be." His mouth curved slowly. "Once you've finished providing me with the quality care I so desperately need." His smile stretched. "As well as deserve."

She crossed her arms over her chest, shaken and more than a little afraid. "Does that mean you'll be working with me this afternoon on your physical therapy?" she asked, finding it so hard to ask the question that her voice was but a whisper.

"No, it means *you* will be working with *me*." He began rolling forward, slowly pushing himself back to the tower rooms. "I imagine it's one now, which means lunch will be served in an hour. I'll meet you for lunch, and we can discuss my thoughts on my therapy then."

Elizabeth spent the next hour in a state of nervous shock. She couldn't absorb anything from the conversation she'd had with Kristian on the patio. Couldn't believe everything she'd thought, everything she knew, was just possibly wrong.

She'd flown Calista into London for her final interview. It had been an all-expenses paid trip, too, and Calista had impressed Elizabeth immediately as a warm, energetic, dedicated nurse. A true professional. There was no way she could be, or ever have been, an exotic dancer. Nor a topless model. Impossible.

Furthermore, Calista wouldn't *dream* of seducing a man like Kristian Koumantaros. She was a good Greek girl, a young woman raised in Piraeus, the port of Athens, with her grandmother and a spinster great-aunt. Calista had solid family values.

And not much money.

Elizabeth closed her eyes, shook her head once, not wanting to believe the worst.

Then don't, she told herself, opening her eyes and heading for her room, to splash cold water on her face. Don't believe the worst. Look for the best in people. Always.

And yet as she walked through the cool arched passages of the tower to her own room a little voice whispered, *Isn't that why you married a man like Nico? Because you only wanted to believe the best in him?*

Forty-five minutes later, Elizabeth returned downstairs, walking outside to the terrace where she'd had a late lunch yesterday. She discovered Kristian was already there, enjoying his coffee.

Elizabeth, remembering her own morning coffee, grimaced inwardly. She'd always thought that Greek coffee— or what was really Turkish coffee—tasted like sludge. Nico had loved the stuff, and had made fun of her preference for *café au lait* and cappuccino, but she'd grown up with a coffee house on every corner in New York, and a latte or a mocha was infinitely preferable to thick black mud.

At her footsteps Kristian lifted his head and looked up in her direction. Her breath caught in her throat.

Kristian had shaved. His thick black hair had been trimmed and combed, and as he turned his attention on her the blue of his eyes was shocking. Intense. Maybe even more intense without sight, as he was forced to focus, to really listen.

His blue eyes were such a sharp contrast to his black hair and hard, masculine features that she felt an odd shiver race through her—a shiver of awareness, appreciation—and it bewildered her, just as nearly everything about this man threw her off balance. For a moment she felt what Calista must have felt, confronted by a man like this.

"Hello." Elizabeth sat down, suddenly shy. "You look nice," she added, her voice coming out strangely husky.

"A good shave goes a long way."

It wasn't just the shave, she thought, lifting her napkin from the table and spreading it across her lap. It was the alert expression on Kristian's face, the sense that he was there, mentally, physically, clearly paying attention.

"I am very sorry about the communication problems," she said, desperately wanting to start over, get things off on a better foot. "I understand you are very frustrated, and I want you to know I am eager to make everything better—"

"I know," he interrupted quietly.

"You do?"

"You're afraid I'll destroy your company." One black eyebrow quirked. "And it would be easy to do, too. Within a month you'd be gone."

There wasn't a cloud in the sky, and yet the day suddenly grew darker, as though the sun itself had dimmed. "Mr. Koumantaros—"

"Seeing as we're going to be working so closely together, isn't it time we were on a first-name basis?" he suggested.

She eyed him warily. He was reminding her of a wild animal at the moment—dangerous and unpredictable. "That might be difficult."

"And why is that?"

She wondered if she should be honest, wondered if now was the time to flatter him, win him over with insincere compliments, and then decided against it. She'd always been truthful, and she'd remain so now. "The name Kristian doesn't suit you at all. It implies Christ-like, and you're far from that."

She had expected him to respond with anger. Instead he smiled faintly, the top of his finger tapping against the rim of his cup. "My mother once said she'd given us the wrong names. My older brother Andreas should have had my name, and she felt I would have been better with his. Andreas—or Andrew—in Greek means—"

"Strong," she finished for him. "Manly. Courageous."

Kristian's head lifted as though he could see her. She knew he could not, and she felt a prick of pain for him. Vision was so important. She relied on her eyes for everything.

"I've noticed you're fluent in Greek," he said thoughtfully. "That's unusual, considering your background."

He didn't know her background. He didn't know anything about her. But now wasn't the time to be correcting him. In an effort to make peace, she was willing to be conciliatory. "So, you are the strong one and your brother was the saint?"

Kristian shrugged. "He's dead, and I'm alive."

And, even though she wanted peace, she couldn't help thinking that Kristian really was no saint. He'd been a thorn in her side from the beginning, and she was anxious to be rid of him. "You said earlier that you were willing to start your therapy, but you want to be in charge of your rehabilitation program?"

He nodded. "That's right. You are here to help me accomplish my goals."

"Great. I'm anxious to help you meet your goals." She crossed her legs and settled her hands in her lap. "So, what do you want me to do?"

"Whatever it is I need done."

Elizabeth's mouth opened, then closed. "That's rather vague," she said, when she finally found her voice.

"Oh, don't worry. It won't be vague. I'll be completely in

control. I'll tell you what time we start our day, what time we finish, and what we do in between."

"What about the actual exercises? The stretching, the strengthening—"

"I'll take care of that."

He would devise his own course of treatment? He would manage his rehabilitation program?

Her head spun. She couldn't think her way clear. This was all too ridiculous. But then finally, fortunately, logic returned. "Mr. Koumantaros, you might be an excellent executive, and able to make millions of dollars, but that doesn't mean you know the basics of physical therapy—"

"Nurse Hatchet, I haven't walked because I haven't wanted to walk. It's as simple as that."

"Is it?"

"Yes."

My God, he was arrogant—and overly confident. "And you want to walk now?"

"Yes."

Weakly she leaned back in her chair and stared at him. Kristian was changing before her eyes. Metamorphosing.

Pano and the housekeeper appeared with their lunch, but Kristian paid them no heed. "You were the one who told me I need to move forward, Cratchett, and you're absolutely right. It's time I moved forward and got back on my feet."

She watched the myriad of small plates set before them. *Mezedhes*—lots of delicious dips, ranging from eggplant purée to cucumber, yoghurt and garlic, cheese. There were also plates of steaming *keftedhes, dolmadhes, tsiros*. And it all smelled amazing. Elizabeth might not love Greek coffee, but she loved Greek food. Only right now it would be impossible to eat a bite of anything.

"And when do you intend to start your…program?" she asked.

"Today. Immediately after lunch." He sat still while Pano moved the plates around for him, and quietly explained where the plates were and what each dish was.

When Pano and the housekeeper had left, Kristian continued. "I want to be walking soon. I need to be walking this time next week if I hope to travel to Athens in a month's time."

"Walking next *week?*" she choked, unable to take it all in. She couldn't believe the change in him. Couldn't believe the swift turn of events, either. From waking him, to the pills being dumped into the fountain, to the revelation about Calista—everything was different.

Everything, she repeated silently, but especially him. And just looking at him from across the table she saw he seemed so much bigger. Taller. More imposing.

"A week," he insisted.

"Kristian, it's good to have goals. But please be realistic. It's highly unlikely you'll be able to walk unaided in the next couple of weeks, but with hard work you might manage short distances with your walker—"

"If I go to Athens there can be no walker."

"But—"

"It's a matter of culture and respect, Ms. Hatchet. You're not Greek; you don't understand—"

"I *do* understand. That's why I'm here. But give yourself time to meet your goals. Two or three months is far more realistic."

With a rough push of his wheelchair, he rolled back a short distance from the table. "Enough!"

Slowly he placed one foot on the ground, and then the other, and then, leaning forward, put his hands on the table. For a moment it seemed as though nothing was happening, and then, little by little, he began to push up, utilizing his triceps, biceps and shoulders to give himself leverage.

His face paled and perspiration beaded his brow. Thick

jet-black hair fell forward as, jaw set, he continued to press up until he was fully upright.

As soon as he was straight he threw his head back in an almost primal act of conquest. *"There."* The word rumbled from him.

He'd proved her wrong.

It had cost him to stand unassisted, too. She could see from his pallor and the lines etched at his mouth that he was hurting, but he didn't utter a word of complaint.

She couldn't help looking at him with fresh respect. What he had done had not been easy. It had taken him long, grueling minutes to concentrate, to work muscles that hadn't been utilized in far too long. But he had succeeded. He'd stood by himself.

And he'd done it as an act of protest and defiance.

He'd done it as something to prove.

"That's a start," she said crisply, hiding her awe. He wasn't just any man. He was a force to be reckoned with. "It's impressive. But you know it's just going to get harder from here."

Kristian shifted his weight, steadied himself, and removed one hand from the table so that he already stood taller.

Silent emotion flickered across his beautiful scarred face. "Good," he said. "I'm ready."

Reaching back for his wheelchair, he nearly stumbled, and Elizabeth jumped to her feet even as Pano rushed forward from the shadows.

Kristian angrily waved both off. *"Ohi!"* he snapped, strain evident in the deep lines shaping his mouth. "No."

"Kyrios," Pano pleaded, pained to see Kristian struggle so.

But Kristian rattled off a rebuke in furious Greek. "I can do it," he insisted, after taking a breath. "I *must* do it."

Pano reluctantly dropped back, and Elizabeth slowly sat down again, torn between admiration and exasperation. While she admired the fact that Kristian would not allow anyone to help him be reseated, she also knew that if he went at his entire therapy like this he'd soon be exhausted, frustrated, and possibly injured worse.

He needed to build his strength gradually, with a systematic and scientific approach.

But Kristian had a different plan—which he outlined after lunch.

Standing—walking—was merely an issue of mind over matter, he said, and her job wasn't to provide obstacles, tell him no, or even offer advice. Her job was to be there when he wanted something, and that was it.

"I'm a handmaid?" she asked, trying to hide her indignation. After four years earning a nursing degree, and then another two years earning a Masters in Business Administration? "You could hire anyone to come and play handmaid. I'm a little over-qualified and rather expensive—"

"I know," he said grimly. "Your agency charged an exorbitant amount for my care—little good did it do me."

"You chose not to improve."

"Your agency's methods were useless."

"I protest."

"You may protest all you like, but it doesn't change the facts. Under your agency's care, not only did I fail to recover, but I was harassed as well as blackmailed. The bottom line, Kyria Hatchet, is that not only did you milk the system—and me—for hundreds and thousands of euros, but you also dared to show up here, uninvited, unwanted, and force yourself on me."

Sick at heart, she rose. "I'll leave, then. Let's just forget this—pretend it never happened—"

"What about the doctors, Nurse? What about those specialists who insisted you come here or I go to their facility in Athens? Was that true, or another of your lies?"

"Lies?"

"I know why you're here—"

"To get you better!"

"You have exactly ten seconds to give me the full name and contact number of the person now responsible for paying my medical bills or I shall begin dismantling your company within the hour. All it will take is one phone call to my office in Athens and your life as you know it will be forever changed."

"Kristian—"

"Nine seconds."

"Kris—"

"Eight."

"I promised—"

"Seven."

"A deal is—"

"Six."

Livid tears scalded her eyes. "It's because she cares. It's because she loves you—"

"Four."

"She wants you back. Home. Close to her."

"Two."

Elizabeth balled her hands into fists. *Please.*

"One."

"Cosima." She pressed one fist to her chest, to slow the panicked beating of her heart. "Cosima hired me. She's desperate. She just wants you home."

CHAPTER FIVE

Cosima?

Kristian's jaw hardened and his voice turned flinty. How could Cosima possibly pay for his care? She might be Andreas's former fiancée and Athens's most popular socialite, but she had more financial problems than anyone he knew.

"Cosima hired you?" he repeated, thinking maybe he'd heard wrong. "She was the one that contacted you in London?"

"Yes. But I promised her—*promised*—I wouldn't tell you."

"Why?"

"She said you'd be very upset if you knew, she said you were so proud—" Elizabeth broke off, the threat of tears evident in her voice. "She said she had to do something to show you how much she believed in you."

Cosima believed in him?

Kristian silently, mockingly, repeated Elizabeth's words. Or maybe it was that Cosima felt indebted to him. Maybe she felt as guilt-ridden as he did. Because, after all, she lived and Andreas had died, and it was Kristian who'd made the decision. It was Kristian who'd played God that day.

No wonder he had nightmares. No wonder he had nightmares during the day.

He couldn't accept the decision he'd made. Nor could he accept that it was a decision that couldn't be changed.

Kristian, wealthy and powerful beyond measure, couldn't buy or secure the one thing he wanted most: his brother's life.

But Elizabeth knew nothing of Kristian's loathing, and anger, and pressed on. "Now that you know," she continued, "the contract isn't valid. I can't remain—"

"Of course you can," he interrupted shortly. "She doesn't have to know that I know. There's no point in wrecking her little plan."

His words were greeted by silence, and for a moment he thought maybe Elizabeth had left, going God knew where, but then he heard the faintest shuffle, and an even softer sigh.

"She just wants what is best for you," Elizabeth said wearily. "Please don't be angry with her. She seems like such a kind person."

It was in that moment that Kristian learned something very important about Elizabeth Hatchet.

Elizabeth Hatchet might have honest intentions, but she was a lousy judge of character.

It was on the tip of his tongue to ask if Elizabeth was aware that Cosima and Calista had gone to school together. To ask her if she knew that both women had shared a flat for more than a year, and had gone into modeling together, too.

He could tell her that Calista and Cosima had been the best of friends until their lives had gone in very different directions.

Cosima had met Andreas Koumantaros and become girlfriend and then fiancée to one of Greece's most wealthy men.

Calista, unable to find a rich enough boyfriend, or enough modeling jobs to pay her rent, had turned to exotic dancing and questionable modeling gigs.

The two seemed to have had nothing more in common after a couple years. Cosima had traveled the world as the pampered bride-to-be, and Calista had struggled to make ends meet.

And then tragedy had struck and evened the score.

Andreas had died in the avalanche, Cosima had survived but lost her lifestyle, and Calista, who had still been struggling along, had thought she'd found a sugar-daddy of her own.

Albeit a handicapped one.

The corner of his mouth curved crookedly, the tilt of his lips hiding the depth of his anger as well as his derision. Calista hadn't been the first to imagine he'd be an easy conquest. A dozen women from all over Europe had flocked to his side during his hospital stay. They'd brought flowers, gifts, seductive promises. *I love you. I'll be here for you. I'll never leave you.*

It would have been one thing if any of them had genuinely cared for him. Instead they'd all been opportunists, thinking a life with an invalid wouldn't be so bad if the invalid was a Greek tycoon.

Again Kristian felt the whip of anger. Did women think that just because he couldn't see he'd lost his mind?

That his inability to travel unaided across the room meant he'd enjoy the company of a shallow, self-absorbed, materialistic woman? He hadn't enjoyed shallow and self-absorbed women before. Why would he now?

"You've met Cosima, then," he said flatly.

"We've only spoken on the phone, but her concern—and she *is* concerned—touched me," Elizabeth added anxiously, trying to fill the silence. "She obviously has a good heart, and it wouldn't be fair to punish her for trying to help you."

Kristian ran his hand over his jaw. "No, you're right. And you said, she seems most anxious to see me on my feet."

"Yes. Yes—and she's just so worried about you. She was in tears on the phone. I think she's afraid you're shutting her out—"

"Really?" This did intrigue him. Was Cosima possibly

imagining some kind of future for the two of them? The idea was as grotesque as it was laughable.

"She said you've become too reclusive here."

"This is my home."

"But she's concerned you're overly depressed and far too despondent."

"Were those her actual words?" he asked, struggling to keep the sarcasm from his voice.

"Yes, as a matter of fact. I have it in my notes, if you want to see—"

"No. I believe you." His brows flattened, his curiosity colored by disbelief. Cosima wasn't sentimental. She wasn't particularly emotional or sensitive, either. So why would she be so anxious to have him return to Athens? "And so," he added, wanting to hear more about Cosima's concern, "you were sent here to rescue me."

"Not rescue, just motivate you. Get you on your feet."

"And look!" he said grandly, gesturing with his hands. "Today I stood. Tomorrow I climb Mount Everest."

"Not Everest," Elizabeth corrected, sounding genuinely bemused. "Just walk in time for your wedding."

Wedding?

Wedding?

Kristian had heard it all now. He didn't know whether to roar with amusement or anguish. His wedding. To Cosima, his late brother's lover, he presumed. My God, this was like an ancient Greek comedy—a bold work conceived of by Aristophanes. One full of bawdy mirth but founded on tragedy.

And as he sat there, trying to take it all in, Cosima and Calista's scheming reminded him of the two Greek sisters: Penia, goddess of poverty, and Amakhania, goddess of helplessness. Goddesses known for tormenting with their evil and greed.

But now that he knew, he wouldn't be tormented any longer.

No, he'd write a little Greek play of his own. And if all went well his good Nurse Cratchett could even help him by playing a leading role.

"Let's not tell her I know," Kristian said. "Let's work hard, and we'll surprise her with my progress."

"So where do we start?" Elizabeth asked. "What do we do first?"

He nearly smiled at her enthusiasm. She sounded so pleased with him already. "*I've* already hired a physical therapist from Sparta," he answered, making it clear that this was not a joint decision, but his and his alone. "The therapist arrives tomorrow."

"And until then?"

"I'll probably relax, nap. Swim."

"Swim?" she asked. "You're swimming?"

Her surprise made his lip curl. She really thought he was in dreadful shape, didn't she? "I have been for the past two weeks."

"Ever since your last nurse left?" she said quietly.

He didn't answer. He didn't need to.

"Maybe you could show me the pool?" she asked.

For a moment he almost felt sorry for her. She was trying so hard to do what she thought was the right thing, but her idea of right wasn't necessarily what he wanted or needed. "Of course. If you'll come with me."

Together they traveled across the stone courtyard with its trellis-covered patio, where they'd just enjoyed lunch, with Kristian pushing his own wheelchair and Elizabeth walking next to him.

They headed toward the fountain and then passed it, moving from the stone patio to the garden, with its gravel path.

"The gardens are beautiful," Elizabeth said, walking

slowly enough for Kristian to push his chair at a comfortable pace.

His tires sank into the gravel, and he wrestled a moment with his chair until he found traction again and pushed faster, to keep from sinking back into the crushed stones. "You'd do better with a stone path here, wouldn't you?" she asked, glancing down at his arms, impressed by his strength.

Warm color darkened his cheekbones. "It was suggested months ago that I change it, but I knew I wouldn't be in a wheelchair forever so I left it."

"So you planned on getting out of your wheelchair?"

His head lifted, and he shot her a look as though he could see, his brow furrowing, lines deepening between his eyes. He resented her question, and his resentment brought home yet again just who he was, and what he'd accomplished in his lifetime.

Watching him struggle through the gravel, it crossed her mind that maybe he hadn't remained in the wheelchair because he was lazy, but because without sight he felt exposed. Maybe for him the wheelchair wasn't transportation so much as a suit of armor, a form of protection.

"Are we almost to the hedge?" he asked, pausing a moment to try and get his bearings.

"Yes, it's just in front of us."

"The pool, then, is to the left."

Elizabeth turned toward her left and was momentarily dazzled by the sun's reflection off brilliant blue water. The long lap pool sparkled in its emerald-green setting, making it appear even more jewel-like than it already was.

"It's a new pool?" she guessed, from the young landscaping and the gorgeous artisan tilework.

"I wish I could say it was my only extravagance, but I've been renovating the monastery for nearly a decade now. It's been a labor of love."

They'd reached a low stone wall that bordered the pool, and Elizabeth moved forward to open the pretty gate. "But why Taygetos? Why a ruined monastery? You don't have family from here, do you?"

"No, but I love the mountains—this is where I feel at home," he said, lifting a hand to his face as if to block the sun. "My mother was French, raised in a small town at the base of the Alps. I've grown up hiking, skiing, rock-climbing. These are the things my father taught us to do, things my mother enjoyed, and it just feels right living here."

Elizabeth saw how he kept trying to shield his eyes with his hand. "Is the sun bothering you?"

"I usually wear bandages, or dark glasses."

"You've that much light sensitivity?"

"It's painful," he admitted.

She didn't want him in pain, but the tenderness and sensitivity gave her hope that maybe, one day, he might get at least a little of his vision back. "Shall I call Pano to get your glasses?"

"It's not necessary. We won't be here long."

"But it's lovely out," she said wistfully, gazing around the pool area and admiring the tiny purplish campanula flowers that were growing up and over the stone walls. The tiny violet-hued blossoms were such a pretty contrast to the rugged rock. "Let me get them. That way you can relax a little, be more comfortable."

"No, just find me a little shade—or perhaps position me away from the sun."

"There's some shade on the other side of the pool, near the rock wall." She hesitated. "Shall I push you?"

"I can do it myself."

But somehow in the struggle, as Elizabeth pushed forward and Kristian grappled for control, the front castors of his chair ran off the stone edge and over the side, and once the front casters went forward, the rest of the chair followed.

He hit the pool with a big splash.

It all happened in slow motion.

Just before he hit the water Elizabeth could see herself grabbing at his chair, hanging tight to the handles and trying to pull him back, but she was unable to get enough leverage to stop the momentum. In the end she let go, knowing she couldn't stop him and afraid she'd fall on him and hurt him worse.

Heart pounding, Elizabeth dropped to her knees, horrified that her patient and his wheelchair had just tumbled in.

How could she have let this happen? How could she have been so reckless?

Elizabeth was close to jumping in when Kristian surfaced. His chair, though, was another matter. While Kristian was swimming toward the side of the pool, his chair was slowly, steadily, sinking to the bottom.

"Kristian—I'm sorry, I'm sorry," she apologized repeatedly as she knelt on the pool deck. She'd never felt less professional in her entire life. An accident like this was pure carelessness. He knew it, and so did she.

"I cut the corner too close. I should have been paying closer attention. I'm so sorry."

He swam toward her.

Leaning forward, she extended her hand as far as it would go. "You're almost at the wall. My hand's right in front of it. You've almost got it," she encouraged as he reached for her.

His fingers curled around hers. Relief surged through her. He was fine. "I've got you," she said.

"Are you sure?" he asked, hand tightening on hers. "Or do I have you?"

And, with a hard tug, he pulled her off her knees and into the pool.

Elizabeth landed hard on her stomach, splashing water wildly.

He'd pulled her in. Deliberately. She couldn't believe it. So much for poor, helpless Kristian Koumantaros.

He was far from helpless. And he'd fooled her three times now.

Spluttering to the surface, she looked around for Kristian and spotted him leaning casually against the wall.

"That was mean," she said, swimming toward him, her wet clothes hampering her movements.

He laughed softly and ran a hand through his hair, pushing the inky black strands back from his face. "I thought you'd find it refreshing."

She squeezed water from her own hair. "I didn't want you to fall in. I'd never want that to happen."

"Your concern for my well-being is most touching. You know, Cratchett, I was worried you might be like my other nurses, but I have to tell you, you're worse."

She swallowed hard. She deserved that. "I'm sorry," she said, knowing a responsible nurse would never have permitted such a thing to happen. Indeed, if any of her nurses had allowed a patient in their care to fall into a pool she'd have fired the nurse on the spot. "It's been a while since I actually did any in-home care. As you know, I'm the head administrator for the company now."

"Skills a little rusty?" he said.

"Mmmm." Using the ladder, she climbed out and sat down on the deck, to pluck at her shirt and tug her soggy shoes off.

"So why are *you* here and not another nurse?"

Wringing water from her skirt, she sighed. Defeated. "The agency's close to bankruptcy. I couldn't afford to send another nurse. It was me or nothing."

"But my insurance has paid you, and I've paid you."

Elizabeth watched the water trickle from her skirt to the

stone pavers. "There were expenses not covered, and those costs were difficult to manage, and eventually they ate into the profits until we were barely breaking even." She didn't bother to tell him that Calista had needed counseling and compensation after leaving Kristian's employment. And covering Calista's bills had cost her dearly, too.

"I think I better get your chair," she said, not wanting to think about things she found very difficult to control.

"I do need it," he agreed. "Are you a strong swimmer?"

"I can swim."

"You're not inspiring much confidence, Cratchett."

She smiled despite herself. "It'll be okay." And it would be. She wasn't going to panic about holding her breath or swimming deep under water. She'd just go down and grab the chair, and haul it back up.

He sighed, pushed back wet hair from his face. "You're scared."

"No."

"You're not a very good swimmer."

She made a little exasperated sound. "I can swim laps. Pretty well. It's just in deep water I get…nervous."

"Claustrophobic?"

"Oh, it's silly, but—" She broke off, not wanting to tell him. She didn't need him making fun of her. It was a genuine fear, and there wasn't a lot she could do about it.

"But what?"

"I had an accident when I was little." He said nothing, and she knew he was still waiting for the details. "I was playing a diving game with a girl I'd met. We'd toss coins and then go pick them up. Well, in this hotel pool there was a huge drain at the bottom, and somehow—" She broke off, feeling a little sick from the retelling. "There was a lot of suction, and somehow the strings on my swimsuit got tangled, stuck. I couldn't get them out and couldn't get my suit off."

Kristian didn't speak, and Elizabeth tried to smile. "They got me out, of course. Obviously. Here I am. But…" She felt a painful flutter inside, a memory of panic and what it had been like. Her shoulders lifted, fell. "I was scared."

"How old were you?"

"Six."

"You must have been a good swimmer to be playing diving games in the deep end at six."

She laughed a little. "I think as a little girl I was a bit on the wild side. My nanny—" She broke off, rephrased. "Anyway, after that I didn't want to swim anymore. Especially not in big pools. And since then I've pretty much stuck to the shallow end. Kind of boring, but safe."

Elizabeth could feel Kristian's scrutiny even though he couldn't see her. He was trying to understand her, to reconcile what he'd thought he knew with this.

"I'll make you a deal," he said at last.

Her eyes narrowed. So far his deals had been terrible. "What kind of deal?"

"I'll go get my own chair if you don't look while I strip. I can't dive down in my clothes."

Elizabeth pulled her knees up to her chest and tried not to laugh. "You're afraid I'll see you naked?"

"I'm trying to protect you. You're a nurse without a lot of field experience lately. I'm afraid my…nudity…might overwhelm you."

She grinned against her wet kneecap. "Fine."

One black eyebrow arched. "Fine, what? Fine, you'll look at me? Or fine, you'll politely avert your gaze?"

"Fine. I'll politely avert my gaze."

"Endaxi," he said, still in the pool. "Okay." And then he began peeling his clothes off one by one.

And although Elizabeth had made a promise not to look,

the sound of wet cotton inching its way off wet skin was too tempting.

She did watch, and as the clothes came off she discovered he had a rather amazing body, despite the accident and horrific injuries. His torso was still powerful, thick with honed muscle, while from her vantage point on the deck his legs looked long and well shaped.

Clothes gone, he disappeared beneath the surface, swimming toward the bottom with strong, powerful strokes. Even though he couldn't see, he was heading in the right direction. It took him a moment to find the chair's exact location, but once he found it he took hold of the back and immediately began to swim up with it.

Incredible.

As Kristian surfaced with the chair, Pano and one of the housemaids came running through the small wrought-iron gate with a huge stack of towels.

"Kyrios," Pano called, "are you all right?"

"I'm fine." Kristian answered, dragging the chair to the side of the pool.

Pano was there to take the chair. He tipped it sideways and water streamed from the spokes and castors. He tipped it the other way and more water spurted from open screwholes, and then he passed the chair to the maid, who began vigorously toweling the wheelchair dry.

In the meantime Kristian placed his hands on the stone deck and hauled himself up and out, using only his shoulders, biceps and triceps. He was far stronger than he let on, and far more capable of taking care of himself than she'd thought.

He didn't need anyone pushing him.

He probably didn't need anyone taking care of him.

If everyone just stepped back and left him alone, she suspected that soon he'd manage just fine.

And, speaking of fine, Elizabeth couldn't tear her eyes

from Kristian's broad muscular back, lean waist, and tight hard buttocks as he shifted his weight around. His body was almost perfectly proportioned, every muscle shaped and honed. He didn't look ill, or like a patient. He looked like a man, an incredibly physical, virile man.

Once his thighs had cleared the water he did a quick turn and sat down. Pano swiftly draped a towel over Kristian's shoulders and threw another one over his lap, but not before Elizabeth had seen as much of Kristian's front as she had seen of his back.

And his front was even more impressive. His shoulders broad and thick, his chest shaped into two hard planes of muscle, his belly flat, lean, and his...

His...

She shouldn't be staring at his lap, it was completely unprofessional, but he was very, very big there, too.

She felt blood surge to her cheeks, and she battled shyness, shame and interest.

His body was so beautiful, and his size, that symbol of masculinity—wow. Ridiculously impressive. And Elizabeth wasn't easily impressed.

No wonder Kristian was so comfortable naked. Even after a year plus in a wheelchair he was still every inch a man.

"I thought we had a deal," Kristian murmured, dragging the towel over his head and then his chest.

"We did. We do." Flushing crimson, Elizabeth jumped to her feet and twisted her damp skirt yet again. "Maybe I should go get some dry clothes."

"A good idea," Kristian said, leaning back on his hands, face lifted. He was smiling a little, a smile that indicated he knew she'd been looking at him, knew she'd been fascinated by his anatomy. "I wouldn't want you to catch a chill."

"No."

His lips curled, and the sunlight played over the carved

planes of his face, lingering on the jagged scar, and she felt her heart leap at the savage violence done to his Greek beauty. "I'll see you at dinner, then."

See her at dinner.

He couldn't see her, of course, but he'd meet her, and her heart did another peculiar flutter. "Dinner tonight?"

"I thought I was to eat all my meals with you," he answered lazily. "Something about you needing to socialize me. Make me civil again."

Her heart was drumming a mile a minute. "Right." She forced a tight, pained smile. "I'll look forward to that...then."

Elizabeth turned so quickly that she stubbed her toe. With a hop and a whimper she set off at a run for the sanctuary of her room, lecturing herself the entire way. *Do not get personally involved, do not get personally involved, no matter what you do, do not get personally involved.*

But as she reached her tower bedroom and began to strip her wet clothes off she almost cried with vexation.

She already was involved.

CHAPTER SIX

OUTSIDE IN THE garden, as Kristian struggled to make his way back to the villa, water dripped from the chair and his cushion sagged, waterlogged.

Thank God he was almost done with this wheelchair.

Falling into the pool today had been infuriating and insightful. He hated how helpless he'd felt as he went blindly tumbling in. He'd hated the shock and surprise as he'd thrashed in his clothes in the water. But at the same time his unexpected fall had had unexpected results.

For one, Elizabeth had dropped some of her brittle guard, and he'd discovered she was far less icy than he'd thought. She was in many ways quite gentle, and her fear about the deep end had struck home with him. As a boy he'd been thrown from a horse, and he hadn't ridden again for years.

Getting back into the wet wheelchair had been another lesson. As he'd been transferred in, he'd realized the chair had served its purpose. He didn't want it anymore—didn't want to be confined or contained. He craved freedom, and knew that for the first time since his accident he was truly ready for whatever therapy was required to allow him to walk and run again.

Water still dripping, he cautiously rolled his way from grass to patio, and from patio toward the wing where his room was.

But as he rolled down the loggia he couldn't seem to find his bedroom door. He began to second-guess himself, and soon thought he'd gone the wrong way.

Pano, who'd been following several paces behind, couldn't keep silent any longer. "*Kyrie,* your room is just here." And, without waiting for Kristian to find it himself, the butler steered the wheelchair around the corner and over the door's threshold.

Kristian felt a tinge of annoyance at the help. He'd wanted to do it alone, felt an increasing need to do more for himself, but Pano, a good loyal employee of the past fifteen years, couldn't bear for Kristian to struggle.

"How did you end up in the pool?" Pano asked, closing the outside door.

Kristian shrugged and tugged the wet towel from around his shoulders. "Ms. Hatchet was pushing me toward the shade and misjudged the distance to the pool's edge."

"*Despinis* pushed you into the pool?" Pano cried, horrified.

"It was an accident."

"How could she push you into the pool?"

"It was a tight corner."

"How can that happen? How is that proper?" The butler muttered to himself as he opened and closed drawers, retrieving dry clothes for his master. "I knew she wasn't a proper nurse—knew she couldn't do the job. I *knew* it."

Kristian checked his smile. Pano was a traditional Greek, from the old school of hearth and home. "And how is she not a proper nurse?"

"If you could see—"

"But I can't. So you must tell me."

"First, she doesn't act like one, and second, she doesn't *look* like one."

"Why not? Is she too old, too heavy, what?"

"*Ohi,*" Pano groaned. "No. She's not too old, or too fat,

or anything like that. It's the opposite. She's too small. She's delicate. Like a little bird in a tiny cage. And if you want a little blonde bird for a nurse, fine. But if you need a big, sturdy woman to lift and carry…" Pano sighed, shrugging expressively. "Then Despinis Elizabeth is not for you."

So she was blonde, Kristian thought after Pano had left him alone to dress.

And Elizabeth Hatchet was neither old nor unattractive. Rather she was fine-boned, slender, a lady.

Kristian tried to picture her, this ladylike nurse of his, who hadn't actually nursed in years, who proclaimed Cosima kind, and as a child had stayed at hotels with a nanny to look after her.

But it was impossible to visualize her. He'd dated plenty of fair English and American girls, Scandinavians and Dutch, but he would have wagered a thousand euros Elizabeth was brunette.

But wasn't that like her? So full of surprises. For example her voice—melodic, like that of a violin—and her fragrance—not floral, not exotic spice, but fresh, clean, grass or melon. And then last night, when she'd leaned close to his bed to adjust his pillows, he'd been surprised she wore her hair down. Something about her brisk manner had made him assume she was the classic all-business, no-nonsense executive.

Apparently he was wrong.

Apparently his Cratchett was blonde, slender, delicate, *pretty.* Not even close to a battleaxe.

In trying to form a new impression of her, he wondered at her age, and her height, as well as the shade of her hair. Was she a pale, silvery blonde? Or a golden blonde with streaks of warm amber and honey?

But it wasn't just her age or appearance that intrigued him. It was her story, too, of a six-year-old who'd once been a daring swimmer now afraid to leave the shallow end, as well as the haunting image of a child trapped, swimsuit ties tangled, in that pool's powerful drain.

In her bedroom, after several lovely long hours devoted to nothing but reading and taking a delicious and much needed nap, Elizabeth was dressing for dinner as well as having a crisis of conscience.

She didn't know what she was doing here. Kristian didn't need a nurse, and he certainly didn't need the round-the-clock supervision her agency and staff had been providing.

How could she stay here? How could she take Cosima's money? It was not as if Kristian was even letting her do anything. He wanted to be in control—which was fine with her if he could truly motivate himself. He really would be better off with a sports trainer and an occupational therapist to help him adapt to his loss of sight rather than someone trained to deal with concussions, wounds, injuries and infections.

And, to compound her worry, she didn't have the foggiest idea how to dress for dinner.

She, who'd grown up in five-star hotels all over the world, was suffering a mild panic attack because she couldn't figure out what to wear for a late evening meal, at an old monastery, in the middle of the Taygetos.

One by one Elizabeth pulled out things from her wardrobe and discarded them. A swingy pleated navy skirt. Too school-girl. A straight brown gabardine skirt that nearly reached her ankles. She'd once thought it smart, but now she found it boring. A gray plaid skirt with a narrow velvet trim. She sighed, thinking they were all so serious and practical.

But wasn't that what she was supposed to be? Serious? Practical?

This isn't a holiday, she reminded herself sternly, retrieving the gray plaid skirt and pairing it with a pewter silk blouse.

Dressing, she wrinkled her nose at her reflection. Ugh. So *not* pretty.

But why did she even care what she was wearing?

And that was when she felt a little wobble in her middle—butterflies, worry, guilt.

She was acting as if she was dressing for a dinner date instead of dinner with a patient. And that was wrong. Her being here, feeling this way, was wrong.

She was here for business. Medicine.

And yet as she remembered Kristian's smile by the pool, and his cool, mocking, "I thought we had a deal," she felt the wobble inside her again. And this time the wobble was followed by an expectant shiver.

She was nervous.

And excited.

And both emotions were equally inappropriate. Kristian was in her care. She'd been hired by his girlfriend to get him back on his feet. It would be professionally, never mind morally, wrong to think of him in any light other than as her patient.

A patient, she reminded herself.

Yet the butterflies in her stomach didn't go away.

With a quick, impatient flick of her wrist she dragged her brush through her hair. Kristian couldn't be an option even if he *was* single, and *not* her patient. It was ridiculous to romanticize or idealize him. She'd been married to a Greek and it had been a disaster from the start. Their marriage had lasted two years but scarred her for nearly seven.

The memory swept her more than ten years back, to when, as a twenty-year-old New York socialite, she had been toasted as the next great American beauty.

She'd been so young and inexperienced then, just a debutante entering the social scene, and she'd foolishly believed everything people told her. It would be three years before she fully understood that she was adored for her name and fortune, not for herself.

"No more Greek tycoons," she whispered to herself. "No more men who want you for the wrong reasons." Besides, marriage to a Greek had taught her that Mediterranean men preferred beautiful women with breasts and hips and hourglass figures—attributes slender, slim-hipped Elizabeth would never have.

With her hair a smooth pale gold curtain, she headed toward the library, since she didn't know where they were to eat tonight as the dining room had been converted into a fitness room.

Be kind, cordial, supportive, educational and useful, she told herself. But that is as far as your involvement goes.

Kristian entered the library shortly after she did. He was wearing dark slacks and a loose white linen shirt, and with his black hair combed back from his face his blue eyes seemed even more startling.

He wasn't happy, though, she thought, watching him push into the room, his wheelchair tires humming on the floor.

"Is something wrong?" she asked, still standing just inside the door, since she hadn't known where to go and didn't feel comfortable just sitting down. This was Kristian's refuge, after all, the place he spent the majority of his time.

He grimaced. "Now that I want to walk, I don't want to use the wheelchair."

"But you can't give up the chair yet. Though I bet you tried," she guessed, her tone sympathetic.

"I suppose I thought that, having stood, I could also probably walk."

"And you will. It'll take some time, but, considering your determination, it won't be as long as you think."

Pano appeared in the doorway to invite them to dinner. They followed him a short distance down the hall to a spacious room with a soaring ceiling hand-painted with scenes from the New Testament, in bold reds, blues, gray-greens and golds, although in places the paint was chipped and faded, revealing dark beams beneath.

A striking red wool carpet covered the floor, and in the middle of the carpet was a table set with two place-settings and two wood chairs. Fat round white candles glowed on the table and in sconces on the wall, and the dishes on the table were a glazed cobalt blue.

"It looks wonderful in here," she said, suddenly feeling foolish in her gray plaid skirt with its velvet trim. She should be wearing something loose and exotic—a flowing peasant skirt, a long jeweled top, even casual linen trousers came to mind. "The colors and artwork are stunning. This is the original ceiling, isn't it?"

"I had it saved."

"Is the building very old?"

"The tower dates to the 1700s while this part, the main monastery building, was put into service in 1802." Kristian drew a breath, held it, and just listened. After a moment he added more quietly. "Even though I can't see what's around me—the old stone walls, the beamed and arched ceilings. I feel it."

"That's good," she answered, feeling a tug on her heart. She could see why he loved the renovated monastery. It was atmospheric here, but it was so remote that she worried that Kristian wasn't getting enough contact with the outside world. He needed stimulation, interaction. He needed…a life.

But he's still healing, she reminded herself as they sat down at the table, her place directly across from Kristian's. Just over a year ago he'd lost his brother, his cousin and numerous friends in the avalanche. He'd been almost fatally injured when his helicopter had crashed trying to look for survivors. Kristian had been badly hurt, and in the blunt trauma to his head he'd detached both retinas.

Sometimes, when she thought about it, it took her breath away just how much he'd lost in one day.

The housekeeper served the meal, and Pano appeared at Kristian's elbow, ready to assist him. Kristian sent him away. "We can manage," he said, reaching for the wine.

Kristian held the bottle toward Elizabeth, tilting it so she could read the label. "Will a glass hurt, Nurse Hatchet?"

His tone was teasing, but it was his expression which made her pulse quicken. He looked so boyish it disarmed her.

"A glass," she agreed cautiously.

He laughed and carefully reached out, found her glass, maneuvering the bottle so it was just over the rim. He poured slowly and listened carefully as he poured. "How is that?" he asked, indicating the glass. "Too much? Too little?"

"Just right."

He slowly poured a glass for himself, before finding an empty spot on the table for the bottle.

The next course was almost immediately served, and he was attentive during the meal, asking her questions about work, her travels, her knowledge of Greek. "At one point I spent a lot of time in Greece," she answered, sidestepping any mention of her marriage.

"The university student on holiday?" Kristian guessed.

She made a face. "Everyone loves Greece."

"What do you like most about it?" he persisted.

A half-dozen different thoughts came to mind. The water. The people. The climate. The food. The beaches. The warmth. But Greece had also created pain. So many people here had turned on her during her divorce. Friends—close friends— had dropped her overnight.

A lump filled her throat and she blinked to keep tears from forming. It was long ago, she told herself. Seven years.

She couldn't let the divorce sour her on an entire country. Maybe her immediate social circle hadn't been kind when she and Nico separated, but not everyone was so judgmental or shallow.

"You've no answer?" he said.

"It's just that I like it all," she said, smiling to chase away any lingering sadness. "And you? What do you like best about your country?"

He thought about it for a moment, before lifting his wine glass. "The people. And their zest for life."

She clinked her glass against his, took another sip, and let the wine sit on her tongue a moment before swallowing. It was a red wine, and surprisingly good. She knew from the label it was Greek, but she wasn't as familiar with Greece's red wines as she was the white, as Nico preferred white. "Do you know anything about this wine?"

"I do. It's from one of my favorite wineries, a local winery, and the grape is *ayroyitiko,* which is indigenous to the Peloponnese."

"I didn't realize there were vineyards here."

"There are vineyards all over Greece—although the most famous Greek wines come from Samos and Crete."

"That's where you get the white wines, right?"

"Samian wine is, yes, and the most popular grape there is the *moshato.* Lots of wine snobs love Samian wine."

It was all she could do not to giggle. Nico, her former husband, was the ultimate wine snob. He'd go to a restaurant, order an outrageously priced bottle, and if he didn't think it up to snuff imperiously send it away. There had been times when Elizabeth had suspected there was absolutely nothing wrong with the wine. It was just Nico wanting to appear powerful.

"You're a white wine drinker?" Kristian asked.

"No, not really. I just had…friends…who preferred white

Greek wine to red, so I'm rather ignorant when it comes to the different red grape varieties."

Kristian rested his forearms on the table. The corner of his mouth tugged. "A friend?" His expression shifted, suddenly perceptive. "A *male* friend?"

"He was male," she agreed carefully.

"And Greek?"

"And Greek."

He laughed softly, and yet there was tension in the sound, a hint that not all was well. "Greek men are sexual as well as possessive. I imagine your Greek friend wanted more from you than just friendship?"

Elizabeth blushed hotly. "It was a long time ago."

"It ended badly?"

Her head dipped. Her face burned. "I don't know." She swallowed, wondered why she was protecting Nico. "Yes," she corrected. "It did."

"Did this prejudice you against Greek men?"

"No." But she sounded uncertain.

"Against me?"

She blushed, and then laughed. "Maybe."

"So that is why I got the fleet of battleaxe nurses."

She laughed again. He amused her. And intrigued her. And if he wasn't her patient she'd even admit she found him very, very attractive. "Are you telling me you didn't deserve the battleaxe nurses?"

"I'm telling you I'm not like other Greek men."

Her breath suddenly caught in her throat, and her eyes grew wide. Somehow, with those words, he'd changed everything—the mood, the night, the meal itself. He'd charged the room with an almost unbearable electricity, a hot tension that made her fiercely aware of him. And herself. And the fact that they were alone together.

"You can't judge all wine based on one vintner or one

bottle. And you can't judge Greek men based on one unhappy memory."

She felt as though she could barely breathe, and she struggled to find safer topics, ones that would allow her more personal distance. "What kind of wine do *you* like?"

"It's all about personal preference." He paused, letting his words sink in. "I like many wines. I have bottles in my cellar that are under ten euros which I think are infinitely more drinkable than some eighty-euro bottles."

"So it's not about the money?"

"Too many people get hung up on labels and names, and hope to impress each other with their spending power or their knowledge."

"We are talking about wine?" she murmured.

"Do you doubt it?" he asked, his head lifting as though to see her, study her, drink her in.

She bit into her lower lip, her cheeks so warm she felt desperate for a frozen drink or a sweet icy treat. Something to cool her off. Something to take her mind off Kristian's formidable physical appeal.

And, sitting there, she could see how someone like Calista, someone young and impressionable, might be attracted to Kristian. But to threaten him? Attempt to blackmail him? Impossible. Even blinded, with shattered bones and scarred features, he was too strong, too overpowering. Calista was a fool.

And, thinking of the girl's foolishness, Elizabeth began to giggle, and then her giggle turned into full blown laughter. "What was Calista thinking?" she wheezed, touching her hand to her mouth to try and stifle the sound. "How could someone like Calista think she could get away with blackmailing *you*?"

Kristian sat across the table from Elizabeth and listened to her laugh. It had been so long since he'd heard a laugh like that, so open and warm and real. Elizabeth in one day had made him realize how much he'd been missing in life. He hadn't even known he'd become so angry and shut down until she'd arrived and begun insisting on immediate changes.

He'd at first resented her bossy manner, but it had worked. He'd realized he didn't want or need someone else giving him orders, or attempting to dictate to him. There was absolutely no reason he couldn't motivate himself.

Although he was still incredibly suspicious of Cosima, and mistrusted her desire to have him walking and returning to Athens, he was also grateful for her interference. Cosima had brought Elizabeth here, and, as it turned out, Elizabeth was the right person at the right time.

He needed someone like her.

Maybe he even needed *her*.

Sitting across the table from her, he focused on where he pictured her to be sitting. He hoped she knew that even if he couldn't see, he was listening. Paying attention.

He'd never been known for his sensitivity. But it wasn't that he didn't have feelings. He just wasn't very good at expressing them.

He liked this room, and he was enjoying the meal. Even if he couldn't see, he appreciated the small touches made by Pano and Atta, his housekeeper—like the low warm heat from the candles, which smelled faintly of vanilla.

He knew they were eating off his favorite plates. He could tell by the size and shape that they were the glazed ceramic dinnerware he'd bought several years ago at a shop on Santorini.

The weave and weight of the table linens made him suspect they were also artisan handicrafts—purchased impulsively on one of his trips somewhere.

Despite his tremendous wealth, Kristian preferred simplicity, and appreciated the talent of local artists, supporting them whenever he could.

"Now you've grown quiet," Elizabeth said, as Atta began clearing their dishes.

"I'm just relaxed," he said, and he was. It had been so long since he'd felt this way. Months and months since he'd experienced anything so peaceful or calm. He'd forgotten what it was like to share a meal with someone, had forgotten how food always tasted better with good conversation, good wine and some laughter.

"I'm glad."

The warm sincerity in her voice went all the way through him. He'd liked her voice even in the beginning, when she had insisted on calling him Mr. Koumantaros every other time she opened her mouth.

He also liked the scent she wore. He still didn't know what it was, although he could name all the other battleaxes' favorite fragrances: chlorine, antiseptic, spearmint, tobacco and, what was probably the worst of all, an annoyingly cloying rose-scented hand lotion.

Elizabeth also walked differently than the battleaxes. Her step was firm, precise, confident. He could almost imagine her sallying forth through a crowded store, decisive and determined as she marched through Fortnum and Mason's aisles.

He smiled a little, amused by this idea of her in London. That was where she lived. His smile faded as the silence stretched. He wished he could see her. He suddenly wondered if she was bored. Perhaps she wanted to escape, return to her room. She had passed on coffee.

As the seconds ticked by, Kristian's tension grew.

He heard Elizabeth's chair scrape back, heard her linen napkin being returned to the table. She was leaving.

Grinding his teeth, Kristian struggled to get to his feet. It was the second time in one day, and required a considerable effort, but Elizabeth was about to go and he wanted to say something—to ask her to stay and join him in the library. It was very possible she was tired, but for him the nights were long, sometimes endless. There was no difference between night and day anymore.

He was on his feet, gripping the table's edge with his fingers. "Are you tired?" he said, his voice suddenly too loud and hard. He hadn't meant to sound so brusque. It was uncertainty and the inability to read her mood that was making him harsh.

"A little," she confessed.

He inclined his head. "Goodnight, then."

She hesitated, and he wondered what she was thinking, wished he could see her face to know if there was pity or resentment or something else in her eyes. That was the thing about not being able to see. He couldn't read people the way he'd used to, and that had been his gift. He wasn't verbally expressive, but he'd always been intuitive. He didn't trust his intuition anymore, nor his instinct. He didn't know how to rely on either without his eyes.

"Goodnight," she said softly.

He dug his fingers into the linen-covered table. Nodded. Prayed she couldn't see his disappointment.

After another moment's hesitation he heard her footsteps go.

Slowly he sat back down in his wheelchair, and as he sat down something cracked in him. A second later he felt a lance of unbelievable pain.

How had he become so alone?

Gritting his teeth, he tried to bite back the loss and loneliness, but they played in his mind.

He missed Andreas. Andreas had been his brother, the last of his family. Their parents had died a number of years earlier—unrelated deaths, but they had come close together—

and their deaths had brought he and Andreas, already close, even closer.

He should have saved Andreas first. He should have gone to his brother's aid first.

If only he could go back. If only he could undo that one decision.

In life there were so many decisions one took for granted— so many decisions one made under pressure—and nearly all were good decisions, nearly all were soon forgotten. It was the one bad decision that couldn't be erased. The one bad decision that stayed with you night and day.

Slowly he pushed away from the table, and even more slowly he rolled down the hall toward the library—the room he spent nearly all his waking hours in.

Maybe Pano could find something on the radio for him? Or perhaps there was an audio book he could listen to. Kristian just wanted something to occupy his mind.

But once in the library he stopped pushing and just sat near his table, with his papers and books. He didn't want the radio, and he didn't want to listen to a book on tape. He just wanted to be himself again. He missed who he was. He hated who he'd become.

"Kristian?" Elizabeth said timidly.

He straightened, sat taller. "Yes?"

"You're in here, then?"

"Yes. I'm right here."

"Oh." There was the faintest hitch in her voice. "It's dark. Do you mind if I turn the lights on?"

"No. Please. I'm sorry. I don't know—"

"Of course you don't know."

He heard her footsteps cross to the wall, heard her flip the switch and then approach. "I'm not really that sleepy, and I wondered if maybe you have something I could read to you. The newspaper, or mail? Maybe you even have a favorite book?"

Kristian felt some of the tension and darkness recede. "Yes," he said, exhaling gratefully. "I'm sure there is."

CHAPTER SEVEN

THAT NIGHT BEGAN a pattern they'd follow for the next two weeks. During the day Kristian would follow a prescribed workout regimen, and then in the evening he and Elizabeth would have a leisurely dinner, followed by an hour or two in the library, where she'd read to him from a book, newspaper or business periodical of his choice.

Kristian's progress astounded her. If she hadn't been there to witness the transformation, she wouldn't have believed it possible. But being here, observing the day-to-day change in Kristian, had proved once and for all that attitude was everything.

Every day, twice a day, for the past two weeks, Kristian had headed to the spacious dining room which had been converted into a rehabilitation room. Months ago the dining room's luxurious carpets had been rolled back, the furniture cleared out, and serious equipment had been hauled up the mountain face to dominate the space.

Bright blue mats covered the floor, and support bars had been built in a far corner to aid Kristian as he practiced walking. The nine windows overlooking the garden and valley below were always open, and Kristian spent hours at a time in that room.

The sports trainer Kristian had hired arrived two days after Elizabeth did. Kristian had found Pirro in Sparta, and he had agreed to come and work with Kristian for the next four weeks, as long as he could return to Sparta on the weekends to be with his wife and children.

During the week, when Pirro was in residence, Kristian drove himself relentlessly. A trainer for the last Greek Olympic team, Pirro had helped rehabilitate and train some of the world's most elite athletes, and he treated Kristian as if he were the same.

The first few days Kristian did lots of stretching and developing core strength, with rubber balls and colored bands. By end of the first week he was increasing his distance in the pool and adding free weights to his routine. At the end of the second week Kristian was on cardio machines, alternating walking with short runs.

From the very beginning Elizabeth had known Kristian would get on his feet again. She hadn't expected it would only take him fifteen days.

Elizabeth stopped by the training room on Friday, early in the afternoon, to see if Pirro had any instructions for her for the two days while he returned to Sparta for the weekend.

She was shocked to see Kristian running slowly on a steep incline on the treadmill.

Pirro saw her enter and stepped over to speak with her. *"Ti Kanis?"* he asked. "How are you?"

"Kalo." Good. She smiled briefly before pointing to Kristian on the treadmill. "Isn't that a bit extreme?" she asked worriedly. "He could hardly stand two weeks ago. Won't the running injure him?"

"He's barely running," Pirro answered, glancing over his shoulder to watch Kristian's progress. "Notice the extreme incline? This is really a cross training exercise. Yes, we're working on increasing his cardio, but it's really to strengthen and develop the leg muscles."

Elizabeth couldn't help but notice the incline. Nor Kristian's intense concentration. He was running slowly, but without support, with his shoulders squared, his head lifted, his gaze fixed straight ahead. And even though sweat poured off him, and his cheeks glowed ruddy red, she didn't think he'd ever looked better—or stronger. Yes, he was breathing hard, but it was deep, regular, steady.

She walked closer to the machine, glanced at the screen monitoring his heart-rate. His heart-rate was low. She returned to Pirro's side. "So it's really not too much?" she persisted, torn between pride and anxiety. She wanted him better, but couldn't help fearing he'd burn out before he got to where he wanted to be.

"Too much?" Pirro grinned. "You don't know Kirie Kristian, do you? He's not a man. He's a monster."

Monster.

Pirro's word lingered in her mind as she turned to leave Kristian to finish his training. It was the same word Kristian had used when she'd first met him—the day he'd torn the bandages from his head to expose his face. Monster. Frankenstein.

Yet in the past two weeks he'd demonstrated that he was so far from either...

And so much more heroic than he even knew.

Soon he'd be returning to Athens. To the woman and the life that waited for him there. He'd eventually marry Cosima—apparently his family had known her forever—and with luck he'd have many children and a long, happy life.

But thinking of him returning to Athens put a heaviness in her heart. Thinking of him marrying Cosima made the heaviness even worse.

But that was why she was here, she reminded herself, swallowing hard around the painful lump in her throat, that lump that never went away. She'd come to prepare Kristian for the life he'd left behind.

And he was ready to go back. She could see it even if he couldn't.

The lump grew, thickening, almost drawing tears to her eyes.

Kristian, the Greek tycoon, had done this to her, too. She hadn't expected to feel this way about him, but he'd amazed her, impressed her, touched her heart with his courage, his sensitivity, as well as those rare glimpses of uncertainty. He made her feel so many emotions. But most of all he made her feel tender, good, hopeful, new. *New.*

"Shall I give him a message for you?" Pirro asked, his attention returning to Kristian.

And Elizabeth looked over at Kristian, this giant of a man who had surprised her at every level, her heart doing another one of those stunning free falls. He was so handsome it always touched a nerve, and that violent scar of his just made him more real, more beautiful. "No," she murmured. "There's no message. I'll just see him at dinner."

But as Elizabeth turned away, heading outside to take a walk through the gardens, she wondered when she'd find the courage to leave.

She had to leave. She'd already become too attached on him.

Putting a hand to her chest, she tried to stop the surge of pain that came with thinking of leaving.

Don't think of yourself, she reminded herself. Think of him. Think of his needs and how remarkable it is that he can do so much again. Think about his drive, his assertiveness, his ability to someday soon live independently.

And, thinking this way, she felt some of her own sadness lifted. He and his confidence were truly amazing. You wouldn't know he couldn't see from the way he entered a room, or the way he handled himself. In the past couple of weeks he'd become more relaxed and comfortable in his own skin, and the more comfortable he felt, the more powerful his physical presence became.

She'd always known he was tall—easily over six feet two—but she'd never felt the impact of his height until he'd begun walking with a cane. Instead of stumbling, or hesitating, he walked with the assurance of a man who knew his world and fully intended to dominate that world once more.

Her lips curved in a rueful smile as she walked through the garden, with its low, fragrant hedges and rows of magnificent trees. No wonder a monastery had been built here hundreds of years ago. The setting was so green, the views breathtaking, the air pure and clean.

Pausing at one of the stone walls that overlooked the valley below, Elizabeth breathed in the scent of pine and lemon blossoms and gazed off into the distance, where the Messenian plain stretched.

Kristian had told her that the Messenian plain was extraordinarily fertile and produced nearly every crop imaginable, including the delicious Kalamata olive. Beyond the agricultural plain was the sea, with what had to be more beautiful beaches and picturesque bays. Although Elizabeth had never planned on returning to Greece, now that she was here she was anxious to spend a day at the water. There was nothing like a day spent enjoying the beautiful Greek sun and sea.

"Elizabeth?"

Hearing her name called, she turned to discover Kristian heading toward her, walking through the gardens with his long narrow cane. He hadn't liked the cane initially, had said it emphasized his blindness, but once he'd realized the cane gave freedom as he learned to walk again, he had adapted to it with remarkable speed.

His pace was clipped, almost aggressive, bringing to mind a conversation she'd had with him a few days ago. She'd told him she was amazed by his progress and his confident stride.

He'd shrugged the compliment off, answering, "Greeks like to do things well or not at all."

She couldn't help smiling as she remembered his careless confidence, bordering on Greek arrogance. But it had been a truthful answer and it suited him, especially now, as she watched him walk through the garden.

"Kristian, I'm here," she called to him, "I'm at the wall overlooking the valley."

It didn't take him long to reach her. He was still wearing the white short-sleeve T-shirt and gray buggy sweat pants he'd worked out in. His dark hair fell forward on his brow and his skin looked burnished with a healthy glow. Her gaze searched his face, looking for signs of exhaustion or strain. There were none. He just looked fit, relaxed, even happy.

"You had a grueling workout," she said.

"It was hard, but it felt good."

"Pirro can be brutal."

Kristian shrugged. "He knows I like to be challenged."

"But you feel okay?"

White teeth flashed and creases fanned from his eyes. "I feel great."

And there went her heart again, with that painful little flutter of attraction, admiration and sorrow. He wasn't hers. He'd never be hers. All she had to do was watch one of his exhausting physical therapy sessions to see that his desire to heal was for his Cosima. And although that knowledge stung, she knew before long she'd be back in her office and immersed in her administrative duties there.

The desk would be a good place for her. At her desk she'd be busy with the phone and computer and email. She wouldn't feel these disturbing emotions there.

"You were in the training room earlier," he said. "Everything all right?"

The soft breeze was sending tendrils of hair flying around

her face, and she caught one and held it back by her ear. "I just wanted to check with Pirro—see if he had any instructions for me over the weekend."

"Did he?"

"No."

"I guess that means we've the weekend free."

"Are you making big plans, then?" she asked, teasing him, knowing perfectly well his routine didn't vary much. He was most confident doing things he knew, walking paths he'd become familiar with.

"I'm looking forward to dinner," he admitted.

"Wow. Sounds exciting."

The corner of his mouth lifted, his hard features softening at her gentle mockery. "Are you making fun of me?"

"Me? No. Never. You're Mr. Kristian Koumantaros—one of Greece's most powerful men—how could I even consider poking fun at you?"

"You would," he said, grooves paralleling his mouth. "You do."

"Mr. Koumantaros, you must be thinking of someone else."

"Mmm-hmm."

"I'm just a simple nurse, completely devoted to your well-being."

"Are you?"

"Of course. Have I not convinced you of that yet?" She'd meant to continue in her playful vein, but this time the words came out differently, her voice betraying her by dropping, cracking, revealing a tremor of raw emotion she didn't ever want him to hear.

Instead of answering, he reached out and touched her face. The unexpected touch shocked her, and she reared back, but his fingers followed, and slowly he slid his palm across her cheek.

The warmth in his hand made her face burn. She shivered

at the explosion of heat within her even as her skin felt alive with bites of fire and ice.

"Kristian," she protested huskily, more heat washing through her—heat and need and something else. Something dangerously like desire.

She'd tried so hard to suppress these feelings, knowing if she acknowledged the tremendous attraction her control would shatter.

Her control *couldn't* shatter.

"No," she whispered, trying to turn her cheek away even as she longed to press her face to his hand, to feel more of the comfort and bittersweet pleasure.

She liked him.

She liked him very much. Too much. And, staring up into his face, she felt her fingers curl into her palm, fighting the urge to reach up and touch that beautiful scarred face of his.

Kristian, with his black hair and noble but scarred face, and his eyes that didn't see.

She began talking, to try to cover the sudden awkwardness between them. "These past two weeks you've made such great strides—literally, figuratively. You've no idea how proud I am of you, how much I admire you."

"That sounds suspiciously like a goodbye speech."

"It's not, but I *will* have to be leaving soon. You're virtually independent, and you'll soon be ready to return to your life in Athens."

"I don't like Athens."

"But your work—"

"I can do it here."

"But your family—"

"Gone."

She felt the tension between them grow. "Your friends," she said quietly, firmly. "And you do have those, Kristian. You have many people who miss you and want you back where you belong." Chief among them Cosima.

Averting his head, he stood tall and silent. His brows tugged and his jaw firmed, and slowly he turned his face toward her again. "When?"

"When what?"

"When do you intend to leave?"

She shrugged uncomfortably. "Soon." She took a quick breath. "Sooner than I expected."

"And when is that? Next week? The week after that?"

She twisted her fingers together. "Let's talk about this later."

"It's that soon?"

She nodded.

"Why?" he asked.

"It's work. I've a problem in Paris, and my case manager is fed up, threatening to walk off the job. I can't afford to lose her. I need to go and try to sort things out."

"So when is this? When do you plan to go?"

Elizabeth hesitated. "I was thinking about Monday." The lump was back in her throat, making it almost impossible to breathe. "After Pirro returns."

Kristian just stood there—big, imposing, and strangely silent.

"I've already contacted Cosima," she continued. "I told her that I've done all I can do and that it'd be wrong to continue to take her money." Elizabeth didn't add that she'd actually authorized her London office to refund Cosima's money, because it was Kristian who'd done the work, not she. It was Kristian's own miracle.

"Monday is just days away," Kristian said, his voice hard, increasingly distant.

"I know. It is sudden." She took a quick breath, feeling a stab of intense regret. She wished she could reach out and touch him, reassure him, but it wasn't her place. There were lines that couldn't be crossed, professional boundaries that she had to respect, despite her growing feelings for him. "You know you don't need me, Kristian. I'm just in your way—"

"*No.*"

"Yes. But you must know I'm in awe of you. You said you'd walk in two weeks, and I said you couldn't. I said you'd need a walker, and you said you wouldn't." She laughed, thinking back to those first two intense and overwhelming days. "You've made a believer out of me."

He said nothing for a long moment, and then shook his head. "I wish I *could* make a believer out of you," he said, speaking so quietly the words were nearly inaudible.

"Monday is still three days from now," she said, injecting a note of false cheer. "Do we have to think about Monday today? Can't we think of something else? A game of blindman's bluff?"

Kristian's jaw drew tight, and then eased. He laughed most reluctantly. "You're a horrible woman."

"Yes, I know," she answered, grateful for humor.

"Most challenging, Cratchett."

"I'll take that as a compliment."

"Then you take it wrong."

Elizabeth smiled. When he teased her, when he played her game with her, it amused her to no end. Moments ago she'd felt so low, and yet she was comforted and encouraged now.

She loved his company. It was as simple as that. He was clever and sophisticated, handsome and entertaining. And once he'd determined to return to the land of the living, he had done so with a vengeance.

For the past week she'd tried to temper her happiness with reminders that soon he'd be returning to Athens, and marriage to Cosima, but it hadn't stopped her heart from doing a quick double-beat every time she heard his voice or saw him enter a room.

"I'm not sure of the exact time," Kristian said, "but I imagine it's probably close to five."

Elizabeth glanced at her silver watch. "It's ten past five now."

"I've made plans for dinner. It will mean dressing now. Can you be ready by six?"

"Is this for dinner here?"

"No."

"We're going *out?*" She gazed incredulously at the valley far below and the steep descent down. Sure, Pirro traveled up and down once a week to work with Kristian. But she couldn't imagine Kristian bumping around on the back of a mule or in a donkey's cart.

His expression didn't change. "Is that a problem?"

"No." But it kind of *was* a problem, she thought, glancing at the dwindling light. Where would they possibly go to eat? It would take them hours to get down the mountain, and it would be dark soon. But maybe Kristian hadn't thought of that, as his world was always dark.

Kristian heard the hesitation in Elizabeth's voice and he tensed, his posture going rigid. He resented not being able to see her, particularly at times like this. It hadn't been until he couldn't see that he'd learned how much he'd depended on his eyes, on visual cues, to make decisions.

Why was she less than enthusiastic about dinner?

Did she not want to go with him? Or was she upset about something?

If only he could see her face, read her expression, he'd know what her hesitation meant. But, as it was, he felt as though he were stumbling blindly about. His jaw hardened. He hated this feeling of confusion and helplessness. He wasn't a helpless person, but everything was so different now, so much harder than before.

Like sleep.

And the nightmares that woke him up endlessly. Or, worse, the nightmares he couldn't wake from—the dreams that haunted him for hours when, even when he told himself to wake, even when he said in the dream, *This is just a dream,* he couldn't let go, couldn't open his eyes and see. Day or night, it was all the same. Black. Endless pitch-black.

"If you'd rather not go…" he said, his voice growing cooler, more distant. He couldn't exactly blame her if she didn't want another evening alone with him. She might say he didn't look like Frankenstein, but the scar on his face felt thick, and it ran at an angle, as though his face had been pieced together, stitched with rough thread.

"No, Kristian. No, that's not it at all," she protested, her hand briefly touching his arm before just as swiftly pulling away. And yet that light, faint touch was enough. It warmed him. Connected him. Made him feel real. And, God knew, between the darkness and the nightmares and the grief of losing Andreas, he didn't feel real, or good, very often anymore.

"I'd like to go," she continued. "I want to go. I just wasn't sure what to wear. Is there a dress code? Casual or elegant? How are you going to dress?"

He pressed the tip of his cane into the ground, wanting to touch her instead, wanting to feel the softness of her cheek, the silky texture that made him think of crushed rose petals and velvet and the softest lace edged satin. His body ached, his chest grew tight, pinched around his heart.

"I won't be casual." His voice came out rough, almost raw, and he winced. He'd developed edges and shadows that threatened to consume him. "But you should dress so that you're comfortable. It could be a late night."

* * *

In her bedroom, Elizabeth practically spun in circles.

They were going out, and it could be a late night. So where were they going and exactly how late was late?

Her stomach flipped over, and she felt downright giddy as she bathed and toweled off. It was ridiculous, preposterous to feel this way—and yet she couldn't help the flurry of excitement. It had been a little over two weeks since she'd arrived, and she was looking forward to dinner out.

Knowing that Kristian wouldn't be dressed casually, she flipped through her clothes in the wardrobe until she decided she'd wear the only dress she'd brought—a black cocktail-length dress with a pale lace inset.

Standing before the mirror, she blew her wet hair dry and battled to keep her chaotic emotions in check.

You're just his nurse, she reminded herself. Nothing more than that. But her bright eyes in the mirror and the quick beat of her pulse belied that statement.

Her hair shimmered. Elizabeth was going to leave it down, but worried she wouldn't appear professional. At the last minute she plaited her hair into two slender braids, then twisted the braids into an elegant figure-eight at the back of her head, before pulling some blonde wisps from her crown so they fell softly around her face.

Gathering a light black silk shawl and her small handbag, she headed for the monastery's library. As she walked through the long arched hallways she heard a distant thumping sound, a dull roar that steadily grew louder, until the sound was directly above and vibrating through the entire estate. Then abruptly the thumping stopped and everything was quiet again.

Elizabeth discovered Kristian already in the library, waiting for her.

He'd also showered and changed, was dressed now in elegant black pants and a crisp white dress shirt, with a fine leather black belt and black leather shoes. With his dark hair combed and his face cleanshaven, Elizabeth didn't think she'd ever met a man so fit, strong, or so darkly handsome.

"Am I underdressed?" he asked, lifting his hands as if to ask for her approval.

"No." Her heart turned over. God, he was beautiful. Did he have any idea how stunning he really was?

Kristian moved toward her, his cane folded, tucked under his arm. He looked so confident, so very sure of himself. "What are you wearing…besides high heels?"

"You could tell by the way I walked?" she guessed.

"Mmmm. Very sexy."

Blushing, she looked up into his face, glad he couldn't see the way she looked at him. She loved looking at him, and she didn't even know what she loved most about his face. It was just the way it came together—that proud brow, the jet-black eyebrows, the strong cheekbones above firm, mobile lips.

"I'm wearing a dress," she said, feeling suddenly shy. She'd never been shy around men before—had never felt intimidated by any man, not even her Greek former husband. "It's black velvet with some lace at the bodice. Reminds me of the 1920s flapper-style dress."

"You must look incredible."

The compliment, as well as the deep sincerity in Kristian's voice, brought tears to her eyes.

Kristian was so much more than any man she'd ever met. It wasn't his wealth or sophistication that impressed her, either—although she did admit that he wore his clothes with ease and elegance, and she'd heard his brilliant trading and investments meant he'd tripled his family fortune—those weren't qualities she respected, much less admired.

She liked different things—simple things. Like the way his voice conveyed so much, and how closely he listened to her when she talked to him. His precise word choice indicated he paid attention to virtually everything.

"Not half as incredible as you do," she answered.

His mouth quirked. "Ready?"

"Yes."

He held out his arm and she took it. His body was so much bigger than hers, and warm, the muscles in his arm dense and hard. Together they headed through the hall to the front entrance, where Pano stood, ready to open the front door.

At the door Kristian paused briefly, head tipped as he gazed down at her. "Your chariot awaits," he said, and with another step they crossed the monastery's threshold and went outside—to a white and silver helicopter.

CHAPTER EIGHT

A HELICOPTER.

On the top of one of Taygetos's peaks.

She blinked, shook her head, and looked again, thinking that maybe she'd imagined it. But, no, the silver and white body glinted in the last rays of the setting sun.

"I wondered how you got up and down the mountain," she said. "You didn't seem the type to enjoy donkey rides."

Kristian's deep laugh hummed all the way through her. "I suppose I could have sent the helicopter for you."

"No, no. I would have hated to miss hours bumping and jolting around in a wood cart.

He laughed again, as though deeply amused. "Have you been in a helicopter before?"

"I have," she said. "Yes." Her parents had access to a helicopter in New York. But that was part of the affluent life she'd left behind. "It's been a while, though."

The pilot indicated they were safe to board, and Elizabeth walked Kristian to the door. Once on board, he easily found his seatbelt and fastened the clip. And it wasn't until they'd lifted off, heading straight up and then over, between the mountain peaks, that Elizabeth remembered that the worst of Kristian's injuries had come from the helicopter crash instead of the actual avalanche.

Turning, she glanced into his face to see what he was feeling. He seemed perhaps a little paler than he had earlier, but other than that he gave no indication that anything was wrong.

"You were hurt in a helicopter accident," she said, wondering if he was really okay, or just putting up a brave front.

"I was."

She waited, wondering if he'd say more. He didn't, and she touched the tip of her tongue to her upper lip. "You're not worried about being in one now?"

His brows pulled. "No. I know Yanni the pilot well—very well—and, being a pilot myself..."

"You're a pilot?"

His dark head inclined and he said slowly, "I was flying at the time of the crash."

Ah. "And the others?" she whispered.

"They were all in different places and stages of recovery." His long black lashes lowered, hiding the brilliant blue of his eyes.

She waited, and eventually Kristian sighed, shifted, his broad shoulders squaring. "One had managed to ski down the mountain to a lower patrol. Cosima..." He paused, took a quick short breath. "Cosima and the guide had been rescued. Two were still buried in snow and the others...were located but already gone."

The details were still so vague, and his difficulty in recounting the events so obvious that she couldn't ask anything else. But there were things she still wanted to know. Like, had he been going back for his brother when he crashed? And how had he managed to locate Cosima so quickly but not Andreas?

Thinking of the accident, she stole a swift side-glance in Kristian's direction. Yes, he was walking, and, yes, he was physically stronger. But what if he never saw again?

What if he didn't get the surgery—or, worse, did have it and the treatment didn't work? What if his vision could never be improved? What then?

She actually thought Kristian would cope—it wouldn't be easy, but he was tough, far tougher than he'd ever let on—but she wasn't so sure about Cosima, because Cosima desperately wanted Kristian to be "normal" again. And those were Cosima's words: "He must be normal, the way he was, or no one will ever respect him."

How would Cosima feel if Kristian never did get his sight back?

Would she still love him? Stay with him? Honor him?

Troubled, Elizabeth drew her shawl closer to her shoulders and gazed out the helicopter window as they flew high over the Peloponnese peninsula. It was a stunning journey at sunset, the fading sun painting the ground below in warm strokes of reddish-gold light.

In her two years of living in Greece she'd never visited the Peloponnese. Although the Peloponnese was a favorite with tourists, for its diverse landscape and numerous significant archeological sites, she only knew what Kristian had been telling her these past couple weeks. But, remembering his tales, she was riveted by three "fingers" of land projecting into the sea, the land green and fertile against the brilliant blue Mediterranean.

"We're almost there," Kristian suddenly said, his hand briefly touching her knee.

She felt her stomach flip and, breath catching, she glanced down at her knee, which still felt the heat of his fingers even though his hand was no longer there.

She wanted him to touch her again. She wanted to feel his hand slide inside her knee, wanted to feel the heat of his hand, his palm on her knee, and then feel his touch slide up the inside of her thigh. And maybe it couldn't happen, but it didn't make the desire any less real.

Skin against skin, she thought. Touch that was warm and concrete instead of all these silent thoughts and intense emotions. And they were getting harder to handle, because she couldn't acknowledge them, couldn't act on them, could do nothing but keep it in, hold it in, pretend she wasn't falling head over heels in love. Because she was.

And it was torture. Madness.

Her heart felt like it was tumbling inside her chest—a small shell caught in the ocean tide. She couldn't stop it, couldn't control it, could only feel it.

With an equally heart-plunging drop, the helicopter descended straight down.

As the pilot opened the door and assisted her and then Kristian out, she saw the headlights of a car in front of them. The driver of the car stepped out, and as he approached she realized it was Kristian's driver.

Whisked from helicopter to car, Elizabeth slid through the passenger door and onto the leather seat, pulse racing. Her pulse quickened yet again as Kristian climbed in and sat close beside her.

"Where are we?" she asked, feeling the press of Kristian's thigh against hers as the driver set off.

"Kithira."

His leg was much longer than hers, his knee extending past hers, the muscle hard against hers.

"It's an island at the foot of the Peloponnese," he added. "Years ago, before the Corinth Canal was built in the late nineteenth century, the island was prosperous due to all the ships stopping. But after the canal's construction the island's population, along with its fortune, dwindled."

As the car traveled on quiet roads, beneath the odd passing yellow light, shadows flickered in and through the windows. Elizabeth couldn't tear her gaze from the sight of his black trouser-covered leg against hers.

"It's nice to be going out," he said, as the car began to wind up a relatively steep hill. "I love living in the Taygetos, but every now and then I just want to go somewhere for dinner, enjoy a good meal and not feel so isolated."

She turned swiftly to look at him. There were no streetlights on the mountain road and she couldn't see his face well. "So you *do* feel isolated living so far from everyone?"

He shrugged. "I'm Greek."

Those two words revealed far more than he knew. Greeks treasured family, had strong ties to family, even the extended family, and every generation was respected for what it contributed. In Greece the elderly rarely lived alone, and money was never hoarded, but shared with each other. A father would never let his daughter marry without giving her a house, or land, or whatever he could, and a Greek son would always contribute to his parents' care. It wasn't just an issue of respect, but love.

"That's why Cosima wants you back in Athens," Elizabeth said gently. "There you have your *parea*—your group of friends." And, for Greeks, the circle of friends was nearly as important as family. A good *parea* was as necessary as food and water.

But Kristian didn't speak. Elizabeth, not about to be put off, lightly touched his sleeve. "Your friends miss you."

"My *parea* is gone."

"No—"

"Elizabeth." He stopped her. "They're gone. They died with my brother in France. All those that perished, suffocating in the snow, were my friends. But they weren't just friends. They were also colleagues."

Pained, she closed her eyes. Why, oh why did she push? Why, oh, why did she think she knew everything? How could she be so conceited as to think she could counsel him? "I'm sorry."

"You didn't know."

"But I thought… Cosima said…"

"Cosima?" Kristian repeated bitterly. "Soon you will learn you can't believe everything she says."

"Even though she means well."

Silence filled the car, and once again Elizabeth sensed that she'd said the wrong thing. She pressed her fists to her knees, increasingly uncomfortable.

"Perhaps I should tell you about dinner," Kristian said finally, his deep chest lifting as he squared his shoulders. "We're heading to a tiny village that will seem virtually untouched by tourism or time. Just outside this village is one of my favorite restaurants—a place designed by a Greek architect and his artist wife. The food is simple, but fresh, and the view is even better."

"You could go anywhere to eat, but you choose a rustic and remote restaurant?"

"I like quiet places. I'm not interested in fanfare or fuss."

"Have you always been this way, or…?"

"It's not the result of the accident, no. Andreas was the extrovert—he loved parties and the social scene."

"You didn't go with him?"

"Of course I went with him. He was my brother and my best friend. But I was content to let him take center stage, entertain everyone. It was more fun to sit back, watch."

As Kristian talked, the moon appeared from behind a cloud. Elizabeth could suddenly see Kristian's features, and that rugged profile of his, softened only by the hint of fullness at his lower lip.

He had such a great mouth, too. Just wide enough, with perfect lips.

To kiss those lips…

Knots tightened inside her belly, knots that had less to do with fear and more to do with desire. She felt so attracted to him it was hard to contain her feelings, to keep the need from showing.

What she needed to do was scoot over on the seat, put some distance between them—because with him sitting so close, with their thighs touching and every now and then their elbows brushing, she felt so wound up, so keenly aware of him.

She looked now at his hand, where it rested on his thigh, and she remembered how electric it had felt when his hand had brushed her knee, how she'd wanted his hand to slide beneath the hem of her dress and touch her, tease her, set her on fire...

That hand. His body. Her skin.

She swallowed hard, her heart beating at a frantic tempo, and, crossing her legs, she fought the dizzying zing of adrenaline. This was ridiculous, she told herself, shifting again, crossing her legs the other way. She had to settle down. Had to find some calm.

"You seem restless," Kristian said, head cocking, listening attentively.

She pressed her knees together. "I guess I am. I probably just need to stretch my legs. Must be the sitting."

"We're almost there."

"I'm not complaining."

"I didn't think you were."

She forced a small tight smile even as her mind kept spinning, her imagination working overtime. She was far too aware of Kristian next to her, far too aware of his warmth, the faint spice of his cologne or aftershave, the formidable size of him...even the steady way he was breathing.

"You're not too tired, are you?" he asked as the car headlights illuminated the road and what seemed to be a nearly barren slope before them.

"No," she said, as the car suddenly turned, swinging onto a narrow road.

"Hungry?"

She made a soft sound and anxiously smoothed the velvet

hem of her dress over her knees. "No. *Yes.* Could be." She laughed, yet the sound was apprehensive. "I honestly don't know what's wrong with me."

He reached out, his hand finding hers in the dark with surprising ease. She thought for a moment he meant to hold her hand but instead he turned it over and put his fingers on the inside of her wrist, checking her pulse. Several seconds passed before his mouth quirked. "Your heart's racing."

"I know," she whispered, staring at her wrist in his hand as the lights of a parking lot and restaurant illuminated the car. His hand was twice the size of her own, and his skin, so darkly tanned, made hers look like cream.

"You're not scared of me?"

"No."

"But maybe you're afraid to be alone with me?"

Her heart drummed even harder, faster. "And why would that be?"

His thumb caressed her sensitive wrist for a moment before releasing her. "Because tonight you're not my nurse, and I'm not your patient. We're just two people having dinner together."

"Just friends," she said breathlessly, tugging her hand free, suddenly terrified of everything she didn't know and didn't understand.

"Can a man and a woman be just friends?"

Elizabeth's throat seized, closed.

The driver put the car into "park" and came around to open their door. Elizabeth nearly jumped from the car, anxious to regain control.

At the restaurant entrance they were greeted as though they were family, the restaurant owner clasping Kristian by the arms and kissing him on each cheek. "Kyrios Kristian," he said, emotion thickening his Greek. "*Kyrie.* It is good to see you."

Kristian returned the embrace with equal warmth. "It is good to be back."

"*Parakalo*—come." And the older man, his dark hair only peppered with gray, led them to a table in a quiet alcove with windows all around. "The best seats for you. Only the best for you, my son. Anything for you."

After the owner left, Elizabeth turned to Kristian. "He called you *son?*"

"The island's small. Everyone here is like family."

"So you know him well?"

"I used to spend a lot of time here."

She glanced out the window and the view was astonishing. They were high on a hill, perched above a small village below. And farther down from the village was the ocean.

The lights of the village twinkled and the moon reflected off the white foam of the sea, where the waves broke on the rocks and shore.

The restaurant owner returned, presenting them with a gift—a bottle of his favorite wine—pouring both glasses before leaving the bottle behind.

"*Yiassis,*" she said, raising her glass and clinking it with his. *To your health.*

"*Yiassis,*" he answered.

And then silence fell, and the stillness felt wrong. Something was wrong. She just knew it.

Kristian shifted, and a small muscle suddenly pulled in his cheek. Elizabeth watched him, feeling a rise in tension.

The mood at the table was suddenly different.

Kristian suddenly seemed so alone, so cut off in his world. "What's wrong?" she asked nervously, fearing that she'd said something, done something to upset him.

He shook his head.

"Did I do something?" she persisted.

"No."

"Kristian." Her tone was pleading. "Tell me."

His jaw worked, the hard line of his cheekbone growing even more prominent, and he laughed, the sound rough and raw. "I wish to God I could see you."

For a moment she didn't know what to say or do, as heat rushed through her. And then the heat receded, leaving her chilled. "Why?" she whispered.

"I just want to see you."

Her face grew hot all over again, and this time the warmth stayed, flooding her limbs, making her feel far too sensitive. "Why? I'm just another battleaxe."

"Ohi." No. "Hardly."

Her hand shook as she adjusted her silverware. "You don't know that—"

"I know how you sound, and smell. I know you barely reach my shoulder—even in heels—and I know how your skin feels—impossibly smooth, and soft, like the most delicate satin or flower."

"I think you've found your old pain meds."

His dark head tipped. His blue eyes fixed on her. "And I think you're afraid of being with me."

"You're wrong."

"Am I?"

"Yes." She reached for her water glass and took a quick sip of the bubbly mineral water, but drank so much that the bubbles ended up stinging her nose. "I'm not afraid," she said, returning the glass to a table covered in white crisp linen and flickering with soft ivory candlelight and shadows. "How could I be afraid of you?"

His lips barely curved. "I'm not nice, like other men."

Her heart nearly fell. She looked up at him from beneath her lashes. "I'm not going to even dignify that with a response."

"Why?"

"Because you're baiting me," she said.

He surprised her by laughing. "My clever girl."

Her heart jumped again, and an icy hot shiver raced through her. Liquid fire in her veins. *His clever girl.* He was torturing her now. Making her want to be more than she was, making her want to have more than she did. Not more things, but more love.

His love.

But he was promised, practically engaged. And she'd been through hell and back with one man who hadn't been able to keep his word, or honor his commitments. Including his marriage vows.

"Kristian, I can't do this." She would have gotten up and run if there had been anywhere to go. "I can't play these games with you."

His forehead furrowed, emphasizing the scar running down his cheek. "What games?"

"These…this…whatever you call this. Us." She shook her head, unable to get the words out. "I know what you said earlier, that tonight we're not patient and nurse, we're just a man and…woman. But that's not right. You're wrong. I *am* your nurse. That's all I am, all I can be."

He leaned back and rested one arm on the table, his hand relaxed. His expression turned speculative. "And will you still be my nurse when you return to London in two days?"

"Three days."

"Two days."

She held her breath, her fingers balling into fists and then slowly exhaled.

His mouth tugged and lines deepened near his lips, emphasizing the beautiful planes of his face. "Elizabeth, *latrea mou,* let us not play games, as you say. Why do you have to go back?"

"I have a business to run—and, Kristian, so do you. Your

officers and board of directors are desperate for you to return to Athens and take leadership again."

"I can do it from Taygetos."

She shook her head, impatient. "No, you can't. Not properly. There are appointments, conferences, press meetings—"

"Others can do it," he said dismissively.

Staring at him, she felt her frustration grow. He'd never sounded so arrogant as he did now. "But *you* are Koumantaros. You are the one investors believe in and the one your business partners want to meet with. *You* are essential to Koumantaros Incorporated's success."

He nearly snapped his fingers, rejecting her arguments. "Did Cosima put you up to this?"

"No. Of course not. And that's not the issue here anyway. The issue is you resuming your responsibilities."

"Elizabeth, I still head the corporation."

"But absent leadership?" She made a soft scoffing sound. "It's not effective, and, frankly, it's not you."

"How can one little Englishwoman have so many opinions about things she knows so little about?"

Elizabeth's cheeks flamed. "I know you better than you think," she flashed.

"I'm referring to the corporate world—"

"I am a business owner."

It was his turn to scoff. "Which we've already established isn't well managed at all."

Hurt, she abruptly drew back and stared at him. "That was unkind. And unnecessary."

He shrugged off her rebuke. "But true. Your agency provided me with exceptionally poor care. Propositioned and then blackmailed by one nurse, and demeaned by the others."

She threw her napkin down and pushed her chair back. "Maybe you were an exceptionally poor patient."

"Is that possible?"

"Possible?" she repeated, her voice quavering with anger and indignation. "My God, you're even more conceited than I dreamed. *Possible?*" She drew a swift breath. "Do you want the truth? No more sugar-coated words?"

"Don't start mincing words now," he drawled, sounding as bored as he looked.

Her fingers flexed, and blood pumped through her veins. She wanted to smack him, she really did. "Truth, Kristian—*you* were impossible. You were the worst patient in the history of my agency, and we take care of hundreds of patients every year. I've had my business for years, and never encountered anyone as self-absorbed and manipulative as you."

She took another quick breath. "And another thing—do you think I *wanted* to leave my office, put aside my obligations, to rush to your side? Do you think this was a holiday for me to come to Greece? No. And no again. But I did it because no one else would, and you had a girlfriend desperate to see you whole and well."

Legs shaking, Elizabeth staggered to her feet. "Speaking of your girlfriend, it's time you gave her a call. I'm done here. It's Cosima's turn to be with you now!"

CHAPTER NINE

ELIZABETH RUSHED OUT of the restaurant, past the three other tables of patrons. But no sooner had she stepped outside into the decidedly cooler night air than she felt assailed by shame. She'd just walked out on Kristian Koumantaros, one of Greece's most powerful and beloved tycoons.

As gusts of wind whistled past the building, perched on the mountain edge, she hugged her arms close, chilled, overwhelmed. She'd left a man who couldn't see alone, to find his own way out. And worst of all, she thought, tugging windblown tendrils behind her ears, she'd left in the middle of the meal. Meals were almost as sacred as family in Greece.

She was falling apart, she thought, putting a hand to her thigh to keep her skirt from billowing out. Her feelings were so intense she was finding it difficult to be around Kristian. She was overly emotional and too sensitive. And this was why she had to leave—not because she couldn't still do good here, but because she wondered if she couldn't manage her own emotions, how could she possibly help him manage his?

In London things would be different.

In London she wouldn't see Kristian.

In London she'd be in control.

A bitter taste filled her mouth and she immediately shook her head, unable to bear the thought that just days from now she'd be gone and he'd be out of her life.

How could she leave him?

And yet how could she remain?

In the meantime she was standing outside Kristian's favorite restaurant while he sat alone inside. God, what a mess.

She had to go back in there. Had to apologize. Try to make amends before the evening was completely destroyed.

With a deep breath, she turned and walked through the front door, out of the night, which was rapidly growing stormy. Chilly. She rubbed at her arms and returned to their table, where Kristian waited.

He was sitting still, head averted, and yet from his profile she could see his pallor and the strain at his jaw and mouth.

He was as upset as she was.

Heart sinking, Elizabeth sat down. "I'm sorry," she whispered, fighting the salty sting of tears. "I'm sorry. I don't know what else to say."

"It's not your fault. Don't apologize."

"Everything just feels wrong—"

"It's not you. It's me." His dense black lashes dropped. He hesitated, as though trying to find the right words. "I knew you'd need to go back, but I didn't expect you'd say it was so soon—didn't expect the announcement today."

She searched his face. It was a face she loved. *Loved.* And while the word initially took her by surprise, she also recognized it was true. "Kristian, I'm not leaving *you*. I'm just returning to my office and the work that awaits me there."

He hesitated a long time before picking up his wine glass, but setting it back down without taking a drink. "You couldn't move your office here?"

"Temporarily?"

"Permanently."

She didn't understand. "I didn't make this miracle, Kristian. It was you. It was your focus, your drive, your hours of work—"

"But I didn't care about getting better, didn't care about much of anything, until *you* arrived. And now I do."

"That's because you're healing."

"So don't leave while I'm still healing. Don't go when everything finally feels good again."

She closed her eyes, hope and pain streaking through her like twin forks of lightning. "But if I move my office here, if I remain here to help you…"

"Yes?"

She shook her head. "What about me? What happens to me when you're healed? When you're well?" She was grateful he couldn't see the tears in her eyes, or how she was forced to madly dash them away before anyone at the restaurant could see. "Once you've gotten whatever you need from me, do I just pack my things and go back to London again?"

He said nothing, his expression hard, grim.

"Kristian, forgive me, but sometimes being here in Greece is torture." She knotted her hands in her lap, thinking that the words were coming out all wrong but he had to realize that, while she didn't want to hurt him, she also had to protect herself. She was too attached to him already. Leaving him, losing him, would hurt so much. But remaining to watch him reunite with another woman would break her heart. "I like you, Kristian," she whispered. "Really like you—"

"And I like you. Very much."

"It's not the same."

"I don't understand. I don't understand any of this. I only know what I think. And I believe you belong here. With me."

He was saying words she'd wanted to hear, but not in the context she needed them. He wanted her because she was convenient and helpful, supportive while still challenging. Yet the relationship he was describing wasn't one of love, but usefulness. He wanted her company because it would benefit him. But how would *she* benefit by staying?

"Elizabeth, *latrea mou*," he added, voice deepening. "I need you."

Latrea mou. Darling. Devoted one.

His voice and words were buried inside her heart. Again tears filled her eyes, and again she was forced to brush them swiftly away. "No wonder you had mistresses on every continent," she said huskily. "You know exactly what women want to hear."

"You're changing the subject."

She wiped away another tear. "I'm making an observation."

"It's not accurate."

"Cosima said—"

"This isn't working, is it? Let's just go." Kristian abruptly rose, and even before he'd straightened the restaurant owner had rushed over. "I'm sorry," Kristian apologized stiffly, his expression shuttered. "We're going to be leaving."

"*Kyrie,* everything is ready. We're just about to carry out the plates," the owner said, clasping his hands together and looking from one to the other. "You are sure?"

Kristian didn't hesitate. "I am sure." He reached into his pocket, retrieved his wallet and cash. "Will you let my driver know?"

"Yes, Kyrie Kristian." The other man nodded. "At least let me have your meal packed to go. Maybe later you will be hungry and want a little plate of something, yes?"

"Thank you."

Five minutes later they were in the car, sitting at opposite ends of the passenger seat as the wind gusted and howled outside. Fat raindrops fell heavily against the windshield. Kristian stonily faced forward while Elizabeth, hands balled against her stomach, stared out the car window at the passing scenery, although most of it was too dark to see.

She didn't understand what had happened in the restaurant tonight. Everything had been going so well until they'd sat down, and then…

And then…what? Was it Cosima? Her departure? What?

As the car wound its way back down the mountain, she squeezed her knuckled fists, her insides a knot of regret and disappointment. The evening was a disaster, and she'd been so excited earlier, too.

"What happened?" she finally asked, breaking the miserably tense silence. "Everything seemed fine in the helicopter."

He didn't answer and, turning, she looked at him, stared at him pointedly, waiting for him to speak. He had to talk. He had to communicate.

But he wouldn't say a word. He sat there, tall, dark, impossibly remote, as though he lived in a different world.

"Kristian," she whispered. "You're being horrible. Don't do this. Don't be like this—"

His jaw hardened and his lashes flickered, but that was his only response, and she thought she could hate him in that moment—hate him not just now, but forever.

To be shut out, to be ignored. It was the worst punishment she could think of. So unbelievably hard to bear.

"The weather is going to be a problem," he said at last. "We won't be able to fly. Unfortunately we are unable to return to Taygetos tonight. We'll be staying in the capital city, Chora."

The driver had long ago merged with traffic, driving into and through a harbor town. If this was the capital city it wasn't very big. They were now paralleling the coast, passing houses, churches and shops, nearly all already closed for the night. And far off in the distance a vast hulking fortress dwarfed the whitewashed town.

As the windshield wipers rhythmically swished, Elizabeth gazed out the passenger window, trying to get a better look at the fortress. It sat high above the city, on a rock of its own. In daylight the fortress would have an amazing view of the coast, but like the rest of Chora it was dark now, and even more atmospheric, with the rain slashing down.

"You've booked us into a hotel?" she asked, glimpsing a church steeple inside the miniature walled town.

"We won't be at a hotel. We'll be staying in a private home."

She glanced at him, her feelings still hurt. "Friends?"

"No. It's mine." He shifted wearily. "My home. One of my homes."

They were so close to the fortress she could see the distinct stones that shaped the mammoth walls. "Are we far from your home?"

"I don't think so, no. But I confess I'm not entirely sure where we are at the moment."

Of course—he couldn't see. And he wouldn't automatically know which direction they were going, or the current road they were traveling on. "We're heading toward a castle."

"Then we're almost there."

"We're staying near the castle?"

"We're staying *at* the castle."

"Your home is a castle?"

"It's one of my properties."

Her brows pulled. "How many properties do you have?"

"A few."

"Like this?"

"They're all a bit different. The monastery in Taygetos, the castle here, and other estates in other places."

"Are they all so...grand?"

"They're all historic. Some are in ruins when I purchase them; some are already in operation. But that's what I do. It's one of the companies in the Koumantaros portfolio. I buy historic properties and find different ways to make them profitable."

Elizabeth turned her attention back to the fortress, with

its thick walls and towers and turrets looming before them. "And this is a real castle?"

"Venetian," he agreed. "Begun in the thirteenth century and finished in the fifteenth century."

"So what do you do with it?"

He made a soft, mocking sound. "My accountants would tell you I don't do enough, that it's an enormous drain on my resources, but after purchasing it three years ago I couldn't bear to turn it into a five-star luxury resort as planned."

"So you stay here?"

"I've reserved a wing for my private use, but I haven't visited since before the accident."

"So it essentially sits empty?"

The wind suddenly howled, and rain buffeted the car. Elizabeth didn't know if it was the weather or her question, but Kristian smiled faintly. "You're sounding like my accountants now. But, no, to answer your question. It's not empty. I've been working with an Italian architect and designer to slowly—carefully—turn wings and suites into upscale apartments. Two suites are leased now. By next year I hope to lease two or three more, and then that's it."

The car slowed and then stopped, and an iron gate opened. The driver got out and came round to open their door. "We're here."

A half-dozen uniformed employees appeared from nowhere. Before Elizabeth quite understood what was happening, she was being whisked in one direction and Kristian in another.

Left alone in an exquisite suite of rooms, she felt a stab of confusion.

Where on earth was she now?

The feeling was strongly reminiscent of how she'd been as a child, the only daughter of Rupert Stile, the fourth richest man in America, as she and her parents had traveled from one sumptuous hotel to the next.

It wasn't that they hadn't had houses of their own—they'd had dozens— but her mother had loved accompanying her father on his trips, and so they had all traveled together, the young heiress and her nannies too.

Back then, though, she wasn't Elizabeth Hatchet but Grace Elizabeth Stiles, daughter of a billionaire a hundred times over. It had been a privileged childhood, made only more enviable when she had matured from pampered daughter status to being the next high-society beauty.

Comfortable in the spotlight, at ease with the media, she'd enjoyed her debutante year and the endless round of parties. Invitations had poured in from all over the world, as had exquisite designer clothes made for her specifically.

It had been so much power for a twenty-year-old. Too much. She'd had her own money, her own plane, and her own publicist. When men wined her and dined her—and they *had* wined and dined her—the dates had made tabloid news.

Enter handsome Greek tycoon Nico. Being young, she'd had no intention of settling down so soon, but he'd swept her off her feet. Dazzled her completely with attention, affection, tender gifts and more. Within six months they'd been engaged. At twenty-three she'd had the fairy-tale wedding of her dreams.

Seven and a half months after her wedding she had discovered him in bed with another woman.

She'd stayed with him because he'd begged for another chance, promised to get counseling, vowed he'd change. But by their first anniversary he'd cheated again. And again. And again.

The divorce had been excruciating. Nico had demanded half her wealth and launched a public campaign to vilify her. She was selfish, shallow, self-absorbed—a spoiled little rich girl intent on controlling him and embarrassing him. She'd emasculated him by trying to control the purse strings. She'd refused to have conjugal relations.

By the time the settlement had been reached, she hadn't been able to stand herself. She wasn't any of the things Nico said, and yet the public believed what they were told—or maybe she'd begun to believe the horribly negative press, too. Because by the end, Grace detested her name, her fortune, and the very public character assassination.

Moving to England, she'd changed her name, enrolled in nursing school and become someone else—someone stable and solid and practical.

But now that same someone was back in Greece, and the two lives felt very close to colliding.

She should have never returned to Greece—not even under the auspices of caring for a wounded tycoon. She definitely shouldn't have taken a helicopter ride to a small Greek island. And she definitely, *definitely* shouldn't have agreed to stay in a thirteenth-century castle in the middle of a thunderstorm.

Exhausted, Elizabeth pivoted slowly in her room like a jewelry box ballerina. Where had Kristian gone? Would she see him again tonight? Or was she on her own until morning?

As if on cue, the bedroom lights flickered once, twice, and then went out completely, leaving her in darkness.

At first Elizabeth did nothing other than move toward the bed and sit there, certain at any moment the power would come back on or one of the castle staff would appear at her room, flashlight, lantern or candle in hand. Neither happened. No power and no light. Minutes dragged by. Minutes that became longer.

Unable even to read her own watch, Elizabeth didn't know how much time had gone by, but she thought it had to have been nearly an hour. She was beyond bored, too. She was hungry, and if no one was coming to her assistance, then she would go to them.

Stumbling her way toward the door, she bumped into a trunk at the foot of the bed, a chair, a table—ouch—the wall, tapestry on the wall, and finally a door.

The hall was even darker than her room. Not a flicker of light anywhere, nor a sound.

A rational woman would return to her room and call it a night, but Elizabeth was too hungry—and a little too panicked—to be rational, and, taking a left from her room, began a slow, fearful walk down the hall, knowing there were stairs somewhere up ahead but not certain how far away, nor how steep the staircase. She couldn't even remember if there was one landing or two.

Just when she thought she'd found the stairs she heard a noise. And it wasn't the creak of stairs or a door opening, but something live, something breathing. Whimpering.

She stopped dead in her tracks. Her heart raced and, reaching for the wall, her hand shook, her skin icy and clammy.

There was something—someone—in the stairwell, something—someone—waiting.

She heard a heavy thump, and then silence. Ears, senses straining, she listened. It was breathing harder, heavier, and there was another thump, a muffled cry, not quite human, followed by a scratch against the wall.

Elizabeth couldn't take anymore. With one hand out, fingertips trailing the wall, she ran back down the hall toward her room—and yet as she ran she couldn't remember exactly where her room was, or where the door was located. She couldn't remember if there were many doors between her room and the stairs, or even if she'd left her bedroom door open or not.

The terror of not knowing where she was, of whatever was in the stairwell and what might happen next, made her nearly frantic. Her heart was racing, pounding as if it would burst, and she turned in desperate circles. Where was her room? Why had she even left it? And was that thing in the stairs coming toward her?

There was a thump behind her, and then suddenly something brushed her arm. She screamed. She couldn't help it. She was absolutely petrified.

"Elizabeth."

"Kristian." Her voice broke with terror and relief. "Help me. Help me, please."

And he was there, hauling her against him, pulling her into the circle of his arms, his body protecting her. "What is it? What's wrong?"

"There's something out there. There's something…" She could hardly get the words out. Her teeth began chattering and she shivered against him, pressed her face against his cheek, which was hard and broad and smelled even better than it felt. "Scary."

"It's your imagination," he said, his arm firmly around her waist, holding her close.

But the terror still seemed so real, and it was the darkness and her inability to see, to know what it was in the stairwell. If it was human, monster or animal. "There was something. But it's so dark—"

"Is it dark?"

"Yes!" She grabbed at his shirt with both hands. "The lights have been out for ages, and no one came, and they haven't come back on."

"It's the storm. It'll pass."

Her teeth still chattered. "It's too dark. I don't like it."

"Your room is right here," he said, his voice close to her ear. "Come, let's get you bundled up. I'm sure there's a blanket on the foot of the bed."

He led her into her room and found the blanket, draping it around her shoulders. "Better?" he asked.

She nodded, no longer freezing quite as much. "Yes."

"I should go, then."

"No." She reached out, caught his sleeve, and then slid her fingers down to his forearm, which was bare. His skin was warm and taut, covering dense muscle.

For a long silent minute Kristian didn't move, and then he reached out, touched her shoulder, her neck, up to her chin. His fingers ran lightly across her face, tracing her eyebrow, then moving down her nose and across her lips.

"You better send me away," he said gruffly.

She closed her eyes at the slow exploration of his fingertips, her skin hot and growing hotter beneath his touch. "I'll be scared."

"In the morning you'll regret letting me stay."

"Not if I get a good night's sleep."

He rubbed his fingers lightly across her lips, as if learning the curve and shape of her mouth. "If I stay, you won't be sleeping."

She shivered even as nerves twitched to life in her lower back, making her ache and tingle all over. "You shouldn't be so confident."

"Is that a challenge, *látrea mou?*"

He strummed her lower lip, and her mouth quivered. The heat in his skin was making her insides melt and her body crave his. Instinctively her lips parted, to touch and taste his skin.

She heard his quick intake when her tongue brushed his knuckle, and another intake when she slowly drew that knuckle into her mouth. Having his finger in her mouth was doing maddening things to her body, waking a strong physical need that had been slumbering far too long.

She sucked harder on his finger. And the harder she sucked

the tighter her nipples peaked and her womb ached. She wanted relief, wanted to be taken, seized, plundered, sated.

"Is this really what you want?" he gritted from between clenched teeth, his deep voice rough with passion.

She didn't speak. Instead she reached toward him, placed her hand on his belt and slowly slid it down to cover his hard shaft.

Kristian groaned deep in his throat and roughly pulled her against him, holding her hips tight against his own. She could feel the surge of heat through his trousers, feel the fabric strain.

Control snapped. He covered her mouth with his and kissed her hard, kissed her fiercely. His lips were firm, demanding, and the pressure of his mouth parted her lips.

She shuddered against him, belly knotting, breasts aching, so that she pressed against him for desperate relief, wanting closer contact with his body, from his thighs to his lean hips to his powerful chest and shoulders. Pressed so closely, she could feel his erection against the apex of her thighs, and as exciting as it felt, it wasn't enough.

She needed him—more of him—more of everything with him. Touch, taste, pressure, skin. "Please," she whispered, circling his waist and slowly running her hands up his back. "Please stay with me."

"For how long?" he murmured, his head dropping to sweep excruciatingly light kisses across the side of her neck and up to the hollow beneath her ear. "Till midnight? Morning? Noon?"

The kisses were making it impossible to think. She pressed her thighs tight, the core of her hot and aching. Years since she'd made love, and now she felt as though she were coming apart here and now.

His mouth found hers again, and the kiss was teasing, light, and yet it made her frantic. She reached up to clasp his head, burying her fingers in his thick glossy hair. "Until as long as you want," she whispered breathlessly.

She'd given him the right answer with her words, and the kiss immediately deepened, his mouth slanting across hers, parting her lips again and drawing her tongue into his mouth. As he sucked on the tip of her tongue she felt her legs nearly buckle. He was stripping her control, seizing her senses, and she was helpless to stop him.

She'd given him a verbal surrender, she thought dizzily, but it wasn't enough. Now he wanted her to surrender her body.

CHAPTER TEN

KRISTIAN FELT ELIZABETH shiver against him, felt the curve of her hips, the indentation of her waist, the full softness of her breasts.

He'd discovered earlier she was wearing her hair pulled back, with wisps of hair against her face. Kissing her, he now followed one of the wisps to her ear, and he traced that before his fingers slid down the length of her neck.

He could feel her collarbone, and the hollow at her throat, and the thudding of her heart. Her skin was even softer than he remembered, and he found himself fantasizing about taking her hair down, pulling apart the plaits and letting her hair tumble past her shoulders and into his hands.

He wanted her hair, her face, her body in his hands. Wanted her bare and against him.

"Kristian," she said breathlessly, clasping his face in her hands.

Instantly he hardened all over again, his trousers too constricting to accommodate his erection. He wanted out of his clothes. He wanted her out of hers. *Now.*

Elizabeth shuddered as Kristian's hand caressed her hip, down her thigh, to find the hem of her velvet dress. As he lifted the hem she felt air against her bare leg, followed immediately by the heat of his hand.

She let out a slow breath of air, her eyes closing at the path his hand took. His fingers trailed up the outside of her thigh, across her hipbone to the triangle of curls between her legs.

Tensing, shivering, she wanted his touch and yet feared it, too. It had been so long since she'd been held, so long since she'd felt anything as intensely pleasurable as this, that she leaned even closer to him, pressing her breasts to his chest, her tummy to his torso, even as his fingers parted her cleft, finding the most delicate skin between. She was hot, and wet, and she pressed her forehead to his jaw as his fingers explored her.

She couldn't help the moan that escaped her lips, nor the trembling of her legs. She wanted him, needed him, and the intensity of her desire stunned her.

Flushed, dazed, Elizabeth pulled back, swayed on her feet. "The bed," she whispered breathlessly, tugging on his shirt. They walked together, reaching the bed in several steps.

As they bumped into the mattress Kristian impatiently stripped her dress over her head. "I want your hair down, too."

Reaching up, she unpinned her hair and pulled the elastics off the plaits. It was hard to pull her hair apart when Kristian was using her own body against her. With her arms up, over her head, he'd taken her breasts in his hands, cupping their fullness and teasing the tightly ruched nipples.

Gasping at the pressure and pleasure, she very nearly couldn't undo her hair. She hadn't worn a bra tonight due to the sheer lace at her bodice, and the feel of his hands on her bare skin was almost too much.

Hair loose, she reached for Kristian's belt, and then the button and zipper of his trousers. Freeing his shaft, she stroked him, amazed by his size all over again.

But Kristian was impatient to have her on the bed beneath him, and, nudging her backward, he sent her toppling down, legs still dangling over the mattress edge. With her knees parted he kissed her inner thigh, and then higher up, against her warm, moist core. He had a deft touch and tongue, and his expertise was almost more than she could bear. Suddenly shy, she wanted him to stop, but he circled her thighs with his arms, held her open for him.

The tip of his tongue flicked across her heated flesh before playing lightly yet insistently against her core. Again and again he stroked her with his tongue and lips, driving her mad with the tension building inside her. She panted as the pressure built, reached for Kristian, but he dodged her hands, and then, arching, hips bucking, she climaxed.

The orgasm was intense, overwhelming. She felt absolutely leveled. And when Kristian finally moved up, over her, she couldn't even speak. Instead she reached for his chest, slid her fingers across the dense muscle protecting his heart, up over his shoulder to pull him down on top of her.

His body was heavy, hard and strong. She welcomed the weight of him, the delicious feel of his body covering hers. Her orgasm had been intense, but what she really wanted—needed—was something more satisfying than just physical satisfaction. She craved him. The feeling of being taken, loved, sated by him.

He entered her slowly, harnessing his strength to ensure he didn't hurt her. Elizabeth held him tightly, awed by the sensation of him filling her. He felt so good against her, felt so good *in* her. She kissed his chest, the base of his throat, before he dipped his head, covering her mouth with his.

As he kissed her, he slowly thrust into her, stretching his body out over hers to withdraw and then thrust again. His chest grazed her breasts, skin and hair rubbing across her sensitive nipples. She squirmed with pleasure and he buried himself deeper inside her.

Elizabeth wrapped her legs around his waist as his hips moved against her. She squeezed her muscles, holding him inside, and the tantalizing friction of their bodies, the warm heated skin coupled with the deep impenetrable darkness, made their lovemaking even more mysterious and erotic.

As Kristian's tempo increased, his thrusts becoming harder, faster, she met each one eagerly, wanting him, as much of him as he would give her.

No one had ever made her feel so physical, so sexual, or so good. It felt natural being with him, and she gave herself over to Kristian, to his skill and passion, as he drove them both to a point of no return where muscles and nerves tightened and the mind shut out everything but wave after wave of pleasure in the most powerful orgasm of her life.

For those seconds she was not herself, not Grace Elizabeth, but bits of sky and stars and the night. She felt thrown from her body into something so much larger, so much more hopeful than her life. It wasn't sex, she thought, her body still shuddering around him, with him. It was possibility.

Afterwards, feeling dazed and nearly boneless, she clung to Kristian and drew a great gulp of air.

Amazing. That had been so amazing. He made her feel beautiful in every way, too. "I love you," she whispered, against his chest. "I do."

Kristian's hand was buried in her hair, fingers twining through the silken strands. His grip tightened, and then eased, and, dropping his head, he kissed her nose, her brow, her eyelid. "My darling English nurse. Overcome by passion."

"I'm not English," she answered with a supremely satisfied yawn, her body relaxing. "I'm American."

He rolled them over so that he was on the mattress and her weight now rested on him. "What?"

"An American."

"You're *American?*" he repeated incredulously, holding her firmly by the hips.

"Yes."

"Well, that explains a lot of things," he said with mock

seriousness. "Especially your sensitivity. Americans are so thin-skinned. They take everything personally."

Her hair spilled over both of them, and she made a face at him in the dark. "I think you were the one who was very sensitive in the beginning. And you were attached to your pain meds—"

"Enough about my pain meds. So, tell me, your eyes... blue? Green? Brown?"

She felt a pang, realizing he might never really know what she looked like. She'd accepted it before, but now it seemed worse somehow. "They're blue. And I'm not that tall—just five-four."

"That's it? When you first arrived a couple weeks ago I was certain you were six feet. That you made Nurse Burly—"

"Hurly," she corrected with a muffled laugh.

"Nurse Hurly-Burly seem dainty."

Elizabeth had to stifle another giggle. "You're terrible, Kristian. You know that, don't you?"

"So you and a half-dozen other nurses keep telling me."

Grinning, she snuggled closer. "So you really had no clue that I was raised in New York?"

"None at all." He kissed the base of her throat, and then up by her ear. "So is that where home is?"

"Was. I've lived in London for years now. I'm happy there."

"Are you?"

"Well, I don't actually live in London. I work in Richmond, and my home is in Windsor. It's under an hour's train ride each way, and I like it. I read, take care of paperwork, sort out my day."

He was stroking her hair very slowly, leisurely, just listening to her talk. As she fell silent, he kissed her again. "My eye specialists are in London."

She wished she could see his face. "Are you thinking of scheduling the eye surgery?"

"Toying with the idea."

"Seriously toying...?"

"Yes. Do you think I should try?"

She considered her words carefully before answering. "You're the one that has to live with the consequences," she said, remembering what Pano had said—that Kristian needed to have something to hope for, something to keep him going.

"But maybe it's better to just know." He exhaled heavily, sounding as if the weight of the world rested on his shoulders. "Maybe I should just do it and get it over with."

Elizabeth put her hand to his chest, felt his heart beating against her hand. "The odds...they're not very good, are they?"

"Less than five percent," he answered, his voice devoid of emotion.

Not good odds, she thought, swallowing hard. "You're doing so well right now. You're making such good progress. If the surgery doesn't turn out as you hoped, could you cope with the results?"

He didn't immediately answer. "I don't know," he said at last. "I don't know how I'd feel. But I know this. I miss seeing. I miss my sight."

"I'm sure you do."

"And I'd love to get rid of the cane. I don't like announcing to the world that I can't see. Besides, I'm sure I look foolish, tapping my way around—"

"That's a ridiculous thing to say!" She pulled away, sat up cross-legged. "First of all, the cane doesn't look foolish, and secondly, it's not about appearances, either. Life and love shouldn't be based on looks. It's about kindness, courage, humility, strength." She paused, drew an unsteady breath. "And you have all those qualities in abundance."

With that, power restored, the lights suddenly flickered and came on.

Elizabeth looked down at them, aware that Kristian couldn't see what she could see and that she should have been embarrassed. They were both naked, he stretched out on his back, she sitting cross-legged, with his hand resting on her bare thigh. But instead of being uncomfortable she felt a little thrill. She felt so right with him. She felt like his— body and soul.

"The power's back," she said, gazing at Kristian, soaking up his dark erotic beauty. His black hair, the strong classic features, impossibly long eyelashes and that sensual mouth of his. "We have lights again."

"Am I missing anything?" he drawled lazily, reaching for her and pulling her back on top of him.

As she straddled his hips he caressed the underside of her breast, so that her nipple hardened and peaked. The touch of his hand against her breast was sending sharp darts of feeling throughout her body, making her insides heat, and clench, and begin to crave relief from his body again.

"No," she murmured, eyes closing, lips helplessly parting as he tugged her lower, allowing him to take her nipple into his mouth. His mouth felt hot and wet against the nipple, and she gripped his shoulders as he sucked, unable to stifle her whimper.

Her whimper aroused him further. Elizabeth could feel him grow hard beneath her. And all she could think was that she wanted him—again. Wanted him to take her—hard, fast— take her until she screamed with pleasure.

He must have been thinking the same thing, too, because, shifting, he lifted her up, positioned her over him and thrust in. She groaned and shivered as he used his hands to help her ride him. She'd tried this position years ago and hadn't liked it, as she hadn't felt anything much but foolish, and yet now the positions and their bodies clicked. Elizabeth's cheeks burned hot, and her skin glowed as they made love again.

She came faster than before, in a cry of fierce pleasure, before collapsing onto his chest, utterly spent.

Her heart hammering, her body damp, she could do nothing but rest and try to catch her breath. "It just keeps getting better," she whispered.

He stroked her hair, and then the length of her back, until his hand rested on her bottom. "I think I've met my match," he said.

She pushed up on her elbow to see his face. "What does that mean?"

He cupped her breast, stroked the puckered aureola with his thumb. "I think you enjoy sex as much as I do."

"With you. You're incredible."

"It takes two to make it incredible." Reaching up, he pulled her head down to his and kissed her deeply, his tongue teasing hers in another sensual seduction.

In the middle of the kiss, her stomach suddenly growled. Elizabeth giggled apologetically against his mouth. "Sorry. Hungry."

"Then let's find our dinner. I'm starving, too."

They dressed in what they'd left strewn about the floor earlier. Elizabeth bent to retrieve their clothes before handing Kristian first his pants and then his shirt. Slipping on her dress, she struggled to comb her hair smooth with her fingers.

"I feel like I'm in high school," she said with a laugh. And then, and only then, it hit her—Cosima.

"My God," she whispered under her breath, blood draining, her body going icy cold. What had she done? What had she just done?

"Elizabeth?"

She pressed her hand to her mouth, stared at him as he struggled to rebutton his shirt. He'd got it wrong.

"What's the matter?" he demanded.

She could only look at him aghast, shocked, sickened.

She'd behaved badly. *Badly.* He wasn't hers. He'd never been hers. All along he'd belonged to another woman….

"Elizabeth?" Kristian's voice crackled with anger. "Are you still here? Or have you left? Talk to me."

He was right. He couldn't see. Couldn't read her face to know what she was thinking or feeling. "What did we just do, Kristian?" *What did I do?*

His hands stilled, the final button forgotten. A look of confusion crossed his features. "You already have…regrets?"

Regrets? She nearly cried. Only because he wasn't hers.

"Do you have someone waiting for you in London?" he asked, his voice suddenly growing stern, his expression hardening, taking on the glacier stillness she realized he used to keep the world at bay.

"No."

"But there is a relationship?"

"No."

Even without sight he seemed to know exactly where he was, he crossed to her, swiftly closing the distance between them. He took her by the shoulders.

She stiffened, fearing his anger, but then he slid his arms around her, held her securely against him. He kissed her cheek, and then her ear, and then nipped playfully at a particularly sensitive nerve in her neck. "What's wrong, *latrea mou?* Why the second thoughts?"

She splayed her fingers against his chest. Her heart thudded ridiculously hard. "As much as I care about you, Kristian, I cannot do this. It was wrong. *Is* wrong. Just a terrible mistake."

His arms fell away. He stepped back. "Is it because of my eyes? Because I can't see and you pity me?"

"No."

"It's something, *latrea mou.* Because one moment you are in my arms and it feels good, it feels calm and real, like a taste of happiness, and now you say it was…terrible." He drew a breath. "A *mistake*." The bitterness in his voice carved her heart in two. "I think I don't know you at all."

Eyes filling with tears, she watched him take another step backward, and then another. "Kristian." She whispered his name. "No, it's not that. Not the way you make it sound. I loved being with you. I wanted to be near you—"

"Then *what?* Is this about Cosima again? Because, God forgive me, but I can't get away from her. Every time I turn around there she is…even in my goddamn bedroom!"

"Kristian."

"*No.* No. None of that *I'm so disappointed in you* garbage. I've had it. I'm sick of it. What is it with you and Cosima? Is it the contract? The fact that she paid you money? Because if it's money, tell me the amount and I'll cut her a check."

"It's not the money. It's…you. You and her."

He laughed, but the sound grated on her ears. "*Cosima?* Cosima—the Devil Incarnate?"

"You're not a couple?"

"A couple? You're out of your mind, *latrea mou*. She's the reason I couldn't get out of bed, couldn't make myself walk, couldn't face life. Why would I ever want to be with a woman who'd been with my brother?"

Her jaw dropped. Her mouth dried. "Your…*brother?*"

Kristian had gone ashen, and the scar on his cheek tightened. "She was Andreas's fiancée. He's dead because she's alive. He's dead because I went to her aid first. I rescued her for him."

Elizabeth shook her head. Her mouth opened, shut. Of course. *Of course.*

Still shaking her head, she replayed her conversations with Cosima over again. Cosima had never said directly that she was in love with Kristian. She said she'd cared deeply for him, and wanted to see him back in Athens, but she never had said that there was more than that. Just that she hoped...

Hoped.

That was all. That was it.

"So, do you still have to go to Paris on Monday? Or was that just an excuse?" Kristian asked tersely, his features so hard they looked chiseled from granite.

"I still have to go," she answered in a low voice.

"And you still have regrets?"

"Kristian—"

"You do, don't you?"

"Kristian, it's not that simple. Not black and white like that."

"So what *is* it like?" Each word sounded like sharp steel coming from his mouth.

"I..." She closed her eyes, tried to imagine how to tell him who she'd been married to, how she'd been vilified, how she'd transformed herself to escape. But no explanation came. The old pain went too deep. The identities were too confusing. Grace Elizabeth Stiles had been beautiful and wealthy, glamorous and privileged, but she'd also been naïve and dependent, too trusting and too easily hurt.

"You *what?*" he demanded, not about to let her off the hook so easily.

"I can't stay in Greece," she whispered. "I can't."

"Is this all because of that Greek *ornio* you met on your holiday?"

"It was more serious than that."

He stilled. "How serious?"

"I married him."

For a long moment he said nothing, and then his lips pulled and his teeth flashed savagely. "So this is how it is."

She took a step toward him. "What does that mean?"

"It means I'm not a man to you. Not one you can trust or respect—"

"That's not true."

"It *is* true." His shoulders tensed. "We spent two weeks together—morning, noon and night. Why didn't you tell me you were married before? Why did you let me believe it was a simple holiday romance, a little Greek fling gone bad?"

"Because I…I…just don't talk about it."

"Why?"

"Because it hurt me. Badly." Her voice raised, tears started to her eyes. "It made me afraid."

"Just like swimming in the deep end of the pool?"

She bit her bottom lip. He sounded so disgusted, she thought. So irritated and impatient.

"You don't trust me," he added, his tone increasingly cold. "And you don't know me if you think I'd make love to one woman while involved with another."

Her heart sank. He was angry—blisteringly angry.

"What kind of man do you think I am?" he thundered. "How immoral and despicable am I?"

"You're not—"

"You thought I was engaged to Cosima."

"I didn't want to think so."

"But you did," he shot back.

"Kristian, please don't. Please don't judge me—"

"Why not? You judged me."

Tears tumbled. "I love you," she whispered.

He shrugged brusquely. "You don't know the meaning of love if you'd go to bed with a man supposedly engaged to another woman."

Elizabeth felt her heart seize up. This couldn't be happening like this, could it? They couldn't be making such a wretched mess of things, could they? "Kristian, I can't explain it, can't find the words right now, but you must know how I feel—how I really feel. You must know why I'm here, and why I even stayed this long."

"The money, maybe?" he mocked savagely, opening the door wider.

"*No*. And there is no money, I'm not taking her money—"

"Conveniently said."

He didn't know. He didn't see. And maybe that was it. He couldn't see how much she loved him, and how much she believed in him, and how she would have done anything, just about anything, to help him. Love him. Make him happy. "Please," she begged, reaching for him.

But there was no reaching him. Not when he put up that wall of his, that huge, thick, impenetrable ice wall of his, that shut him off from everyone else. Instead he shrugged her off and walked down the hall toward the distant stairwell.

His rejection cut deeply. For a moment she could do nothing but watch him walk away, and then she couldn't just let him go—not like that, not over something that was so small.

A misunderstanding.

Pride.

Ego.

None of it was important enough to keep them apart. None of it mattered if they truly cared for each other. She loved him, and from the way he'd held her, made love to her, she knew he had to have feelings for her—knew there was more to this than just hormones. For Pete's sake, neither of them were teenagers, and both of them had been through enough to know what mattered.

What mattered was loving, and being loved.

What mattered was having someone on your side. Someone who'd stick with you no matter what.

And so she left the safety of her door, the safety of pride and ego, and followed him to the stairs. She was still wiping away tears, but she knew this—she wasn't going to be dismissed, wasn't going to let him get rid of her like that.

She chased after him, trailing down the staircase. Turning the corner of one landing, she started down the next flight of stairs even as a door opened and footsteps crossed the hall below.

"Kristian!" a man said, his voice disturbingly familiar. "We were just told you'd arrived. What a surprise. Welcome home!"

Nico?

Elizabeth froze. Even her heart seemed to still.

"What are *you* doing here?" Kristian asked, his voice taut, low.

"We—my girlfriend and I—live here part-time," Nico answered. "Didn't you know we'd taken a suite? I was sure you'd been told. At least, I know Pano was aware of it. I talked to him on the phone the other day."

"I've been busy," Kristian murmured distractedly.

Legs shaking, Elizabeth shifted her weight and the floorboard squeaked. All heads down below turned to look up at her.

Elizabeth grabbed the banister. This couldn't be happening. Couldn't be.

Nico, catching sight of her, was equally shocked. Staring up at Elizabeth, he laughed incredulously. "Grace?"

Elizabeth could only stare back.

Nico glanced at Kristian, and then back to his ex-wife. "What's going on?" he asked.

"I don't know," Kristian answered tightly. "You tell me."

"I don't know either," Nico said, frowning at Elizabeth. "But for a moment I thought you and Grace were…together."

"Grace who?" Kristian demanded tersely.

"Stile. My American wife."

Kristian went rigid. "There's no Grace here."

"Yes, there she is," Nico answered. "She's standing on the landing. Blonde hair. Black lace dress."

Elizabeth felt Kristian's confusion as he swung around, staring blindly up at the stairwell. Her heart contracted. "Kristian," she said softly, hating his confusion, hating that she was the source of it, too.

"That's not Grace," Kristian retorted grimly. "That's Elizabeth. Elizabeth Hatchet. My nurse."

"Nurse?" Nico laughed. "Oh, dear, Koumantaros, it looks like she's duped you. Because your Elizabeth is my ex-wife, Grace Stile. And a nasty gold-digger, too."

CHAPTER ELEVEN

KRISTIAN FELT AS though he'd been punched hard in the gut. He couldn't breathe, couldn't move, could only stand there, struggling to take in air.

Elizabeth wasn't Elizabeth? Elizabeth was really Grace Stile?

He tried to shake his head, tried to clear the fuzz and storm clouding his mind.

The woman he'd fallen in love with wasn't even who he thought she was. Her name wasn't even Elizabeth. Maybe she wasn't even a nurse.

Maybe she was a gold-digger, just like Nico said.

Gold-digger. The word rang in Elizabeth's head.

Shocked, she went hot, and then cold, and hot again. "I'm no gold-digger," she choked, finally finding her voice. Legs wobbling, she took one step and then another until she'd reached the hall. "*You* are," she choked. "You, you… you're…" But she couldn't get the words out, couldn't defend herself, could scarcely breathe, much less think.

Nico had betrayed *her.*

Nico had married *her* for her money.

Nico had poisoned the Greek media and public against her.

Stomach roiling, she was swept back into that short brutal marriage and the months following their divorce.

He'd made her life a living hell and she'd been the one to

pay—and pay, and pay. Not just for the divorce, and not just his settlement, but emotionally, physically, mentally. It had taken years to heal, years to stop being so hurt and so insecure and so angry. *Angry*.

And she had been angry because she'd felt cheated of love, cheated of the home and the family and the dreams she'd cherished. They were supposed to have been husband and wife. A couple, partners.

But she'd only been money, cash, the fortune to supplement Nico's dwindling inheritance.

Nico, though, wasn't paying her the least bit of attention. He was still talking to Kristian, a smirk on his face—a face she'd once thought so handsome. She didn't find him attractive anymore, not even if she was being objective, because, next to Kristian, Nico's good looks faded to merely boyish, almost pretty, whereas Kristian was fiercely rugged, all man.

"She'll seduce you," Nico continued, rolling back on his heels, his arms crossed over his chest. "And make you think it was your idea. And when she has you in bed she'll tell you she loves you. She'll make you think it's love, but it's greed. She'll take you for everything you're worth—"

"That's enough. I've heard enough," Kristian ground out, silencing Nico's ruthless character assassination. He'd paled, so that the scar seemed to jump from his cheekbone, a livid reminder of the tragedy that had taken so much from him over a year ago.

"None of it is true," Elizabeth choked, her body shaking, legs like jelly. "Nothing he says—"

"I said, *enough*." Kristian turned away and walked down the hall.

Elizabeth felt the air leave her, her chest so empty her heart seized.

Somehow she found her way back to her room and stumbled into bed, where she lay stiff as a board, unable to sleep or cry.

Everything seemed just so unbelievably bad—so awful that it couldn't even be assimilated.

Lying there, teeth chattering with shock and cold, Elizabeth prayed that when the sun finally rose in the morning all of this would be just a bad, bad dream.

It wasn't.

The next morning a maid knocked on Elizabeth's door, giving her the message that a car was ready to drive her to meet the helicopter.

Washing her face, Elizabeth avoided looking at herself in the mirror before smoothing the wrinkles in her velvet dress and heading downstairs, where the butler ushered her to the waiting car.

Elizabeth had been under the impression that she'd be traveling back alone, but Kristian was already in the car when she climbed in.

"Good morning," she whispered, sliding onto the seat but being careful to keep as much distance between them as she could.

His head barely inclined.

She ducked her head, stared at her fingers, which were laced and locked in her lap. Sick, she thought, so sick. She felt as though everything good and warm and hopeful inside her had vanished, left, gone. Died.

Eyes closing, she held her breath, her teeth sinking into her lower lip.

She only let her breath out once the car started moving, leaving the castle for the helicopter pad on the other side of town.

"You were Nico's wife," Kristian said shortly, his deep rough voice splitting the car's silence in two. There was a brutality in his voice she'd never heard before. A violence that spoke of revenge and embittered passion.

Opening her eyes, she looked at Kristian, but she couldn't read anything in his face—not when his fiercely handsome features were so frozen, fixed in hard, remote, unforgiving lines. It was as if his face wasn't a face but a mask.

The car seemed to spin.

She didn't answer, didn't want to answer, didn't know *how* to answer—because in his present frame of mind nothing she said would help, nothing she said would matter. After all, Kristian Koumantaros was a Greek man. It wouldn't matter to him that she was divorced—had been divorced for years. In his mind she'd always be Nico's wife.

Elizabeth glanced down at her hands again, the knuckles white. She was so dizzy she didn't think she could sit straight, but finally she forced her head up, forced the world's wild revolutions to slow until she could see Kristian on the seat next to her, his blue eyes brilliant, piercing, despite the fact that she knew he couldn't see.

"I'm waiting," he said flatly, finality and closure in his rough voice.

Tears filling her eyes, she drew another deep breath. "Yes," she said, her voice so faint it sounded like nothing.

"So your name isn't really Elizabeth, is it?"

Again she couldn't speak. The pain inside her chest was excruciating. She could only stare at Kristian, wishing everything had somehow turned out differently. If Nico hadn't been one of the castle's tenants. If Cosima hadn't stood between them. If Elizabeth had understood just who and what Cosima really was...

"I'm still waiting," Kristian said.

Hurt and pain flared, lighting bits of fire inside her. "Waiting for what?" she demanded, shoulders twisted so she could better see him. "For some big confession? Well, I'm not going to confess. I've done nothing wrong—"

"You've done *everything* wrong," he interrupted through gritted teeth. "Everything. If your name isn't really Elizabeth Hatchet."

Colder and colder, she swallowed, her eyes growing wide, her stomach plummeting.

"If Nico was your husband, that makes you someone I do not know."

Elizabeth exhaled so hard it hurt, her chest spasming, her throat squeezing closed.

When she didn't answer, he leaned toward her, touched the side of her head, then her ear and finally her cheekbones, her eyes, her nose, her mouth. "You are Grace Stile, aren't you?"

"Was," she barely whispered. "I was Grace Stile. But Grace Stile doesn't exist anymore."

"Grace Stile was a beautiful woman," he said mockingly, his fingertips lingering on the fullness of her soft mouth.

She trembled inwardly at the touch. "I am not her," she said against his fingers. Last night he'd made her feel so good, so warm, so safe. *Happy.* But today…today it was something altogether different.

He ground out a mocking laugh. "Grace Stile, daughter of an American icon—"

"No."

"New York's most beautiful and accomplished debutante."

"Not me."

"Even more wealthy than the Greek tycoon she married."

Elizabeth stopped talking.

"Your father, Rupert Stile—"

She pulled her head away, leaned back in her seat to remove herself from his touch. "Grace Stile is gone," she said crisply. "I am Elizabeth Hatchet, a nursing administrator, and that is all that is important, all that needs to be known."

He barked a laugh, far from amused. "But your legal name isn't even Elizabeth Hatchet."

She hesitated, bit savagely into her lower lip, knowing she'd never given anyone this information—not since that fateful day when everything had changed. "Hatchet was my mother's maiden name. Legally I'm Grace Elizabeth."

He laughed again, the sound even more strained and incredulous. "Are you even a registered nurse?"

"Of course!"

"Of course," he repeated, shaking his head and running a hand across his jaw, which was dark with a day's growth of beard.

For a moment neither spoke, and the only sound was Kristian's palm, rubbing the rough bristles on his chin and jaw.

"You think you know someone," he said, after a tense minute. "You think you know what's true, what's real, and then you find out you know nothing at all."

"But you do know I am a nurse," she said steadfastly. "And I hold a Masters Degree in Business Administration."

"But I don't know that. I can't see. You could be just anybody…and it turns out you are!"

"Kristian—"

"Because if I weren't blind you couldn't have pulled this off, could you? If I could see I would have recognized you. I would have known you weren't some dreary, dumpy little nursing administrator, but the famously beautiful heiress Grace Stile."

"That never crossed my mind—"

"No? Are you sure?"

"Yes."

He made a rough, derogatory sound. His mouth slanted, cheekbones pronounced. The car had stopped. They were at the small airport, and not far from their car waited the helicopter and pilot. As the driver of the car turned off the ignition, Kristian laid a hand on Elizabeth's thigh.

"Your degrees," he said. "Those are in which name?"

She felt the heat of his hand sear her skin even as it melted her on the inside. She cared for him, loved him, but couldn't seem to connect anything that was happening today with what had taken place in her bed last night.

"My degrees," she said softly, referring to her nursing degree and then the degree in Business Administration, "were both earned in England, as Elizabeth Hatchet."

"Very clever of you," he taunted, as the passenger door opened and the driver stood there, ready to provide assistance.

Elizabeth suppressed a wave of panic. It was all coming to an end, so quickly and so badly, and she couldn't figure out how to turn the tide now that it was rushing at her, fierce and relentless.

"Kristian," she said urgently, touching his hand, her fingers attempting to slide around his. But he held his fingers stiff, and aloof, as though they'd never been close. "There was nothing clever about it. I moved to England and changed my name, out of desperation. I didn't want to be Grace Stile anymore. I wanted to start over. I *needed* to start over. And so I did."

He didn't speak again. Not even after they were in the helicopter heading for Athens, where he'd told her a plane awaited. He was sending her home immediately. Her bags were already at Athens airport. She'd be back in London by mid-afternoon.

It was a strangely silent flight, and it wasn't until they were on the ground in Athens, exiting the helicopter, that he broke the painful stillness.

"Why medicine?" he demanded.

Kristian's question stopped her just as she was about to climb the private jet's stairs.

Slowly she turned to face him, tucking a strand of hair

behind her ear even as she marveled all over again at the changes two weeks had made. Kristian Koumantaros was every inch the formidable tycoon he'd been before he was injured. He wasn't just walking, he stood tall, legs spread, powerful shoulders braced.

"You didn't study medicine at Smith or Brown or wherever you went in the States," he continued, naming universities on the East Coast. "You were interested in antiquities then."

Antiquities, she thought, her teeth pressed to the inside of her lower lip. She and her love of ancient cultures. Wasn't that how she'd met Nico in the first place? Attending a party at a prestigious New York museum to celebrate the opening of a new, priceless Greek exhibit?

"Medicine's more practical," she answered, eyes gritty, stinging with tears she wouldn't let herself cry.

And, thinking back to her move across the Atlantic, to her new identity and her new choices, she knew she'd been compelled to become someone different, someone better... more altruistic.

"Medicine is also about helping others—doing something good."

"Versus exploiting their weaknesses?"

"I've never done that!" she protested hotly.

"No?"

"No." But she could see from his expression that he didn't believe her. She opened her mouth to defend herself yet again, before stopping. It didn't matter, she thought wearily, pushing another strand of hair back from her face. He would think what he wanted to think.

And, fine, let him.

She cared about him—hugely, tremendously—but she was tired of being the bad person, was unwilling to be vilified any longer. She'd never been a bad woman, a bad person. Maybe at twenty-three or twenty-four she hadn't known better than to accept the blame, but she did now. She was a woman, not a punching bag.

"Goodbye," she said *"Kali tihi."* Good luck.

"Good luck?" he repeated. "With what?" he snapped, taking a threatening step toward her.

His reaction puzzled her. But he'd always puzzled her. "With everything," she answered, just wanting to go now, needing to make the break. She knew this could go nowhere. Last night she should have realized that nothing good would come out of an inappropriate liaison, but last night she hadn't been thinking. Last night she'd been frightened and uncertain, and she'd turned to him for comfort, turned to him for reassurance. It was the worst thing she could have done.

And yet Kristian still marched toward her, his expression black. "And just what is *everything?*"

She thought of all he had still waiting for him. He could have such a good life, such a rich, interesting life—sight or no sight—if he wanted.

Her lips curved in a faint, bittersweet smile. "Your life," she said simply. "It's all still before you."

And quickly, before he could detain her, she climbed the stairs, disappearing into the jet's cool, elegant interior where she settled into one of the leather chairs in the main cabin.

Except for the flight crew, the plane was empty.

Elizabeth fastened her seatbelt and settled back in the club chair. She knew it would be a very quiet trip home.

Back in London, Elizabeth rather rejoiced in the staggering number of cases piled high on her desk. She welcomed the billing issues, the cranky patients, the nurses needing vacations and personal days off, as every extra hour of work meant another hour she couldn't think about Kristian, or Greece, or the chaotic two weeks spent there.

Because now that she was back in England, taking the train

to work at her office in Richmond every day, she couldn't fathom what had happened.

Couldn't fathom how it had happened.

Couldn't fathom why.

She wasn't interested in men, or dating, or having another lover. She wasn't interested in having a family, either. All she wanted was to work, to pay her bills, to keep her company running as smoothly as possible. Her business was her professional life, social life and personal life all rolled into one, and it suited her just fine.

Far better to be Plain Jane than Glamorous Grace Stile, with the world at her feet, because the whole world-at-your-feet thing was just an illusion anyway. As she'd learned the hard way, the more people thought you had, the more they envied you, and then resented you, and eventually they lobbied to see you fall.

Far better to live simply and quietly and mind your own business, she thought, shuffling papers into her briefcase.

She was leaving work early again today, tormented by a stomach bug that wouldn't go away. She'd been back home in England just over two months now, but she hadn't felt like herself for ages. Since Greece, as a matter of fact.

Her secretary glanced up as Elizabeth opened the office door.

"Still under the weather, Ms. Hatchet?" Mrs. Shipley asked sympathetically, pushing her reading glasses up on her head.

Mrs. Shipley had practically run the office single-handedly while Elizabeth was gone, and she couldn't imagine a better administrative assistant.

"I am," Elizabeth answered with a grimace, as her insides did another sickly, queasy rise and fall that made her want to throw up into the nearest rubbish bin. But of course she never had the pleasure of actually throwing up. She wasn't lucky enough to get the thing—whatever it was—out of her system.

"If you picked up a parasite in Greece, you'll need a good antibiotic, my dear. I know I'm sounding like a broken record, but you really should see a doctor. Get something for that. The right antibiotic will nip it in the bud. And you need it nipped in the bud, as you look downright peaky."

Mrs. Shipley was right. Elizabeth felt absolutely wretched. She ached. Her head throbbed. Her stomach alternated between nausea and cramps. Even her sleep was disturbed, colored with weird, wild dreams of doom and gloom.

But what she feared most, and refused to confront, was the very real possibility that it wasn't a parasite she'd picked up but something more permanent. Something more changing.

Something far more serious.

Like Kristian Koumantaros's baby.

She'd been home just over two months now and she hadn't had her period—which wasn't altogether unusual, since she was the least regular woman she knew—but she couldn't bring herself to actually take a pregnancy test.

If she wasn't pregnant—fantastic.

If she was:...

If she was?

The next morning her nausea was so severe she huddled next to the toilet, managing nothing more than wrenching dry heaves.

Her head was spinning and she was gagging, and all she could think was, What if I really am pregnant with Kristian Koumantaros's baby?

Kristian Koumantaros was one of the most wealthy, powerful, successful men in Europe. He lived in ancient monasteries and castles and villas all over the world. He traveled by helicopter, private jet, luxury yacht. He negotiated with no one.

And she knew he wouldn't negotiate with her. If he knew she was pregnant he'd step in, take over, take action.

And, yes, Kristian *ought* to know. But how would he benefit from knowing? Would the baby—if there really was a baby—benefit?

Would *she?*

No. Not when Kristian viewed her as a heartless mercenary, a gold-digger, someone who preyed upon other's weaknesses.

Elizabeth somehow managed to drag herself into work, drag listlessly through the day, and then caught the train home to Windsor.

Sitting on the train seat, thirty minutes away from her stop, it hit her for the first time. She was pregnant. She knew deep down she was going to have a baby.

But Kristian. What about Kristian?

A wave of ice flooded her. What would he say, much less do, if he knew about the baby? He didn't even like her. He despised her. How would he react if he knew she carried his child?

Panic flooded her—panic that made her feel even colder and more afraid.

She couldn't let him find out. She wouldn't let him find out.

Stop it, she silently chastised herself as her panic grew. It's not as though you'll bump into him.

You live on opposite ends of the continent. You're both on islands separated by seas. No way to accidentally meet.

As heartless as it sounded, she'd make sure they wouldn't meet, either.

He'd take the baby. She knew he'd take the baby from her. Just the way Nico had taken everything from her.

Greek men were proud, and fierce. Greek men, particularly Greek tycoons, thought they were above rules and laws. And Kristian Koumantaros, now that he was nearly recovered, would be no different.

Elizabeth's nausea increased, and she stirred restlessly in

her seat, anxious to be home, where she could take a long bath, climb into bed and just relax.

She needed to relax. Her heart was pounding far too hard.

Trying to distract herself, she glanced around the train cabin, studying the different commuters, before glancing at the man next to her reading a newspaper. His face was hidden by the back of the paper and her gaze fell on the headlines. Nothing looked particularly interesting until she read, *Koumantaros in London for Treatment*.

Koumantaros.

Kristian Koumantaros?

Breath catching, she leaned forward to better see the article. She only got the first line or two before the man rudely shuffled the pages and turned his back to her preventing her from reading more.

But Elizabeth didn't need to read much more than those first two lines to get the gist of the article.

Kristian had undergone the risky eye surgery at Moorfield's Hospital in London today.

CHAPTER TWELVE

WALKING FROM THE train station to her little house, Elizabeth felt her nerves started getting the best of her. For the past three years she'd made historic Windsor her home, having found it the perfect antidote to the stresses of her career, but today the walk filled her with apprehension.

Something felt wrong. And it wasn't just thinking about the baby. It was an uneasy sixth sense that things around her weren't right.

Picking up her pace, she tried to silence her fears, telling herself she was tired and overly imaginative.

No one was watching her.

No one was following her.

And nothing bad was going to happen.

But tugging the collar of her coat up, and crossing her arms over her chest to keep warm, she couldn't help thinking that something felt bad. And the bad feeling was growing stronger as she left the road and hurried up the crushed gravel path toward her house.

Windsor provided plenty of diversion on weekends, with brilliant shopping as well as the gorgeous castle and the riverside walks, but as she entered her house and closed the door behind her, her quiet little house on its quiet little lane seemed very isolated.

If someone had followed her home, no one would see.

If someone broke into her house, no one would hear her cries for help.

Elizabeth locked the front door, then went through the kitchen to the back door, checking the lock on that before finally taking her coat off and turning the heat up.

In the kitchen she put on the kettle for tea, and was just about to make some toast when a knock sounded on her door.

She froze, the loaf of bread still in her hands, and stood still so long that the knock sounded again.

Putting the bread on the counter, and the knife down, she headed for the door, checking through a window first before she actually opened it.

A new model Jaguar was parked out front, and a man stood on her doorstep, his back to her as he faced the car. But she knew the man—knew his height, the breadth of his shoulders, the length of his legs, the shape of his head.

Kristian.

Kristian here.

But today was his surgery…he was supposed to have had surgery…the paper had said…

Unless he'd backed out.

But he wouldn't back out, would he?

Heart hammering, she undid the lock and opened the door, and the sound of the lock turning caught his attention. Kristian shifted, turning toward her. But as he faced her his eyes never blinked, and his expression remained impassive.

"Kristian," she whispered, cold all over again.

"Cratchett," he answered soberly.

And looking up into his face, a face so sculpturally perfect, the striking features contrasted by black hair and blue eyes, she thought him a beautiful but fearsome angel. One sent to judge her, punish her.

Glancing past him to the car, the sleek black Jaguar with

tinted windows, she wondered how many cars he had scattered all over the world.

"You're...here," she said foolishly, her mind so strangely blank that nothing came to her—nothing but shock and fear. He couldn't know. He didn't know. She'd only found out today herself.

"Yes, I am." His head tipped and he looked at her directly, but still without recognition. She felt her heart turn over with sympathy for him. He hadn't gone through with the surgery. He must have had second thoughts. And while she didn't blame him—it was a very new, very dangerous procedure—it just reaffirmed all over again her determination to keep the pregnancy a secret...at least for now.

"How did you know I lived here?"

"I had your address," he said blandly.

"Oh. I see." But she didn't see. Her home address was on nothing—although she supposed if a man like Kristian Koumantaros wanted to know where she lived it wouldn't take much effort on his part to find out. He had money, and connections. People would tell him things, particularly private detectives—not that he'd do that...

Or would he?

Frowning, bewildered, she stared up at him, still trying to figure out what he was doing here in Windsor—on her doorstep, no less.

From the kitchen, her kettle began to whistle.

His head lifted, his black brows pulling.

"The kettle," she said, by way of explanation. "I was just making tea. I should turn it off." And without waiting for him to answer she went to the kitchen and unplugged the kettle, only to turn around and discover Kristian right there behind her, making her small, old-fashioned kitchen, with its porcelain farm sink and simple farmhouse table, look tired and primitive.

"Oh," she said, taking a nervous step back. "You're here."

The corner of his mouth twisted. "I appear to be everywhere today."

"Yes." She pressed her skirt smooth, her hands uncomfortably damp. How had he made his way into the kitchen so quickly? It was almost as if he knew his way already—or as if he could actually see...

Could he?

Her pulse quickened, her nerves strung so tight she felt disturbingly close to falling apart. It had been such an overwhelming day as it was. First her certainty about the baby, and now Kristian in her house.

"Have you been in England long?" she asked softly, trying to figure out just what was going on.

"I've spent part of the last month here."

A month in England. Her heart jumped a little, and she had to exhale slowly to try to calm herself. "I didn't know."

One of his black eyebrows lifted, but he said nothing else. At least some things hadn't changed, she thought. He was still as uncommunicative as ever. But that didn't mean she had to play his game.

"The surgery—it was scheduled for today, wasn't it?" she asked awkwardly.

"Why?"

"I read it in the paper...actually, it was on the train home. You were supposed to have the treatment done today in London."

"Really?"

She felt increasingly puzzled. "It's what the paper said," she repeated defensively.

"I see." He smiled benignly. And the conversation staggered to a stop there.

Uncertainly, she turned to pour her tea.

Good manners required her to ask if he'd like a cup, but the last thing she wanted to do was prolong this miserable visit.

She wrestled with her conscience. Good manners won. "Would you like some tea?" she asked, voice stilted.

White teeth flashed in a mocking smile. "I thought you'd never ask."

Hands shaking, she retrieved another cup and saucer from the cupboard before filling his cup.

He couldn't see…could he?

He couldn't possibly see…

But something inside her, that same peculiar sixth sense from earlier, made her suspicious.

"Toast?" Her voice quavered. She hated that. She hated that suddenly everything felt so wildly out of control.

"No, thank you."

Glancing at him, she put the bread away, too nervous now to eat.

"You're not going to eat?" he asked mildly.

"No."

"You're not hungry?"

Her stomach did another uncomfortable freefall. How did he know she wasn't going to eat?

"The surgery," she said. "You didn't have it today."

"No." He paused for the briefest moment. "I had it a month ago."

Her legs nearly went from beneath her. Elizabeth put a hand out to the kitchen table to support herself. "A month ago?" she whispered, her gaze riveted to his face.

"Mmmm."

He wasn't helping at all, was he? She swallowed around the huge lump filling her throat. "Can you, can you…see?"

"Imperfectly."

Imperfectly, she repeated silently, growing increasingly light-headed. "Tell me…tell me…how much do you see?"

"It's not all dark anymore. One eye is more or less just shadows and dark shapes, but with the other eye I get a bit more. While I'll probably never be able to drive or pilot my own plane again, I can see you."

"And what do you see...now?" Her voice was faint to her own ears.

"You."

Her heart was beating so hard she was afraid she'd faint.

"The colors aren't what they were," he added. "Everything's faded, so the world's rather gray and white, but I know you're standing near a table. You're touching the table with one hand. Your other hand is on your stomach."

He was right. He was exactly right. And her hand was on her stomach because she felt like throwing up. "Kristian."

He just looked at her, really looked at her, and she didn't know whether to smile for him or burst into tears. He could see. Imperfectly, as he'd said, but something was better than nothing. Something meant he'd live independently more easily. He'd also have more power in his life again, as well as control.

Control.

And suddenly she realized that if he could see her, he'd eventually see the changes in her body. He'd know she was pregnant...

Her insides churned.

"Is that why you're here tonight?" she asked. "To tell me your good news?"

"And to celebrate your good news."

She swayed on her feet. "My good news?"

"You do have good news, don't you?" he persisted.

Elizabeth stared at Kristian where he stood, just inside the kitchen doorway. Protectively she rubbed her stomach, over her not yet existent bump, trying to stay calm. "I...I don't think so."

"I suppose it depends on how you look at it," he answered. His mouth slanted, black lashes lowering to conceal the startling blue of his eyes. "We knew each other only two weeks and two days, and that was two months and two weeks ago. Those two weeks were mostly good. But there was a disappointment or two, wasn't there?"

She couldn't tear her eyes off him. He looked strong and dynamic, and his tone was commanding. "A couple," she echoed nervously.

"One of the greatest offenses is that we flew to Kithira for dinner and we never ate. We were in my favorite restaurant and we never enjoyed an actual meal."

Elizabeth crossed her arms over her chest. "That's your *greatest* disappointment?"

"If you'd ever eaten there, you'd understand. It's truly great food. Greek food as it's meant to be."

She blinked, her fingers balling into knuckled fists. "You're here to tell me I missed out on a great meal?"

"It was supposed to be a special evening."

He infuriated her. Absolutely infuriated her. Pressing her fists to her ribs, she shook inwardly with rage. Here she was, exhausted from work, stressed and sick from her pregnancy, worried about his sight, deeply concerned about the future, and all he could think of was a missed meal?

"Why don't you have your pilot take you back to Kithira and you can *have* your delicious dinner?" she snapped.

"But that wouldn't help you. You still wouldn't know what a delicious meal you'd missed." He gestured behind him, to the compact living room. "So I've brought that meal to you."

"What?"

"I won't have you flying in your state, and I'm worrying about the baby."

"What baby?" she choked, her veins filling with a flood of ice water.

"Our baby," he answered simply, turning away and heading for the living room, which had been transformed while they were in the kitchen.

The owner of the Kithirian restaurant, along with the waiter who had served them that night, had set up a table, chairs, covering the table in a crisp white cloth and table settings for two. The lights had been turned down and candles flickered on the table, and on the side table next to her small antique sofa, and somewhere, she didn't know where, music played.

They'd turned her living room into a Greek taverna and Elizabeth stood rooted to the spot, unable to take it all in. "What's going on?"

Kristian shrugged. "We're going to have that dinner tonight. Now." He moved to take one of the chairs, and pulled it out for her. "A Greek baby needs Greek food."

"Kristian—"

"It's true." His voice dropped, and his expression hardened. "You're having our baby."

"My baby."

"Our baby," he corrected firmly. "And it is *our* baby." His blue gaze held hers. "Isn't it?"

With candles flickering on the crisp white cloth, soft Greek music in the background, and darkly handsome Kristian here before her, Elizabeth felt tears start to her eyes. Two months without a word from him. Two months without apology, remorse, forgiveness. Two months of painful silence and now this—this power-play in her living room.

"I know you haven't been feeling well," he continued quietly. "I know because I've been in London, watching over you."

Weakly she sat down—not at the table, but on one of her living room chairs. "You think I'm a gold-digger."

"A gold-digger? Grace Stile? A woman as wealthy as Athina Onassis Roussel?"

Elizabeth clasped her hands in her lap. "I don't want to talk about Grace Stile."

"I do." He dropped into a chair opposite her. "And I want to talk about Nico and Cosima and all these other sordid characters appearing in our own little Greek play."

The waiter and the restaurant owner had disappeared into the kitchen. They must have begun warming or preparing food, as the smell coming from the back of the house made her stomach growl.

"I know Nico put you through hell in your marriage," Kristian continued. "I know the divorce was even worse. He drove you out of Greece and the media hounded you for years after. I don't blame you for changing your name, for moving to England and trying to become someone else."

She held her breath, knowing there was a *but* coming. She could hear it in his voice, see it in the set of his shoulders.

"But," he added, "I minded very much not being able to see you. Much more not being able to see—and assess—the situation that night at the Kithira castle for myself."

She linked her fingers to hide the fact they were trembling. "That evening was a nightmare. I just want to forget it. Forget them. Forget Grace, too."

"I can't forget Grace." His head lifted and his gaze searched her face. "Because she's beautiful. And she's you."

The lump in her throat burned, swelled, making everything inside her hurt worse. "I'm not beautiful."

"You were beautiful as a New York debutante, and you're even more beautiful now. And it has nothing to do with your name, or the Stile fortune. Nothing to do with your marriage or your divorce or the work you do as an administrator. It's you. Grace Elizabeth."

"You don't know me," she whispered, trying to silence him.

"But I do. Because for two weeks I lived with you and worked with you and dined with you, and you changed me. You saved me—"

"No."

"Elizabeth, I didn't want to live after the accident. I didn't want to feel so much loss and pain. But you somehow gave me a window of light, and hope. You made me believe that things could be different. Better."

"I wasn't that good, or nice."

"No, you weren't nice. But you were strong. Tough. And you wouldn't baby me. You wouldn't allow me to give up. And I needed that. I needed you." He paused. "I still do."

Her eyes closed. Hot tears stung her eyelids.

He reached over, skimmed her cheeks with his fingers. "Don't cry," he murmured. "Please don't cry."

She shook her head, then turned her cheek into his palm, biting her lip to keep the tears from falling. "If you needed me, why did you let me go?"

"Because I didn't feel worthy of you. Didn't feel like a man who deserved you."

"Kristian—"

"I realized that night that if I'd been able to see, I would have been in control at the castle in Kithira. I could have read the situation, understood what was happening. Instead I stood there in the dark—literally, figuratively—and it enraged me. I felt trapped. Helpless. My blindness was creating ignorance. Fear."

"You've never been scared of anything," she protested softly.

"Since the accident I've been afraid of everything. I've been haunted by nightmares, my sleep disturbed until I thought I was going mad, but after meeting you that began to change. I began to change. I began to find my way home—my way back to me."

She simply stared at him, her heart tender, her eyes stinging from unshed tears.

"I am a man who takes care of his woman," he continued quietly. "I hated not being able to take care of you. And you are my woman. You've been mine from the moment you arrived in the Taygetos on that ridiculous donkey cart."

Her lips quivered in a tremulous smile. "That was the longest, most uncomfortable ride of my life."

"Elizabeth, *latrea mou,* I have loved you from the very first day I met you. You were horrible and wonderful and your courage won me over. Your courage and your compassion. Your kindness and your strength. All those virtues you talked about in Kithira. You told me appearances didn't matter. You said there were virtues far more important and I agree. Yes, you're beautiful, but I couldn't see your beauty until today. I didn't need your beauty, or the Stile name, or your inheritance to win me. I just needed you. With me."

"Kristian—"

"I still do."

Eyes filmed by tears, she looked up, around her small living room. Normally it was a rather austere room. She lived off her salary, having donated nearly all of her inheritance to charity, and it never crossed her mind to spoil herself with pretty things. But tonight the living room glowed, cozy and intimate with candlelight, the beautifully set table and strains of Greek music, even as the most delectable smells wafted from the kitchen.

The restaurant owner appeared in the doorway. "Dinner is ready," he said sternly. "And tonight you both must eat."

Elizabeth joined Kristian at the table, and for the first time in weeks she enjoyed food. How could she not enjoy the meal tonight? Everything was wonderful. The courses and flavors were beyond brilliant. They shared marinated lamb, fish with tomatoes and currants, grilled octopus—which Elizabeth did pass on—and as she ate she couldn't look away from Kristian.

She'd missed him more than she knew.

Just having him here, with her, made everything feel right. Made everything feel good. Intellectually she knew there were problems, issues, and yet emotionally she felt calm and happy and peaceful again.

It had always been like this with him. It wasn't what he said, or did. It was just him. He made her feel good. He made her feel wonderful.

Looking across the table at him, she felt a thought pop into her head. "You know, Cosima said— " she started to say, before breaking off. She'd done it again. Cosima. Always Cosima. "Why do I keep talking about her?"

"I don't know. But you might as well tell me what she said. I might as well hear all of it."

"It's nothing—not important. Let's forget it."

"No. You brought it up, so it's obviously on your mind. What did Cosima say?"

Elizabeth silently kicked herself. The dinner had been going so well. And now she'd done the same thing as at the castle in Kithira. Her nose wrinkled. "I'm sorry, Kristian."

"So tell me. What does she say?"

"That before you were injured you were an outrageous playboy." She looked up at him from beneath her eyelashes. "That you could get any woman to eat out of your hand. I was just thinking that I can see what she meant."

Kristian coughed, a hint of color darkening his cheekbones. "I've never been a playboy."

"Apparently women can't resist you…ever."

He gave her a pointed look. "That's not true."

"So you didn't have two dates, on two different continents, in the same day?"

"Geographically as well as physically impossible."

"Unless you were flying from Sydney to Los Angeles."

Kristian grimaced. "That was a one-time situation. If it hadn't been for crossing the time zones it wouldn't have been the same day."

Elizabeth smiled faintly, rather liking Kristian in the hot seat. "Do you miss the lifestyle?"

"No—God, no." Now it was his turn to smile, his white teeth flashing against the bronze of his skin. Sun and exercise had given him the most extraordinary golden glow. "Being a playboy isn't a picnic," he intoned mockingly. "Some men envied the number of relationships I had, but it was really quite demanding, trying to keep all the women happy."

She was amused despite herself. "You're shameless."

"Not as shameless as you were last August, checking me out by the pool...*despite* us having a deal."

"I *wasn't* looking."

"You were. Admit it."

She blushed. "You couldn't even see."

"I could tell. Some things one doesn't need to see to know. Just as I didn't need to see you to know I love you. That I will always love you. And I want nothing more than to spend the rest of my life with you."

Elizabeth's breath caught in her throat. She couldn't speak. She couldn't even breathe.

Kristian stood up from the table and crossed around to kneel before her. He had a ring box in his hand. "Marry me, *latrea mou,*" he said. "Marry me. Come live with me. I don't want to live without you."

His proposal shocked her, and frightened her. It wasn't that she didn't care for him—she did, oh, she did—but *marriage.* Marriage to another Greek tycoon.

She drew back in her chair. "Kristian, I can't... I'm sorry, I can't."

"You don't want to be with me?"

All she wanted was to be with him, but marriage terrified her. To her it represented an abuse of power and control, and she never wanted to feel trapped like that again.

"I do want to be with you—but marriage…" Her voice cracked. She felt the old pressure return, the sense of dread and futility. "Kristian, I just had such a terrible time of it. And it shattered me when it ended. I can't go that route again."

"You can," he said, rising.

"No, I can't. I really can't." She slid off her chair and left the table. She felt cornered now, and she didn't know where to go. He was in her house. The restaurant owner and the waiter were in her house. And it was a little two-bedroom house.

Elizabeth retreated to the only other room—her bedroom—but Kristian followed. He put his hand out to keep her from closing the door on him.

"You accused *me* of being a coward by refusing to recover," he said, holding the door ajar. "You said I needed to get on my feet and back to the land of living. Maybe it's time you took your own advice. Maybe it's time you stopped hiding from life and started living again, too."

Firmly, insistently, he pushed the door the rest of the way open and entered her room. Elizabeth scrambled back, but Kristian marched toward her, fierce and determined. "Being with you is good. It feels right and whole and healthy. Being with you makes me happy, and I know—even if I couldn't see before—it made you happy, too. I will not let happiness go. I will not let you run away, either. We belong together."

She'd backed up until there was nowhere else to go. She was against her nightstand, cornered near her bed, her heart thundering like mad in her chest.

"You," he added, catching her hands in his and lifting them to his mouth, kissing each balled fist, "belong with me."

And as he kissed each of her fists she felt some of the terrible tension around her heart ease. Just his skin on hers calmed her, soothed her. Just his warmth made her feel safe. Protected. "I'm afraid," she whispered.

"I know you are. You've been afraid since you lost your parents, the year before your coming-out party. That's why you married Nico. You thought he'd protect you, take care of you. You thought you'd be safe with him."

Tears filmed her eyes. "But I wasn't."

He held her fists to his chest. "I'm not Nico, and I could never hurt you. Not when I want to love you and have a family with you. Not when I want to spend every day of the rest of my life with you."

She could feel his heart pounding against her hands. His body was so warm, and yet hard, and even with that dramatic scar across his cheek he was beautiful.

"Everything I've done," he added, tipping his head to brush his lips across her forehead, "from learning to walk again to risking the eye surgery, was to help me be a man again—a man who was worthy of you."

"But I'm not the right woman—"

"Not the right woman? *Latrea mou,* look at you! You might be terrified of marriage, but you're not terrified of me." His voice dropped, low and harsh, almost mocking. "I know I'm something of a monster, I've heard people say as much, but you've never minded my face—"

"I *love* your face."

His hands tightened around hers. "You don't bow and scrape before me. You talk to me, laugh with me, make love with me. And you make me feel whole." His voice deepened yet again. "With you I'm complete."

It was exactly how he made her feel. Whole. Complete. Her heart quickened and her chest felt hot with emotion.

"You make sense to me in a way no one has ever made sense," he added, even more huskily. "And if you love me, but really can't face marriage, then let's not get married. Let's not do anything that will make you worry or feel trapped. I don't need to have a ceremony or put an expensive ring on your finger to feel like you're mine, because you already are mine. You belong with me. I know it, I feel it, I believe it— it's as simple and yet as complicated as that."

Elizabeth stared up at him, unable to believe the transformation in him. He was like a different man—in every way— from the man she'd met nearly three months ago.

"What's wrong?" he asked, seeing her expression. "Have I got it wrong? Maybe you don't feel the same way."

The sudden agony in his extraordinary face nearly broke her heart. Elizabeth's chest filled with emotion so sharp and painful that she pressed herself closer. "Kiss me," she begged.

He did. He lowered his head to cover her mouth with his. The kiss immediately deepened, his touch and taste familiar and yet impossibly new. This was her man. And he loved her. And she loved him more than she'd thought she could ever love anyone.

Kissing him, she moved even closer to him, his arms wrapping around her back to hold her firmly against him. His warmth gave her comfort and courage.

"I love you," she whispered against his mouth. "I love you and love you and love you."

She felt the corner of his mouth lift in a smile.

"And I don't care if we get married," she added, "or if we just live together, as long as we're together. I just want to be with you, near you, every day for the rest of my life."

He drew his head back and smiled down into her eyes. "They say be careful what you wish for."

"Every day, forever."

"Grace Elizabeth…"

"Every day, each day, until the end of time."

"Done." He dropped his head and kissed her again. "There's no escaping now."

She wrapped her arms around him, reassured by the wave of perfect peace. "I suppose if you're not going to let me escape, we might as well make it legal."

Kristian drew his head back a little to get a good look at her face. "You've changed your mind?"

A huge knot filled her throat and she nodded, tears shimmering in her eyes. "Ask me again. Please."

"Will you marry me, *latrea mou?*" he murmured, his voice husky with emotion.

"Yes."

He kissed her temple, and then her cheek, and finally her mouth. "Why did you change your mind?"

"Because love," she whispered, holding him tightly, "is stronger than fear. And, Kristian Koumantaros, I love you with all my heart. I don't want to be with anyone but you."

* * * * *

COMING NEXT MONTH from Harlequin Presents®
AVAILABLE MARCH 19, 2013

#3129 MASTER OF HER VIRTUE
Miranda Lee

Shy, cautious Violet has had enough of living life in the shadows. She resolves to experience all that life has to offer, starting with internationally renowned film director Leo Wolfe. But is Violet ready for where he wants to take her?

#3130 A TASTE OF THE FORBIDDEN
Buenos Aires Nights
Carole Mortimer

Argentinian tycoon Cesar Navarro has his sexy little chef, Grace Blake, right where he wants her—in his penthouse, at his command! She should be off-limits, but Grace has tantalized his jaded palette, and Cesar finds himself ordering something new from the menu!

#3131 THE MERCILESS TRAVIS WILDE
The Wilde Brothers
Sandra Marton

Travis Wilde would never turn down a willing woman in a king-size bed! Normally innocence like Jennie Cooper's would have the same effect as a cold shower, yet her determination and mouth-watering curves have him burning up all over!

#3132 A GAME WITH ONE WINNER
Scandal in the Spotlight
Lynn Raye Harris

Paparazzi darling Caroline Sullivan hides a secret behind her dazzling smile. Her ex-flame, Russian businessman Roman Kazarov, is back on the scene—is he seeking revenge for her humiliating rejection or wanting to take possession of her troubled business?

HPCNM0313RA

#3133 HEIR TO A DESERT LEGACY
Secret Heirs of Powerful Men
Maisey Yates

When recently and reluctantly crowned Sheikh Sayid discovers his country's true heir, he'll do anything to protect him—even marry the child's aunt. It may appease his kingdom, but will it release the blistering chemistry between them...?

#3134 THE COST OF HER INNOCENCE
Jacqueline Baird

Newly free Beth Lazenby has closed the door on her past, until she encounters lawyer Dante Cannavaro who is still convinced of her guilt. But when anger boils over into passion, will the consequences forever bind her to her enemy?

#3135 COUNT VALIERI'S PRISONER
Sara Craven

Kidnapped and held for ransom... His price? Her innocence! Things like this just don't happen to Maddie Lang, but held under lock and key, the only deal Count Valieri will strike is one with an *unconventional* method of payment!

#3136 THE SINFUL ART OF REVENGE
Maya Blake

Reiko has two things art dealer Damion Fortier wants; a priceless Fortier heirloom and her seriously off-limits body! And she has no intention of giving him access to either. So Damion turns up lethal charm to ensure he gets *exactly* he wants....

You can find more information on upcoming Harlequin® titles, free excerpts and more at www.Harlequin.com.

REQUEST YOUR FREE BOOKS!

2 FREE NOVELS PLUS
2 FREE GIFTS!

YES! Please send me 2 FREE Harlequin Presents® novels and my 2 FREE gifts (gifts are worth about $10). After receiving them, if I don't wish to receive any more books, I can return the shipping statement marked "cancel." If I don't cancel, I will receive 6 brand-new novels every month and be billed just $4.30 per book in the U.S. or $4.99 per book in Canada. That's a saving of at least 14% off the cover price! It's quite a bargain! Shipping and handling is just 50¢ per book in the U.S. and 75¢ per book in Canada.* I understand that accepting the 2 free books and gifts places me under no obligation to buy anything. I can always return a shipment and cancel at any time. Even if I never buy another book, the two free books and gifts are mine to keep forever.

106/306 HDN FVRK

Name _____
                          (PLEASE PRINT)

Address _____ Apt. # _____

City _____ State/Prov. _____ Zip/Postal Code _____

Signature (if under 18, a parent or guardian must sign) _____

Mail to the **Harlequin® Reader Service:**
IN U.S.A.: P.O. Box 1867, Buffalo, NY 14240-1867
IN CANADA: P.O. Box 609, Fort Erie, Ontario L2A 5X3

Are you a current subscriber to Harlequin Presents books
and want to receive the larger-print edition?
Call 1-800-873-8635 or visit www.ReaderService.com.

* Terms and prices subject to change without notice. Prices do not include applicable taxes. Sales tax applicable in N.Y. Canadian residents will be charged applicable taxes. Offer not valid in Quebec. This offer is limited to one order per household. Not valid for current subscribers to Harlequin Presents books. All orders subject to credit approval. Credit or debit balances in a customer's account(s) may be offset by any other outstanding balance owed by or to the customer. Please allow 4 to 6 weeks for delivery. Offer available while quantities last.

Your Privacy—The Harlequin® Reader Service is committed to protecting your privacy. Our Privacy Policy is available online at www.ReaderService.com or upon request from the Harlequin Reader Service.

We make a portion of our mailing list available to reputable third parties that offer products we believe may interest you. If you prefer that we not exchange your name with third parties, or if you wish to clarify or modify your communication preferences, please visit us at www.ReaderService.com/consumerchoice or write to us at Harlequin Reader Service Preference Service, P.O. Box 9062, Buffalo, NY 14269. Include your complete name and address.

SPECIAL EXCERPT FROM

HARLEQUIN

Presents

*These two men have fought battles, waged wars and won.
But when their command—their legacy—is challenged by
the very women they desire the most...who will win?*

*Enjoy a sneak peek from HEIR TO A DESERT LEGACY,
the first tale in the potent new duet,*
SECRET HEIRS OF POWERFUL MEN,
by USA TODAY *bestselling author Maisey Yates.*

* * *

CHLOE stood up quickly, her chair tilting and knocking into
the chair next to it, the sound loud in the cavernous room.
"Sorry, sorry." She tried to straighten them, her cheeks
burning, her heart pounding. "I have to go."

Sayid was faster than she was, his movements smoother.
He crossed to her side of the table and caught her arm, drawing her to him, his expression dark. "Why are you running
from me?" he asked, dipping his face lower, his expression
fierce. "It's because you know, isn't it? You feel it?"

"Feel what?" she asked.

"This...need between us. How everything in me is demanding that I reach out and pull you hard against me. And
how everything in you is begging me to."

"I don't know what you're talking about," she said.

"I think you do." He lowered his hand and traced her
collarbone with his fingertip, sliding it slowly up the side of
her neck, along her jawbone.

She shook her head, pulling away from him, from his touch. "No," she lied, "I don't."

She didn't understand what was happening with her body, why it was betraying her like this. She'd never felt this kind of wild, overpowering attraction for anyone in her life. But if she was going to, it would have been for a nice scientist who had a large collection of dry-erase pens and looked good in a lab coat.

It would not be for this rough, uncivilized man who believed he could move people around at his whim. This man who sought to control everything and everyone around him.

Unfortunately, her body hadn't asked her opinion on who she should find attractive. Because that was most definitely what this was. Scientific, irrefutable evidence of arousal.

* * *

Will Chloe give in to temptation? And will she ever be able to tame the wild warrior?

Find out in HEIR TO A DESERT LEGACY,
available March 19, 2013.

* * *

"It won't work," she said, her voice fiercer than she'd
thought she could manage at that moment.

Roman cocked an eyebrow. "What won't work, darling?"

A shiver chased down her spine. Once, he'd meant the
endearment, and she'd loved the way his Russian accent
slid across the words as he spoke. It was a caress before the
caress. Now, however, he did it to torment her. The words
were not a caress so much as a threat.

She turned and faced him head-on, tilting her head
back to look him in the eye. He stood with his hands in his
pockets, one corner of his beautiful mouth slanted up in a
mocking grin.

Evil, heartless. That was what he was now. He wasn't
here to do her any favors. He would not be merciful.

Especially if he discovered her secret.

"I know what you want and I plan to fight you," she said.

He laughed. "I welcome it. Because you will not win.

Not this time." His eyes narrowed as he studied her. "Funny, I would have never thought your father would step down and leave you in charge. I always thought they would carry him from his office someday."

A shard of cold fear dug into her belly, as it always did when someone mentioned her father these days. "People change," she said coolly.

"In my experience, they don't." His gaze slid over her again, and her skin prickled.

"Then you must not know many people," she said. "We all change. No one stays the same."

"No, we don't. But whatever the essence was, that remains. If one is heartless, for instance, one doesn't suddenly grow a heart."

Caroline's skin glowed with heat. She knew he was speaking of her, speaking of that night when she'd thrown his love back in his face. She wanted to deny it, wanted to tell him the truth, but what good would it do? None whatsoever.

* * *

Find out if Roman is seeking revenge or seduction in
A GAME WITH ONE WINNER, available March 19, 2013.

HARLEQUIN *Presents*®

Discover the first book in a red-hot
new duet from *USA TODAY*
bestselling author Carole Mortimer.

Buenos Aires Nights
*After dark with Argentina's most
infamous billionaires!*

World-renowned Argentinean Cesar Navarro has
sexy chef Grace Blake right where he wants her—in
his penthouse, at his command! She should be
off-limits, but Grace has tantalized his jaded palate,
and Cesar finds himself craving…

A TASTE OF THE
FORBIDDEN

Pick up a copy March 19, 2013,
wherever books are sold!